K.D. Richards is a native of̶ ̶
who now lives outside Toront̶ ̶
sons. You can find her at kdrichardsbooks.com

New York Times and *USA Today* bestselling, award-winning
author **Lisa Childs** has written more than eighty-five
novels. Published in twenty countries, she's also appeared
on the *Publishers Weekly*, Barnes & Noble and Nielsen
Top 100 bestseller lists. Lisa writes contemporary romance,
romantic suspense, and paranormal and women's fiction.
She's a wife, mom, bonus mom, avid reader and less avid
runner. Readers can reach her through Facebook or her
website, lisachilds.com

Also by K.D. Richards

West Investigations
Shielding Her Son
Dark Water Disappearance
Catching the Carling Lake Killer
Under the Cover of Darkness
A Stalker's Prey
Silenced Witness
Lakeside Secrets
Under Lock and Key
The Perfect Murder

Also by Lisa Childs

Bachelor Bodyguards
Bodyguard Under Siege
Hostage Security
Personal Security

Hotshot Heroes
Hotshot Hero on the Edge
Hotshot Heroes Under Threat
Hotshot Hero in Disguise

The Coltons of Owl Creek
Colton's Dangerous Cover

Discover more at millsandboon.co.uk

KILLER ON THE POTOMAC

K.D. RICHARDS

THE UNKNOWN COLTON

LISA CHILDS

MILLS & BOON

First Published in Great Britain 2025
by Mills & Boon, an imprint of HarperCollins*Publishers* Ltd
1 London Bridge Street, London, SE1 9GF

www.harpercollins.co.uk

HarperCollins*Publishers*
Macken House, 39/40 Mayor Street Upper,
Dublin 1, D01 C9W8, Ireland

Killer on the Potomac © 2025 Kia Dennis
The Unknown Colton © 2025 Harlequin Enterprises ULC

Special thanks and acknowledgment are given to Lisa Childs for her contribution to *The Coltons of Alaska* series.

ISBN: 978-0-263-39728-4

0925

KILLER ON THE POTOMAC

K.D. RICHARDS

Chapter One

It was nearly five in the morning. He'd gotten a much later start than he'd planned, but the moon hid behind clouds still shrouding the city park in near darkness as he pulled into the empty lot and cut his engine. He'd done his homework and knew that the two cameras hanging high above on either end of the lot had long ceased to work. He'd broken the bulb in the lone streetlight two nights earlier and was relieved to see the city had yet to switch it for a new one.

"Everything's coming up roses," he sang softly.

He continued humming the tune as he got out of the car, opened the trunk, and lifted the body out of it. He cradled it close as he made his way along the path. Fallen leaves swirled in a breeze. He'd scouted the location extensively and knew exactly where he was headed. He passed the playground and the basketball courts and stepped onto the soft grass in the open field, passing an empty picnic table. The night was unusually balmy, and they were due for rain, but the ground was hard and dry now. He'd chosen her final resting place well.

He wished this one had been the one. He'd been

searching for so long and had finally thought he'd found her. His Sarah. But once again, he'd been wrong. He hadn't thought it would be so difficult.

When he arrived at his chosen spot, he lowered the body to the ground. He took his time positioning her, then snapped a photo with the phone that only he knew about. Even though she wasn't the one he was looking for, she was still so beautiful. It almost hurt to leave her. But he knew he couldn't stay. He needed to move quickly. The last thing he wanted was to be spotted by some vagrant or early-morning jogger running through the park. He had to be long gone, preferably back home and in his bed, when the body was found.

A sliver of moon broke through the cloud-covered sky, casting a glowing light on the body. He couldn't help himself; he knew he should leave. Instead, he crouched down, fluffing the hair he'd fanned out around her and running his fingers over her cheek and down the side of her neck one last time. "I'm sorry we couldn't be together forever. I will miss you."

He'd have to keep searching. The thought made him smile as he turned and walked back along the path to his car, humming his favorite song.

Chapter Two

A 6:00 a.m. summons to a crime scene gave new meaning to the saying "Mondays are murder," Detective Dora Madison thought as she drove to the small park nestled in the Adams Morgan neighborhood in Washington, DC. It was rare to get a call out to this area, much less one about a body found in the park. The city's homicide rate had been trending downward for several years, but in the last month she'd caught two homicides that had a grown a hole in the pit of her stomach. From the scant details that the dispatcher had given her about the crime scene, that hole was about to get deeper.

Half a dozen police cruisers blocked the park's entrance when she arrived. She paused in front of the baby-faced officer, flashed her badge, and made her way back along an asphalt walkway that passed by a playground, a softball field, and a basketball court to her crime scene. She slipped her hands into nitrile gloves as she made her way down the path. There was a buzz of activity—forensics techs and more uniformed officers—on the open lawn to her right, about fifty feet off the path. Yellow police tape wound around a tree, to a picnic table,

Killer on the Potomac

around a stick that someone had seen fit to plunge into the ground and back to the tree, forming a misshapen triangle around the body lying on the dew-covered grass.

A red-faced man with dark, hair and a Mediterranean brown complexion strode toward her. He wore a tired black suit, off the rack, a white shirt, a striped blue-and-white tie, and well-worn loafers. His eyes were dark and grim, and his lips were pressed together into a harsh line. She recognized him as a detective out of the Third District, which usually caught all the cases originating in the Adams Morgan neighborhood, but for the life of her, she couldn't remember his name.

He reached for her and extended his hand. "Detective Madison? I'm Detective Wendell Keene." His glove-clad handshake was firm. Keene looked to be in his early thirties, with short brown hair cut in a fashion that told her he'd been in the military. He was only slightly taller than her five feet, ten inches, but he carried himself with a confidence that couldn't be taught.

"Nice to meet you, albeit under these less-than-ideal circumstances," Dora said. "What do we have?"

Keene turned on his heel, and together they walked toward the body, Keene reading from the small notebook in his hand. "Dispatch took a call at approximately five forty this morning. A jogger the park encountered a woman running from the direction of the body. She was visibly upset and said there was a body on the other side of the park. The jogger called 911, and officers were dispatched. They found a woman, late teens or early twenties, deceased." Keene looked up from his notes. "The officers immediately noted the flower in the victim's hair."

Dora let out a deep sigh. "Which is why I was called."

Keene nodded. "Yes. I got the call because that's standard operating procedure, but my lieutenant instructed me to bring you in immediately."

She was sure he had. The press was already grumbling about the rise in crime and the possibility of a serial killer stalking the streets of the nation's capital. It had been plain bad luck that she'd caught the first murder, a grocery store cashier with a flower in her hair. The second victim, a waitress, had been found three weeks later in the same neighborhood, although one of Dora's colleagues had been on duty when that call came in. Both victims were brunettes with slim, athletic builds and were in their early twenties. Once they had confirmed that the second victim had the same flower in her hair, their boss, Lieutenant Tracy Crenshaw, had made Dora the lead detective in both cases. Crenshaw was as close to a mentor as Dora had. The lieutenant had made it through the ranks at record speed, traversing all the diplomatic stuff as well as men who still had problems with women on the force, especially those reaching for rank. But Crenshaw had managed it all and was clearly still on her way up. She'd seen something in Dora and given her a shot, and more than anything Dora wanted to prove that the lieutenant's faith in her wasn't misplaced. Too often lately, she'd felt like she was failing.

And now they had a third victim. Official serial-killer territory. Although she doubted very much, she'd hear those two words cross Lieutenant Crenshaw's lips.

Solve this fast. I'm counting on you had been Lieutenant Crenshaw's exact words when she'd dropped the second case onto Dora's desk, but apparently Dora wasn't moving fast enough. Crenshaw had been on her for the last week, demanding daily, sometimes twice daily, updates on cases. It was becoming harder and harder to spin bupkis into something that sounded hopeful.

"Where are the jogger and the woman who found the body?"

"I had officers take them both to the Third District station. I can have them transported to you at the Sixth if you'd prefer to interview them there."

Dora shook her head. "No. I'll swing by the Third when we're finished here."

A forensic technician stepped aside as she and Keene approached the body. Dora examined the body with practiced eyes for several long moments. The young woman was on her back, her eyes vacantly gazing at the leafy tree branches above her. The woman's chocolate-brown hair fanned out around her head, and twigs and a leaf entwined in its strands, but the glossy sheen of her professional blowout was still ascertainable. Her face was made up—black mascara, gold sparkly eyeshadow, expertly applied and blended foundation, and the remains of what would have been a vibrant red lipstick clinging to her lips. The makeup seemed too heavy for a day at the office. It was more likely their victim had been out or was about to go out on a night out on the town. Her clothing confirmed that assessment. Black skintight leather pants with a sparkly gold top and strappy high-heeled sandals that looked more like torture devices than shoes.

"What happened to you?" Dora murmured, circling the body.

"Cause of death?"

"We don't know. There are no signs of trauma on the body."

Just as with the other victims. If this was the same killer, they'd find that this woman, like the others, had been drowned, most likely in a bathtub, while she'd been sedated. "Have you started a search of the park?"

"We have officers fanned out, searching the park and two blocks in each direction right now."

Dora stared off beyond the trees. This was a mixed residential and commercial area, with mostly apartments and condos. That meant many people were coming and going.

"Do we know when the body was placed here?" Because she was sure forensics would determine the victim had been placed just like the other two victims.

"Not yet."

She fought to hold back a frown. "Have we found any evidence at all?"

Keene's voice held more than a hint of irritation. "Still looking. There are multiple entrances to this park. No gates, although there are signs informing the public that the park is closed after dark."

Yeah, Dora was sure that did absolutely nothing to keep people out of the park at night.

"You came from the west entrance, so you know there's a parking lot there," Keene continued. "Whoever left her could have parked in the lot and carried her here."

"Possible." Dora frowned. "But he or she would have had to be strong."

"Or they could have used something to make the trip easier," Keene responded. "We've had a few dry days. The ground is hard. I've got uniforms looking for any sign of a vehicle or drag marks, but it might not be possible to discern any from the general wear and tear in the park."

That was always the trouble with a crime scene in a public place. So many people came through that it was nearly impossible to figure out what was evidence and what wasn't. Something their perpetrator obviously knew.

"Cameras?"

Keene shot her a forlorn look. "Two in the parking lot, but…"

She didn't need him to finish the sentence to know its ending. "They aren't working."

He shook his head. "Haven't been for more than a year."

It was long enough for anyone who lived in the area— heck, even many who didn't—to know.

"Let's assume our killer brought the victim in through the west entrance. It's the closest, and it makes the most sense based on what we know now. That means he or she could have been in and out of here in, what, ten minutes?"

Keene shrugged. "Maybe less. I think it's safe to say our guy scouts his dump sights and he—"

"Or she," Dora interjected.

"Or she, although female serials are less common," Keene added.

"I think both our commanding officers would have your head for uttering the *S*-word, but point taken."

"Our perp," Keene continued, opting for the safest description of their killer, "appears to be organized and has his or her crimes well thought out."

"I agree. And if their pattern holds, we'll find that

our victim has been missing for three days." Dora stared at the body. The woman had been well groomed, her clothes were designer, her hair done in a salon or at least by someone who'd known what they were doing. Not the type of person who could typically go missing for three days without someone knowing. "Three days. We need to be looking at missing person's reports."

"Already got someone on it," Keene said.

"Make sure to expand the search into Northern Virginia and Maryland. We'll start with the DMV, but it's possible she came into the city from farther away." The DMV, as it was affectionately called by those who lived in the area, was the region surrounded by Interstate 495 also known as the Beltway—although its borders were constantly shifting outward as the suburbs expanded and more and more people found it palatable to commute to the city from farther away.

"Got it," Keene answered.

She nodded toward the pathway that jutted from the one she'd used to trek from the parking lot to the crime scene where the apartment buildings stretched over the tops of the trees. "We need to canvass every unit in those apartment buildings."

Keene groaned.

Dora answered with a shrug. It would be a pain, but... "That's what uniforms are for. Someone might have seen something that puts us on our killer's tail. Or our killer could live in one of those buildings."

It wasn't out of the question. Most killers stayed close to home. It was one of the reasons some killers were so hard to catch. Their friends and neighbors just never thought of them as a killer.

Dora squatted next to the body. The woman's hands had been crossed one over the other and placed between her breasts. Her legs were similarly crossed at the ankle. Just like the first two victims. She touched the dead woman's forearm. It was stiff. "Rigor has set in. She's been dead for at least twenty-four hours."

"She hasn't been here for twenty-four hours. No way she wouldn't have been noticed."

"No." Dora got to her feet. "She hasn't been here that long. Hopefully, the canvass will give us a better idea about the much use this park gets." She made a mental note to question the jogger who'd called in the body too. How many people usually walked or jogged the path? Were there more in the mornings or the evenings? Was it a frequent lunchtime spot for workers in the area? "She was most likely placed here in the wee hours of this morning when the body would have still been flexible enough for her killer to pose like this. But that also leads me to believe our guy—"

"Or gal," Keene interjected with a mirthless smile.

"*Or gal* knows something about forensic science."

Their killer was smart. College educated, maybe. Or maybe he or she was just very skilled at killing. Just because they only had three bodies didn't mean their killer had only killed three people. She could be running even further behind than she'd realized.

Dora scanned the body as thoroughly as she could without touching it. No scratches on the skin were visible. The polish on her nails was chipped, but the nails themselves remained intact. There were no defensive wounds that Dora could see. If this woman had been drowned, she'd likely been sedated first, just like the other two victims.

"Have you had any luck running down the flower?" Keene asked.

"No." The single word came out as a growl, but Dora's frustration wasn't aimed at Keene as much as the situation. She'd never given much thought to flowers, but there were over four hundred thousand species of flowers and several dozen garden centers and nurseries in the DC metropolitan area. She'd keep pushing on the lead, but their perp could have gotten the flower from almost anywhere.

Keene cleared his throat. "I know it's your case, but if you wouldn't mind, I'd like to stay on."

She studied him for a moment before nodding. "I could use all the help I can get. I think this one is going to take its toll before it's wrapped up."

"I've already put a call in to the medical examiner," he said. "He should be here soon to pick up the body. Would you mind if I observe the autopsy with you?"

Observing autopsies was one of her least favorite parts of the job, but they often revealed information and leads that were vital to catching a killer. "Sure. Why don't you stay on top of that and let me know when the medical examiner has it scheduled?"

Keene glanced down at the body once more. "What kind of sicko does something like this?"

Twelve years on the force and she didn't have an answer for him. "Let's check with the uniforms, see if they've turned up—"

As if he'd heard the words she'd been speaking, a baby-faced officer jogged around the bend in the pathway, a large plastic evidence bag in his hands. "Detectives!"

Dora approached the officer, with Keene at her side. His breastplate gave his last name as King. "Officer King, have you got something for us?"

Officer King held out the evidence bag. Inside, there was a small black purse encrusted with rhinestones. "Found this about a quarter mile away in some bushes. I got the techs to take photos before I bagged it."

"Good work, Officer," Keene said, taking the bag and carefully opening it.

Whether it was a natural male aversion to going through a woman's purse or because she was the lead detective, Keene passed the purse to Dora.

The usual necessities for a night out were inside: Lipstick. Cell phone. A hair tie. And a wallet. Dora snapped open the wallet and slid the driver's license out of the first slot.

Michelle Quitoni.

Dora passed the license to Keene, and the hole in her stomach opened into a chasm.

"Quitoni. Like that senator who has been all over the news lately?"

Dora slid the photograph that was in the slot behind the driver's license out. "Not *like* that senator. That senator's daughter." She held the photograph so that she and Keene could study it together. Senator Preston Quitoni and the woman lying in the field just feet from them smiled back at them.

Chapter Three

It was just after two in the afternoon when Special Agent Logan Elkins found himself pausing outside of the conference room at the Sixth District station where the chief of police, the deputy chief of police, the deputy mayor, and the lead detective on the case he'd just been assigned to waited for him. The main players were all different now. It had been over seven years since he'd left the Metropolitan Police Department, so that was to be expected. The MPD, as it was colloquially called, had a storied history. The department was more than a hundred and fifty years old, making it one of the oldest in the country. It was in a unique position, being a police department in a federal city, but it was still the primary policing authority in the area with law enforcement professionals who were second to none.

What he hadn't counted on was the bout of nerves he'd been fighting since pulling into the police parking lot. He couldn't remember the last time he'd been nervous walking into a meeting about a case, but it wasn't the case that had him on edge. It was seeing Detective Dora Madison again. The last time they'd spoken, over two years ago now, it had not gone well. He'd known his reassignment back to DC and her promotion to detective meant it was possible that their professional paths might cross at some point. Washington, DC, might have been the nation's capital, but it had a lot in common with small towns. But he and Dora were both professionals with a common goal: getting a killer off the streets.

He straightened his back, squared his shoulders, and reached for the conference room door. All the heads in the room turned toward him as he strode through the door. Despite his little pep talk in the hall, he scanned the faces for Dora and let out a sigh that was part relief and part disappointment when he realized she wasn't among the people in the room.

The chief stood up from his position at the head of the long, rectangular table that dominated the space and came forward. Chief of Police Stefon Bayne was a short African American man with a stocky build and, if rumors were true, a Napoleon complex. He wore his dress blues along with a scowl. "Special Agent Elkins," he said crisply, thrusting out his hand. "Thank you for coming."

"Of course. I'm happy to do whatever I can." The chief's hand was sweaty enough that Logan had to fight the urge to wipe his hand on his pant leg when the man let go.

"I understand you used to be part of the Metropolitan Police Department."

"It's been a few years, but I started my career here before moving on to the FBI."

"Well, we're happy to have you back helping on this case," Bayne answered, sounding anything but happy to have his help.

Murder, including serial murders, fell under the purview of the local police. The Federal Bureau of Investigation provided help, usually profiling and forensic work and occasionally manpower, when requested by the locals. But Chief Bayne hadn't requested the FBI's help. Senator Quitoni had insisted the FBI be brought in to assist. That made the situation awkward, to say the least. But it wasn't the first time Logan had been tasked to work with hostile locals, and it wouldn't be the last time. He'd use this meeting to work out the power dynamics among the group—who he could sway to his side, who he could trust, and who he couldn't.

He cataloged the names and titles of each of the people in the room as they introduced themselves. The deputy chief of police, Tina Linuesa, and two of her aides. The deputy mayor, Carl Simone, with one aide. An attorney from the US Attorney's Office for the District of Columbia. A police press officer. The mayor's press officer. There were too many politicians and administrators and not enough of the people who were going to be doing the real work of finding a killer.

He was just about to ask if the detectives assigned to the case were going to be joining them when the conference room door opened.

"Ah, perfect timing, Lieutenant Crenshaw," Chief Bayne said with a disapproving frown. "We were just about to get started, Detectives."

"Sorry we're late. Got stuck in traffic." Crenshaw strode to the table with the confidence that she could have only been born out of years of dealing with men like Bayne. Her gaze hopped over each of the people at the table before landing on Logan. "Special Agent Elkins." She gave a tight-lipped smile. "Good to see you again."

Tracy Crenshaw had been a detective when he'd joined the force as a rookie. She looked as if she'd aged ten years since he'd last seen her, but he supposed that was a hazard of her job. Her hair was grayer than the red it had once been. She wore it in a bun, coiled tightly at the nape of her neck. Her suit was boxy, hiding any curves she might have had. A purposeful choice, Logan deduced. She didn't want the men she worked with to see her as a woman as much as a boss. He'd never worked with Crenshaw directly, but she had a reputation as a solid cop who put in the work. He was more than a little surprised that she knew of him, though.

He heard himself telling the lieutenant to please call him Logan, but his gaze was pinned over the lieutenant's shoulder at the woman who was obviously trying to look anywhere but directly at him.

"Let me introduce Detective Wendell Keene, on loan to us from the Third District until we catch this guy," Crenshaw said.

He didn't know if Keene had been on the force at the same time as he had, but the man's name and face weren't ringing any bells. Keene reached a hand across the table.

Logan felt himself taking the man's hand and shaking it, almost as if he was in a daze.

"And this is the lead detective on the case, Detective Dora Madison," Crenshaw continued.

Dora finally met his gaze head on. "Agent Elkins and I have met." Dora's expression gave nothing away. Was she happy to see him? Angry? Indifferent? There was a time when he could have read every thought she had and every emotion, but those days were long gone.

What he did know was that she was still a knockout. Her ebony skin glowed, and he wondered if it was as soft now as it had been two years ago. She'd allowed her dark brown hair to grow down below her shoulders in loose ringlets. She wore a dark pantsuit that accentuated her generous curves and low-heeled boots. And she still wore the freesia-scented perfume that drifted toward him and fired his blood.

Crenshaw looked from him to Dora. "You two worked together in the past?"

"Something like that," Dora said, her light brown eyes hard.

Dora marched past him to the conference room table, her tailored dark green suit hugging her slim figure. She was still as lovely as he'd ever seen her.

Dora held his gaze for a moment longer before looking away.

"Well then, let's get started." Chief Bayne waved the newcomers to the empty seats at the table and began the meeting.

Logan supposed he should be thankful that no one seemed to have noticed the tension between him and Dora.

"I've got a press conference scheduled in less than an hour," Bayne said, the statement sounding almost like a threat. "I need to let the city know we are on top of this. That we won't rest until we have this psychopath in custody. What do we have so far?"

Dora briefed the group on that morning's 911 call, the

witness, and the results so far on the door-to-door canvass of the neighborhood.

"What can I take to the press?" Bayne said after Dora
had been speaking for nearly ten minutes. "Did the witness give us a description of the perp? Do we have any
solid evidence? DNA?"

Logan frowned. The 911 call about the body had only
come in about eight hours earlier. Even if the cops had
collected a DNA sample, Bayne had to know there was
no way they'd have processed it yet. Even the FBI lab—
one of the best in the world—couldn't have gotten results that quickly.

"We're still processing the evidence from the scene,
sir," Dora responded. "The witness is…distraught. We
spoke to her a little before she was transported to the
hospital, where the doctors felt it was best to sedate her.
Detective Keene and I are heading back to the hospital
to speak to her after this meeting."

"Did the autopsy turn up anything useful?" Bayne
pressed.

"It's scheduled for an hour from now."

"Her phone? The search of her house? The canvass?"

Keene stepped up to the plate this time. "Techs are
working on unlocking the phone, sir. We have a team
searching Ms. Quitoni's condo as we speak. The canvass is ongoing."

"So, I have to go out there and tell the press you have
nothing." Bayne threw the pen he'd been tapping against
the table down.

Jerk. The thought popped into Logan's mind unbid-
den. He pushed it aside and said, "Actually, Chief Bayne,

I would suggest you hold off on telling the press anything at the moment."

Bayne's gaze whipped to him. "And why is that Special Agent Elkins? The public is rightly terrified that we have a serial killer stalking the streets of DC."

"You have a killer who is obviously seeking attention. He leaves his victims in public places where he knows they will be found. He also takes a considerable risk in being seen doing so. That tells me he craves an audience. That he might even seek a confrontation. If you go to the press now, you might give him exactly what he wants."

Bayne's eyes narrowed, his shoulders hunching forward. "And the people of this city? Am I just supposed to let them think the police don't care?"

You mean let them think you don't care? That wouldn't be good for whatever aspirations you have beyond being chief of police, now, would it?

"No, but I am saying that giving this killer what he's looking for will probably put the residents of this city in more danger, not less." Logan fought to keep his temper in check. It wouldn't do anyone any good to start off on the wrong foot. "If you feel you must speak to the press, simply assure them you are doing everything you can. Encourage anyone who may have been in the area of this third crime scene last night or this morning and saw something suspicious to come forward. Do the same for potential witnesses to the first two crimes and show photos of those victims. Hopefully, it will jog someone's memory."

"Do you really think it's wise to so explicitly connect

the first two crimes to this one?" Deputy Mayor Carl Simone spoke up.

Of course the mayor's office would want to downplay the serial aspect of the case. It was bad for business. Tourists shied away from cities that had serial killers roaming the streets.

"The press is already connecting it for us," Dora chimed in, saving him from having to state the obvious. "Three women with the same exotic flower in their hair, a fact we'd been trying to keep out of the press. I'd love to know who leaked it," she added bitterly, "but the fact is, it's out there now."

The Metropolitan Police Department's press liaison cleared his throat. "My office has started getting questions about whether the department dropped the ball on the first two murders and whether we prioritize solving the murders of prominent victims over crimes against average citizens."

Bayne let out a string of curses. "Elkins, I can't go out there and just say some version of 'If you've seen something, say something.' The press would eat me alive."

"You can and you should," Logan shot back. "Isn't that what they pay you the big bucks for? To take the heat. If you go out there and goad this killer, the press could be the least of your worries."

Bayne glared across the table at him.

Logan held his gaze steady on the chief. He'd been brought in to do a job, and while he couldn't make Bayne take his professional advice, he wouldn't let the chief stop him from giving it.

"Can I just play devil's advocate here?" The deputy chief of police, Tina Linuesa, spoke up, her voice cutting through the tension in the room. "Is it possible that not giving the killer the attention he craves might anger him, thus driving him to commit even more murders?"

"It is possible," Logan conceded. "But he's already killed three women, and in killing Michelle Quitoni, he'll be getting more attention than he garnered after the first two murders, no matter what we do. I'm merely suggesting we don't throw gas on the fire."

Linuesa nodded in apparent agreement, but Bayne's frown didn't budge.

"Fine," Bayne growled after a minute of silence. "I'll keep the press conference brief and the details sparse. Madison, Keene, what did you get out of the witness?"

"Well, as I mentioned, she was very distressed," Dora started. "She was able to give us a general description of a Caucasian man, medium height, that she watched carry the body across the lawn."

"That's it? A white man of medium height. That could be anyone. Hell, that could be two of the people in this room," Bayne boomed, pointing from Carl Simone to one aide at the table. "Who is this woman? Why was she in the park so early in the morning?"

Keene and Dora shared a look.

"That's one thing we hope to ask her when we speak with her this afternoon. She would only give us her first name, Becky."

Bayne threw up his hands. "Great."

"There is something else you could speak about at your press conference, Chief," Tina Linuesa said, drawing all the eyes in the room to her. "Senator Quitoni has offered to post a two-hundred-fifty-thousand-dollar reward for anyone who has information leading to the arrest of his daughter's killer."

Logan hadn't spoken to Senator Quitoni, although he knew the senator had spoken to his boss and the director of the FBI briefly. Interviewing Michelle Quitoni's family and close friends was on his rapidly expanding to-do list.

He'd had enough experience with the parents of murder victims to know that they always wanted answers quickly, and given his prominent position and power, Logan knew the politician would be a thorn in his side until he got those answers. It was no surprise that Senator Quitoni had put up such a whopping reward. Powerful people thought money would bring all the answers. But in cases like the one they faced, a reward of that size was more likely to be a hindrance than a help.

"I'd advise against making the reward that big," Logan said.

"Of course you do," Bayne spat.

To Logan's surprise, Dora spoke up. "It will bring every crank and crook out of the woodwork. We'll get thousands of false leads, all of which we'll have to spend time and manpower running down."

Linuesa cocked her head to one side. "Maybe a more modest number, then?"

"Ten thousand," Logan said. "It's enough to catch the public's attention but not enough to have a con salivating."

Linuesa nodded. "I'll let Senator Quitoni know."

"Should the arrangements to take Senator Quitoni's statement be made through your office?" Keene asked Linuesa.

Logan noted the downturn in Dora's mouth. She didn't like that there would be a middleman between her and her victim's family, but it was an allowance regularly made for powerful or connected people, and a senator qualified as both.

"The senator passed along the contact information for his personal aide." Linuesa slid a business card from the leather portfolio in front of her onto the table. "You can call her to arrange to speak with the senator."

"I'd like to go with you when you conduct that interview, if you don't mind," Logan said.

Dora's mouth tugged down into a genuine frown now, but she nodded. "Of course."

"Take Special Agent Elkins with you when you interview the witness too," Lieutenant Crenshaw said. "It will be good to have his impressions of the woman if we are going to be relying on her description to catch our perp. The last thing we want to do is have the whole damn city on the lookout for the wrong man."

Bayne nodded. "Absolutely not. If she gives you enough for a composite sketch, get one, but don't release it without clearing it through my office first."

Crenshaw sat up straighter in her chair. "That's not our standard protocol."

"I don't care what standard protocol is. This case is too important to screw up. I'm the one that will be standing at that podium taking heat from the press, so I'm going to be riding herd on this one, Lieutenant. Understand?"

"Yes, sir," Crenshaw answered tightly.

"Good. Anything else?" Bayne asked, but he was already out of his seat. "We're adjourned."

Bayne strode from the room without a backward glance. Tina Linuesa and Carl Simone were only steps behind him.

Logan moved around the table and caught Dora's arm before she could exit the room.

"Dora. Got a moment?"

"Sure," she clipped, pulling her arm from his grasp.

"I just wanted to make sure our past isn't going to—"

"Our past," she said, cutting him off in a low voice while glancing around the room. Most of the meeting attendees had filed out of the room, but two of the chief's aides were conversing in low voices on the opposite side of the room. "Is just that. In the past. I have a job to do, and so do you."

He raised his hands. "I didn't mean to upset you."

"You haven't upset me," she said, her voice rising enough to draw a glance from one aide. She blew out a deep breath. "You haven't upset me," she repeated more quietly. "I would simply prefer it if we kept our discussion strictly in the professional realm from this point forward. I think it's best."

Dora didn't meet his gaze. He couldn't say he didn't deserve her anger.

They'd met right after he'd applied to the FBI. He'd fully expected the relationship to go the way most of his relationships had prior to that. They'd spend a few great weeks together, maybe a month or two, and then things would start to peter out. Or in some cases, explode in a fiery mess that usually ended with lots of name calling and door slamming. Either way, he hadn't expected to spend nine pretty great months with Dora. To be honest, he'd been thinking about the future, their future—but then he'd gotten the call to interview with the FBI.

Things had moved fast after that. Joining the Bureau had been a dream of his since he'd decided on a career in law enforcement, but he hadn't told anyone other than his brother, Landon. He hadn't mentioned it to Dora at all. What it had come down to was that he'd felt he'd had to choose between his career and Dora. Nine months might have been a long time for him to have a relationship, but it wasn't long enough to expect her to put her life on hold for him. So, he'd taken the job, broken up with Dora, and headed out to his new duty station in Arizona.

It had not taken long before he realized what he'd left behind. As much as he loved the job and the Bureau, and he did, he'd missed Dora. And the longing for her hadn't dissipated at all as first one year and then another had passed.

He'd considered calling her when he'd gotten word that he was being transferred back to Washington, DC, but frankly, he'd been too ashamed of how he'd left. He'd convinced himself that she'd moved on with her life, had gotten over him, and that he needed to do the same. He'd even been proud of himself for not googling her like some lovesick teenager.

But fate had other plans. Now that he'd seen her and was going to be working side by side with her, he knew that what he wanted most in the world was another chance. He just hoped she wanted the same thing.

"Whatever you think is best," he responded through clenched teeth.

"Good." She glanced at her watch. "I want to see if

the medical examiner has anything for me yet. Would you like to go with me?"

It was rare for him to attend an autopsy. Usually, he had to rely upon the medical examiner's report, but viewing the victim could give him some insight into the killer's mind and certainly his signature.

He nodded. "Yes."

"Fine, then." Dora returned his nod. "Let's go."

Chapter Four

Dora skimmed emails and dodged pedestrians on the short walk from the station to the medical examiner's office. Anything to avoid making small talk with Logan. Why couldn't he have grown a beer belly and receding hairline in the last two years? How did he manage to get even more handsome—heck, she'd say it but only to herself—sexy? Broad shoulders, tapered hips, and lips that were made for kissing.

Don't think about kissing!

She stole a glance at Logan. He'd buttoned his coat up to his neck, but it was an unusually warm January day. A thin sheen of perspiration had begun blooming on the brown skin on his forehead.

The man looks good even when he's sweating. She heard the words in her mother's voice, and a ping of yearning shot through her. She missed her mother, but after raising a child all on her own, Pearl Madison deserved to live her life for herself. Dora just wished her mother had found happiness in Washington, DC, or at least on the East Coast. Five years ago, her mother had gone on a cruise and met Felix Mayberry. The two had fallen for each other fast and, just four months after meeting, had gotten married. Despite the speed of their courtship, Dora thought Felix was a great guy and a great guy for her mother. His one flaw was that he lived in San Francisco. Her mother had decided if she was going to go on the adventure, she was going to go all the way and had moved across the country.

Dora made a mental note to call her mother. She was sure Pearl had some words of wisdom that would help settle the emotions churning inside Dora at the moment.

They arrived at the medical examiner's office and signed in before heading to the basement, where the autopsies were done. She and Logan slid their arms through thin protective gowns and snapped booties over their shoes before pushing through the heavy swinging doors that led into the medical examiner's lab.

Dean Schroff, the medical examiner, looked up from the victim he'd been examining on the table as they entered, his clear blue eyes landing on Dora. Dean was one of the youngest medical examiners at thirty-two, but he was also one of the best. He shook his curly, dirty blond hair out of his eyes and said, "I'm not finished my exam." He turned back to the body on the table.

Dora snagged the tube of menthol from Dean's desk. She dabbed a bit under her nose before passing the tube to Logan, who did the same. "I'll take whatever you have so far."

"Who's he?" Dean asked. Dean had only taken the job of head medical examiner for the District of Columbia a year earlier, right after Logan had gone over to the FBI, so their paths would not have crossed before.

"Logan Elkins. I'm former MPD and currently a profiler with the FBI here to help Detective Madison on this case."

Dean glanced up again, studying Logan for a long moment.

"Dean," Dora said when Dean's inspection had gone on long enough to be awkward, "have you got anything for me or not?"

Dean slowly slid his gaze from Logan to Dora. "I told you I'm not finished—"

Dora opened her mouth to protest, but Dean stopped her.

"But I have found some interesting details." Dean moved from the head of the steel table to the midpoint. "The victim wasn't beaten or sexually assaulted. There's some bruising, but that is probably from the victim struggling against restraints."

"So just like the other victims," Logan said. "He doesn't hurt them physically if he can help it."

Dean gave a nod. "I found this tangled in the victim's hair."

Dean held the jar out to Dora. She took it and held it up so Logan could examine the contents at the same time she did.

"It's a flower," Logan said.

"The exotic and not easily found in Washington, DC, desert rose, to be exact," Dean repeated. "Just like with the first and second victims found tangled in the hair."

"We've kept that quiet," Dora said at Logan's confused expression. "We don't want the media to get wind of it."

Logan nodded his understanding. "Something to weed out the fake reports."

"Exactly," Dora responded. "Both victims were found in the park, and the second victim was found in a field overrun with the stuff."

"Do you think a third victim with it in their hair will finally get the brass to use the dreaded term *serial killer*?" Dean questioned.

She had her doubts. "I don't know."

"There's one other thing I want to show you," Dean said. He rolled the victim onto her side so that Dora and Logan could see the words written on her back. The killer had written on the victim: *Protect the innocent*.

Dora made no attempt to hide her fury and disgust. From the look on their faces, Dean and Logan felt similarly. "I really want to catch this guy."

"And I really hope you do." Dean lowered the body onto her back once again. "And quickly," he added pointedly.

Dora didn't need to ask why. A killer with this much rage…wouldn't stop until they were stopped.

True to form, Crenshaw barely let Dora get to her desk before calling for an update on the case. Dora motioned for Logan, who had somehow managed to secure himself the empty desk facing her own, to follow her. When they arrived at the lieutenant's office, they found the small space already bursting at the seams. The lieutenant's office was designed like a fishbowl, with glass walls running along three sides. However, Crenshaw's organizational skills left much to be desired. Five-drawer vertical file cabinets ran the length of one wall, blocking most of the view of the right side of the bullpen. A low credenza stacked high with files, notebooks, and other papers occupied the other side of the office allowing a slightly less obstructed view of the left side of the bullpen, but only slightly. Crenshaw sat behind her desk. Keene sat in one of the visitor's chairs facing the lieutenant, while Detective Bill Roberts leaned against a tall file cabinet, a steaming mug in his hands.

Roberts was nearing his twenty years and, rumor had it, on the way out. Dora had worked with him on two or three cases over the years and hadn't been impressed. He wasn't a bad cop, but he tended to miss details and to go into situations with preconceived notions. She held in a sigh. She'd have to be careful how she used him on this case. She couldn't afford mistakes or setbacks.

"Madison, Elkins, come in." Lieutenant Crenshaw waved them into the office as if there was plenty of space for two more bodies.

Logan nodded to the second unoccupied chair in the room, but Dora gave a slight shake of her head. She preferred to stand when she was making her reports.

Logan gave a small shrug and sat.

"Elkins, the big guy behind you with a mug of green tea is Detective Roberts. I'm assigning him to the case along with you, Dora, and Keene. I have every confidence that with my best detectives and an FBI profiler we can get this case solved ASAP." Crenshaw glared from across her desk. "Okay, so where are we?" Crenshaw asked with a hint of irritation in her tone.

Dora felt a matching flicker of irritation rumble in her own chest. They'd discovered their most recent victim less than six hours earlier, and Logan still needed to get up to speed. They were nowhere, the same as they'd been for weeks now.

But she couldn't say that to the lieutenant, so instead she said, "Logan and I were just with Dean." She ran through what the Dean had told them about the manner of death being strangulation and his official determination of homicide.

Keene whispered a low curse, but Crenshaw didn't bother to whisper.

"Damn it." The lieutenant slapped her palm against her desk, then swung her eyes to Logan. "That's three. So, we've officially got a serial killer, right?"

"Well, it's not that easy," Logan answered, before quickly adding, "but I am inclined to think that the same person killed all three of your victims, yes."

"'Inclined to think.'" Crenshaw shot the words like daggers back at Logan. "Okay, tell us why you are *inclined to think* that."

"You have three victims—Monica Gonzalez, Alicia Jones, and Michelle Quitoni. All between the ages of twenty-five and thirty-five, and all brunettes. None were what we'd consider high risk. Based on the reports forwarded to me, none of our victims had ever been involved in drugs or gambling. No one had ever reported an abusive husband or boyfriend. No issues at work. Monica was a cashier, Alicia was a preschool teacher, and Michelle was an investment banker. Nothing in any of their backgrounds that we've discovered so far would suggest they'd meet the end they did."

"And yet they did."

"Yes, but that tells us something. These women may not have been at high risk, but each of them crossed paths with the killer at some point."

"I have only been on the case for an hour, so I'm still

catching up," Roberts spoke up from his perch against the filing cabinets, "but I did skim Dora's interim reports on the first two victims. She hadn't found anything that suggested the victims knew each other."

Logan turned in his chair so that he was looking at Roberts when he answered. "They didn't have to know each other. Their paths just had to cross each other, and not even at the same time. They might not have even been aware of it."

Dora nodded, catching on to the thread of Logan's thoughts. "Like they both could use the same grocery store or beautician. They might not know they patronize the same place, but our killer does."

Logan shifted again, his gaze falling on her, and smiled. Her heart fluttered.

"Exactly," he said, holding her gaze for one moment longer before turning back around to face Crenshaw.

The lieutenant was not smiling. "Then how exactly do we find this guy?"

"We need to learn as much as we can about each of the victim's daily habits. Where they shopped, where they went for lunch, their favorite coffee shop—everything. And we need to know if there had been any changes in their habits lately. Even something small or innocuous like changing dry cleaners might have put them in the path of our unsub."

Keene groaned. "Do you know how many man hours compiling that kind of information for three people will eat up?"

Logan patted the younger detective on the back. "Sorry, but profiling is not like they make it out on television. It is mostly collecting and shifting through mounds of data until I can paint a vivid enough picture to see the unsub."

"There was one other piece of information we got from Dean that might help with painting that picture," Dora offered.

Lieutenant Crenshaw arched her brow.

"The killer wrote a message on Michelle Quitoni."

"He wrote on her?" Keene said, his eyes wide with shock.

His surprise reminded Dora just how green the detective was. She nodded. "Yes."

"What did he write?" Roberts asked in a wary tone. He'd been on the force the longest of all of them, even longer than Crenshaw. Dora wouldn't be surprised if nothing shocked him. She had once overheard one of the other detectives ask Roberts why he hadn't tried to rise higher in the ranks. Roberts had responded with a detailed cost benefit analysis which had amounted to *it wasn't worth the headache*. At the time, she'd marked Roberts as lacking ambition, but the longer she was in the job the more she understood where he was coming from. She was no longer sure she wanted to become one of the brass, pushing paper and worried about politics day in and day out. Doing the real work of putting the bad guys away meant being in the trenches.

"Dora?" Crenshaw barked.

Dora jerked out of her thoughts. "Sorry. He wrote 'Protect the innocent,'" Dora added.

"This sicko has got some messed-up definition of protecting the innocent," Keene spat.

"Maybe, maybe not," Logan said. "The question is whether the killer sees these women as innocent or not.

If he thinks they are innocent, he may also think that by killing them he is protecting them."

Dora felt her mouth turn down in a frown. "And if he doesn't think his victims are innocent?"

Logan turned in his chair, looking at her again. "He may feel as if, by killing them, he *is* protecting the innocent."

"So, either way he's delusional," Roberts offered.

Logan shrugged facing forward again. "Serial killers aren't known for their rational behavior, Detective."

"All right," Crenshaw said, running her hands through her already messy hair and leaning back in her chair. "Whatever his reason, motivations, or mental state, we need to find this guy, like yesterday. Have you talked to our witness again?"

Dora stood up straighter. "That's my next stop."

"Good." The lieutenant swept her gaze over each of them in turn. "The four of you go do whatever you have to do to get this guy off the street."

Chapter Five

Their witness, Randi Singer, was seventeen and homeless, which Logan knew created an additional layer of problems for any investigation, not the least of which was finding stable housing for the duration of the investigation. Dora had successfully found Randi a bed at Sunset House, a halfway house for women and children in need.

Sunset House turned out to be a large colonial in an older modest neighborhood. The street was quiet, and trees lined it. There was nothing at all to indicate that the home served as a refuge, which was the point. Hiding in plain sight, so to speak.

Dora had called before they'd left the police station to let Randi and Violet Fullerton, the halfway house Dora had found for Randi, know they were coming. Violet Fullerton answered the door and led them down a short hallway. Randi was waiting for them in the living room, which had obviously been furnished with hand-me-down furniture but also included a large flat-screen television that was mounted to the wall over a stone fireplace. Randi still looked much older than her seventeen years, but she at least looked rested now. Violet had gotten her some clean clothes, and it looked as if she'd gotten her hair washed and trimmed.

"Randi, hi," Dora said, entering the room and pulling her badge out of her jacket pocket. "I don't know if you remember me, but I'm Detective Dora Madison."

Randi chewed the nail on her index finger. "I remember you." Her gaze shifted to Logan.

"And I'm Logan Elkins. I'm working on the case with Detective Madison."

Randi cocked her head to the side. "Are you her partner?"

Logan slid a look at Dora.

"No," Dora answered quickly. "Special Agent Elkins is with the FBI."

Randi's head tilted even farther, but she didn't offer a response.

Dora took a seat perched in the easy chair opposite the sofa. Logan sat in the armchair to her right.

"Randi, we know you've been through a lot. We were hoping that you could answer a few questions for us, though. Would that be okay?"

"More questions," Randi whined, reminding Logan that the girl was a mere seventeen years old. She was only a year older than his own niece.

"It would be really helpful," Logan offered gently. "We really need to catch this guy before he hurts someone else."

Randi hesitated for a moment longer before giving a faint nod.

"Thank you." Dora took a small notebook from her jacket pocket and uncapped a pen.

He preferred a more hands-free approach. "Randi, do you mind if I record the conversation? Just to make it easier for me to remember things later. I won't share the recording with anyone not investigating the case."

Randi nodded. "Sure, yeah, whatever."

Logan hit the Record button on his cell phone and waited. Dora was the lead investigator. It was her show.

"Let's start with something easy," Dora said. "Where are you from?"

Randi brought her index finger to her mouth again. "Lots of places. My father moved us around a lot before he died."

"When did your father pass away?" Logan asked.

"Two years ago." She ducked her head, trying to hide the shimmer of tears, but he'd seen it. So, she wasn't a runaway but a kid who had suffered a hard knock early in life and was finding it hard to recover on her own.

"What about your mother?"

Randi shrugged. "Don't know her. Dad said she abandoned us when I was too young to remember."

Dora scribbled a note on her pad. "Do you know her name? Where she lives? Maybe we can contact her for you."

"No." The single word left no room for negotiation. Randi was seventeen, almost an adult legally. If she didn't want her mother in her life, there was nothing Dora or anyone else could do to force her.

"Okay. Could you tell us why you were in the park last night?"

Randi's eyes narrowed with suspicion. "What does that matter?"

Logan cleared his throat. "It helps us understand the circumstances surrounding the night—that's all."

Randi was quiet for a beat more before she spoke again. "I was just hanging out."

That could mean a whole host of things—drugs, alcohol, meeting a john—the one thing it most likely didn't include was simply chatting with friends.

He shot another look at Dora, but she remained focused on her witness.

"Okay," Dora said, scratching another note on the page in front of her. "Could you tell us what you saw?"

Randi shifted on the sofa, her knee bouncing in time to some unheard music. "I already told you everything I know."

"I know we spoke yesterday." Dora kept her voice low and gentle, but Logan could hear the edge of annoyance in her tone.

No doubt Randi did too. Her knee bounced faster.

He slid forward in his chair and clasped his hands in front of him. "Sometimes a good night's rest helps us to recall little details we don't think about in the initial moments after an event." He smiled encouragingly at the young woman across from him. "Anything you can tell us now will be so helpful, Randi."

He watched as Randi's body visibly relaxed. He'd been told he had a way with interviews. It was part of what made him a good profiler. He was excellent at reading people. And what he read when he looked at Randi was that she was a scared young woman who'd been through more than her fair share of crap in her short life. It wasn't fair that they were asking even more of her now, but it was necessary if they wanted to catch a killer.

"I was hanging out in the park just walking around—"

"Was anyone with you?" Dora interrupted.

Randi shook her head. "No. I'm kind of a loner. Safer that way."

Logan wasn't sure that was true at all, but it wasn't worth mentioning it now.

"I saw a man and a woman. At least I thought it was a woman. They were on the ground. I thought they were…" Randi's face flushed. "You know. I was about to turn away, but something seemed…off."

"Off? Off how?" Logan interrupted this time.

Randi's face scrunched up, her gaze going up and to the left as if she was trying to grasp onto the words to answer his question but couldn't quite catch them. "I'm not sure. Just off."

"That's okay," Dora said. "Sometimes 'off' is just our subconscious telling us to be careful."

"I guess." Randi's finger went back to her mouth. "I just knew that I shouldn't let the man know that I was there, you know? I hid behind this big tree and watched him."

"What did he do?" Dora had scooted to the edge of the easy chair now as well.

"He was petting her." Randi shivered at the memory. "Like smoothing her clothes and making sure she looked okay, I think. He tucked something into her hair, and then he kissed her on the lips and walked away toward the parking lot."

She swallowed hard. "That's when I realized this wasn't some freaky date night. The woman didn't get up and go with him. She didn't move at all. I wasn't sure if I should go over to her—like, if she might yell at me or whatever—but she was so still. I thought she might need help."

"You did exactly the right thing," Logan said.

Randi's eyes locked onto him. He could see the fear she must have felt in those moments reflected in her eyes now. "I knew she was dead when I got a good look at her, so I ran."

"To the convenience store?" Dora said softly.

Randi's head bobbed up and down. "Yeah. The night manager there lets me use the ladies' room even though he's not supposed to unlock the door for anyone after ten. He let me in, and he called the cops when I told him what I saw."

He'd read the responding officer's report. The convenience store manager hadn't provided anything helpful. He'd called the cops when Randi arrived, and they'd both waited at the store for help.

"Can you remember anything else?" Dora asked now. "Any sounds? Smells? See anyone else at all?"

Randi's gaze fell to the floor. "No."

There was something there. Something she didn't want to say.

Logan glanced at Dora again. This time she met his gaze, the look on her face indicating that she was thinking exactly what he was.

"Would you be willing to work with a sketch artist, Randi?"

"I… I don't know. I already told you. It was dark. The guy was white, kind of tall, but other than that I didn't see anything."

Somewhere in the house a door slammed. Randi startled, her eyes darting around the room.

Logan gave her a moment to settle before he said, "You'd be surprised what a sketch artist can pull from your memory. Why don't you give it a try? I'm sure Detective Madison will even spring for lunch afterward."

Dora's smile was tight enough that he knew he'd pay for the suggestion later. "Sure. What do you say, Randi?"

"I guess. At least I'll have something to do. How long am I going to have to stay at this place?"

"Do you have someplace else you can go?" Logan asked gently.

Randi didn't answer, which was an answer in itself.

"I've arranged for you to stay here for the time being. I'm sure that Violet could use some help around here. There's always something that needs doing."

Randi scratched her elbow. "Yeah, maybe."

Dora's smile this time was genuine, and it hit him like a punch to the gut. He'd forgotten how beautiful she was when she smiled.

Now is not the time.

"Great," Dora said rising. Logan followed suit. "I'll pick you up tomorrow at ten. You decide where you'd like to have lunch."

For the first time since they'd entered Sunset House, Randi smiled. "Anywhere?"

Dora let out a small groan, but the smile remained on her lips. "Anywhere that is manageable by a cop's salary."

"Oh." Randi turned to Logan. "I bet FBI agents make more than DC cops." Her brows rose.

"Oh, they definitely do." Dora clapped a hand on Logan's shoulder. "And I know Special Agent Elkins wouldn't miss lunch with you for the world."

Dora turned her smile on him directly, and there wasn't much he wouldn't have promised to keep it there. "Sure. Lunch is on me tomorrow. Anywhere you want, Randi."

Chapter Six

Dora drove to a nearby family-owned Chinese restaurant that served an amazing dim sum. The interior of the restaurant was warm and welcoming. She and Logan followed the hostess to a table.

Dora was a regular and didn't need to look at the menu before ordering. Logan placed an order for dumplings and sweet-and-sour pork, and they both got oolong tea.

"So how long have you been back in town?" Dora asked, jumping right in. If they were going to be working together, she wanted to get the awkward questions out of the way.

"Not long. A couple of months." Logan held her gaze. "I wanted to call you, but I didn't know if I should."

She didn't respond. Mostly because she didn't know how she would have reacted if he had called. Instead, she cleared her throat and changed the subject.

"How are Lisa and Landon? Is Landon still catching the bad guys and Lisa still fighting cybercrime?" she asked, keeping her tone light. Landon, his older brother and an investigative reporter, seemed to be more open-minded about his sister's role in the justice system.

"They're both good, work wise at least. Layla is sixteen, and she and Lisa are butting heads more often now."

Dora had trouble imagining Logan's niece, a pretty, shy young girl the last time Dora had seen her, pushing back against her mother, but she had heard that the teen years could be hard on mothers and daughters.

"Wow. Sixteen. Time flies."

"That it does," Logan concurred. "Layla seems to have made it through her parent's divorce relatively unscathed."

"I remember Lisa and Charles's marriage was on rocky ground when…" *When we'd been together*, but instead of saying the words she let the rest of the statement trail off.

Logan gave her a look. "Yeah, they decided to call it quits. It was rough for everyone, but they seem to have found a system that works for them. Charles and Lisa were never a good fit for each other, but they both unequivocally love Layla more than anything else. They've been committed to getting her through this period with as little trauma as possible. They're good parents."

"That's good." Dora swallowed and reached for her water. Something about the conversation was feeling a little too intimate, too much like a conversation between two people in a personal relationship. But that was not what they were. They were colleagues and colleagues only. It looked like she was going to have to remind herself of that often while they were working together.

She searched her brain for another topic of conversation. Her gaze landed on the plates on the table in front of them.

Dora chuckled. "I'm sure I'd forgotten how much you eat."

"Fast metabolism." Logan dug into his food. "I remember that you'll work until you drop."

Their server, the owner's grandson, brought out their orders.

"You sure you don't need more to eat?" Logan asked, eyeing her single plate before glancing back at his multiple dishes, I seem to remember you forgetting to eat more than once."

"I eat when necessary." Dora speared a pork dumpling. She chewed, ignoring Logan's skeptical look. "What do you think of the case so far?" she asked, changing the subject once again.

"We're still early."

"I know, but I'm just wondering what you're thinking. Are we headed in the right direction? Is there any way to narrow down the pool of suspects?"

Logan sighed. "Dora, I can't just wave a magic wand. Profiling isn't an exact science. The more evidence we gather, the more I'll be able to refine the profile of our killer, but I'll never be able to give you a name and address. Only good old-fashioned police work will get you that."

Dora scowled. "More evidence likely means another woman will be killed. I want to avoid that."

Logan lowered his chopsticks. "I do too, but one thing I've had to come to terms with in this job is that, more often than not, I'll be too late to save the victim. The only thing I can do is use my skills to potentially save the next one."

"What if I don't think that's good enough?"

"It has to be," Logan shot back. "You know that. If you let yourself get consumed with the ones you couldn't save, you'll drive yourself mad."

Dora's scowl only deepened. She knew he was right, but that didn't stop her from feeling responsible. She was supposed to catch the bad guys, and so far, it was bad guy three, Dora zero. She pushed her half-eaten lunch to the side. "We should get back to work."

Logan sighed again and wiped his hands on his napkin.

Dora got the waiter's attention, signaling that they were ready for the check. The server quickly brought over the bill, handing it to Logan even though she had called for it.

She stretched her hand across the table, but Logan snatched the bill before she could reach it.

Her scowl deepened. "What's my part come to?"

He took several bills out of his wallet and placed them inside the folder. "Don't worry about it. My treat."

Dora sat up straighter in her chair. "That's nice of you," she said deservedly, "but I like to pay my own way."

Logan rolled his eyes. "Your part came to next to nothing compared to mine, and I was the one who insisted on stopping to eat. Let me get this."

Dora started to argue again.

"Dora, I got this. You can get the next one, okay?"

She wasn't happy about it, but it wasn't worth arguing about any further. Not when they had work to do. "Okay," she responded grudgingly. After another beat, she added, "Thank you."

"You're welcome," Logan replied as they rose and headed to the car. "Now, where to next?"

WHEN LOGAN TRIED to arrange a meeting with Senator Quitoni and his wife, he'd been told that the senator and Mrs. Quitoni were too distraught. He was told to call the next day to see if the senator was feeling strong enough to speak to them.

Logan was frustrated by the senator putting them off. He'd have thought that Michelle's parents would want to do everything they could to find their daughter's killer. But he understood that diplomacy would be needed here. The senator was powerful, and powerful people often had to be treated with kid gloves. He'd call tomorrow, but if the senator "wasn't up for speaking to them" then, he'd have a talk with Lieutenant Crenshaw and his own bosses.

He and Dora spent the rest of the day reviewing the reports from the witness canvasses, attempting to identify anyone who saw something that would warrant a second interview and trying to nail down Michelle's movements over her last days. It was the tedious, unsexy work that often led to a suspect but never made it onto the television and movie screens. It was the kind of work that showed the mettle of a good cop, and Dora was a good cop. Methodical, thoughtful, and attentive to the smallest details. When he finally knocked off for the night, Dora was still at her desk.

His older brother, Landon, had sent a text earlier that afternoon asking if Logan could stop by when he had a chance. Logan was still too wired to go home, so he pointed his car in another familiar direction. His parents had bought their Brightwood Park home more than forty years earlier. A short walk away from the Fort Totten metro station, it was a sleepy neighborhood filled with families. When they'd purchased the home, they couldn't have imagined how much it would appreciate over the succeeding four decades.

He found a parking space at the end of the street and walked back to the house, using his key to let himself in. Logan stuffed his gloves and hat into the pocket of his coat and tossed the coat over the arm of the sofa. He made his way past boxes of flooring into the kitchen.

"The remodel is coming along," Logan said by way of greeting his older brother. Landon flashed a quick smile from his seat at the kitchen table. He'd been focused on something on his laptop screen. Landon had taken after their father and become an investigative reporter.

"It's getting there," his brother said.

The footprint of the kitchen would always be small—that was the way it was with row houses. But the space now boasted brand-new top-of-the-line appliances and sparkling white granite countertops.

"Still getting it all together," Landon said, pointing to the upper cabinets which waited to be hung on the floor against the kitchen wall.

Logan wrapped a bottle of water from the fridge and took a long swig, sitting at the table next to his brother. "I'd help you put them up, but I just caught a case that's going to tie up most of my time for a while."

"Don't worry about it." Landon closed the laptop. "I can handle it myself."

"Yeah, but you shouldn't have to," Logan said, feeling guilty not for the first time.

All three of the siblings had inherited the home after their mother's death. Landon had taken responsibility for it since Lisa owned her own place and Logan had moved to Arizona. Landon's plan was to renovate the house, which they'd all agreed to since their mother hadn't so much as painted since the early nineties. Once the work was done, they hoped to sell the place for a good sum. College-fund money, as Lisa had labeled it.

Landon reached over and clasped Logan on the shoulder. "Listen, don't worry about it. I got it."

Logan nodded, but the guilt was still there.

"I'm glad you could make it over tonight," Landon said.

"Your text made it seem important."

Landon stood. "I think it could be. I found something."

Logan followed Landon back into the living room.

Landon sat on the sofa and pulled a strongbox that Logan had passed unnoticed when he entered the house across the coffee table. Logan sat next to his brother.

"I found this in the attic."

"What were you doing in the attic?" Logan asked.

"It's a good space. You can stand up there—in most spots at least. I thought it might make a good office or spare room."

It had been years since Logan had ventured into his mother's attic. The thing he remembered most about it was the cobwebs and how creepy it felt to him. But if Logan said it was usable and, more importantly, valuable space, Logan didn't doubt him.

"So, what is this?" Logan asked, turning the conversation back to the strongbox in front of them.

Landon opened the box. Inside was an old notebook, and beside it was a handgun.

Logan leaned forward to look at the contents more

closely but didn't touch them. "Where did you find this exactly?"

"In a crawl space in the attic. I'm not sure I ever knew it existed before today, but when I moved some of the boxes Mom had stashed up there the cover to the crawl-space fell off."

The layer of dust that covered the contents had been disturbed.

"You check the gun?"

Landon nodded. "Unloaded."

"I'm not sure why you are showing this to me," Logan said again.

"I think this stuff belongs to Dad. In fact, I'm sure of it. The writing in the notebook is definitely his."

Landon had been fifteen, Logan thirteen, when their father was murdered. They were old enough to have lasting memories of their father, including being able to identify his handwriting on sight.

Logan reached for the notebook and flipped it open. Most of the text was indecipherable, written in some sort of code, but Landon was right. The handwriting was that of their father's.

"You think the gun was Dad's too?" Logan queried.

"Seems that way. It makes sense. I know he'd been threatened once or twice over a story. I heard him and Mom arguing about it when I was younger."

Logan hadn't known that, but he knew his father had been a dogged reporter who had taken on some powerful people in Washington, DC, from time to time to get a story. Samuel Elkins's mantra had been to "speak truth to power." Logan knew from experience that "power" didn't always appreciate hearing the truth.

"Okay, I'm still not sure why you're showing me all this," Logan said.

"Look here," Landon said, pointing to the only two words on the page that didn't appear to have been written in code. "There are names—William Burgess and Addison Kober."

Logan looked up at the ceiling, thinking. "Burgess. Burgess."

"William Burgess is the Australian ambassador, though he wasn't when Dad would have written this."

"If this note refers to the same man. You have no way of knowing that," Logan pointed out.

"But it's possible, and that's enough reason for me to check it out. Especially when I factor in Addison Kober."

That was a name he knew. Addison Kober had disappeared shortly before their father's death. She'd been fifteen, the same age as Landon at the time, and her disappearance had been all over the Washington, DC, media for weeks.

"Why would he hide this? I mean, I get why he'd stash the gun with us kids in the house. But what about the journal?" Landon said.

"I…don't know. We may never know."

Their father had been dead for twenty years, and their mother, who might have been able to answer these questions for them, had been dead for two years now. Time had dulled the pain of their father's loss, but just the memory of his mother, Carolyn, was still strong enough to send a bolt of grief through Logan strong enough to snatch his breath away.

It was a moment before his lungs began to function again.

"I think these notes—" Landon held up the journal, seemingly unaware of Logan's swirling emotions "— might help us figure out what Dad was working on when he was killed. And maybe who could have killed him."

Logan sighed. He knew that Landon had been carrying on his own side investigation into their father's murder for years. Hell, he wasn't ashamed to admit that he had pulled some strings himself when he'd worked for the MPD and looked at the report on the investigation, such that it was. The file had been sparse on facts, witnesses, and evidence.

His father's body had been found in an alleyway with several stab wounds. One witness, a woman living in an adjacent apartment building, had thought she might have heard yelling, but she didn't see anyone or recognize the voices. The cops confirmed that Samuel had been at his favorite bar, O'Sullivan's, earlier that night. There hadn't been anything out of the ordinary, according to the regular bartender. Around midnight, his father had received a call on his cell phone. He closed his tab and left soon after. The bartender had not known who the call came from, and if the cops had looked into it any further, that information hadn't found its way into the file. Their father's cell phone, watch, and wallet were missing when his body was found. General consensus was that the murder had been a random robbery homicide, and the case had gone cold.

Landon had never bought that explanation, and Logan wasn't sure he did either. But he wasn't going to let the unanswered questions consume his life. Not like his father's stories had consumed him. And not like their father's unsolved murder appeared to be slowly consuming Landon's life.

"Look, Lan, I know it's hard to make peace with the fact that we may never have answers about Dad's death—"

"Murder," Landon interrupted, his voice hard. "Dad was murdered. And we could have answers if anyone bothered to look."

Logan held his hands out. "I don't want to argue with you. I'm just saying cold cases aren't as easy to solve as the television shows make it seem."

"I'm an investigative reporter." Landon glared. "Don't you think I know that?"

Logan wasn't sure, but he knew he'd do whatever he could to help his brother. "What do you want for me?"

"Do you think you could get me a copy of the MPD file on Dad's murder?"

"Landon—"

"I know it's a big ask, but—"

"It's a huge ask. I don't have direct access to the MPD's system anymore. And even when I did, there was a firewall between me and all the information on Dad's case."

"But you're working with the MPD now, right? Couldn't you ask Dora—"

Logan shot his brother a look. "Don't go there."

"Look, I wouldn't ask if it wasn't important. No one else cares about finding his killer anymore, if they ever did. I'm all that he has if he's going to get any justice."

"You're not all he has," Logan growled, standing.

Landon had the decency to look embarrassed. "I didn't mean it like that. It's just... Maybe you're right.

Maybe I'm a little obsessed, but I can't let it go. Not without doing everything I can to find his killer. You understand that, right?"

Because he did understand, most of Logan's ire toward his brother faded away. "No promises," Logan said, grabbing his coat and heading for the front door. "I'll see what I can do."

Chapter Seven

Logan was happy to discover a text letting him know that Senator Quitoni and his wife were ready to speak to him. The Senator had insisted that the "conversation," as his people had termed it, be held at the Senator's residence. Since he firmly believed beggars couldn't be choosers, he met Dora at the police station, and they drove to the Senator's house together.

Senator Preston Quitoni lived on a sprawling estate in Great Falls, about thirty-five minutes from Capitol Hill. A tall iron fence ran around the tree-spotted property. The red-brick colonial sat two full football fields back from the street.

Dora swung the unmarked police sedan past the multiple news vans parked at the curb along the street from the corner and down past the senator's property. Cameras had been set up alongside the vans on the sidewalk. A half dozen reporters milled about on their phones, chatting, waiting for something to happen. They looked up as the car rolled by. The two bravest made their way toward the driveway, but two very large men materialized out of a gatehouse that blended into the line of cedar trees so well that Dora hadn't even noticed it at first.

"I bet the neighbors are loving this," Logan deadpanned.

Dora snorted. "I'm sure the local precinct is getting an earful, but it's a public street, so…" She shrugged and turned the sedan into the driveway, stopping beside an intercom.

A voice crackled from the speaker. "May I help you?"

"Detective Dora Madison from the Washington, DC, Metropolitan Police Department and Special Agent Logan Elkins of the FBI here to speak with Senator and Mrs. Quitoni."

The intercom crackled again. "Please hold your credentials up to the camera."

They did as requested, and after a moment, the disembodied voice said, "Very well."

The intercom clicked off, and the gates in front of them opened.

A young woman in black slacks and a white apron answered the door. Dora and Logan stepped into a large foyer with honey-brown teak flooring, wood-paneled walls, and an elaborate chandelier hanging overhead.

The maid led them to a sitting room larger than Dora's entire apartment. She recognized the man and woman sitting on the sofa as Senator and Mrs. Quitoni. The other man in the room she didn't know, but she didn't need to know his name to know that he was a lawyer. The thousand-dollar suit and constipated expression were dead giveaways.

The suit stepped forward, extending his hand. "Detectives, I am Cory Mase, of Mase, Black, and Glass. I'm the Quitonis' personal attorney."

Dora shook Mase's hand. "I'm the detective." She

hooked her thumb at Logan. "He's a special agent with the FBI."

"Yes, of course, my apologies. Special Agent Elkins, is it?"

Logan gave Mase's hand a cursory shake. "Yes."

"Special Agent, Detective, my clients have been through an extraordinary loss. I've advised them to take more time to grieve before speaking to you, but the senator has insisted on doing whatever it takes to help you find the monster who did this to his daughter."

"Well, we appreciate that," Logan said. "The more information we can get, the better chance we will have at catching your daughter's killer," Dora said.

"Of course. I just ask that you respect the Quitonis' precarious emotional state at the moment."

Dora nodded noncommittally. The law might treat every person the same in theory, but in practice she was sitting in front of a man with vast power.

Mase stepped back beside the sofa his clients were sitting on. Dora sank into an armchair across from the sofa, and Logan took the matching chair beside her. A coffee table in a rich, dark mahogany separated the armchairs and sofa.

"First, please let me extend condolences on behalf of myself and the Metropolitan Police Department," Dora started.

"Thank you, Detective," Mrs. Quitoni replied.

The maid strode back into the room carrying a silver serving tray laden down with a coffee pot and several coffee mugs. Dora studied the senator and his wife as the maid poured five cups of coffee. The senator looked broken and more than a little devastated. The senator's eyes were red rimmed, and it was clear he'd been crying. His wife was also visibly upset, but Mrs. Quitoni's expression was determined, her eyes were clear, and her makeup was perfect. They were both wearing suits, but the senator looked like he had slept in his while Mrs. Quitoni looked ready to hit the campaign trail.

The maid finished serving and left the room quickly.

Dora ignored her cup of coffee. "We'd like to ask you a few questions about your daughter."

Senator Quitoni sank deeper into the sofa, but his wife's back straightened. "Our daughter didn't do anything to deserve this."

"Of course she didn't, but knowing as much about her as possible might help us to locate the person who took her life."

Mrs. Quitoni frowned.

"We'll tell you whatever you want to know," Senator Quitoni said in a scratchy voice.

"Of course," Mrs. Quitoni quickly answered. "I'm just not sure we know anything that will help you."

Logan smiled tightly. "You'd be surprised about what could be helpful."

"When was the last time either of you saw your daughter?"

"Two nights ago. She came over for dinner."

"And how did she seem then?" Dora asked.

"Fine," the senator responded. "She seemed fine. Happy. She had plans to meet up with some friends after dinner."

"Do you know who those friends were?"

The senator shrugged. "Michelle was a grown woman. We tried not to pry into her life."

"You could try asking Eisha Steele. That's Michelle's best friend. They went to school together."

Dora jotted the name down. "And Michelle had been working at the Leonard Art Gallery, correct?" Dora had her notebook out and was taking notes.

"Yes. Michelle was an art history major at Georgetown." Senator Quitoni rubbed his temples.

"She got her MBA at George Mason last year," Mrs. Quitoni rushed to add. "She had plans to own her own gallery. She didn't just want to look at pretty things her whole life—she had real plans for success."

"Veronica," the senator hissed at his wife.

It sounded as if Mrs. Quitoni wasn't totally on board with her daughter's career choices. It might be worth looking more closely into the family's dynamics. Discreetly, of course. She made a mental note of that thought rather than writing it down.

Dora plowed ahead with her questions. "Michelle had recently moved out on her own, I understand."

Senator Quitoni nodded. "Yes. She lived here through undergraduate and graduate school, but she was twenty-six. She wanted her own space. We bought her a town house downtown, not far from the gallery."

Which would have cost big bucks, probably well into the millions. She wasn't exactly making it on her own.

"You must have been close." She had to tread carefully, but Michelle's parents were two of the last people who'd seen her alive. Dora needed to get a better picture of the dynamics of their relationship. As sick as it sounded, most murder victims were killed by the people closest to them—husbands, wives, lovers, siblings, even children. It would not be the first time that a parent had killed a child.

Senator Quitoni focused on the wall of glass windows looking out onto a pool and beyond. "Our relationship was fine. Maybe a little complicated."

Mrs. Quitoni tensed at her husband's words. He might have been the elected representative, but it was clear she was the power behind the couple.

"Michelle is our only child, Detective," the Senator continued. "We were close when Michelle was young. Then I decided to run for office when she was a teenager. All the attention was difficult for her."

"She hated it," Mrs. Quitoni said, as if a teenage girl not liking media attention was some sort of sacrilege. Dora wasn't sure there were any teens who would appreciate going through puberty under a media microscope.

The room was silent for a moment.

"Is that why Michelle moved to London?"

"Yes," the senator answered.

"No," Mrs. Quitoni said at the same time.

Dora shared a look with Logan.

Mrs. Quitoni shot a glare at her husband, and he shrunk even farther into the sofa cushions. "Michelle got a fellowship at the Louvre. It was an opportunity of a lifetime."

"She went to London to get away from the media frenzy around my last campaign. It was bruising. My opponent accused me of accepting bribes in exchange for voting on certain bills. There was no evidence, of course, because it didn't happen, and the Senate ethics committee cleared me, but the media spent weeks speculating. It almost certainly would have cost me the election if it hadn't come out that my opponent was the one actually taking bribes."

"What is it they say?" Mrs. Quitoni smirked. "Every accusation is a confession."

Politics was hard to avoid in Washington, DC, especially when a sitting congressman was accusing the senator from his own state of taking bribes. The scandal had been in the news for weeks before the election, and the late-night comedians had a field day when it came out that the congressman was arrested for bribery. He'd resigned his seat and slunk out of Washington, leaving the field clear for the senator's reelection.

"And she moved back to Washington six months ago?"

"Yes, her supervisor at the Louvre recommended her for the job at the Leonard Gallery."

"Did Michelle mention having any problems with anyone at the gallery? Or anyone at all?"

"No," the senator breathed. "She loved that job. Only had good things to say about it."

"What about someone special in her life? A boyfriend or girlfriend?" Logan pressed.

"No." Mrs. Quitoni waved the suggestion away. "Michelle was focused on her career. She didn't have time for romance."

Dora and Logan shared another look. Young women didn't always share their love lives with their parents. They'd have a talk with Michelle's coworkers and best friend. They'd likely know if there was a special someone in Michelle's life.

Senator Quitoni dropped his head into his hands as if it was all too much. His wife patted his shoulder absentmindedly, the first show of affection Dora had seen between the couple since the interview had started.

"We understand you have identified a witness. Have they been able to tell you anything about the person who did this to our daughter?" Mrs. Quitoni turned her hard gaze on Dora.

Irritation stabbed through Dora's gut. They hadn't released information about a witness, for obvious reasons. That the Quitonis knew about the witness wasn't a shock, but it did mean that someone in the department was telling tales out of school. And because she had no doubt that someone had probably been in the morning meeting and sat several notches above her in the food chain, there wasn't likely to be a whole lot she could do about it.

"I'm not at liberty to discuss the details of the investigation."

"This is our daughter!" Mrs. Quitoni's voice shook.

"I understand that, ma'am. And I am going to do everything I can to bring her killer to justice."

"We understand that you want answers," Logan jumped in, "but revealing details could jeopardize the case."

The senator lifted his head and speared Dora with a look. "You can't believe we'd do anything that might let this animal get away with what they did to our—" Senator Quitoni's voice broke.

"Of course they don't." Mrs. Quitoni's patting picked up speed. Anger flashed in her eyes. "I think my husband needs to rest now. You two can see yourselves out."

She said it like a woman who was used to people doing what she told them.

Dora and Logan rose.

"Again, we are sorry for your loss," Logan said. "And we'll be doing everything we can to find out who took her from you."

"What do you think?" Logan said after they'd slid back into the sedan.

Dora started the car before turning in her seat to face him. "I think there's a lot the Quitonis aren't telling us."

Logan's smile was grim. "I think you're right."

Chapter Eight

The Sutton Place townhomes were modern builds with gray stones and faux-wood doors with solar panels on their roofs. They reminded Logan of *The Jetsons*. It was a secure community, but there had been no one at the guard's hut when they drove through the open gates. But when they pulled to a stop in front of Michelle's unit, a small electric vehicle stopped behind them and a man in khakis and a polo shirt with *Sutton Place* etched over his left breast got out.

"This is a private community. You need to leave," he said, storming toward the sedan as soon as Dora stepped out of the car. He was in his early thirties, with wavy dark brown hair and dark eyes to match. He wore a pronounced scowl.

She held out her badge. "I'm Detective Madison. This is Special Agent Elkins."

"Oh." The man visibly relaxed. "Sorry. I've been dealing with calls from the residents about the press sneaking in here all day." The man swiped at the sweat beading on his forehead. "The homeowners don't want me to close the gates. They'd have to use their key card, and that would be an inconvenience to them. Tell me how I'm supposed to keep people out, then, huh?"

"I'm sorry to hear that Mr.—" Dora said.

"Waylen Osvolo. I'm the property manager here." Osvolo's eyes narrowed. "So, you're the detective in charge of Michelle's case?"

"I am," Dora responded.

"And you're FBI?" Osvolo turned to Logan.

"I am."

"Well, how can I help? Michelle was a nice girl. I couldn't believe it when I heard—"

Dora rounded the car and headed for the front walk. Logan and Osvolo followed. "How did you hear about Michelle's murder?"

It hadn't escaped Logan's notice that Osvolo was referring to Michelle by her first name. It raised questions, like how well did the property manager know Michell Quitoni? He'd have to wait until Dora finished her line of questioning to get his answers, though.

"One of the vultures. They've been hanging around since early this morning, looking for anyone who will talk to them. One even tried to bribe me into letting them into Michelle's unit." Osvolo puffed out his chest. "Of course, I said no. Told that creep if I caught him around here again, I'd call the cops on him."

"As you should have," Dora responded.

Osvolo's chest puffed out more.

"Mr. Osvolo, these are town houses." Logan stopped at the bottom of the staircase leading to the front door of the unit. Dora started up the stairs but turned back when he spoke. "What sort of property management do you do for the residents?"

"Anything that needs doing." He chuckled. "The people that live here are rich—like, seriously rich. They don't want to worry about yard maintenance or busted pipes or missing roof shingles. The management company offers full-service property upkeep and maintenance. We take care of hiring contractors for your everyday maintenance, like mowing the lawn in the summer and shoveling the walkways in the winter, as well as plumbing, heating, and electrical emergencies. All the homeowner has to do is give me a call. We have a bevy of contractors on retainer."

"Sounds like my kind of homeownership," Dora quipped.

"And how much does service like that run the homeowners?" Logan asked.

"Well, the monthly homeowner's association fees run twenty-three hundred a month, not including special assessments."

Dora let out a low whistle. "Never mind."

Logan chuckled. "What kind of special assessments?"

"Well, if the pipe in your home burst, it wouldn't be fair for all the homeowners to pick up the cost."

"So, twenty-three hundred is your base cost per month. You'd likely have additional charges during a year because something is always going wrong in a house."

Osvolo nodded. "Exactly." The property manager leaned in and dropped his voice. "Some of the homeowners are constantly calling for one thing or the other. Little things. Like, just the other day, Mrs. Celetano called me to change her light bulb. Can you believe it? The management company charges a hundred fifty dol-

lars every time I step foot into a unit, and she called me
to change a light bulb. Rich people." Osvolo shook his
head in disgust.

"Mr. Osvolo, you seem to know Michelle Quitoni
pretty well," Logan said while the other man's head was
still going back and forth.

Osvolo startled, just as Logan had hoped. He wanted
to catch the man off guard and gauge his reaction to the
question.

Osvolo's neck pinked. "I… I don't know what you
mean. She was a homeowner here. We were friendly,
but nothing more than that."

Logan leaned against the stair railing. "You seem
more than just friendly. For instance, you referred to
Mrs. Celetano using an honorific and her last name, but
you call Miss Quitoni by her given name, Michelle."

"I… It's… She told me to. It's not against the rules!"
The pink from Osvolo's neck crawled upward.

"No one is suggesting you broke any rules, Mr. Osvolo." Dora stepped down a stair. "We're just trying to
get a mental picture of Michelle's life. She has friends
and acquaintances. The people she came into contact
with regularly."

"Well, I only saw her on maintenance calls or if I
happened to be driving by or manning the guard booth.
That's all."

"Was she friendly with any neighbor in particular?"

He shook his head, still upset. "Not that I know of. I
don't spy on the residents."

"We're not suggesting you do," Logan said in his most
soothing voice. Osvolo certainly riled quickly.

"Did you ever see Miss Quitoni with anyone in particular? A boyfriend? A girlfriend?"

Another head shake. "No boyfriend. There is a girl sometimes, a woman, about the same age. They seemed like friends, though."

"Can you describe her?" Dora took out her notebook.

Osvolo's brow scrunched. "Blond hair, about down to here." He dusted his shoulder with his hand. "Close to Michelle's height. Pretty enough. Slim. Dressed really nice. That's about all I remember. I only saw her a couple of times."

"This is great—thanks. And when was the last time you saw Miss Quitoni?" Dora asked, not looking up from her notebook.

Logan couldn't help but admire her technique. Slipping in the real question she wanted answered so smoothly.

Osvolo's body tensed. "I already told the officers that came by this morning. I was in bed asleep with my wife when Michelle was killed."

Dora lifted her head and pinned Osvolo in her gaze. "We don't know when Miss Quitoni was killed. Do you?"

"I… I meant…" Osvolo sputtered, and Dora let him. "Of course not. You're trying to confuse me. The reporters said you found her this morning. I meant to say I was in bed when you found her. And I'm sure I have an alibi for whenever she was killed—not that I need one. I didn't kill her!"

The slam of a car door had him spinning. Logan looked over Osvolo's shoulder. Three houses down, a woman wrangled a car seat out of the back of a Mercedes SUV. She didn't seem to be paying any attention to them.

Osvolo faced Logan and Dora again. "Look, I... I've told you everything I know."

Dora smiled. "But you haven't, Mr. Osvolo. You haven't answered my last question."

"Your question?" He wiped the sweat from his brow with his forearm. "What question?"

"When did you last see Miss Quitoni?"

"Um...maybe two, three days ago. In passing," he hurried to add. "It was trash day. Mr. Levin uses a walker and can't get around too well anymore, so I pull his trash cans to the curb for him. I headed to his house around seven that morning to make sure the trash got out before the men came for it, and I saw Michelle getting into her car. I waved, and she waved back. Her car was gone when I came back down the street about ten minutes later. I assumed she'd left for work."

Dora finished noting everything he'd said and closed her notebook. "Thank you very much, Mr. Osvolo. If I have any more questions for you, I know how to contact you."

It was a dismissal, and Osvolo seemed more than happy to heed it. He bounded down the walk. His car peeled away as Dora keyed in the code to get the key for the lock the uniforms had put on Michelle's door earlier that day.

Police protocol would have had uniforms out to Michelle's house soon after her body was identified to secure it.

Logan accepted the nitrile gloves Dora handed him as they passed through the doorway and snapped them over his hands.

The main floor was open space with the living area

flowing into the dining area and into the kitchen. It wasn't a large space, but whoever had designed it had done the most with what they had. The space could have used some interior decorating. It looked more like a showroom than a home. A beige silk sofa sat atop a soft chenille rug with a glass coffee table anchoring the space. The obligatory flat-screen television was mounted on the wall across from the sofa. Under the large window, looking out onto the front lawn, sat a white desk, its top devoid of anything other than a small gold lamp.

"What are we looking for?" Logan asked.

Dora strode forward, speaking to him without turning around. "You know as well as I do it's always somewhat of a 'you'll know it when you see it' situation. Mostly, I just wanted to see Michelle's living space. Get a feel for how she lived." Dora glanced at him over her shoulder. "I figured you'd want to do the same, profiler."

Logan felt his brow arch.

"I may have read one or two of your papers." She turned around, but before he caught the hint of a smile on her face.

He couldn't help but feel good that she'd thought about him after they'd broken up, at least enough to keep up with his career after their breakup. He'd thought about her a lot. More than he cared to admit, even to himself.

"CSI has already been here and collected Michelle's tablet."

Logan opened the drawer of the desk seated under the window. Monogrammed letterhead and envelopes, paperclips, two pens with *Leonard Gallery* spelled out in cursive on their sides, and a highlighter were all that was inside the drawer.

The bookshelves on the opposite side of the room were orderly, organized by the author's last name. One shelf held a photo of Michelle and her parents and another of Michelle and a blonde woman, both women smiling widely and wearing bikinis on what looked like a very expensive yacht.

Logan picked up the photo. "This could be the blonde woman that Osvolo saw." He took his phone from his jacket pocket and snapped a photo before passing the photo to Dora, who did the same.

"Could be the best friend, Eisha Steele, that her parents told us about. I'll check into it when we get back to the station."

She replaced the photo on the shelf and headed for the stairs.

Logan followed.

There were three bedrooms upstairs, although one of the three was tiny. Michelle seemed to have agreed. She'd turned it into a closet.

Dora made a circle around the room. "If I counted all the clothes I've ever owned together, I don't think it would amount to this much."

Logan couldn't disagree. It was a lot of clothing. Dresses, skirts, and tops. Fancy, business, or casual. Michelle Quitoni could have opened a boutique just consisting of her wardrobe. It was overkill if you asked him. He had five suits—two black, two blue, and one tan.

They left the closet and headed for Michelle's bedroom. Like the rest of the house, it looked unused. The bed was made with military-sharp corners. End tables stood on either side, but their tops were clear of clutter.

Dora opened the closet door. Shelves of shoes stared back at her.

Logan went to the end tables. If there was anything to be found in a bedroom, the end tables, closets, and between the mattresses were where it would be found. The drawers in the end table were empty. Dora helped him shove the mattress to the side even though she protested that if there had been something to find, CSI would have found it. He didn't doubt CSI's professionalism, but he wanted to see it with his own eyes. There was nothing.

The attached bathroom and second bedroom were equally devoid of anything that could be useful.

"There is nothing here," Dora said once they'd descended the stairs.

"Yes and no," Logan responded.

Dora gave him a silent look.

"A home this clean, this unlived in tells me quite a bit about its inhabitant."

Dora fisted a hand on her hip and smirked. "Oh, really, and what had it been saying to you?"

Logan couldn't help grinning. "It tells me that Michelle was well ordered, likely a creature of habit. She liked that her life was orderly and neat. She's not likely to take many risks or veer off the path that she's set for herself."

"Okay." Dora drew out the word, letting him know that she wanted him to say more.

"I don't see her going off with someone she didn't know."

"So, she likely knew her killer, or at least was familiar with the person."

"I'm still gathering information, but this house—" he

did a three sixty turn "—is the house of a woman used to being in control of her life. A woman that most likely sticks to a strict self-imposed schedule."

Dora clucked her tongue and headed for the front door. "Well, that's good at least. It means we just have to keep digging into Michelle's life. That's where we'll find our killer."

THE ITCH WAS BACK. That need. It was almost a command.

Find her.

He could feel it slowly rising up, humming through his body. Demanding action. He had to keep going until he found her. He had to keep going until he saved her. Then they could be together again.

A family, just like they used to be. He'd been mistaken about the others. He thought they were pure, like his own Sarah. But he was wrong.

He couldn't be wrong this time. He'd find her.

And then he would finally be free.

Chapter Nine

Landon felt bad about having Logan ask Dora for a favor. He knew his brother still had feelings for the pretty police detective. He hoped they could work out their differences. His brother deserved happiness, and Dora seemed to make him happy. It helped that the detective wouldn't stand for Logan's broody, silent act.

But it had been twenty years of not knowing exactly what had led to his father's death. Landon had always wondered. He'd always had his suspicions that his father's murder hadn't been a random robbery, and when he'd found his dad's hidden journal, his concerns had heightened even more. Well, he was an investigative reporter, after all. It was in his blood to sniff out a story.

So, he'd do what he had to do and make his apologies later, he thought as he headed to the basement of *The District Sun*'s offices.

The long windowless corridor leading to the *Sun*'s archive room was desolate so late in the evening. *The District Sun* was a small, though highly regarded, operation. What it lacked in operating funds, it made up for by hiring dogged, experienced professionals. But that meant savings had to be found wherever possible, and one area was with respect to archiving old articles and editions of the paper. There was no money for cloud storage for everything, so the publisher kept files from the early 2000s on an in-house hard drive. It was rudimentary, but it worked. Articles from 2002, the year Addison Kober had gone missing, would be found on that hard drive.

The door to the archive room was kept locked, but Landon had gotten the key from the *Sun*'s receptionist before she left for the evening. The unfinished, dimly lit room was an open cavernous space that held rows of steel shelving with cardboard boxes stacked on them. Landon ignored the shelves and boxes. They held old, printed newspapers, notes of long-dead reporters, and who knew what else. What he needed might not have been accessible on the cloud, but it was accessible on the hard drive of the archive's old IBM computer.

The computer sat in the corner of the room on a beat-up wooden desk, beige monitor and matching beige keyboard.

Landon had to wait for what felt like a lifetime for the computer to boot up, but the screen finally lit up with the paper's logo and a box asking for his username and password. He entered his information, and after several more painstaking seconds, the search page appeared. He started with a broad search, entering the name *Addison Kober*. The search returned more than a dozen results. For the *Sun*, that was a lot of stories on the same topic. But the disappearance of Addison Kober had been big news in the Washington, DC, area two decades earlier.

He read through several of the articles, sending them

all to his email before also sending them to the aged printer next to the desk.

He'd go through them all again more carefully, but for now, he wanted to gather as much information as possible. He noted the dates on the articles and the fact that as time wore on, fewer and fewer articles had been written about Addison. The last article written appeared approximately three months after Addison had gone missing. Three months. That was all the time it had taken for most of the world to forget about the disappearance of a fifteen-year-old girl.

He did another search, this one combining Addison's name with *William Burgess*. There were no hits. He tried similar searches with all the Burgesses and got the same result.

So, what had his father known that no one else did?

Landon logged off the computer and headed back upstairs to his desk. He wanted to do the same searches in the broader multi-newspaper databases that the *Sun* subscribed to, but he was sure those searches would return hundreds of results, if not more. He'd need to read through all of them. He'd learned early in his career to take nothing for granted. You never knew where the key to a story would be found. He'd pull every thread until he was sure where it led. Especially since he suspected one of the threads would lead him to his father's killer.

"I CAN'T BELIEVE this is happening." Eisha Steele took another tissue from the box on the coffee table in front of the couch where she sat.

Dora had called ahead to let her know she and Logan would be stopping by, but Eisha had still burst into tears the moment she'd opened the door to them. She was clearly a woman overcome with grief, but she'd assured them that she would do whatever she could to help find Michelle's killer.

And Dora was hopeful Eisha knew something that would help. She was the last person that they know of to have seen or spoken to Michelle before she was killed.

Dora sat beside Eisha on the sofa while Logan discretely roamed the living room.

"I'm sorry." Eisha sniffed. "It's just so unbelievable. Michelle is dead. No matter how many times I say it, it just doesn't feel real."

"Give it time. Let yourself grieve."

"Thank you."

"I'm sorry to have to do this now, but the sooner we can get some answers, the more likely we'll find the person that did this to Michelle."

Eisha nodded. "I totally understand. I want to help you."

"Thank you. Can you tell me how long you and Michelle have been friends?" She found it was somewhat easier to talk to family and friends of victims in the present tense, especially when the loss was hitting them hard. The past tense was a reminder that could sometimes overwhelm the person before she'd finished her questioning.

"We met in grad school. We were both getting our MBAs and had a couple of classes together. We hit it off and kept up the friendship after we graduated last year."

"Do you go out together a lot?"

"I wouldn't say a lot. We both have full-time jobs now. It's not like being in school. But we get together a couple times a month, usually for dinner but sometimes to hit a club, like the other night."

Dora made a note, then said, "Can you take me through what you two did, from the moment you met until you parted?"

Eisha took a deep breath and let it out slowly. "I'd gotten two VIP tickets to Vibe." She must have read the incomprehension on Dora's face because she followed up with, "It's this new club in Northeast. Everyone's been talking about it, but it's pretty hard to get in, especially to the VIP section, where everyone wants to be seen. Anyway, this guy from work has been chatting me up, and I think he is working up to asking me out and wants to impress me. When he offered to get me two passes, to be honest, I didn't think he would do it, but I was super excited when he did."

"And Michelle went with you."

Eisha nodded. "She didn't really want to. I had to beg her to go, but she finally agreed."

"Why didn't she want to go?"

Frown lines formed on Eisha's forehead. "She'd been kind of weird lately. Like, not wanting to go out much. Preoccupied. At first, I thought it was just work, but she never wanted to talk about it when I asked, and that wasn't like her."

"Not to talk about her feelings?"

"Not talking about her feelings about work. She loved her job, even though she always butted heads with her boss about the best way to run the gallery." Eisha's gaze darted away before landing on Logan and Dora again. "John Leonard knows his art, but he's not a very good businessman. Michelle was always proposing new ways to get people into the gallery to get the gallery out in the community. But Leonard wanted to be exclusive. Very elite, but elite wasn't paying the bills."

"The gallery was in trouble?" Logan plucked a book from the bookshelf across from the sofa.

Eisha looked at him, a flash of surprise crossing her face as if she'd forgotten he was in the room. "*Trouble* may be overstating it. John comes from money, so I doubt he's in any danger of having to close, but the gallery isn't running in the black—that's for sure. Michelle was very vocal about what she would do differently when she had her own gallery. And now she'll never—" Eisha choked off a sob.

Dora gave her a minute to pull herself together before getting the interview back on track. "So, while you were at the club, any behavior in particular stand out at all to you?"

Eisha dabbed at her eyes. "I mean, Michelle was quieter than usual. She's usually up for dancing, but she rejected every guy that asked. She drank more than usual."

Dora jotted that information down. "How many drinks would you say?"

"Oh, I'm not sure. I didn't keep an eye on her all night. Now I wish I had." Eisha swallowed hard. "I know she had at least three over the night."

"And how long were you two there?"

"We got there about eleven. Dylan, the guy I mentioned, the one who gave me the tickets, was there. I ended up hanging out with him for a long time." She blushed. It seemed that the tickets had worked their magic. "I guess it was about one when Michelle said she was ready to leave. I was still having a good time and didn't want to go. Dylan offered to drive me home, so Michelle left."

"You two drove in her car to the club?" Logan said, giving Dora a pointed look.

"Yes. Michelle insisted." Eisha pulled a face. "I figured it was because she planned to leave early, which is why I wasn't that upset when she said she was going."

They hadn't found Michelle's car, and the killer would have had to get her to the park somehow.

"Do you remember anyone at the club paying special attention to Michelle? Asking her to dance a lot? Buying her drinks? Or just maybe hanging around?"

Eisha chuffed a laugh. "It's a club, Detective, and we were dressed for going out. Lots of guys paid Michelle special attention. I can't think of anyone that seemed creepy, though, and I'm sure she would have mentioned it if anyone had given her the willies."

"Okay, what about Michelle's love life more generally? Had she been seeing anyone lately?"

Eisha shook her head. "No. She'd gone on a few dates in the last year, but since grad school she hadn't seen anyone seriously. She, and I," she hurried to add, "have been mostly focused on our careers. There hasn't been time for romance."

"Is Michelle close to anyone else? Maybe someone from her job?"

"I think there's a part-time person that covers for Michelle when she takes a day off or when John goes out of town on a buying trip." Eisha didn't look at them while she answered.

Dora's cop instinct pinged. She shared a look with Logan and gathered that he'd also gone on alert. Eisha wasn't telling them something. She'd also looked away when she'd mentioned Michelle's contentious relationship with her boss.

Dora cleared her throat. "And her boss, John Leonard? You mentioned that Michelle butted heads with him. Was there more to their relationship?"

Eisha continued to avoid looking at either of them. "I'm not sure what you mean."

"I think you are," Logan responded.

Eisha heaved a sigh. "Look, John and Michelle spend a lot of time together at the gallery. I wasn't lying when I said they were at odds about how to run the place, but you know there's a thin line between love and hate and all that. She and John had gotten together a few times."

"Gotten together," Dora pressed. "You mean they were having an affair?"

Eisha rolled her eyes. "Affair may be too strong a word for it. They hooked up whenever the mood struck. It wasn't like they were in a relationship or anything though. I know Michelle saw other people. And John is technically married."

Dora wondered how someone could be technically married. In her book, you either were or were not married—it was pretty simple. But Eisha Steele's philosophy on commitment wasn't relevant to the case so she let it go. John Leonard was already on the growing list of people Dora needed to speak with.

"The only other person that Michelle talks about is her psychiatrist," Eisha added.

"Michelle was seeing a psychiatrist?" Logan sat the book down and moved over to the sofa. "Do you know why?"

Eisha shifted on the couch. "Not exactly."

Dora shot Logan a look she hoped he read correctly as *Back off* before focusing back on Eisha. "Eisha, I'm sure that you want to protect Michelle, but holding back information from us now doesn't protect her. But it may protect the person that killed her."

Eisha hesitated for a moment longer.

"I know Michelle struggled some with anxiety and depression while we were in graduate school. Her parents, her mother especially, put a lot of pressure on her to be perfect. The perfect student. The perfect business-woman. To never do anything that anyone could perceive as embarrassing to the senator. Especially during his last campaign. The media was brutal, and Michelle didn't escape their glare."

"Did anything in particular happen during the senator's campaign that Michelle was concerned about?" Logan pressed.

Eisha shrugged. "I mean, the usual. Reporters followed her everywhere she went after the allegations against the senator came out. The campus police had to ban them, but that didn't help when she wasn't on campus."

"Do you know Michelle's psychiatrist's name?"

"Dr. Najimy."

Dora jotted down the name. "Did her parents know she was seeing a psychiatrist?"

"Definitely not," Eisha said emphatically. "Her parents wanted everyone to think they were this close, happy family, but Michelle could barely stand her mother, and she thought her father was weak and needed to stand up to her more."

Mrs. Quitoni definitely drove the relationship, based on what Dora had seen. Maybe the picture that the Quitonis had painted of their family wasn't as rosy as they'd have liked Dora to believe.

"So, Michelle left the club about two in the morning," Dora said, wanting to make sure that she didn't miss any of the details. "Did you speak with her or communicate with her at all after that?"

"I sent her a text just after four, letting her know I'd gotten home safely. We always did that for each other. I didn't hear back from her. Come to think of it, she never sent me a text telling me that she'd made it home safely. I should have noticed." Tears streamed down her face. "I could have called the police earlier, maybe…"

Dora reached for the woman's hand. "None of this is your fault, and I am sure that Michelle wouldn't want you blaming yourself."

Eisha's tears kept coming.

Dora suspected she wasn't going to get anything else out of her until she'd had more time to process her loss.

Chapter Ten

Logan wished he could say he was shocked by the news that Michelle might have been having an affair with her boss, but he wasn't. The picture of Michelle Quitoni that was emerging was that she was a woman with secrets. Dora got the contact information for John Leonard, owner of the Leonard Gallery and Michelle's boss, but he did not answer his cell or his office number. She left messages on both voicemails.

They had better luck when it came to Michelle's psychiatrist, Bruce Najimy. He agreed to fit them in between patients. They headed for his offices in Arlington, Virginia, after leaving Eisha.

Najimy's office was on the third floor of a medical building that housed a medical practice, psychotherapist's office, and a physiotherapist. The building was just on the other side of the Potomac from Washington, DC, in Virginia. Dr. Bruce Najimy was in a session when Logan and Dora arrived. Najimy's secretary, a rail-thin young man in his twenties with jet-black hair, offered coffee and tea and, after they'd declined, left them to wait in an elegantly furnished waiting area. The door to the interior office opened ten minutes later, and Dr. Bruce Najimy stepped out. A large window in the area overlooked the Potomac, a view that Logan was sure had added a few thousand dollars a year to the rent on the space.

"Detective Madison, please come in. Sorry for the wait." Dr. Bruce Najimy ushered them into the office. He waved them to the visitor's chairs in front of his desk. On the other side of the large office was a plush, upholstered sofa that faced a straight-backed armchair. End tables stood on either side of the armchairs with a brass lamp on one. This was obviously the space in the office where the doctor met with his patients.

"Thank you for seeing us on short notice, Dr. Najimy. This is Special Agent Logan Elkins. He's assisting the department with this case. He's a profiler with the FBI."

Logan shook the hand the doctor had offered.

"Happy to be of help, as you know, Detective," Dr. Najimy said.

"In addition to his private practice, Dr. Najimy assists the department from time to time when we need a psych evaluation."

"Forensic psychology has always fascinated me," he explained. "I enjoy the work, and it makes me feel as if I'm contributing to making the world a better place, so why not?"

"The department is lucky to have you," Dora said with a tense smile. "Hopefully, you can help us out with our investigation into Michelle Quitoni's murder."

"As much as I would like to help you, Detective Madison, Michelle was my patient. There's not a lot I can say given doctor-patient confidentiality."

"Your patient is dead, Doctor," Logan said, letting the irritation he felt creep into his tone. "I'd think that would take precedence."

"Special Agent Elkins, as a profiler, I'm sure you know that confidentiality doesn't end with the patient's death. Unless Michelle or her representative gives me permission, I am limited in what I can say to you."

"Michelle is dead," Logan shot back bluntly. "I'm sure she would like her killer to be found and held responsible. Preferably before he or she kills again."

"Logan," Dora hissed, shooting him a quelling look before turning to the doctor. "Doctor Najimy, please, whatever you can tell us would be helpful."

"I'll do what I can."

"Could you tell us how long Michelle had been seeing you?"

"About six years." Najimy said.

"Six years?" Dora said, surprised.

So, while Michelle was an undergraduate, which most likely meant her parents knew about the therapy. After all, how would a college student have afforded the bill on her own?

Dora must have been thinking along the same lines. "Did Michelle's parents know she was seeing you?"

"I assume so. My bills are sent directly to Senator Quitoni's accountant and are always promptly paid."

"Do you know how she found you?" Logan asked.

Najimy leaned back in his chair and looked up at the ceiling in thought. After a moment, he said, "I believe it was through a referral, although I can't tell you who exactly."

Can't or *won't*. Either way Logan was sure it didn't

matter. Najimy wasn't going to give them any more information than he wanted to, and he didn't appear to want to give them much. The psychiatrist was smug.

"How was Michelle's relationship with her parents?" Logan asked.

Najimy held up a finger and waved it from side to side. "Ah, ah, ah. That would be crossing the line."

"How about something easier?" Dora interjected before Logan could tell the psychiatrist where he could stick his finger. "When was the last time you saw Michelle?"

"I saw her twice a week, on Wednesdays and Fridays at noon."

"That doesn't answer the question," Logan shot back.

Najimy smiled. "You're correct, Special Agent Elkins. My apologies for not being precise. The last time I saw Michelle was Friday morning. It was our regularly scheduled appointment."

"Did she seem worried or upset?" Dora pressed. "Anything at all out of the ordinary with her?"

"Again, I can't get into the details of our session."

Logan started to speak.

Najimy forged ahead. "But Michelle seemed the same as she always did."

"Dr. Najimy, Michelle's best friend told us that she was seeing you for anxiety and depression."

Najimy blinked but did not speak.

Logan sighed. "Look, can you at least tell us if you'd prescribed any medications for her? We'll find out whether she was on anything when the toxicology report comes back, but it would help to know what medications were supposed to be there to weed out those that shouldn't."

Najimy hesitated for a moment. "I have prescribed fluoxetine and diazepam."

Logan knew enough about pharmaceuticals to recognize the medications: Prozac and Valium.

"Do you know if she was having trouble with anyone? A boyfriend or lover? Maybe someone who wanted to be in those categories?"

"Not that I know of, but…" Najimy broke off. He stroked his beard with one hand.

"Doctor," Logan pressed.

"This is probably crossing a line, but Michelle had mentioned feeling as if someone was watching her."

Dora leaned forward in her chair. "Did she say who?"

"No, and to be honest, I didn't think much of it. Her father's election scandal was not easy for Michelle. The press was relentless. They followed her for weeks. For someone already suffering from anxiety and depression, it was trying."

Logan fought back a smile. Najimy didn't seem to realize he'd confirmed that Michelle was seeing him for anxiety and depression, though the medications he had her on were evidence enough.

"So, you don't think Michelle was actually being followed?"

Najimy held his hands up. "I don't know now."

A familiar hum vibrated in Logan's chest. This could be important. "And she gave you no indication of who she suspected of following her?"

"None whatsoever." The phone on the doctor's desk buzzed. "I'm sorry, Detective, Special Agent. My next patient is here." He rose and extended his hand over the desk. "If there is anything else I can do for you, please don't hesitate to let me know."

They shook hands, and Najimy led them to a different door than the one they'd come into the office through. It led directly into the building's hallway.

"What do you think?" Dora asked as they headed for the elevators.

"I think I don't like the good doctor."

She chuckled. "I'm with you there, but I meant what do you think of what the doctor told us. About someone possibly watching Michelle."

"I don't know what to think. Najimy all but said Michelle was seeing him for anxiety and depression. It's possible she was paranoid."

"Possible, but you don't think so." The elevator doors opened, and they stepped out into the building's main lobby.

Logan watched Dora fall into step beside him. "I think it's all we have to go on right now."

MERCY'S BAR AND GRILL was located on Wisconsin Avenue in the upscale Friendship Heights neighborhood. The restaurant was already pretty busy by the time Dora arrived to meet with her best friend, Special Victims Unit Detective Noreen Montgomery. Noreen had already arrived and gotten a table for them.

Dora greeted her friend and took a seat, ordering a prosecco when the waitress stopped by the table. Noreen already had a glass of red wine in front of her.

While they waited for the waitress to return with Dora's drink, Noreen asked, "So, how are you doing?"

"The case? It's taxing. I can't stop thinking about the next victim."

"You never do. I've never met a more compassionate cop than you, even though you tried to hide it. But I was talking about how you are doing with Logan being back."

Dora rolled her eyes. "Of course you already know. Do you have spies everywhere?"

"Yes." Noreen laughed.

The waitress returned with Dora's drink and took their orders. They both got the surf and turf. When the waitress left, Noreen turned the conversation back to Logan.

"Okay, now spill. Is he still hot?"

"That is irrelevant," Dora replied, heat rising in her cheeks.

"You're blushing," Noreen teased, "so I'm going to take your nonanswer as a yes."

"Logan and I are over."

"Okay," Noreen said, incredulously taking a sip of her wine.

"It's been two years, Nor. I'm over him."

"It's been two years, but you are definitely not over him. You haven't seriously dated anyone since Logan moved to Arizona."

"That has nothing to do with him. I've been focused on my job."

"Yeah, right." Noreen snorted. "Keep telling yourself that. Maybe you'll believe it soon."

"It's true."

"Okay, listen, maybe it wouldn't be all that bad for you to explore a bit when it comes to Logan."

"Explore."

"Yes, I mean he's moved back to DC, right?"

"Yes."

"Well, if you wanted something to happen with him, the long-distance thing isn't an issue."

"He dumped me."

"I get it, and he's a fool for that. But did you tell me he said he was ending the relationship because he didn't think he could do long distance? That's not an issue now is all I'm saying."

"Maybe," Dora said, mostly because she didn't know if she wanted to go down that road. It might've been two years, but it wasn't all that easy to put herself out there again.

Noreen held her hands out in a surrender pose. "Okay, I'll back off. Just don't let the past be a barrier to your future."

Noreen didn't wait a beat before she launched into a story about her most recent date. Purposely changing the subject, Dora knew. For all her encouragement to get back together with Logan, Noreen enjoyed dating more than she enjoyed being in long-term relationships.

Dora listened and responded appropriately, but her mind still replayed what Noreen had said.

Was she letting her past with Logan keep her from envisioning what a future could be for them? More importantly, did she even want a future with him?

Chapter Eleven

When he'd informed his older brother, Landon, that he was moving back to Washington, DC, Landon had offered Logan the use of one of the spare rooms in his house. It was a nice offer and probably the only way he'd get to spend a good deal of time with his busy journalist brother, but Logan hadn't been able to see himself moving back into his childhood home. Especially not now when both his parents were gone. Just visiting Landon there brought back memories that could sometimes be overwhelming. He couldn't imagine living there again.

Instead, he'd rented an apartment in Southwest. The rent was a little pricy, but the neighborhood was convenient, and his building was only a two-block walk to the metro station. It meant he rarely had to drive the car he paid a small fortune to park in the building's garage. His sister, Lisa, had been after him to buy a house and really put down roots. He knew it made sense—more sense at least than paying rent forever. But he wouldn't consider buying a house until he was married and ready to start a family. And he'd only ever envisioned it hap-

pening in fleeting moments in what seemed to be a lifetime ago with Dora.

He strode through the building lobby and took the
elevator to the seventh floor, heading for his corner
apartment. He could hear movement inside as soon as
he opened the door. Someone was in his kitchen. He
sniffed. Cooking.

Logan shut the door to his apartment and stepped into
the galley kitchen. His niece, Layla, stood barefoot in
front of the stove.

"Hi, Uncle Logan." Layla flashed a brilliant smile
that turned his heart to putty. No matter how old she
got, he'd always see the little girl that he'd bounced on
his knee and given piggyback rides when she was little.

"I got hungry. I'm making pancakes." Layla expertly
flicked her wrist, sending the pancake in the pan on the
stove into the air and catching it like a pro. His niece
loved to cook, much like her mother, and had recently
begun thinking about going to culinary school when she
graduated from high school in two years' time.

Logan dropped a kiss onto Layla's forehead. "Hmm.
Smells good. Do you have enough for your old uncle?"

"Sure."

"Sweetheart, you know you're always welcome, but
refresh my memory—did we have a playdate scheduled?"

Layla looked so much like her mother, his sister,
Lisa. But she reminded Logan more of his older brother,
Landon. Self-assured. Dogged when they thought they
were right. Stubborn, even. It was that self-assuredness
and doggedness that had made Landon a great investigative reporter. And it was Landon's stubborn streak

that had kept him from giving up on investigating the nearly twenty-year-old murder of their father.

Layla rolled her eyes at him in perfect teenage fashion. "I am too old for playdates. Mom is making dinner for Edgar, and I didn't want to be there for that."

Logan's sister, Lisa, hadn't dated for years after her divorce, but she recently began venturing back onto the dating market. Edgar was a coworker that Lisa had begun seeing quite a bit of, much to her daughter's dismay.

"Ah, so you decided to pay me a visit. I'm sorry I wasn't here."

"It's no problem. I just borrowed the spare set of keys Mom has. Actually, I was supposed to go to Julia's house, but…" Layla shrugged.

Logan had spent enough time with the teen to know when a shrug was more than just a shrug. Julia was Layla's best friend, he'd gleaned from the number of times her name had appeared in Layla's stories.

"But what?" he pressed.

Layla shrugged again. "Julia is being kind of weird is all."

"Kinda weird how?"

"I don't know, just kind of…mean lately."

"She's being mean to you?" Logan's protective instincts piqued, though he reminded himself that Julia was a sixteen-year-old girl.

"Don't go all FBI man on me, okay?" Layla plated two pancakes and slid them across the bar to Logan. She grabbed her own plate and slid onto the bar stool next to him.

"I don't know what's going on with Julia." Layla

spoke around the piece of pancake she just popped into her mouth. "She started hanging out with these other two girls, Marleen and Elyse."

Layla stuck her forefinger into her mouth and made a gagging noise.

Logan chuckled but kept eating. He'd learned it was best to let Layla talk things out herself. She was a bright girl who usually made it to the right decisions on her own.

"I don't know what Julia sees in them. They barely come to school. I think they both had to do summer school, like, every year since the ninth grade. And they smoke, which is just gross." Layla made a face.

Logan's brow rose. "Smoke what?"

"Cigarettes is all I've seen them smoke, but I wouldn't be surprised if they smoked weed too. And…" Layla held up a hand. "Before you get upset, no, I have never and will never smoke cigarettes. They are truly nasty."

He thought about pressing the obvious omission of weed from her statement but then thought better of it, remembering Lisa saying she had to pick her battles.

"I don't know," Layla said forlornly. "I'm not sure Julia and I are friends anymore."

"I'm sorry, sweetheart. I think it would be Julia's loss, but I know saying that doesn't make it any easier when it feels like a friend is pulling away."

Layla wiped her eyes with the heel of her hand. Logan put down his fork and wrapped an arm around his knees. Despite all the talking she'd done, she also managed to clear her plate.

"Hey, I think I got some Ben and Jerry's Cherry Garcia in the back of the freezer."

The ends of Layla's mouth turned out just as he knew they would. Cherry Garcia was her favorite flavor of ice cream, which was why he always kept some on hand.

"What do you say you grab it and pick a movie to watch together?"

Layla pressed a quick kiss to his cheek before hopping from her stool and heading to the kitchen.

While she rooted through the freezer, he shot a quick text to Lisa, letting her know Layla was at his place and that he would drop her off at home after the movie. He'd missed a lot of time with his family while he'd been in Arizona, and he was happy to be making up for that now. He was getting closer to his sister and Layla, even if he still only saw Landon sporadically.

Dora's face flitted through his mind's eye. Hopefully, his family members weren't the only people he could rebuild bonds with.

"JUST RELAX. YOU'RE SAFE. No one can harm you here," Forensic artists Jacob Colson said in a calming voice.

Randi let out a shuddering breath.

"I want you to close your eyes and think back to Friday night," Jacob said. Dora knew there was much more to getting a good sketch from a witness than simply drawing. Jacob was one of the best sketch artists and interviewers on the force. If anyone could get Randi to give them something they could work with, it was Jacob.

Randi closed her eyes.

"Keep breathing. You're safe."

Randi took a deep breath and let it out.

"Tell me what you see."

"Nothing. It's dark."

"Okay. Where are you exactly?"

"At a picnic table." Randi's shoulders tensed and her face reddened. "I was smoking a joint."

"You're doing great, Randi." Dora spoke softly and encouragingly. Nobody in the department was going to care about their witness smoking weed. Not when a senator's daughter had been murdered.

"What do you hear?" Jacob continued the interview.

Randi frowned. "Cars, but they aren't close."

"Good. What else?"

"Something rustled in the bushes nearby. A squirrel or something."

"Good. Anything else?"

Randi sat up straighter. "A car door slammed."

That was new information.

"Okay. You're doing an amazing job," Jacob encouraged. "Now, when did you first notice the man?"

"I'm not sure. He was just there all of a sudden. Carrying something. I didn't know what."

"When did you realize he was carrying someone?"

"I didn't. I just… I don't know how to explain it. I just knew that he couldn't see me, so I ducked down under the table."

"All right. What happened next?"

"I watched from under the table. I remember thinking that he was going to hear me breathing. It sounded so loud to my ears."

"That's very common when we're in high-stress situations," Jacob assured her.

"I just stayed huddled under the table. He put her down on the grass and, like, smoothed her clothes. It looked like he might have put something in her hair, but I can't be sure. He…" Randi paused, a shiver rolling through her body. "He kissed her. Then he walked away. I… I stayed under the table for a while. I wasn't sure if he was going to come back or…or what."

"That's totally understandable. Smart. You did the right thing, protecting yourself."

"I didn't hear the car drive away or anything, but after a while I figured it was okay to come out. I wanted to run away, but I thought the woman might need help, so I went over to where she was. But she didn't look…"

Randi didn't have to finish the sentence. The first time seeing a dead body was traumatic. Heck, it was still traumatic for her, and she'd seen plenty of dead bodies. It never got easier realizing what humans were capable of doing to each other.

"I ran. I ran to the convenience store and called the police."

"Exactly what you should have done," Jacob said. "Can you tell me whether the man you saw was white, Black, or Hispanic?"

"It was a white guy."

"Okay." Jacob picked up his pencil. "And how about his size? Was he a large man? Thin? Tall? Short?"

Jacob led Randi through a series of questions, at times flipping through the extensive facial-identification book that she used to get facial features correct. The sketch took a little more than two hours, sketching and revising. The man had been wearing a knit cap, so they didn't have his hair style or color, and it had been too dark to see his eye color, but Jacob was knowledgeable in biometrics. Given the shape of the suspect's face, other features that Randi was able to pull from her memory

and the fact that the overwhelming majority of people
had brown eyes, Jacob sketched the man with darker
irises. They'd leave eye color off the official description, though.

"What happens now?" Randi asked as Dora led her
to the desk of the uniformed officer tasked with driving
her back to Violet's house.

"Now you go home and get some rest."

Randi frowned. "I meant with the case."

Dora bit back a sigh. "I'm going to keep investigating."

Randi chewed on her fingernail. "Do you think my
sketch is going to help you catch the guy?"

The truth was the sketch was pretty generic. A white
man, average height, not thin, strong enough to carry
dead weight about seventy-five yards from the park's
parking lot to the field, possibly with dark features. It
described a good portion of the male population.

"You've been a big help, Randi."

Randi crossed her arms over her chest. "I just want
my life back. I know it might not seem like much, but
I don't want to cower in some stranger's home with her
hovering over me. I could have stayed at home with my
mother if I'd wanted that."

That was probably exactly where she should have
been. As was standard operating procedure, Keene had
run a criminal background check on Randi. She'd grown
up in a West Virginia suburb and had run away right
before graduating from high school. Keene had tried
reaching her mother, but the phone number they had
was out of service. The local cops had gone to the last
address on file, but the home was empty and didn't look

to have been lived in for some time. So, Randi had become Dora's problem. Her criminal record indicated that she'd been arrested once for loitering and once for possession. Both charges were filed when she'd been a juvenile, and both charges had been dropped.

"Listen, we are going to everything in our power to find this guy. The best thing you can do is to go back to Violet's house. Stay there for the time being, so I know how to get in touch with you if I need you." An idea popped into Dora's head. "You know what? Wait here for a moment."

Dora hurried to her sergeant's desk. The department kept a few disposable cell phones on hand for use by confidential informants. Sergeant Harris wasn't at his desk, but everyone knew he kept the phones in the lower drawer of his desk. She plucked one from the desk, leaving a note for the sergeant to let him know she'd taken one of the phones, then headed back to Randi.

"Take this phone. You can use it to call me if you remember anything or if you need someone to talk to." Dora handed her the phone and another one of her business cards.

Randi turned the box over in her hands. "How do I even use it?"

"The instructions are in the box. It's easy. Come on." Dora put a hand on Randi's shoulder and led her to the uniformed officer.

Randi followed the officer out of the station, still looking skeptically at the cell phone box. At least it would give her something to do for a while.

Dora headed back to her desk. Logan sat at his desk, waiting.

"Jacob left copies of the sketch." Logan passed the sketch over to her.

She was struck again by the genericness of the likeness.

"Not much to work with," Logan said.

Dora massaged her temple. "No, no, it isn't. You want to come with me to tell Crenshaw the good news?"

"Uh…"

She dropped her hands to her side and gave him a pointed look. "Get up, Special Agent."

Logan grinned and stood.

Together, they marched across the bullpen floor. Crenshaw waved them in through the glass door.

"What do you have for me?"

Dora handed over the sketch.

Crenshaw studied the picture for a moment before tossing it onto her desk. "What the hell is this?"

Dora stood at attention in front of the lieutenant's desk. "The witness did the best she could, Lieutenant."

Crenshaw stabbed a finger at the sketch. "If this was her best, I'd hate to see her worst. This could be any white man in Washington, DC." Crenshaw threw up her hands. "It could be *every* white man in Washington, DC."

Logan sat in a visitor's chair and crossed one leg over the other. "Lieutenant, your witness is a homeless seventeen-year-old young woman. It was dark, and she was scared. I'm surprised she was able to give us as much as she has. It is possible that, given some time, she'll remember more."

Crenshaw glared at Logan. "Special Agent Elkins, I—we—haven't been afforded that kind of time. The chief, the mayor, hell, I've even gotten calls from DC's congressional delegation. They are all on me to solve this thing. Now, today."

"In my opinion, we shouldn't release the sketch," Dora said. "You're right. It's too generic. All it's going to do is have every nosy Rosy calling in about their middle-aged male neighbor. We'll give her a few days. Maybe Logan is right, and Randi will be able to give us more detail."

Crenshaw shook her head and reached for the bottle of Tylenol on her desk. She swallowed two of them without water before speaking again. "I can't hold back the sketch." She held up a hand to hold off Logan's protest. "You should remember how things work around here. There's no way that half the bullpen doesn't already know about the sketch, which means that I can expect a call from the chief any moment now demanding a copy."

Logan groaned. "And there's no way he won't want to go out with it. Show the public that his department is making progress on the high-profile case."

Crenshaw pointed at him. "Exactly."

"We could try explaining to the chief. He understands how investigations go. The need to keep some information close to the vest."

Crenshaw scowled. "I know you aren't that naive, Madison, so I'm going to chalk that comment up to exhaustion. Too bad you don't have time to rest up." The lieutenant planted her palms on the desk and pushed herself to her feet. "Look, the sketch is going out, probably by this afternoon, and it's going to be a crap fest. Prepare yourselves and keep doing your job. Dismissed." She sat back down heavily.

"Well, that went well," Logan said as they headed back to their desks.

Dora slid him a look. "It actually went better than I expected. Let's call the team together and do our jobs, Elkins."

Chapter Twelve

Dora headed back to her desk.

Logan followed her, thinking about his conversation with Landon. Now was as good a time as any to ask for a favor, he supposed. "I have a favor to ask," Logan said.

Dora didn't respond other than to raise her brows.

"You know about my father's murder, I assume."

He was sure she did. She was a cop, after all, and it would only take a Google search to find out about his father's murder. Logan hadn't spoken about it much at all while they'd been together. But she had mentioned once that he'd mumbled in his sleep, grief-stricken nightmares of a thirteen-year-old boy who lost his father.

Dora nodded.

"Landon wants to take a look at the police file. He's convinced he might see something no one else has that could maybe jump-start the case."

Dora was shaking her head before he finished the statement. "You know I can't do that. It is against a dozen rules and I'm not sure why he thinks he can find something no one else could. And find it twenty years later."

"I know it's a longshot and so does he. It's a huge ask. You don't owe me or my brother anything, but please, would you just think about it? I think if Landon could see the file, see that there is nothing there that could help him, maybe he could move on."

Lieutenant Crenshaw's voice boomed before Dora could speak again. "Madison. Elkins. Are you two going to join us, or what?"

Dora stood and hurried toward the conference room for the task-force meeting that was starting now.

Logan sighed, the weight on his shoulders growing, and followed her. Inside the conference room, he surveyed the attendees. Dora, Keene, Roberts, and Lieutenant Crenshaw were all present to get an update on where the case stood and get their marching orders. He was impressed with how Dora had handled the case so far, even if it hadn't completely been smooth sailing between them.

Dora started them off with an update on the toxicology report that had come in earlier that morning. The medical examiner had found antidepressants and anti-anxiety medications just like Najimy had warned. But the medical examiner had also found a mild sedative in Michelle's system that couldn't be explained. Michelle's car was also still missing, but they had received her phone records from her cell phone carrier. Eisha had told the truth about texting Michelle and not receiving a reply. Between late Friday night when Michelle and Eisha were at the club and when they had found Michelle's body, there were no outgoing calls or texts from the phone.

As they had feared, the brass had released the sketch

of the suspect and the station's phones had been ringing off the hook since. Crenshaw had added several uniforms to the team, who had been tasked with weeding through the information that came in on the tip line and passing on anything that warranted further investigation.

After going over all the new and not terribly helpful information, Dora handed the meeting over to Logan.

"Let me start by saying that this is all preliminary. As we know more, I'll be refining and hopefully giving you a more helpful profile. Our witness reports seeing a white male. That's in keeping with the profile of the majority of serial killers. Our guy is probably between thirty and forty-five years old. He's going to be strong, strong enough to carry deadweight some distance, but unlikely to stand out in a crowd. All the victims are similar in age, size, and coloring—that is Caucasian females with brown hair. There's no known connection between the females, but when we catch the guy, we are likely to find some tenuous connection."

"Tenuous as in what?" Dora was taking notes.

"Something like all the women went to the same gym chain, even if not the same location. Or they all frequented the same coffee shop downtown. Something that is very difficult for the police to hit on but becomes obvious once you're told about it."

"But why these women specifically?" Detective Roberts asked.

Logan shifted his gaze to Roberts. "It's hard to say exactly, but since there is no obvious connection, most likely the women represent someone in the killer's life. Someone they love or loved, I'd think."

"Someone they loved," Keene said disbelievingly.

"There's a reason for the saying 'there's a thin line between love and hate,'" Logan responded. "Both can be very strong emotions."

He couldn't help a glance at Dora, but she did not look up from her notes. He continued.

"But in this case, the writing on the victims—'Protect the innocent'—would suggest the killer sees these women as somehow wholesome or pure."

Roberts frowned. "But how would killing the women be protecting them?"

Logan was used to dealing with skeptics. Not everyone believed that profiling was real police work. He kept his voice measured. "Only the killer could answer that question for sure, but it could be any number of things. He could believe he's saving the women from having their innocence corrupted by killing them. Or he could believe them innocent when he kidnaps them, but then, for some reason, they displease him, and they are no longer pure in his eyes. I'm leaning in the direction of the latter explanation more than the former."

"Or," Roberts interrupted, "he could choose these women because he thinks that he is protecting some other person by killing them."

"That's possible," Logan conceded, even though his professional ire was up. "But I don't think it's likely in this case. Think about how he stages the bodies. He takes great care to dress them, pose them, and leave a flower in their hair, and even after he's brutalized them. That suggests feelings of rage and kindness in turn."

"It suggests to me that he's a sick monster," Roberts spat.

"That too. But he's also smart, probably employed,

a seemingly normal guy," Logan said, getting back to his preliminary profile. "He has been smart enough to avoid leaving any evidence that could identify him. He plans these kidnappings and killings. So far, we have no witness to the actual abduction. He has to have somewhere safe and secure to take the women back to since he keeps them for two to three days. Probably a house, maybe in nearby Virginia or Maryland, since he would want some space to be sure the neighbors didn't see or hear anything suspicious."

Keene leaned forward in his chair. "We've got a witness now."

"Yes, and that might scare our guy. He's been getting bolder. He probably didn't expect anyone in the park the night he left Michelle. If your sketch is accurate—"

"A big if," Roberts interjected.

"If it's accurate, the unsub may panic. That could lead him to act out or to go into hiding."

"Not terribly helpful," Dora said.

"Sorry." Logan shrugged. "Again, not an exact science."

The meeting broke up soon after that. Dora sent Keene and Roberts out to re-canvass Michelle's neighborhood with the sketch in hopes that it would rekindle someone's memory. Michelle's boss, John Leonard, had finally responded to Dora's message, saying that he could meet with her at noon that day. She and Logan were bound for that meeting.

"You really know your stuff, Elkins," Dora said after everyone else had left the room.

"Did you almost choke on those words?" Logan teased.

A thin but genuine smile graced Dora's face.

Warmth bloomed in Logan's chest.

"Not as much as I thought I would have," she shot back. "I'm serious. You're very good at this."

"Thank you. You've done a fantastic job on this case."

The smile fell from Dora's face, and she sighed. "I feel like I am no closer to finding our killer than I was when we found our first victim. And that I'm running out of time before he takes his next victim."

"That's not on you. The killer is responsible for his actions."

"Yeah, well, tell that to the media, the public, and the Quitonis. If we don't find this guy soon, they are going to have all of our heads."

"Well, we'd better get to work, then."

"Kaj, just the man I'm looking for."

Kaj Ryland looked up from his computer and grinned. "Oh boy, now I know I'm in trouble."

The FBI's best tech analyst stood. It was like watching one of those tube men you saw in front of car dealerships unfold upward. Before joining the FBI, Kaj had played basketball in the Euro League. At seven feet two inches, a sitting Kaj was almost as tall as Logan, but a standing Kaj towered over both him and Dora. Basketball aside, Kaj had one of the finest minds for technology that Logan had ever encountered. He'd done wonders with video-enhancing technologies, including creating groundbreaking software. Rumor had it that Kaj was filthy rich and didn't have to work at all, much less for a federal salary. But he did it because he wanted to serve his country, which Logan could respect.

Kaj grabbed Logan's hand, pulling a man for a quick

handshake and pat on the back before stepping back and taking in Dora.

Logan noted the pang of jealousy that shot through him and realized he didn't have a right to it. Still, he'd heard more than one of his female coworkers mention how attractive Kaj's wavy blond locks and blue eyes were.

"And who is this lovely lady?"

"Detective Dora Madison with the DC Metropolitan Police Department," Dora answered before Logan could.

"Well, Detective Madison, what can I do for you?"

"You can call me Dora."

Kaj's smile widened. "Dora, how may I be of service?"

"We need a video image cleared up, hopefully enough to make out the face of the person in it," Logan answered.

Kaj rolled his eyes. "Oh, is that all? You guys think this stuff is so easy. You just pop in here with a grainy video from some convenience store robbery and poof. I'm just supposed to pull whatever you need from it," Kaj said, just enough just to let Logan know that he wasn't really too put out.

"I don't think it's easy at all," Logan responded. "That's why I bring it to you, a master at what you do."

"Yes, yes, I'm Mr. Master Wizard. If you think flattery will get your job done faster, think again. Two tickets to next week's Washington Commanders game. On the fifty-yard line."

Logan crossed his arms over his chest and gave his friend a look. "That's blackmail and not only unbecoming of a federal employee, it's illegal."

"Well, I wouldn't want to break any laws. To the back

of the line with you. Let's see… I should get to your case, oh, six months from Tuesday." Kaj grinned.

Logan tried and failed to beat back his own smile. "You're something else, you know that? I'll see what I can do, but they definitely won't be on the fifty-yard line. I'm collecting a civil-servant salary just like you."

"That sounds suspiciously like I shouldn't hold my breath," Kaj sighed dramatically. "What do you have for me?"

"It's a video of a female we believe is our victim being followed by an unidentified male," Dora answered.

Kaj's eyes lit with understanding. "Is this the serial killer case?"

"It is."

"Damn." Kaj looked from Dora to Logan. "You should have led with that. Forget the tickets. I want to get this guy off the street as much as anyone else. I have three sisters. How do you know the victim is in the video?"

"Well, as I said, it's grainy," Logan started.

"But," Dora interjected, "we know the store was the last place our victim was seen and based on the size, shape, and clothing of the female image in the video, we're pretty sure it's her."

"Okay." Kaj took the USB drive Logan handed to him. "I'll try to clean up the entire frame so you can be sure of both your victim and your unsub. I make no promises, and it may take a while. I have to get in there to see what I'm working with. Though store cameras are notoriously bad."

"I'd be grateful for whatever you could do." Dora smiled back at Kaj, and another jolt of jealousy hit Logan. He beat it back a second time.

"We have a forensic artist's rendering of a suspect from our witness," Logan said, forcing himself to focus on the case. He pulled out his phone and shot the sketch to Kaj's email.

The computer on the desk let out a jingling chime a moment later. Kaj reached for the mouse, opened the email, and popped the sketch up on the large monitor in front of them. He frowned. "You think this is your guy in the video?"

"Could be," Logan hedged.

"Kind of generic, but I'll keep it in mind."

"Thanks, Kaj."

"No problem." Kaj waved as they exited the office.

"This is the best evidence we have. Do you really think your guy can clean up the video enough for us to get a look at our suspect?"

"If anyone can do it, it's Kaj."

Chapter Thirteen

Another one had failed. He watched the light drain from her eyes with sadness in his heart. Would he ever find someone worthy?

It wasn't enough that they look like his Sarah. His Sarah had been pure. Good. These women, they weren't good. They fought him. Even when he tried to explain he wouldn't hurt them. Not unless they didn't cooperate. Not while they behaved. But they never behaved.

Sometimes they pretended for a while. But they all tried to escape eventually. And that was when he knew. They would never measure up to Sarah.

That was when they had to go.

Michelle had been especially defiant. If he had known who she was, he would have never grabbed her.

He'd been more careful with this one. Christine. But it hadn't mattered in the end. He'd been forced to kill her too.

He took one last look at the dead woman. Her eyes were open, staring back at him.

The sound of footsteps startled him. He'd gotten a late start moving Christine's body to the park. It was starting to get light, which meant people.

The footsteps got louder. Closer. There wasn't time to lay this one out like the others.

He swore silently. He couldn't get caught. He needed to find his Sarah. He glanced one more time at the body in the trunk of the car, dismayed Christine wouldn't get the send-off she deserved.

Then he ran.

Hours of additional research had led Landon to Carisse Lynn's small sandwich-and-coffee shop in the Petworth neighborhood. The neighborhood was mostly residential, with many of the iconic row houses that frequently make their way into photos of Washington, DC. One of the main commercial areas ran along Georgia Avenue, which was where Carisse's sandwich shop, the Upper Crust, was located.

She'd been listed as the owner and manager on the website he found. Carisse had been a maid for the Burgesses around the time that his father appeared to have been investigating William Burgess. Questioning Carisse was a long shot, but it wouldn't be the first time that a long shot had paid off for him. And most people, especially rich people like the Burgesses, underestimated just how much of their business the hired help was privy to. Hopefully, Carisse could at least point him in the right direction. Any direction at all would be helpful at this point in his investigation. He felt like the investigation into his father's death was running on fumes.

The coffee shop was bright with tables covered with red-and-white checked tablecloth and a comfortable homey vibe. Midday on a weekday, it was fairly full, with most of the tables occupied and two people waiting in line when Landon entered.

He waited his turn and when he got to the head of the line, he ordered the most expensive sandwich on the menu, artisan roast beef, and a root beer before asking for Carisse.

He took a seat at one of the last open tables and waited. After about ten minutes, a brunette woman in jeans, a white blouse, and sensible black sneakers headed toward his table with a loaded plate and a can of A&W root beer.

"Roast beef and a root beer. Don't get many requests for that anymore. Or many requests to see the manager before the customer has even gotten their food." Carisse eyed him warily. "How can I help you?"

"I'm sure the food is excellent. But I was hoping to speak to you about the time you worked for William Burgess," Landon said.

Carisse drew back in surprise. "Now, there's a name I haven't heard in decades. You know he's an ambassador to Ecuador or Iceland or somewhere."

"Australia," Landon corrected. "I'm an investigative reporter so I also know that you were a housekeeper for the Burgesses."

"More than twenty years ago. While I was in college. I needed a job to help cover my expenses, and Mrs. Burgess was looking for cheap labor. Why are you asking?"

"Please, could you sit a minute?"

Carisse hesitated for a moment, but Landon saw the minute her curiosity overtook her skepticism. She sat.

"My father was a reporter for the *Post*. He was killed twenty years ago while, I have reason to believe, looking into a story concerning Ambassador Burgess."

"Mr. Burgess was a partner at some hoity-toity law firm then."

Landon knew that. It had been easy to get background information on Burgess. The son of an oil tycoon in Texas, Burgess had gone to all the right schools from birth, including Harvard for undergraduate and law. He had accepted a job at a prominent Washington, DC law firm at graduation, working on driving policy—a polite way to say *lobbying*—for his daddy's oil company. Burgess had married his wife, an equally accomplished lawyer, who'd stopped working two years after their marriage and given him three children, two boys and a girl. The Burgesses lived a privileged life among Washington, DC's wealthy, and two years ago Burgess had been appointed to his ambassadorship. It was said he had his eye on higher office, not for himself but for his oldest son, William Burgess Junior, who had followed in his father's footsteps and become a partner at Daddy's law firm.

"Can you tell me what you remember about working for the Burgesses?"

Carisse sighed. "You're a reporter, so I guess you know why I got fired."

That had taken a little more digging, but Landon had eventually determined that Mrs. Burgess had accused Carisse of stealing a necklace.

"It was a stupid mistake, and if I could take it back, I would. School was just so expensive. I didn't have any help, and the Burgesses had so much. At the time I thought…" She shrugged. "I guess I didn't think. Mrs. Burgess confronted me the day after I took the necklace, and I fessed up and gave it back right away. That's the only reason she didn't report me to the cops, but of course, she fired me on the spot. Can't say I blame her. I'd do the same thing if I caught one of my employees stealing from me." She glanced at the counter where the line of customers was being helped.

"How long did you work for the Burgesses?" Landon asked.

"About five months. I wasn't a very good house-keeper. The Burgesses had several, two to three for each floor—if you can believe it. But the house, if you can call it that, it was more like a palace. It was huge. I only worked three days a week, helping the full-timers." Carisse looked as if she was recalling a memory. "I remember not long after I started, I accidentally broke a lamp. It was an ugly, ornate-looking thing, so you know it was expensive. I thought I was going to be fired right then and there, but the head housekeeper didn't even bat an eye. She just went into the basement storage area and came back with an exact replica of the lamp I had broken. Who keeps spare matching lamps in storage like toilet paper or soap? Rich people, that's who."

Landon wondered what the head housekeeper had been through to get to the point where she kept spare lamps on hand, but that was a question for another time.

"It wasn't exactly clear why my father was looking into Ambassador Burgess, but there was another name in his journal." Landon hesitated. Anyone living in Washington, DC, twenty years ago would have known the name *Addison Kober*. She was fifteen when she went missing. Her family had not achieved the same status as the Burgesses, but they'd been upper-middle class—the father a surgeon, the mother a successful Realtor. And Allison had made a picture-perfect victim for the media.

A blonde, blue-eyed cheerleader with a smile that lit up the camera. Her disappearance had dominated the airwaves for weeks, Landon recalled. Eventually, the story had faded from the public eye, but Addison had never been found dead or alive.

"The other name in my dad's journal was *Addison Kober.*"

Carisse's expression went from confusion to recognition in a couple of seconds. "The missing girl?"

Landon nodded. "Do you know if the Burgesses knew Addison or anyone in her family?"

Carisse shook her head. "I don't. I'm sure I would've remembered if I'd seen her at the house or heard her mentioned. Especially with all the media attention about her going missing. Wow, I feel bad. I'd forgotten about that poor girl. They never found her, did they?"

"No, no, they didn't," Landon confirmed.

Carisse tsked. "That's too bad I have a son now. He's four, and if anything like that ever happened to him…"

She didn't finish the statement, but she didn't have to. Their child going missing was every parent's nightmare.

Landon asked a few more questions trying to pry loose from Carisse's memory anything that might explain his father's notes, but either Carisse knew nothing that could help them, or he just didn't have enough information to hit upon the right questions to pull the answers from her memory. After a while, Carisse stood, announcing that she had to get back to work.

Landon had lost his appetite. He wrapped his sandwich in a napkin and took his root beer to go. It looked like he was going to have to dig deeper to figure out what exactly his father had been doing that had gotten him murdered.

JOHN LEONARD, Michelle's boss and owner of the Leonard Gallery, sat behind his desk in his small, cramped office. Leonard hadn't done a thing to make the space feel welcoming. The walls were bare despite the assortment of artwork just outside the door. The space was a mess, with files overflowing Leonard's desk and the small round table in the corner. A leather sofa was wedged into a corner, but it, too, was covered in files that looked like art catalogs and other papers. Leonard had gone out of the office and dug up a single folding chair, which Dora took. Logan stood at her side, making her regret sitting. It felt as if he was in charge of the interview.

Leonard had already heard about Michelle's murder and after a round of "Unbelievable" and "Can't be happening," Dora had finally gotten him to focus on her questions, although he did appear unusually anxious. It could have been nothing, but her instincts weren't leading her in that direction.

"How long have you known Ms. Quitoni?" Dora asked.

"Just since she started working here two years ago. She came highly recommended. Had both art and business experience and was from the area. It seemed like a perfect fit."

"Seemed like?" Logan said, pouncing on the equivocation.

Leonard folded his hands on the desk, then unfolded them and folded them again. "It was. It was a perfect fit."

"Has Michelle had any trouble with anyone in particular? Maybe a buyer—"

"Client." Leonard's back straightened. "We call the people that honor us by purchasing from us *clients*."

Dora gave him a tight smile. "Oh, sorry. Had there been any clients that Michelle had difficulty with? Maybe one that showed her too much or unwanted attention?"

Leonard frowned. "No. Absolutely not. I wouldn't have stood for it."

"That's an interesting way to phrase that." Logan cocked his head to the side, drawing Leonard's full attention to him. "You wouldn't have stood for it. Why? What would you have done, Mr. Leonard?"

"I… I just mean that I'm the owner. Michelle's boss. Ultimately, I'm responsible for her safety while she is within these walls. I wouldn't have tolerated a client harassing her."

"So, there was never a client that asked Michelle out for coffee or anything?" Dora pressed.

"No," Leonard said vehemently. "Fraternizing with the clients is not permitted."

Dora didn't look over at Logan, but she could feel him vibrating with the same excitement she felt. They just had to dig it out of Leonard. "Well, I can understand why you might have the rule, but come on, Mr. Leonard. Michelle is a beautiful young woman, and I'm sure a lot of the men that come in here are pretty well off. That can be attractive."

"Michelle wouldn't do that." Leonard was nearly yelling.

Dora studied the gallery owner, sure now that Eisha Steele was right about the affair between Michelle and her boss. Now she just needed Leonard to confirm it.

"Why wouldn't a young woman accept a date from a handsome, wealthy man?"

Logan shot her a quick look. She was goading Leonard, but he was on the cusp of cracking.

Possibly realizing his reaction to the question had been over-the-top, Leonard stiffened. He smoothed his tie, visibly setting his expression to neutral. "I... It's not. I just meant Michelle wasn't the kind of young woman that dated around."

"We aren't here to upset you, Mr. Leonard."

"I've just found out my assistant manager was murdered. This whole situation is upsetting."

"Especially since you were having an affair with her. That must make it even more upsetting."

Leonard's cheeks were mottled with color. "I can't... That you'd even suggest... I'm a married man... I..."

Dora held up a hand to stop the sputtering man. "Mr. Leonard, I have no intention of embarrassing you or passing judgment. But I am going to get to the truth and find the man who took Michelle's life. And right now, I have to tell you, your lack of cooperation is doing you no favors."

Leonard visibly deflated. "If my wife finds out..."

"Of course we'll do our best to be discreet," Logan jumped in, with a chummy one guy to another smirk. "We only care about finding the murderer."

Leonard dropped his gaze to the desktop. "We had been having an affair. Michelle broke it off a couple weeks ago."

Dora's instincts buzzed. "Michelle broke it off?"

Leonard stiffened. "If you are suggesting that I

would— Maybe I need to consult a lawyer before speaking to you further."

"That is your prerogative. If you could call your lawyer now and have him meet you down at the station…?" Dora started to stand.

Leonard swallowed hard. "Now? I… I can't just leave the gallery."

"Well, I'm sorry," Logan said, all traces of friendliness gone from his voice. "If you won't talk to us here, you'll have to speak to us at the station. With your lawyer, of course."

"Okay, okay, wait. I'll answer your questions."

Dora reclaimed her chair. "So, as you were saying, Michelle broke things off a few weeks ago."

"Yes," Leonard spat. "She wanted me to end my marriage. She was tired of sneaking around. I couldn't do that."

Breaking things off might have made Leonard angry enough to stalk Michelle. He'd certainly have the opportunity knowing her work schedule and all. "Have you been following Michelle? Stalking her?"

"What? No! I wouldn't. Look, I didn't want the thing with Michelle to end, but I couldn't leave my wife. She would have taken half of everything. The house. This gallery. I've worked too hard to lose it."

Dora disliked John Leonard more with each passing minute.

"So, your wife doesn't know about your affair?"

The look of horror on the man's face could not have been faked. "No. No. And I don't want her to. It was a stupid mistake." He turned to look at Logan pleadingly. "You can't ruin my life over a mistake."

The way Dora saw it, it was Leonard who'd ruined his own life. She had no sympathy for cheaters. And if Leonard's wife knew about the affair, she had a motive to want Michelle dead, although she doubted the woman would kill two other innocent women. But she could have killed her husband's mistress and left a trail, making it look like a serial killer was responsible. But that wasn't what Dora's gut was saying. It was saying that as much as she didn't like Leonard, he nor his wife had anything to do with Michelle's death. Still, she'd have to speak to Mrs. Leonard. If that put John in a bad spot, well, it was no less than he deserved for his actions.

"Mr. Leonard, where were you between nine p.m. Friday night and six a.m. Monday morning?"

Leonard let his head fall into his hands. "I can't believe this."

"Mr. Leonard, please answer my question."

"Friday night I was home with my wife and kids all night. I got home around six, and I was with them all weekend. I left for work around seven thirty Monday morning." He lifted his head. "Are we done?"

"For now," Dora said. She and Logan rose and went to the office door. At the door, she turned back. "You know, Mr. Leonard, in my experience, the truth has a way of coming out. It might be better for you if your wife heard the truth from you before it does."

"It's looking more and more like Michelle Quitoni wasn't the perfect senator's daughter that her parents wanted everyone to believe she was," Logan said once they'd gotten back into the car and were headed out of the parking lot.

"No, she wasn't." Dora agreed. "But I don't know if

any of it has anything to do with her murder. I don't see how anything we've learned really helps us. We'll look into whether Leonard might have had something to do with the murder, but my gut is saying no."

She was sure that Michelle was the victim of the serial killer currently stalking Washington, DC's streets, but she had to cover all her bases. It was possible that Michelle had known her killer and that he or she had patterned the murder to look like the other two murders that had been in the news. Possible, but not likely in Dora's professional opinion.

"My gut is saying 'Feed me,'" Logan said, pulling her back into the conversation she'd been having with him before her thoughts wandered. "We haven't had lunch. How about stopping some place?"

Dora shot him a look as she made a right turn onto Georgia Avenue.

"What? We both have to eat."

"Fine. Do you have any particular place in mind?"

Logan grinned. "I do know a place, and it's not that far."

Chapter Fourteen

Logan was thrilled that Dora had accepted his invitation to lunch. Maybe with time, she would see her way to forgiving him. Maybe even giving him a second chance. It was a long shot, maybe the longest shot he'd ever taken, but he knew he had to take it. He'd been wrong to run away from what they'd had, and he was ready to atone for that. If she let him. That, he knew, was still an open question.

He directed her to a seafood restaurant on Water Street in the Southwest Waterfront neighborhood of DC. The neighborhood had seen an economic boom over the last decade, with restaurants, bars, and posh hotels popping up along the mile long stretch of land fronting the Potomac River. It had bought new life to the iconic area, but the downside had been an increase in the cost of living in the area pushing out many of the older, longer time residents.

Whaler's Seafood had survived the changing times, remaining family owned, and Logan did his best to support it, eating there at least once a week. He'd discovered the restaurant not long after moving back to the city. It was new, but the chef knew his business. As far as Logan was concerned, there wasn't better calamari in the city and the blackened swordfish was awe-inspiring.

Once seated at a table by the window, he ordered the calamari for him and Dora to share and the swordfish for his entrée.

"May as well go big since the FBI is paying," Dora said with a playful grin on her face.

Logan laughed. "Order whatever you want. It's on me."

Somehow, talking about the case in such a nice restaurant didn't feel appropriate. Or maybe they both just needed a break. In any case, the conversation moved in the direction of two old colleagues catching up. He told her about Arizona and the FBI, caught her up on his sister, Lisa's, life post-divorce, and Landon's travels all over the world as an investigative reporter.

"And what about you? Anyone special in your life?" Dora asked.

He couldn't tell from her inflection if she was just making idle chitchat or if there was a more personal reason for her question, though he hoped it was the latter.

"No wife. No girlfriend. No one special." Was that relief he saw on her face, or was it just wishful thinking on his part? "I haven't seen anyone seriously since we broke up."

"It wasn't really a breakup, though, right?" Dora said. "I mean, we weren't serious, as it turned out."

"Dora, I'm sorry if I made you feel that way. I do value our relationship. I still do."

She brought the water to her lips and looked away. "Maybe we should talk about something else."

"What if I don't want to talk about something else?" Then, to lighten the tone, he added, "I told you my relationship status. It's only fair you tell me yours."

Dora sighed. "Single," she said, cutting into her steak. "The last guy I was seeing decided to go back to his former girlfriend." She flinched, and he wondered if that meant she'd cared for him or that she still did. "It wasn't serious," she said, almost as if she had read his mind. "We'd only been seeing each other for a few weeks. It seems as if I have a type. Men who don't stick."

"That guy was an idiot."

Dora shot him a look. "There are a lot of idiots out there."

Logan set his fork down and pushed his plate to the side. "I know you don't want to hear this, but you're right. I was an idiot. Instead of talking to you about what I was feeling, about the grief over losing my mother, I shut down and closed myself off to you and to my family. I made drastic changes to my life—some good, others I deeply regret."

"You don't have to—"

"Yes, I do. I have to say that I'm sorry I hurt you. And I miss you. I want to make it up to you and prove I can be the man you deserve. I want to try again." There. He'd said it.

He reached across the table and covered her hand with his. His heart leapt when she let him. He held her in a heated gaze that they didn't break off until the waiter came back to check on them.

Dora moved her hand from under his. "I think we should focus on the case," she said, reaching for her water again.

"And after the case?"

She didn't answer. They ate the rest of their lunch in silence. Logan paid the bill, and they made their way out of the restaurant and back to the car.

He stopped at the driver's-side door beside Dora. "I don't want to upset you, but I want to be clear that I meant what I said. I want a second chance for us, and I'll do whatever you need me to do to prove it."

"I don't know if you can," Dora said softly.

He brought his hand to her cheek and gazed into her eyes. "Will you let me try?"

The seconds ticked by, but Dora finally nodded and the knot in his chest unraveled. He bent his head to kiss her, but her phone trilled before he had a chance to taste her lips.

Dora stepped back and pulled her phone from her purse. "Madison." She listened to whatever was being said on the other end of the phone, a smile slowly blowing across her face. "That's great work, Roberts. Text me the address, will you? Logan and I will go check it out."

"What's up?" Logan asked back in FBI mode, even though the thought of their almost kiss lingered in his mind.

"Roberts found a flower shop in Arlington that recently sold several desert roses."

Logan felt a smile that matched Dora's smile spread across his face. "Sounds like a lead to me. Let's go check it out."

A TALL, MUSCLED Black man in his thirties stood behind the counter of the flower shop. He had a round face, dark brown eyes, and black locs pulled back in a bun at the nape of his neck. He wore a green apron over a gray T-shirt and jeans. He finished ringing up the purchases of a young man before turning to Logan and Dora.

"How can I help you?" he asked in a friendly voice.

Dora and Logan held up their identification. "Detective Dora Madison with the DC Metropolitan Police Department. And this is Logan Elkins with the FBI. Are you Darice Thompson?"

"I am." His eyes narrowed. "What is this all about?"

"We're investigating the murder of several women that occurred in the city recently. We contacted Markham Blooms Wholesalers, and they mentioned that you had ordered a large quantity of desert-rose seeds about two months ago."

His features softened. "What does that have to do with a serial killer?"

"We are hoping you can clear up a few things for us," Logan said without answering Darius's question.

"I'll answer whatever questions you have. I don't have anything to hide." Darius held his hands up, palms out, as if to emphasize his statement.

"So, about these desert-rose seeds."

"Oh, yeah, well, obviously, we order a lot of seeds." He gestured to the flower shop.

"The wholesaler said you'd never ordered these particular kinds of seeds before," Dora shot back.

Darius's face scrunched up. "Well, no, let me take a look in our system." He turned to the computer he'd used moments before to ring up the previous customer. "Two months ago, you said?"

"Approximately," Dora responded.

"Ah, here it is. Yeah, I remember this order now. It

was a special order for the customer. One hundred seeds of the Never Forget You variety. Paid in cash."

Of course it was paid in cash, because nothing could ever be easy for her, Dora thought.

"Never forget you?" Logan said.

"Well, that's what some people call this particular color of the flower. Because of the deep purple color at the tips of the pink petals, some people interpret it as a little bit of sadness amongst the brightness. They are often sent to people who have just suffered a loss." Darius shrugged.

Logan shot Dora a look that told her he was thinking along the same lines as her. Was it a message of some sort from the killer to his victims? That he would never forget them?

"Does the customer on that order have a name?" Dora asked.

"John Smith." Darius cringed, possibly realizing what Dora instinctively knew. The name *John Smith* was undoubtedly an alias.

"What about a phone number?" Logan asked.

"Yeah, yeah, right here." Darius rattled off the number, and Dora took it down in her notebook.

"Would you mind making me a copy of what you have there, Mr. Thompson?"

"No problem. Anything I can do to help." He hit a couple buttons on the keyboard, and a few seconds later, the printer behind him whirled to life. He passed the still warm sheet of paper to Dora. "Anything else I can do for you, Officers?"

Dora ignored being called Officer. She'd learned long ago that most people didn't mean it as a slight. They just saw all law enforcement the same. Officers, detectives, FBI agents—they were all just cops to the general public.

"You could tell us where you were Friday evening through Monday morning."

Darius his eyes went wide. "I am…" He stopped, then started again, giving a detailed accounting of his whereabouts for the time period.

Even though Randi had identified the man she saw leaving Michelle in the park as a white man, Dora had to make sure she had all her bases covered. Darius had access to the seeds, and the customer's name was an obvious fake. Maybe he was working with a partner. It was unlikely, but she wasn't willing to leave any stone unturned.

She showed Darius a photo of the sketch of their suspect on her phone. "Do you recognize this man? Could he be the person who ordered the seeds?"

Darius studied the phone screen for several long moments before shaking his head. "Sorry. We get a lot of people in here, and it was two months ago."

Dora and Logan thanked him and then headed back to the car.

"Mr. Smith is our guy," Logan said when they were back in the car.

"Yeah." Dora started the engine. "But who is he?"

Chapter Fifteen

Logan stood next to Dora, both of them under the glaring sunlight, watching the activity around the crime scene. Another woman was dead. Senselessly murdered by a madman. He could feel the rage, frustration, and, yes, despair rolling off Dora in waves. If she didn't learn to compartmentalize, she wasn't going to make it in this career. She'd been visibly angry since they'd gotten the call that another woman's body had been found. He was going to have to find a way to force Dora to get some rest and unwind, but he knew that wouldn't be easy as long as this killer was on the loose.

He focused his attention back on the crime scene in front of him. The similarity to the previous scenes was jarring. The woman had been found posed with a desert rose in her hair and the words *Protect the innocent* written on her left side. She'd been strangled, just like the killer's other victims. The one difference: The victim hadn't been found for several days. The killer must not have known that the area of the park that he left the body in was closed to foot traffic or maintenance on a crumbling walking path. The woman hadn't been found until a work crew had arrived to complete the work.

"Who are you?" Dora mumbled.

They hadn't found any identification, at least not yet. Logan wasn't sure the question was directed at the killer or their victim, but from the intensity with which Dora gazed at the medical examiner and his assistant as they hunched over the body, he guessed the latter. "We will figure out who she is and make sure whoever did this to her is brought to justice."

Dora didn't respond. Instead, she headed for the medical examiner's side. "What can you tell me, Dean?"

"Not a whole lot yet," Dean said. "I'm ready to move her to my office. I'll get started on the autopsy right away. We need to catch this monster."

"From your lips," Logan said.

Dean stood to his full height. "I can tell you that she fought him. Hard. I've got bruises on her arms and legs and chipped fingernails."

"DNA?" Logan asked.

"Possibly, but I'd need something to match it to unless we get lucky, and our guy is already in the system."

They wouldn't get that lucky; Logan was sure of that. But if Dean found DNA this time, they'd at least have some hard evidence when they had a suspect in custody.

"I'm pretty sure she died by strangulation, based on the bruising around her neck, and her hyoid bone is fractured."

The DNA. The dumpsite that had been closed. Their killer was getting sloppy. Was the attention getting to him? Or was it something else? And more importantly, how would it change his behavior? One thing that profiling counted on was a killer's consistency. If their killer was unraveling… Who knew what that meant or their investigation. Or future victims.

"How about an estimate on time of death?" Dora asked Dean, bringing Logan's focus back to the moment.

"Well, she's been exposed to the elements for at least twenty-four hours, based on the decomposition and rigor, but thankfully, the cold has preserved a lot."

Yes, thankfully. A small shiver snaked its way down Logan's spine. Medical examiners were necessary, but he could have never done the job himself.

Dean motioned for his assistant.

Logan was following Dora back to the car when his phone rang.

He answered while he was walking.

"Where are you?" Kaj's voice rang excitedly over the line. "I've got something for you from the video."

"We're on our way."

They made the drive to Kaj's office in record time.

Kaj was waiting for them in his office when they arrived.

"Finally!" he said.

"I'm here. Finally."

"Okay, what's on this video that's got you so worked up?" Dora stepped over to the desk.

Logan stood behind her.

"I got you a clear shot of your guy." Kaj opened the laptop and pressed the space bar.

Grainy black-and-white footage played on the laptop screen. The front yard of a house similar to Michelle's was visible. A car drove past.

Logan glanced away from the screen at Kaj. "I hope it gets more exciting than this."

"Just wait for it." He was practically vibrating.

Ten more seconds passed, and another car came into the frame. This time, the car stopped at the curb in front of the house and a man got out of the driver's side. It was late, but the streetlights provided enough light to illuminate the man's face.

Logan leaned forward in his chair. "That's—"

"Leonard," Dora interrupted with a hard grimace. "And check the date-time stamp."

Saturday, August 12, 2:07 a.m. The night Michelle went missing.

Logan's pulse quickened. "Where exactly was this video taken?"

"Keene said he got it from a neighbor three blocks north of Michelle's house."

Three blocks.

Leonard was three blocks away during the time frame when Michelle went missing. That couldn't be a coincidence.

"Rewind it," Logan ordered. His heart was pumping so fast that he had to take slow deep breaths to try and slow his breathing while he watched the video a second time.

Kaj dragged his finger over the mouse, and the vehicle pulled up again with Leonard's car coming to a stop at the curb once again.

There wasn't much to it. Leonard got out of the car, looked both ways down the street, then disappeared around the side of the house. He was dressed in all black—black jeans, a top, even black boots. Which alone didn't mean much, but the flinty look he shot up and down the street was more than just a little suspicious.

As was the fact that he parked three blocks from Michelle's house. It might have just been because the two were having an affair and he didn't want his car to be seen in her driveway at that hour. But that didn't explain why Leonard hadn't mentioned this little trip when he and Dora had questioned him.

"We need to bring Leonard in right now," Logan barked.

"Agreed," Dora said, already pulling out her phone. "But I don't know. Does this feel too easy to you?"

"I wouldn't call anything about this case easy," Logan responded. "But this video puts Leonard at Michelle's house on the night she went missing. Making him potentially the last person to see her alive. And he lied to us—or at least he didn't tell us about it."

Dora punched the screen on her phone as she headed for the office door. "Let's go see what Mr. Leonard has to say for himself."

TWENTY MINUTES LATER, Logan pulled to a stop in front of a modest two-story house where John Leonard lived with his wife, Felicia. The grass in the front yard could have used a cut, but the house looked well-kept and loved. The home was in the expensive Chevy Chase neighborhood, so the Leonards weren't doing too badly for themselves.

Dora pointed to the colorful flower beds on either side of the main door. "Someone likes to garden."

Logan leaned over her, peering out of the passenger side window.

She breathed in the scent of his spicy, masculine cologne. Thankfully, he didn't seem to notice.

"Interesting, although I don't see any blooms that look like our desert rose."

"No," Dora agreed, grateful when Logan sat back in the driver's seat, to temper the effects he'd been having on her body. "But it may be worth asking a few questions of Leonard about his garden."

Logan shot her a smile before they both got out of the car.

Rain had been threatening for days, and the dark gray clouds floating across the sky promised to make good on the threat sooner rather than later. She could only hope they were back at the station by then.

"What do we know about the wife?" Logan asked as they made their way to the front door.

"She's thirty-two. A nurse. No criminal record." Dora repeated what she knew about Felicia Leonard, which wasn't much. Neither of the Leonards had criminal records. But that didn't mean John Leonard wasn't their guy. It just meant he'd never been caught.

She and Logan climbed the stairs of the wide porch and flanked the door before knocking. Seconds turned into a full minute, and when no one responded, Dora knocked again.

"No one home?" Logan said.

"Maybe," Dora responded, but her senses were tingling. She tried to see inside through the sidelights next to the door, but the frost was too heavy to detect any movement.

She pressed her ear to the door and heard the sound of someone moving inside. "There's someone in there."

She knocked again harder, the sound almost blocking out the sound of another door opening.

"He's running," Logan said, already moving down the porch stairs.

Dora followed him. They rounded the side of the house.

Leonard was already behind the wheel of a black Mercedes. He looked up, fear and determination hardening the planes of his face.

Dora held up her badge with one hand, the other poised on the butt of her gun. "Police. Freeze!"

Leonard started the car's engine and hit the gas.

Dora leapt out of the way but not before the side of the car clipped her. She hit the grassy lawn face-first. She flipped over.

"Are you okay?" Logan ran at her from the other side of the driveway, where he'd darted out of the way of the Mercedes.

Her hip throbbed where the Mercedes nicked her. "Yeah, I'm good."

Logan's gaze swept over her, ensuring that she was, in fact, fine. He extended a hand and pulled her to her feet. She flinched.

"You need medical attention."

"I need to catch this guy."

The Mercedes sped down the residential street.

"Let's go!" Dora yelled, ignoring the pain as she ran back toward the car.

Logan moved behind the wheel of the police sedan as she jumped into the car, fastening her seat belt with one hand as he wheeled away from the curb after the Mercedes.

Leonard sped up. Logan stayed with him.

Dora gripped the bar above the door tightly enough

that her knuckles whitened. "He's going to get someone killed."

Luckily, they were the only two cars on the residential street at this point in the midday, but that wasn't likely to last. They were only a few blocks from the main thoroughfare, where Leonard could end up killing someone with the way he was driving.

Dora turned on the sirens and lights, then radioed their position, calling for backup.

About three car lengths ahead, Leonard careened into the intersection, turning left onto Connecticut Avenue, barely missing sideswiping a minivan.

"Damnit," Logan followed, slowing his pace slightly.

Leonard jerked the Camaro onto the wrong side of the road. Horns blared.

"He's going to get himself killed!" Dora exclaimed.

The Mercedes rocketed to the front of the line of traffic. The cars in front of Dora and Logan responded much more slowly to the sound of their sirens.

"We're losing him!" Dora yelled.

"I can see that, but there's nothing I can do unless you want me to drive as recklessly as Leonard."

They heard the crash before they saw it.

The Mercedes had swerved into oncoming traffic again. Only Leonard misjudged the amount of space he had to get back on the right side of the road. He slammed head on into the back of a box truck, knocking the Mercedes into and then over the curb.

Pedestrians scattered, and Dora said a quick thank-you to the gods that none of them seemed to have been hit. The Mercedes had been moving fast enough that jumping the curb didn't slow it much at all. It kept moving forward, right into a low brick wall that surrounded a parking lot.

Tires screeched as drivers came to abrupt stops on the street and screams filled the air.

Logan punched the brake, stopping the car in the middle of the street. They both threw their doors open and ran for the wreck.

The front of the car had folded like an accordion.

People drew forward, many of them with their cameras out and recording.

Dora silently cursed them. She reached through the shattered driver's-side window and pressed two fingers against the side of Leonard's neck. There was a pulse— a faint one, but it was there.

"He's alive." Dora pulled her hand back. "Call for an ambulance."

Logan pulled out his phone and made the call.

They'd have to wait for the EMTs to get Leonard out of the car. It was too dangerous to move him.

Dora's legs gave out, and she went down onto her knee. It was then that she realized that she was bleeding as well.

"Dora!" Logan was beside her in an instant.

She pressed a hand to her side and pulled it back bloody.

"You're hurt. I'm going to call for another ambulance," Logan pronounced, fear lacing his words.

She had no desire to go to the hospital and was just about to tell him that when a wave of dizziness hit her. "I think that's probably a good idea."

Chapter Sixteen

John Leonard had survived surgery, but he was in critical condition. Logan was happy to hear it. Hopefully, Leonard would be able to answer some questions soon. He and Dora had plenty of them for him.

Luckily, Dora's injury was minor. Her bleeding at the scene of the accident had come from a scratch on her side. The emergency room doctor theorized that the wave of dizziness had resulted from an adrenaline crash. He'd discharged her with orders to take ibuprofen if her side bothered her and to take it easy. She took the ibuprofen without argument but taking it easy was a different story. Keene, Roberts, and Crenshaw had put in appearances at the hospital while he'd waited for Dora to be discharged.

The hours waiting at the hospital had also given Logan a chance to check in with his colleagues at the FBI. He was surprised to find out that John Leonard wasn't unknown to the Bureau. In fact, he was the subject of an ongoing investigation into money laundering. Logan had to wonder if Leonard running from them had more to do with that than their serial killer case. Leonard didn't exactly fit the profile he was working up on their serial killer. But all those questions would have to wait until Leonard regained consciousness.

After four hours at the hospital, Dora's doctor finally discharged her. Logan had the foresight to get Landon to drop off his personal vehicle so that he could drive Dora home. He led Dora into her house. "Are you hungry?" he asked. He knew he was. He hadn't wanted to leave Dora to find the hospital's cafeteria, so he'd had to make do with a bag of stale chips from the vending machine.

Dora stopped him from trekking to the fridge with a hand on his arm. "I don't want food."

Heat filled her eyes. She brought her lips to his gently.

The surprise that flooded through him quickly changed to desire. He forced himself to pull back, though. "Dora, wait. I'm not sure you're thinking this through."

"I don't want to think right now. I want to feel. We could have been killed today."

He rested his hands on her waist. "I don't want you to regret anything."

"No regrets," she promised.

Logan turned his face into her hand, his lips brushing her palm. His feelings churned through him even as he reminded himself that this was real. Dora was really in his arms.

A moment later, she stretched up on her toes and brushed her lips over his.

When she pulled back, he searched her face and saw joy, awe, and fear—all the same feelings that were swirling inside of him. He wrapped his arms around her, pulling her against his chest, and kissed her with everything he was feeling.

Dora groaned against his lips and snaked her fingers around his neck.

"Let me stay the night," Logan panted against her lips. "Please." He didn't care about the desperation in his voice. He simply knew he needed to be with Dora.

A smile stretched across Dora's face, and she nodded, drawing him in for another kiss before leading her through to the back of the small house where her bedroom was located. He moved to her toward the bed, cupping her cheeks. He kissed her deeply. He hadn't realized how desperately he missed her kiss. He missed the way her lips moved against his and the smell of her floral perfume circling around him.

He stopped bedside, his hands moving to the buttons of her shirt and undoing each in turn, baring her chest to the cool air. His body warmed as the blouse slid from her shoulders onto the floor. He stepped back from her, his eyes roved her body. Her cheeks pinked.

"You are beautiful," he whispered.

Dora unclasped the buttons on her slacks and let them slide down her legs before reaching around her back and unsnapping her bra. It hit the floor only seconds before her panties, and he thought his heart might actually stop. She let him look his fill for several long moments before stepping into him. He reached a hand around her waist, tucking his head into her shoulder and stroking his tongue over the spot on her neck in the way he remembered she loved.

Her body trembled, and Logan held her tighter to him. He let his hand drift lower until it skimmed the apex of her thighs. The contact made her gasp in a little breath. He smiled into her neck as he lavished it with kisses. He slid his finger over the sensitive nerves between her legs, eliciting another moan from her. Her head fell onto his shoulder.

"Logan, I can't. It's too much."

"Just relax. I've got you." There was nothing he wanted more in life at that moment than to bring her to her release.

His hand worked between her thighs while his lips continued to caress her neck.

Dora's breath came in quick pants now, and he knew she was close. He snaked his free hand from around her waist and to her breast. He twirled his finger over her nipple, drawing another moan from her. He curled the finger inside of her and built up speed, drawing another moan from her even as he felt her tightening around his fingers. Her moan turned into a cry, and her body spasmed. He moved his arm back around her waist, holding her up as he wrung every drop of pleasure from her. When she finally went limp in his arms, he laid her across the bed and quickly disposed of his own clothes.

Desire still coursed through his veins. He wasn't anywhere near done with the pleasure he planned for both of them to enjoy that night. He wasn't sure he'd ever tire of exploring her body. He removed his trousers, kicking them away without his eyes leaving her face.

"I want you. So much," he said, climbing onto the bed and stretching out over her.

His mouth collided with hers in a claiming kiss. His manhood pressed against her stomach. He felt his body harden against her belly. He hovered over her, his manhood nudging at her entrance. They stared at each other as he pushed into her, moving slowly at first, her body opening to him and stretching to accommodate him. Each inch filled his own heart with more of her until he was sure it would burst. When he was fully seated, he stilled. It wasn't the right time to say it, but he knew, without a doubt, this…this was right. This, Dora was everything, and he loved her. Had loved her from almost the moment they met.

Then she reached up, cupping his cheek, drawing him in even deeper, and his control shattered. He moved faster, each thrust leading to her making little mewling sounds that only drove his desire higher. She clutched at his backside, demanding his hips move faster and harder.

"Does it feel good to have me inside of you again?" Logan growled against her lips.

"Yes," she panted. "God, yes."

Her affirmation drove him closer to his release. He thrust into her, saying with his body what he wasn't yet ready to say with his words. She broke. His lips collided with hers, swallowing her moans of ecstasy as she continued to writhe beneath him. His last driving thrusts pushed him over the edge, and he moaned her name as he followed her over the cliff. They toppled over and over, shattering before coming back together. Together.

It was the first time in a long time that he'd felt whole.

They lay in each other's arms, not speaking, just holding each other, being together until Dora's breathing evened out. She hadn't asked him to leave, so he pulled her in closer and let his body relax into sleep, wondering if he just might get lucky and convince her to end every night just like this for the rest of their lives.

DORA WOKE WITH what felt like a boulder on her chest. Logan's warm breath tickled her ear. She slid from under the weight of his arm.

His eyes fluttered open. "Hey, where are you going?"

She hastily threw on her undergarments and slid into her jeans. She did a full three-hundred-sixty-degree turn looking for her shirt. "I have to go...you have to go."

Logan sat up in the bed, his mouth turning into a frown. "Dora?"

This had been a mistake. A huge mistake. She'd clearly learned nothing from their past. Not to mention that they were working together again. What was it they said about fools making the same mistakes over and over? Clearly, she was such a fool.

"Listen, we need to get into the station. There's a lot to do today. I know you probably want to go home to shower and change before going in, so I ordered an Uber. It should be here in a few minutes."

She left the room without giving him a chance to respond.

She made coffee, continuing to chastise herself as she did. *God, how stupid do you have to be to fall into bed with the man who broke your heart?*

Logan padded into the kitchen fully dressed but without his shoes. "So, we're not going to talk about it?"

The coffee maker hissed before the brown liquid began dripping into the carafe.

"There's nothing to talk about," Dora said, not daring to look at him. "It was a mistake. It won't happen again. No one needs to know."

"I know. You know."

She did look at him now, and she let her anger fuel

her. "Logan, I am not going down this road with you again. It was just sex. That's all it can be."

"That's all you wanted to be, but that's not all it was. I think you know that."

Dora frowned. "Let's not do this."

"Do what, Dora? Care about each other?"

She threw up her hands. "Fall into this trap of thinking that this time things are going to be different."

"They can be different this time. Our relationship ended because I had to move to Arizona for work."

"Is that why it ended, though? I mean, we could have tried the long-distance thing. I offered to try, and you said no."

"Long distance is—"

She moved in closer to him, crowding him. "Is what, Logan? People do it. People who really want to be together. People who are committed to trying. That was our problem. Not the distance. Not the jobs. You weren't committed to us."

She looked into his eyes, waiting for an answer. Waiting for him to tell her she was wrong, but he seemed to be struggling with the ability to speak.

"Nothing? Really." She shook her head. "Last night was…was great, but it was last night. A onetime thing. I'd like to keep it that way." She unplugged the coffee machine. "My car should be outside. I'll see you later."

She brushed past him, grabbing her purse, and left the kitchen without another word.

"THE WITNESS COULDN'T describe the man she saw. Not in any detail." The killer listened to the two officers talking to one another, leaning forward, ignoring the pounding of his heart. He had to stay calm and not look as if he were eavesdropping even though he was. No one in the police station paid him much attention. It was one of his gifts. He looked as if he belonged no matter where he was. So, nobody noticed when he stopped abruptly, having overheard the officers talking at their desks. He needed to get as much information as possible about this witness.

"Detective Madison has her holed up somewhere supersecret. She's hoping once the witness feels safe, she will be able to give the task force more details about the man she saw."

"It's possible," the other cop responded.

The first nodded. "Let's hope so. We really need to catch this monster." One of the officers' phones rang, ending their conversation.

There was a witness, but she hadn't given the police anything. Yet.

He had to find her before she did. He needed more time to find his Sarah.

Detective Madison. The cops had said Madison had stashed the witness somewhere safe. Which meant Madison was the key.

He had to be careful, but if he followed Madison, she'd eventually lead him to the witness. And then he'd take care of her, just like he'd taken care of the others.

Chapter Seventeen

Monica Gonzalez, their first victim, had been found in a park in the trendy Foggy Bottom neighborhood, making the case a Metropolitan Police case. But her parents lived in Wheaton, Maryland, a middle-class suburb about ten miles north of DC. It was a diverse community with good schools and an abundance of single-family homes. The kind of place parents moved to give their kids the best start they could in life. But as the Gonzalezes had tragically discovered, no neighborhood was completely safe from life's dangers.

"Monica had gotten her life back on track," Lupe Gonzalez insisted. Mrs. Gonzalez taught third grade, which undoubtedly meant she was made of stern stuff. But her hands shook as she brought the coffee, she'd insisted on making for them to her lips. Dr. Gonzalez placed a meaty hand on his wife's shoulder and squeezed. When Dora had called to ask if she and Logan could drop by to speak with the couple, Mrs. Gonzalez had agreed but said her husband was at work at his dentistry practice. Robert Gonzalez must have canceled his afternoon appointments after his wife's call and come straight home because he answered the door of their brick rambler when Dora and Logan rang the bell.

"She was an all-state runner," Mrs. Gonzalez continued. "Did you know that? In high school. We were so proud. She went to College Park," the woman continued, using the shorthand for the University of Maryland's flagship campus. "Monica wanted to be a doctor, but then she met Augustine." Mrs. Gonzalez said the name as if it was an epithet.

"Augustine Salerno." Dr. Gonzalez picked up the narrative with only slightly less disgust in his tone. "Monica was enchanted. She focused so much on track and her grades in high school. I think this was her first taste of puppy love and it was overwhelming for her." Dr. Gonzalez's eyes filled with tears.

"I could tell he was no good from the start. He'd been in school for four years when Monica met him and still wasn't anywhere close to graduating. I told Monica she should stay away from him. But she thought she could help him. Save him, you know what I mean?" Mrs. Gonzalez's eyes bore into Dora's.

She did know what the woman meant. Monica wasn't the first and she wouldn't be the last woman to give her best trying to save a man who didn't want saving. But Dorothy also knew Augustine Salerno had nothing to do with Monica Gonzalez's death. She had thoroughly investigated the man right after they found Monica's body. He struggled with a drug addiction and had physically, mentally, emotionally, and financially abused Monica and several of the women who he'd been living off of. But at the time of Monica's death, he'd been in Rio de

Janeiro, and there was no indication that he had contact with Monica four months prior to her death.

Still, Dora waited patiently, listening to the Gonzalezes rail about the man they blamed for their daughter's death. She knew they needed to get it out of their system before they could be able to help her investigation. If they could be of any help. That remained to be seen.

Once the Gonzalezes' rage had run cold, Dora went through the series of questions she asked them in the days right after Monica's murder, hoping time had jarred loose new details that might put them on the killer's trail. Unfortunately, the Gonzalezes' answers shed no new light on their daughter's murder or the subsequent murders.

"We've answered all these questions already," Lupe said impatiently. "How come you didn't care this much when it was just our daughter who'd been murdered? Nobody cared."

"I assure you that is not true, Mrs. Gonzalez," Logan said.

"Isn't it? I didn't see you here then, Mr. FBI Special Agent. The cops didn't care anything about our Monica. They just saw her as a druggie, even though she'd kicked her addiction by the time that monster took her from us. She'd done rehab and had been keeping up with her therapy for almost a year. But all you saw was a junkie," Lupe spat at Dora.

Dora didn't contradict the grieving mother. She knew that there was nothing she could say that would stem the hurt and anger at her loss. As she knew there was nothing, she could say that wouldn't sound like an excuse. That she hadn't known she was dealing with a serial killer at the time. That she'd gone by the book, treating Monica like every other victim. That she'd looked into any possible drug-related angle and found, as Mrs. Gonzalez said, that Monica had kicked her habit. It was all true and none of it mattered. Monica was dead, and because Dora hadn't found her killer quickly enough, two other women were also now dead.

Dora showed both the Gonzalezes the sketch of their suspect. Neither recognized the man.

Doro and Logan left the couple to try to reseal the wound they just ripped open again.

"You know she's a grieving mother and that nothing she said about your work on the case is true," Logan said as they made their way across the Gonzalezes' lawn to the car.

"No, I don't know that." Dora held up her hand to stop Logan's protest before they got started. "I know I did the best I could with the information I had at the time, but—" Dora stopped and turned to him as they reached the car. "If Monica Gonzalez had been a senator's daughter or if Michelle Quitoni had been the first victim instead of the third, would the FBI have sent you to me sooner? Would my department have put together a task force with four detectives immediately?"

Logan deflated. "Probably. Yes, they would have."

"Exactly." Dora shucked her chin in the direction of the rancher they had just left. Mrs. Gonzalez stood in the front window watching them, her arms crossed across her chest, abject grief covering her face. "And she knows that too."

DORA SPENT THE rest of the workday into the evening at her desk, poring over every bit of information they

had on each of the homicides. There appeared to be little commonality among the murder victims, apart from
their looks. Michelle was an investment banker, Monica
Gonzalez had been a cashier, and Alicia Jones was a preschool teacher. There was no sign that the women knew
each other or had ever crossed paths with each other.
Logan had pointed out that the similarity in appearance
between the victims showed an undeniable pattern, but
there was nothing to connect the victims in any other
way. And there was nothing she could find that would
lead them to their killer. What was she missing? There
must've been something.

Logan sat at the desk across from her, the spicy,
musky scent of his cologne gently tickling her nose.
Her mind wandered to the memory of their night together. She'd forgotten how Logan was in bed and how
wonderful it felt to wake up beside him. A flicker of desire coursed through her, but she pushed it down as far
as she could force it. Their night had been a one-time
thing. She couldn't let it happen again.

She focused back on the case, continuing her search
for anything, any miniscule thing, that might lead her
to her serial killer.

Logan's cell phone rang, and he answered it. Dora
only had to hear his end of the conversation to know
that he was speaking to his sister, Lisa.

"I'm sorry I forgot about dinner. I'm at the station, but
I'll leave now." Logan went silent, but his gaze skimmed
over Dora. "Yes, she's here." He fell silent for another
moment. "I'm not sure she'll want to."

There was another, longer silence from Logan, and

then he sighed. He pulled the phone from his ear, punching the speaker button.

"Dora?" Lisa's voice came loud and clear from the other side of the phone.

"Lisa, ah, hi. How are you?"

"I'm great. How are you?"

"I'm doing well," Dora responded, shooting a look at Logan over the top of her computer monitor. He shrugged and kept holding his phone out.

"Listen, Logan is heading to my house for dinner. I'm inviting you as well."

"Oh, that is so…nice," Dora said, surprised. She hadn't spoken to Lisa since the breakup. "I really have a lot of work to do here. I'm not sure…"

"I'm not going to take no for an answer. I haven't seen you in ages, and no matter how much work you have to do, you also have to eat."

Dora gave Logan another beseeching look that he ignored.

"So, hop in the car with Logan." Lisa bulldozed ahead. "I'll see you both in a half hour." The phone went dead.

"I could have used a little help." Dora glared at Logan.

He shrugged. "Lisa is right. You do have to eat. And you know my sister. If you aren't at her table in exactly thirty minutes, she'll just come down here with a bunch of Tupperware and feed you anyway."

That did sound like Lisa Elkins. She tended to get what she wanted. It was what made her a good attorney.

"Come on. It's just dinner. And maybe taking your mind off the case for a bit will shake something you've missed loose," Logan cajoled.

As if in agreement, her stomach grumbled. She was

hungry. And, as she remembered, Lisa was an amazing cook.

"Okay, fine, but I'm taking these files home with me."

Logan shook his head. "Has anyone ever told you you're a workaholic?"

A tentative smile curled Dora's lips. "It's been mentioned a time or two."

The drive to Lisa's Takoma Park neighborhood, just south of Catholic University, took less than thirty minutes. The house hadn't changed much since the last time Dora had visited. It was a modest, brick, two-story colonial in Takoma Park, not far from the border with Maryland. A big picture window looked out onto a wide front porch and the street beyond.

Logan pulled to the curb, and they got out, walking up the tidy concrete walkway.

Logan pressed his hand to the small of Dora's back, guiding her up the steps of the front porch. He opened the front door without knocking or using a key. The sound of laughter and Alicia Keys's "Fallin'" on the radio followed them into the house as they entered.

Lisa Elkins stuck her head around the corner leading from the kitchen, a dishrag slung over her shoulder.

A smile bloomed on her face when her gaze landed on Dora. "Dora, it's good to see you."

The scent of roast beef and sweet potatoes encircled Dora as Lisa pulled her into a full-body hug.

"It's good to see you too," Dora responded against Lisa's shoulder.

"Lisa, let her breathe," Logan said, easing Dora from his sister's arms.

Lisa let go of Dora and turned back toward the kitchen, calling out, "Landon, Dora is here!"

Landon Elkins strode into the foyer. The eldest Elkins, Landon was built broader than his younger brother but exuded a quiet strength that neither of his brasher younger siblings had. All three Elkins shared the same dark brown skin, matching dark brown eyes and high cheekbones, though. No one would doubt they were siblings.

"Hey there. Long time no see, stranger." Landon pulled Dora into a quick one-armed hug.

A high-pitched teenage voice preceded the teenager it came from into the foyer. "What's going on? I thought we were about to eat. Oh!" The teenage girl stopped short.

It had been years since Dora had seen Layla Williamson. The young girl had grown into quite a beauty.

"Hi, Layla. I'm Dora. We met, but you probably don't remember me."

"Yeah, I do remember, kind of. Hi. Can we eat now?"

Lisa rolled her eyes at her daughter but moved back toward the kitchen. "We can sit down. The food is ready."

The group trooped into the dining room where the table had already been set. Just off of the dining room in the large family room, the family's Christmas tree still stood even though they'd officially made it to mid-January.

"You still have your Christmas tree up," Dora noted, surprised.

Layla groaned, but Lisa chuckled. "Yes, much to my daughter's horror."

"She keeps it up until, like, Valentine's Day. It's so embarrassing."

"Your mom doesn't keep it up quite that long," Landon contradicted his niece.

"But almost," Logan said, joining the family fray.

"Hey, the way I see it, we should hold on to the Christmas spirit for as long as we can," Lisa said in a way that let Dora know this wasn't the first time she'd uttered that statement.

"It's a gorgeous tree," Dora said, feeling more than a little out of place among the family's easy banter.

She never had this for herself. As a single mom, her mom had had to work multiple jobs to keep a roof over their heads. As a child in her teens, she'd eaten most of her meals in front of the television, alone. From the moment she stepped into the house, she'd been enveloped in a feeling of warmth and family that she had no real reference point for. It was like walking into a Norman Rockwell painting.

Not that she'd never thought about it, having a large loving family. Especially when she and Logan had dated. She'd even begun to let herself hope that one day his family might become hers.

But she needed to remember that was never to be, especially now. Especially after last night. She and Logan were not a couple. They would never be one again. She couldn't let herself get caught up in her feelings for him or fairy-tale dreams.

Heat suddenly flashed through her.

She pushed her chair back away from the table quickly, causing the Elkins' banter to cut off abruptly.

"I think I need a little air."

She darted from the room and to the sliding glass door off of the living room without giving anyone at the table a moment to speak or stop her.

On the back deck, Dora took a deep breath. Someone clearly enjoyed gardening, and it showed in the vibrant colors bursting from the flowerbeds in the backyard.

Behind her, the sliding glass door opened. She was surprised when she glanced over her shoulder and found Lisa stepping out onto the deck instead of Logan.

Lisa handed her a full wineglass. "Are you okay?"

"Yeah." Dora took a big sip of wine. "It was a bit over-whelming, I guess. I'm not used to a large family." *Or any family*, she thought to herself.

"It can be a bit much sometimes, but I wouldn't have it any other way." Lisa smiled. "I'm glad to see you, though. Happy to see you're doing so well."

Dora let her eyes fall to the wood boards of the deck floor. She and Lisa had become something like friends while she and Logan dated. But after the breakup, Dora had stopped taking Lisa's calls. She hadn't wanted to hear the pity in Lisa's voice. Now she wondered if she'd been too quick to toss away the friendship.

"I'm sorry I didn't return your calls after Logan and I…"

Lisa waved away the apology. "You have nothing to apologize for. Breakups are hard. Truth be told, I let Logan know he was an idiot for leaving you, especially in such a cowardly way."

Dora glanced at Lisa, surprised. "You did?"

"Of course." Lisa sighed. "Our family has been through a lot. We're tough, we get through it, but not without scars and making our fair share of mistakes," Lisa said pointedly.

Dora stayed quiet, thinking about her words.

"I'm pretty sure Logan would take back leaving you if he could."

Dora opened her mouth to respond, although she had no idea what she would say.

Lisa held up her hand, warding off Dora's words. "I know I should stay out of it, and I will. But just think about whether you could forgive him. It might be worth it."

Lisa gave her a one-armed hug and headed back into the house as Logan stepped out onto the deck. Lisa winked at him as she passed by and tapped a light punch to Logan's shoulder.

A wink and a punch, Dora thought. Siblings were so confusing.

"Are you okay?" Logan asked.

"Yeah. Just need a little air."

"What were you and my sister talking about so intently out here?"

Dora slid a sidelong glance at him. "You."

"I'm not sure if that's good news or bad news."

Dora chuckled. "Me either."

Logan braced his hand on the deck's railing and leaned closer, desire in his eyes. "Dora, I'm so sorry for leaving."

Dora's heart beat wildly. "Logan…"

He didn't respond. His gaze stayed locked on hers. Her eyes fell to his lips, and she shivered with anticipation. She took a step forward.

The heat from his body enveloped her. He traced her jaw with his thumb.

His lips grace hers, soft, gentle, tentative, as if he couldn't believe she was letting him kiss her. Something familiar stirred inside her, and she leaned in. She kissed him with all the passion and desire that she had been fighting since he walked into the police station's conference room.

He pulled her closer. She shifted, pressing against him and eliciting a groan while his mouth was still pressed against hers.

"Give me a second chance," he said, his arms still around her, his voice low and laced with desire.

"Logan—"

"No, don't answer now. Think about it. I know I messed up. Give me a chance to make it up to you. Give us a chance."

Logan stepped back, though it looked as if it took a fair amount of strength.

Dora watched him disappear, his words playing in her mind. His kiss was still sweet on her lips.

Chapter Eighteen

Despite barely being able to keep her eyes open, Dora slept fitfully. Her dreams were filled with Logan. Somehow, the kiss they'd shared on his sister's deck had gotten to her more than their night of unbridled passion. Sleeping together had brought out something raw and instinctual between them. But the kiss they'd shared… That kiss had burrowed deep inside her and broken feelings open that had been locked up tight for years. Feelings she'd ignored even when they'd been together. The more she relived the kiss, the more right being in Logan's arms—being with him—felt. Although she knew she wasn't ready to tell him that. She wasn't sure when, or if, she ever would be. Opening herself up to him again and trusting him would be one of the hardest things she ever did. She wasn't sure she was brave enough to take the risk, even if she could feel herself falling for him all over again.

Despite the sleepless night, she met Noreen at the gym at 7 am. She hated the gym, but she hadn't found a better way to decompress after a trying day. For her part Noreen loved working out. She said it helped her deal with her aggressions. They ran on side-by-side treadmills, Dora working to keep Logan off her mind by running through the details of the case with Noreen, hoping that her friend and fellow detective might have some advice on how to proceed.

"I'm nearly pulling my hair out," Dora said. "The press, the chief, even Lieutenant Crenshaw…everyone is all over me to find this guy," Dora complained. "He's making the department look like fools."

"High-profile cases are the worst," Noreen agreed.

Dora concurred with Logan's assessment that the killer wouldn't stop until he was caught, but they weren't close to catching him. No matter what they did, he always seemed to stay a few steps ahead of their efforts to capture him. "The fact that the killer appeared to have kidnapped some of his victims in broad daylight is what really has me worried," Dora said. "It means this guy is either extremely confident or insanely reckless. Either way, it makes him very dangerous."

"I wish I had some easy answers for you. I want you to catch this guy as much as everyone else in the department, but you have to just put your head down and keep doing the work."

"You sound like Logan now."

"Oh, I do, do I?" Noreen grinned.

Dora blushed.

"Did something happen between you and the hunky FBI agent?"

Dora stayed silent and ran a little faster.

"It has." Noreen slapped the arm of her machine. "Tell me."

She could resist, but she knew Noreen wouldn't stop her barrage of questions until she got what she wanted.

"We slept together," Dora said, keeping her voice low so no one else would hear.

Too bad Noreen didn't take the hint. Her friend hooted loudly, drawing the attention of the one other woman in the treadmill section. "I knew it. I knew you two were going to get back together."

"We are not back together," Dora protested, but the words sounded weak to her ear.

"Headed that way."

"We aren't headed anywhere. I think sleeping with him was a mistake. I'm not going to do it again."

Noreen sighed. "Yes, you are."

"What?"

Noreen stopped her machine, and Dora reluctantly followed suit.

"Look, Logan may have moved, but whatever you two had never really ended. It just went dormant for a while. It's obvious you two still have feelings for each other. I know you didn't ask, but I'm taking best-friend privileges and telling you your business anyway. You should see whatever this is with Logan out to the end. Maybe it will be a love affair for the ages. Maybe it peters out once you solve the case, but I think you owe it to yourself to find out. Don't you?"

Dora didn't have time to answer the question before her phone rang.

"Madison," she answered in a tone that was a heavy mix of exhaustion and irritation.

"Dora, we've just gotten a report of another missing woman that fits the profile of our serial killer's victims."

Dora swore, punching the button on the treadmill to stop the machine's belt and hopping off.

"Christine Belgrade," Keene continued. "Reported missing by her boss Tuesday afternoon."

"Yesterday? Why am I just hearing about this now?"

"Damn rookie took the report over the phone but didn't elevate it. The night sergeant caught it and sent it to me."

Later, when she had time, she and that rookie were going to have a serious chat.

Dora glanced at the time on her phone as she headed back to the locker rooms trailed by Noreen who'd received enough sudden phone calls of her own to recognize when duty called. 7:35 a.m. So much for a workout.

She asked Keene to give Logan a call, update him on the situation, and have him pick her up from her house. She pushed her way into the locker room while sending up a quick prayer that they weren't too late to find Christine Belgrade alive and well.

Dora was waiting for him on her front porch when he pulled to a stop in front of her house. He drove them to Wynette Accounting, just blocks from the iconic Union Station where Christine Belgrade worked as a junior accountant. Her boss, Rashida Edwards, had reported her missing. Ms. Edwards had agreed to meet them at her office before it officially opened for business that day. Given the current situation, they were wasting no time in beginning an investigation. Hopefully, Christine was off somewhere taking an impromptu vacation or with a paramour, but she fit the description of their killer's prior victims and Logan had a bad feeling about her disappearance.

He and Dora sat in Rashida Edwards's office.

"Thanks for coming so quickly, Detectives. I'm really worried about Christine," Ms. Edwards said.

"Of course," Dora responded. "When was the last time you saw Christine?"

While Dora did the questioning, Logan took in the woman in front of them. Rashida Edwards was in her mid-forties, slender with the first touches of gray at her temples. Her light brown eyes were shaded and filled with concern behind horn rimmed glasses.

"Yesterday. Christine was only in for a half day. She said she needed the afternoon off."

"Did she say why?"

Rashida shook her head. "No, and I didn't ask. She had the time, so I approved the request. But when she didn't show up for work this morning, I got concerned."

"And you tried to call her?"

"I've called several times, and I went to her house myself. No one answered the phone or the door."

"Could Christine simply have gotten confused? Maybe she thought she'd taken more time off than she actually requested."

"If you knew Christine, you'd know she takes her job very seriously. She's meticulous. You have to be with the job she holds."

"Could there have been some kind of family emergency? Does she have any family that you could check with?"

"She's not married, but she does have a brother. We have an emergency contact for her. I didn't want to worry him unnecessarily." Rashida handed a piece of paper with the name and number on it across her desk to Dora.

Logan understood why the accountant wouldn't want to be the one to make the call letting a brother know his sister might be missing.

"We'll check with her family." Dora slipped the blue sheet of paper between the folds of her notebook and stood. Logan followed. "And I'll need Christine's address."

Ms. Edwards pulled up the map application on her phone and rattled off the address.

"We'll give Christine's house another look and check with her family to see if they have heard from her," Dora said.

Ms. Edwards's brow furrowed. "Please keep me posted. Everyone here loves Chris, and we're all understandably concerned."

She didn't have to add that the serial killer roaming the streets only heightened that concern.

"We'll let you know what we can," Dora promised.

Their next stop was Christine Belgrade's modest, two-bedroom clapboard home just outside of Washington, DC, in the family-friendly suburb of Silver Spring. The driveway was empty, and the house appeared unoccupied from the outside.

On the drive over, Dora placed a call to Christine's emergency contact, her brother, Philip, who lived in Philadelphia. He hadn't heard from Christine in several weeks but claimed that was not unusual for the siblings. He'd been mildly concerned, enough that he told them where to find the spare key to Christine's house and had authorized them to enter to do a wellness check.

Dora headed for the backyard, where she found the hiding rock with the key. "Nothing looks out of place back there," she said, rejoining Logan at the front door.

They made entry, calling out for Christine as they went from room to room through the small house. There was no one there, and it looked as if Christine hadn't slept in her own bed or used the kitchen or bathroom that morning.

"This is not good," Logan stated the obvious.

"No, no, it isn't." Dora pulled her phone from her pocket. "I'm going to put out an APB on Christine's car."

The phone rang in Dora's hand before she made the call.

"Madison," she answered.

Her face blanched and then hardened as she listened to the person on the other end of the line. "We're on our way." She ended the call.

"What is it?" Logan asked, already following her to the door.

"Michelle Quitoni's car was found in Garfield Park. A body was found in the trunk."

DORA DROVE TO Garfield Park in Southeast DC, where Michelle's car had been found. She had a sick feeling in the pit of her stomach that the body that had been found in the car was Christine Belgrade's. But if so, that meant their killer had evolved. Or devolved. That was a question for Logan. Unfortunately, they hadn't said more than to subsist to each other since that morning. How could she have been so stupid? Falling back into bed with him. Clearly, she learned nothing from their disastrous prior relationship and was a glutton for punishment.

I should have moved faster, Dora thought to herself, even though she knew there was nothing she could have done. She pulled up to the curb of the street running alongside the park. She spotted two patrol cars, lights flashing, parked haphazardly. Two male officers were talking to a young woman with hot-pink hair and wearing multicolored leggings. Michelle's car had been found on a service road used by city employees that ran along the southern edge of the park grounds.

Dora and Logan got out of the car and headed toward the officers. She didn't recognize either of them, but one stepped up to her and Logan as they approached. She flashed identification. "Detective Madison. What do we have?"

The twentysomething male officer squinted at her identification before responding, "A female deceased in the trunk. She appears to have been strangled. ME is on his way."

"Do we have a name?" Dora held her breath.

"The car comes back to a Michelle Quitoni." The narrow-eyed look the uniform shot at her let her know he made the obvious connection. "But the identification in the purse in the trunk indicates our body is Christine Belgrade."

"Damn," Logan swore next to Dora.

She shared his frustration but simply pressed her lips together tightly and said a silent prayer for Christine.

Dora nodded at the officer and began walking again along the service road. Logan followed. They hadn't gone far along the road when they spotted the black Audi with silver rims. The trunk was open, and an MPD evidence technician was studiously snapping photos. Curled into a fetal position and wearing a business suit, she was a slender female with dark brown hair. She looked to be in her early thirties. Her eyes were closed and, but for the grayish pallor of her face and her location, it would have been possible to believe she was only sleeping. A red leather purse lay beside her.

A chill ran through Dora as she stared at the woman, who she could not save. She turned toward Logan, who was studying her with concern written all over his face.

"What do you make of the change in MO?"

Logan thought for a moment. "This road is somewhat hidden. My educated guess is he intended to leave the body in the park as he usually does but something happened to interrupt him."

"Something like what?"

"Your guess is as good as mine. Maybe he heard something or got spooked by an animal."

Dora turned to look the way they'd come. "A car could have pulled into the parking lot."

"It's possible," Logan agreed.

"We should check for security video and with patrol units. See if they have reports of anyone being here last night. They might have seen something."

"Okay, so he gets spooked and just leaves Christine here. And why did he still have Michelle's car? I would have thought he'd have dumped it by now."

"All good questions and I'm sorry I can't answer them for you. I can only speculate."

"Speculate away. It's all I got at the moment."

"Well, he could have hung on to the car as a sort of trophy. Or he could have simply not had any idea how to get rid of it without leaving a trail."

"Okay, I'll buy either of those explanations. What concerns me most is how fast he moved on from Michelle to Christine. We only found Michelle's body Monday. There were almost six weeks between our first and second and our second and third victims."

"He's escalating. Possibly devolving. The high he gets from killing is wearing off faster. The media attention may also be affecting him."

"Affecting him how?"

"Contrary to popular belief, not all serial killers relish attention. Or at least not media attention. It makes it harder for them to do what they do. More eyes are looking out for aberrant behaviors. He might feel threatened."

"Great. I take it a serial killer under pressure is—"

"Dangerous. Many can be even more dangerous and unstable than normal, yes."

"Detectives." The officer that had been speaking with the young woman in the leggings when Dora and Logan arrived at the crime scene jogged over to them. "The woman who called the body in would like to be released to go to work."

"I'd like to speak to her first," Dora said. She made her way to where the woman stood chewing on her nail. "Hello. I'm Detective Dora Madison. This is my colleague, Special Agent Elkins. I understand you need to get to work, but I'd like to ask you a few questions."

"I already answered the other agent's questions."

Dora tried to smile, though it was difficult under the circumstances. "I get that. This will be quick, I promise."

The young woman nodded reluctantly.

"Miss…"

"Yvette Jarvis."

"Miss Jarvis, how did you come to be on the service road this morning?"

As unlikely as it was that their killer was a woman, Dora couldn't dismiss any possibility out of hand.

"I always take this route to work. I live in the apartments over there." Yvette waved vaguely to the throng of buildings at her back. The uniform had no doubt gotten the woman's contact information, and Dora would make sure he checked it out. "I work at Nail Serenity, just on the other side of the park. This is the quickest way to work, and I get my steps in."

"Did you see anything or anyone as you walked to work this morning?" Logan stepped in.

"No. No one. Everything was just as it always was until I saw the car. I knew something was up then. Sometimes I see government vehicles on the road. Usually, trucks with garbage or landscaping tools, you know. But never Audis, and mostly on my walk home from work. Almost never in the morning."

"You walk this route home too? Did you come this way yesterday evening?"

Yvette nodded. "Sure did. And before you ask the same question as the other police officer, that car wasn't here."

"What time did you come through here last night?" Dora asked.

Yvette looked up at the sky. "I got off at six, so probably six fifteen, six twenty. Somewhere around there."

She made the call to 911 at 7:50 a.m., so sometime between 6:30ish the night before and 7:50 this morning, their killer had been here. And it was safe to say he'd come after dark, but Dora would put some uniforms on

canvassing to see if they could find anyone to defini-
tively narrow down that time frame and, if they were
really lucky, give them a description of the perpetrator. She didn't have a lot of faith that they would find
working security cameras in the park, not with the city
constantly slashing the budget, but she'd get a uniform
on finding out for sure. So much work to do. And Dora
couldn't help but feel they were miles behind a killer
poised to strike again.

Chapter Nineteen

The killer watched gleefully as law enforcement worked around Michelle Quitoni's car. Several of the uniformed officers looked shellshocked, but Detective Dora Madison appeared to be angry. No, not just angry—enraged.

The killer smiled. He'd never been one to hang around and watch the police. It always seemed like a waste of time and an unnecessary risk. He knew the cops kept an eye out for bystanders who appeared a little too interested in their work. It was why he made sure to position himself so he was sure he couldn't be seen from the service road where he'd left Michelle's car.

He watched Detective Madison now. She was with the FBI agent, Elkins. Even though he could tell their conversation was intense, there was also an intimacy about it between them.

Interesting.

So far, following the detective hadn't gotten him much. But he was nothing if not persistent. And it didn't seem like Madison had any idea she was being followed. Some detective. He just needed to be patient. If there was one thing his search for Sarah had taught him, it was patience. It had always paid off for him. He wasn't about to doubt it now.

THE IMAGE OF Christine Belgrade's body folded into the trunk of the Audi gnawed at Dora as Logan drove them to Gabriel Owens's Mount Vernon Square address. Rashida Edwards might not have been aware of Christine's personal relationships, but it was difficult to keep one's personal life completely separate from their professional life. Another coworker had been able to provide Christine's boyfriend's name and address. Keene was back at the station and Dora had him run a quick background check on Gabriel Owens. Other than a charge for misdemeanor drug possession when he was in college, his record was clear. Gabriel was a budding journalist with a handful of bylines to his credit and no steady employment, renting a rundown garden-level apartment.

Logan pulled into the apartment building's parking lot next to a beige Cadillac, and together they headed up the walkway to Gabriel's apartment. It was never easy to deliver the news that a loved one had died. Even worse when a loved one had been taken violently.

"I hate death notifications," Dora said.

"Me too," Logan concurred. "It's the worst part of the job."

Dora rang the bell. A moment later, the apartment door opened. Standing there was a tall and muscular man in his mid-twenties with dark disheveled hair and a thick beard. "Yes?"

Dora and Logan introduced themselves and flashed their credentials. "Mr. Owens?"

The man in front of them hesitated. "Yes. Do you want to tell me what this is about?"

"Can we come inside? Please?" Dora added when the man in front of them still hesitated.

"It's about Christine Belgrade," Logan added.

"Yeah, come in." He held the door open for them to pass through.

They stepped through the door, and Dora glanced around the small, slightly musty-smelling apartment. The furnishings were sparse. A well-loved sofa sat across from a flat-screen and a card table served as a dinner table. Very *bachelor lives here*. A Jack Russell terrier lay beside the sofa. He lifted his head when Logan and Dora entered but apparently found them uninteresting and lowered it a moment later.

"What's her name?" Logan nodded at the dog.

Gabriel glanced over at the sofa. "Jack. Not very original, I know. I'm sorry—I'm a little frazzled. Would either of you like something to drink?"

"No, that's okay," Dora said. "Can we sit?" Dora gestured to the sofa.

Gabriel led them to the sofa. "What is this about Chris? Is she okay?"

"Unfortunately, she isn't." Dora had learned long ago that it was best to rip the Band-Aid off when delivering bad news. "I regret to inform you she has been killed."

Gabriel blinked rapidly. "Dead? How?"

"We're still very early in our investigation, but it looks like she was murdered. I'm sorry," Dora said again.

Gabriel's shoulders slumped, and an expletive slipped from his lips.

Dora gave him a moment to process the news before asking, "When did you last see Christine?"

Gabriel ran a hand across his beard. "A few days ago. Saturday. We went to the farmer's market. And we spoke Monday morning."

"Weren't you concerned about not having heard from her?"

"Not at all," Gabriel replied. "We don't speak every day. In fact, we can go for several days without speaking. We had agreed to keep our relationship casual for now."

Dora regarded the man in front of her skeptically. "Do you mind telling us where you were last night?"

"I was out with some friends at Carmella's, a bar on U Street. We had drinks, then went to dinner. We met there at around seven and were together until around eleven. I know I got home just before midnight."

Dora got the names and contact numbers for Gabriel's friends. She'd have his alibi checked out, but her gut told her that Gabriel Owens wasn't their guy. He seemed genuinely upset about Christine's death.

"Christine's boss told us that Christine took Monday afternoon off from work. Do you have any idea where she was going?"

Gabriel rubbed his beard again. "I'm not exactly sure. I know she said she had a doctor's appointment, though."

Gabriel wasn't able to tell them the name of the doctor, but it was something to look into.

He was unable to provide them any more information that they found helpful.

Dora's phone rang as they left Gabriel's apartment. The conversation was brief.

"That didn't sound good," Logan said when she ended the call.

"It wasn't. Lieutenant Crenshaw wants to see us. Now."

LATE THAT AFTERNOON, the task force met again. Dora stood in front of the assembled group: Lieutenant Crenshaw, Roberts, Keene and Logan. She briefed on what little information they had at the point and Christine Belgrade's murder. She and Logan had already met with Lieutenant Crenshaw privately, where the lieutenant had recounted the not-so-pleasant call she'd received from the chief on behalf of Senator Quitoni. Not surprisingly, the senator and his wife were furious that Dora hadn't arrested their daughter's killer yet. They wanted her taken off the case. Dora had held her breath, waiting for Crenshaw's dismissal to slam into her. Surprisingly, the chief hadn't given in, standing behind his lieutenant and the department. But Crenshaw had warned that support was soft and could disappear at any moment. As if Dora wasn't under enough pressure. All she could do was do her job, so she got to it. She turned her attention to the monitor on the wall of the conference room.

She brought up images of the third and fourth victims, Michelle and Christine. "Christine Belgrade was murdered sometime between Monday afternoon when she left work early and this morning when her body was found in the trunk of Michelle Quitoni's car. The medical examiner is working on the autopsy, but there was writing on Christine's legs—the same phrase found on the other three bodies. A desert rose was found in the front passenger seat of the car. We believe the killer was spooked prior to setting out the body as he usually does. Evidence techs are gathering evidence at the scene and towing the car to their facility for further processing. So far, there is no known connection between Christine and any of our prior victims."

She went over all the victims' vital information again, the location of the murders, and the efforts thus far to gather evidence and interview witnesses, including the improbability of John Leonard being their killer. She did not try to hide her own frustration with the pace of the investigation and the lack of a viable suspect.

Dora swallowed as she looked at Logan.

He gave her a nod and stood, taking her place at the front of the room. "Losing another woman was something none of us wanted to happen. But this recent murder tells us a lot about our killer." He reiterated the points he made to Dora earlier about the murderer possibly evolving in his methods. "One thing I am sure of is that this killer has no intention of stopping—not until we stop him."

Dora stepped up next to Logan, and they fielded questions from the room. Most of which came from Lieutenant Crenshaw, and many of which they had no answers for yet. The meeting began to wind down as Keene's phone beeped.

The frown that bloomed on Keene's face was enough to have Dora moving across the room to his side before he finished reading the text message.

"What is it?" she asked him, something more than seeing Logan reach her side.

Keene looked up from his phone. "It's the media. They've gotten Randi Singer's name."

DORA HAD LOGAN drive her to Violet Fullerton's house after the task-force meeting broke up. Randi was understandably upset and scared. It had taken an hour to calm her down and convince her that she was still safer at Violet's house than out on the street by herself. She finally agreed to remain at Violet's house, but Dora wasn't sure how much longer Randi would be willing to be "held prisoner," as she'd described it. But for now, she was safe. The press might have had her name, but they didn't know where she was, and they wouldn't if Dora had anything to say about it.

It was after eight when Logan finally pulled the car into her driveway. Without asking he walked her to her door following her inside. She didn't have the energy or desire to stop him.

She headed back to the kitchen.

"You've been quiet all day," Logan said, taking off his suit jacket and tossing it over a chair at the kitchen table.

"Just thinking about everything." She reached into the fridge and grabbed a bottle of water. "This case is…"

"A tough one. For everyone. But I don't think that's all this is. You've been avoiding me."

She closed the fridge door with more force than she'd intended. "What are you talking about? We've been working together all day."

"Yes, and you've barely looked at me and only spoken to me when you absolutely had to."

"That's not avoiding you."

Logan shook his head, a rueful smile on his face. "It's not going to work, you know."

"What's not going to work?" Dora crossed her arms over her chest.

"Ignoring me. Pushing me away."

"I'm not doing any of that. I just need to solve this case. This maniac is killing women in my city."

"You are one of the best cops I know. One of the best detectives in this city. But this is not about the case. This is about us."

"There is no *us*."

He took a step closer to her. "You may want that to be the case, but I think we both know it isn't. Not only is there an *us*, I think there is always going to be an *us*. We've gotten under each other's skin in a way that doesn't dim. It doesn't falter. It doesn't go away. It just is. We can try to ignore it, but I don't want to, and I don't think you do either."

She huffed a laugh. "You're pretty full of yourself."

His smile turned seductive, and despite everything she'd just said to him, her body reacted.

"I care about you, Dora."

His words sent emotions swirling inside of her including fear. Because he wanted her to admit that she cared about him too. Which she did, but she didn't know if she could get over the fear that he'd leave again, and she didn't know if she could stand losing him a second time.

"You left. And I didn't hear from you for two years."

Logan took another step closer to her. They were only inches apart now. "The biggest mistake of my life. If I could do it over again I would. But I can only promise you that if you give us a second chance, I will never hurt you again."

She rested her forehead against his. "I'm afraid."

He huffed a laugh. "Me too." He brushed a strand of hair back from her face. "So, let's be afraid together."

He didn't move, and she knew he was waiting for her. He was waiting for her to decide if they would move forward together or go on with their lives separately but always wondering what might have been. What if she'd opened up her heart again? What if she'd forgiven him? Yes, he had hurt her when he'd left, but he was there now. They had this second chance. If she didn't take it, she'd be the one hurting them both. Because she was sure he was right. They had gotten under each other's skins in a way that was irreversible. He was her person. The one she was supposed to walk through this life with. She just had to reach out and grab him.

She lifted her gaze, a single tear sliding down her cheek as she pressed her lips to his.

He stood frozen for a moment more before, wrapping his arms around her and pulling her tightly against his chest.

She could feel how much he wanted her, his desire matched only by her own.

Dora took his hand and led him to the bedroom. Moments later they were on the bed, stripping each other of their clothing. Then they were tangled together, Logan's weight pressing her down into the mattress.

Dora wrapped her legs around Logan's waist and took him into her body in one smooth movement. He filled her, and they moved together, their desire building in waves until it reached an explosive crescendo.

Then they were over the peak and free-falling, holding on to each other more tightly than she'd ever held on to anything before.

Chapter Twenty

When she woke the next morning, contentment had given way to concern. She'd promised herself that this would be nothing more than a casual fling. Once they caught their killer, she'd go back to her life, and he'd go back to his. But that was a lie—maybe it had always been. Because what she was feeling wasn't casual. It was so much more than that. So much more intense and…real. And once again she feared her heart was on the line, ready to be crushed a second time.

Her phone rang, and as she sat up to get it, Logan reached out for her, attempting to tug her back down on the bed. She evaded his grasp. The phone was still in her jacket pocket, which lay tossed haphazardly on the floor next to the bed. Aware that she was naked, she slipped the jacket on before she pulled her phone out of the pocket and accepted the call.

Keene was on the other end of the line. He started speaking without preamble. "The evidence technicians found something in Michelle Quitoni's car."

"Do you want to tell me what it is?" Dora said.

"Let me have my moment." Another short pause. "It's a pill bottle."

"There better be more," Dora growled.

"Patience. Patience. The bottle was wedged under the driver seat, which is why we didn't see it at the scene. It's the name on the bottle though that's important," Keene said, on a roll now. "It's not Michelle's. It's Waylen Osvolo's."

Dora's heartbeat quickened with excitement she recognized as born from having finally caught a break. "Now, why would Osvolo's prescription bottle be in Michelle's car?" She felt the bed move as Logan stood up. She felt rather than saw that he was also now fully engaged in her and the phone call.

"Well, that's something I'm sure you want to find out." Dora could hear the smile in Keene's voice.

"You're right about that."

"You want me to call Elkins for you?"

Dora glanced over her shoulder again. Logan was shrugging into his shirt, having already pulled on his pants. She took a moment to admire his sculpted abs before the fabric hid them from her view. "No, I'll call in. I still don't have a car, so I'll need him to pick me up anyway. We'll go pick up Osvolo and bring him in." She ended the call with Keene, then relayed what he had said to Logan, though he had picked up on most of it already.

She glanced at the bedside clock. It was after eight in the morning, and they still needed to shower before they could go get their suspect.

"We should shower, then try to find Osvolo at his job."

Logan circled the bed to come stand in front of her. "I like the sound of a shower, especially if you share it with me."

Dora's eyes shifted away from his. "I don't know if that's a good idea. We need to focus on this case."

Logan reached out and cupped her cheek. "I know I messed up last time, but I'm not going to make the same mistake twice. I think we have something here. And I think you know that. Whatever you have to do to prove to you that I'm not the same guy that ran away from you... I'll do it."

She wanted to believe him. Even if it didn't work out, she didn't want to give up whatever time she had with Logan now.

Dora stepped around him and headed for the en suite bathroom. At the door she turned, unsurprised to find Logan watching her. She let the jacket fall off her shoulders and onto the floor. She arched her back. "I thought you wanted to shower. What are you waiting for?"

THE SHOWER WAS quick but very satisfying. Logan had trouble forcing himself to focus on the task at hand even as he pulled the car to the gates of the Sutton Place community. This time the gatehouse was manned by a rent-a-cop who directed them to the management offices.

A woman in her early sixties with a platinum-blond bob and too much makeup met them in the management office. She introduced herself as Geraldine Steward.

"Mr. Osvolo has been let go."

"Let go?" Dora said incredulously.

Logan shared her incredulity. They finally had a good lead, and now they didn't know where to find him.

"Yes, as of two days ago."

"May I ask why?" Dora bit out.

"Well, we don't usually discuss personnel matters,

but as you are the police… We discovered Mr. Osvolo stealing from one of the residents."

"Stealing? Stealing what? There was no report made to the police department." She knew that if there had been, Osvolo's name would have triggered an alert to her since he was a person of interest in a murder investigation.

"No, the board thought it best not to report it, and the homeowner agreed. The community doesn't need any more bad press."

Bad press, Logan assumed, was referring to Michelle Quitoni, as if the most important thing regarding the murder of one of her neighbors was the inconvenience to her. He felt his mouth turn down in a frown. "What did Mr. Osvolo steal?" he asked instead of saying what he wanted to say to the woman.

"Clothing."

"He broke into someone's house?"

"Not exactly," the woman said.

"Mrs. Steward, I'm sure it will be more than just bad press for your neighborhood if I have to arrest you for impeding a criminal investigation," Dora said.

"You wouldn't dare." The older woman glared at Dora.

"Try me," Dora spat back. "Now, what is this about Osvolo stealing clothes?"

Mrs. Steward huffed. "A resident put a bag of clothes out on her stoop to be picked up by a charity. She went out to run some errands, and when she returned Mr. Osvolo was on her property going through the bags. It was clear he was taking out things he intended to keep for himself. She reported the attempted theft, and of course, the board agreed we had to act swiftly. We can't have anyone untrustworthy working for us."

"Do you have any idea where Mr. Osvolo is now?"

Mrs. Steward shook her head. "None."

Dora and Logan left the office and stepped back into the warm morning sunlight. Dora slipped her sunglasses on. "They never make it easy, do they?"

"I'M DETECTIVE DORA Madison." Dora held her badge out for Waylen's wife, Cindy, to peer at it through the screen door. The address on Waylen Osvolo's driver's license belonged to a small clapboard house in the family-friendly neighborhood of Woodridge.

"Are you Mrs. Cindy Osvolo?"

"Yes."

"We need to speak to your husband. Is he here?"

"He doesn't live here anymore. He hasn't lived here for almost four months now."

Logan could feel his frustration growing.

"Do you mind if we come in and take a look around?" Dora asked.

Cindy hesitated for a moment before pushing the screen door open and standing aside. The house was lived in, with shoes lined up at the door and mismatched furniture in the living room. Dora could see into the eat-in kitchen with its yellow appliances and scarred linoleum floors.

But Osvolo was not inside.

Logan and Dora made their way back to the living room where Cindy waited. "I told you he wasn't here."

"Do you have any idea where he might be?"

Cindy shook her head. "Waylen hasn't been around

for months. Not since I kicked him out for cheating on me. The best I can tell you is that he always has liked Miller's Bar over on U Street. You might find him there."

Dora made a note of it in her notebook.

"Mrs. Osvolo—"

"I'm changing my name back to *Fairmont* just as soon as the divorce is final."

"Ms. Fairmont," Logan started again, "have you ever heard the names *Christine Belgrade* or *Michelle Quitoni*?"

Cindy's face scrunched in thought. "No, I don't think so."

Logan tossed out the two other victims' names, but Cindy didn't recognize them either. There was nothing else to get from Osvolo's estranged wife, so he thanked Cindy for her time and left.

The door closed behind them before they made it off the front stoop.

"I take it Miller's Bar is our next stop," Logan said as they made their way to the car.

Dora nodded. "Third time. It's got to be the charm, right?"

Logan hoped she was right.

MILLER'S BAR OPENED at five in the afternoon, but a brief chat with the owner and weekday bartender revealed that most of the regulars like Osvolo didn't put in an appearance before eight in the evening. Dora stationed a couple of rookie detectives in plain clothes in the bar right after opening just in case Osvolo made an early appearance. She and Logan arrived just before eight and ordered drinks taking them to a booth in the back corner. The two detectives she had on duty were relieved by two fresh pairs of eyes, and then they waited.

Dora scanned the growing group of patrons with sharp eyes. She started when Logan reached across the table and took her hand in his.

"You need to relax. Osvolo isn't here yet, but if he's our killer, he might make a run for it he spots us."

Dora took a deep breath and let it out, sliding her hand from under Logan's. He was right about relaxing, but there was no way she could do that with her hand in his.

"We need to be ready. We have to assume that he's armed and dangerous."

"True, which is why we can't scare him off. We need to take him down as quickly and quietly as possible."

"Maybe we should have tried to catch him as he came in," she said. "He'd have been easier to spot." Dora second-guessed herself.

They spent the hours between talking to Osvolo's wife and getting to the bar, running through the best scenarios for the takedown. Miller's was a popular place on a street full of popular establishments. Even on a weekday evening the pedestrian traffic was fixed. The team had ultimately agreed it would be safest to corner Osvolo inside the bar rather than outside.

"There's no looking back now," Logan said. "We just need to do what we do best."

"Agreed," Dora said.

"Good. Just make sure you stay close to me," he added. "Everyone goes home in one piece tonight."

Holding his gaze, she understood that he was probably thinking about their last outing to bring in a suspect and their subsequent car crash. She knew he wanted to protect her, and she felt the same way about him, but this was the job. For both of them.

Dora's eyes roamed over the crowd, on the lookout again for Osvolo. Maybe he wasn't coming tonight. He had just lost his job. Maybe he'd decided to tighten his belt, lay off the boozing and bars until he found a new one.

Or maybe not. Dora homed in on the man who had just come through the doors and was sidling up to the bar.

"That's him," she said, already sliding out of the booth.

Logan followed. "Hopefully, Osvolo will come quietly."

Osvolo spotted them then. He jumped up from the bar stool he'd been sitting on, pushing through a group of women who'd approached the bar, and ran.

"Spoke too soon," Logan deadpanned.

Dora took off after Osvolo with Logan hot on her heels. They dodged bar goers as they tried to reach Osvolo before he made it back onto the street. It was slow going as many of the patrons were clueless to what was going on. And it didn't appear that the other two detectives she had in the bar were having any easier time reaching their suspect.

Just when Osvolo made it to the front entrance of the bar, a burly security guard stepped in his path. Osvolo bounced off the man comically. The barman reached out to steady him but held on to him while Osvolo struggled.

Nora reached the bear, taking Osvolo from the bouncer and twisting his arms behind his back, cutting him.

"Waylen Osvolo, you are being arrested on suspicion of murder."

OSVOLO'S ATTITUDE HADN'T improved at the police station. He was still defiant, proclaiming that he'd had nothing to do with Michelle's murder and that he was going to sue the department, the FBI, and a host of other people. He was speaking to them, though, so Dora was willing to put up with his puffery.

Logan and Dora sat on one side of the table in the interrogation room. Osvolo was seated on the opposite side of the table with a dour expression on his face. He looked as if he had a rough go of it, which, Logan realized, was true. Osvolo sported a scruffy beard and bloodshot eyes. He looked as if he hadn't slept in days.

Logan had noted a small cut on the back of Osvolo's right hand when he cuffed him to the table and pointed it out to Dora. Could it have possibly happened when he killed Christine? Maybe they get lucky and there would be DNA this time.

Osvolo had declined to have a lawyer present, so Dora got right to the questioning. "Mr. Osvolo, you are being held on suspicion of having a hand in the murder of Michelle Quitoni."

Osvolo's nostrils flared. "I had nothing to do with any murders. I didn't kill anybody."

"Where were you from Monday at noon until Tuesday at eight in the morning?" Dora's tone gave nothing away, but she narrowed her eyes at Osvolo, studying him.

He provided an answer that amounted to "Alone at home," so he had no real alibi.

"Where is home these days, Mr. Osvolo?" Logan said. "We understand from your wife that you no longer reside with her."

"I've been bunking on a buddy's sofa ever since that witch put me out of my own house."

Dora and Logan had been switching off on the questioning in an attempt to keep Osvolo off-kilter.

Logan tsked. "Things haven't been going so well for you lately, Waylen. We understand you've lost your job," Logan said.

"What about it?" Osvolo shot back

"Well, Geraldine Steward said you were caught stealing. Is that true?"

"It wasn't stealing. How can you steal something from someone giving the thing away?"

"Fair point," Dora said, taking the good cop role for a moment. "Let's call it 'taking,' then. Have you ever taken anything else that belongs to a resident in the neighborhood where you previously worked?"

"I don't know what you mean."

"Say a car, perhaps," Logan jumped in again.

"Now you're accusing me of being a car thief. I guess it's better than a murderer." Osvolo scowled.

"It doesn't have to be one or the other. You could have murdered Michelle Quitoni, then kept her car to make it easier to grab and transport your next victim," Dora responded.

"I told you I didn't murder anyone."

"Then how did this—" Dora slapped a photo of the pill bottle down on the table "—pill bottle, get into Michelle Quitoni's car?"

Osvolo visibly swallowed. "I don't know anything about that. I don't even know what it is." But beads of sweat had broken out on his forehead.

"You don't know, huh?" Logan picked up the questioning. "Let me help you, then. It's a prescription bottle of Oxy with your name on it, and I bet you can guess where we found it."

"Why should I… How could I know?"

"We found it in Michelle Quitoni's car. Where we also found the body of Christine Belgrade."

"I don't know anyone named Christine Belgrade," Osvolo yelled. "And I didn't kill anyone. Stop saying that I did."

"How did the pill bottle get into Michelle's car?" Logan pressed.

Osvolo was close to cracking. "I don't know… I don't know."

Dora slammed her palm against the metal table. "Don't give us that. We got a pill bottle with your name on it in a dead woman's car with another dead woman in the trunk. You are in this up to your eyeballs. If you aren't a serial killer, I'd bet dollars to doughnuts you know who is."

"Look, I don't know anything about murder. I admit I sold the Oxy to Michelle. She came asking if I knew anyone who could sell her something more recreational than weed. I've been prescribed Oxy for a back injury— I got in a car accident last year. I didn't like how the pills made me feel, but a buddy of mine bought them off me for a decent chunk of change. I found a doctor that didn't ask too many questions, and I kept buying them for my buddy, so when Michelle asked, I offered. That's all I know."

"So, you lied about how close you and Michelle were earlier. You aren't just the property manager. You were her dealer," Dora said.

"I'm not a drug dealer or a killer."

Logan cocked his head to the side, studying their prime suspect. There was a lot to suggest they had their guy, but something wasn't sitting right with him. "What about a voyeur? Are you still a Peeping Tom, Waylen?"

They found the juvenile record right before coming into the interrogation room. It wouldn't be admissible in court, but that didn't mean they couldn't use it to break Osvolo. Whatever it took, if he was their serial killer. Osvolo stilled, his face going blank. It was as if he'd gone somewhere else.

"Mr. Osvolo, could you answer the question?" Logan pressed.

Osvolo snapped back to attention. "No, no, I don't think I will. In fact, I want my lawyer. Now."

They had no choice but to end the interview.

Lieutenant Crenshaw met them in the hallway. "We can hold him on charges stemming from selling the Oxy, but we don't have enough to arrest him for the murders."

"We'll get enough," Dora declared. "This is our guy. I can feel it."

"I'm not so sure," Logan replied hesitantly. He didn't want to undermine Dora in front of her superior, but there were quite a few holes in the tale of Osvolo as a serial killer.

"What do you mean?" Dora argued.

"It's just I don't think we should get out ahead of our skis here. The lieutenant is right about the evidence being insufficient for charges, and Osvolo doesn't fit the profile of our serial killer."

"What are you talking about? White male between

the ages of twenty-nine and forty-five. He's even got a peeping charge, and who knows what else we'll find?"

"Superficially, yes, he could be our guy, but we have no connection between him and the other victims. And usually, serial killers have some kind of trauma that leads them down the road of killing. We found nothing like that in Osvolo's past."

"We will," Dora gritted out.

"Fine." Crenshaw put her hands up, signaling to cease the bickering. "Well, find the evidence, then. If Osvolo is our guy, I want to nail him to the wall."

Chapter Twenty-One

The killer had been right about following the detective paying off. Detective Madison had led him right to her witness, thanks to some help from the press. It was about time they did something besides turn up the heat on him.

He'd been by the house where Detective Madison's witness was staying several times in the last twenty-four hours. He had to be careful. Despite what some law enforcement thought about serial killers, generally he had no desire to get caught. But now it was time to put his plan into motion.

The killer made his way around the side of the small home he had followed Detective Madison to the day before. The interior was dark. He watched a middle-aged woman and a second young woman in her late teens leave minutes earlier. He couldn't imagine what a middle-aged woman would have been doing in the park in the middle of the night, which meant the witness was probably the younger woman. Not that it mattered. He'd take care of both of them. No loose ends.

He made his way to the back door of the house. It

was easy to force the door open with a heavy rock he
took from the garden. Inside, he found a small func-
tional space. He didn't need to turn on any lights, and
he was careful not to touch anything. As long as the
occupants of the home came in through the front door,
they wouldn't realize anyone was here until it was too
late. He planned to take care of the middle-aged woman
first, but as soon as he saw the younger one, he'd known
that it was no coincidence that she was the one who'd
spotted him the night he left Michelle. It had been fate.

She looked just like his Sarah.

He passed the kitchen and the living room and
climbed the stairs to the second floor of the home. There
were three bedrooms, although one was more the size
of a closet. Someone had turned that room into an office. The largest bedroom was easily identifiable as the
older woman's. The bed was made and covered with a
crocheted blanket. The dresses in the closet were sensible and hung above equally sensible shoes.

The last bedroom was a woman's as well but clearly
a younger woman's space. A pair of jeans lay thrown
across the bottom of an unmade bed, and the dresser
drawer hung partially open. There was a small armoire,
but it was empty inside. A notebook sat on an otherwise
empty desk.

He fingered through it quickly, becoming bored with
the overwrought complaints that the younger woman
seemed to have with the old one. There'd be no need
for his Sarah to worry after tonight. Not after he got her
home. Then she would have everything she needed, and
she'd be happy.

So would he.

The killer smiled.

It wouldn't be long now.

DORA WORKED WELL into the evening, digging through Osvolo's recent and distant past, looking for some connection to any of the victims other than Michelle and a trigger for his homicidal tendencies. She found nothing. Osvolo might have been a threat, but there was nothing in his past that she could find to prove he was a murderer. She was frustrated. Even more so because she was beginning to wonder if Logan was right and Osvolo wasn't their guy, after all.

At nine that night, Logan shut down his laptop and stood. "We should go home."

"You go. There is still some stuff I want to get done here."

"Dora, I had to give my professional opinion. It's what your department is paying me the big bucks for."

"Of course you did."

Logan sighed heavily. "You're going to burn out if you don't get some rest."

"I'll rest when we know our serial killer is behind bars."

"Let me take you home."

"The requisitions department issued me a shiny new police sedan." A clerk had dropped off the keys when Logan had stepped out to get dinner, an invitation that Dora had declined. "I can get myself home now. But thanks for all the rides."

Logan sighed again. "Then let me come home with you."

Dora glanced around the bullpen. Most of the detectives had gone home hours ago, but the skeleton night crew was there. No one seemed to be paying her or Logan any attention, though.

"I don't think that's a good idea," she said, keeping her voice low. Then, before he could speak again: "I need time and space to think. I can't do that with you around. Anyway, you probably want to stop by Landon's place on your way home anyway."

Logan cocked his head to the side, confused.

"Look in your bag. I think you have something for him," Dora said, before turning back to her computer monitor.

Logan reached into his bag and found a single manila folder that hadn't been there before. He fingered through the first pages, recognizing them as the twenty-year-old report on his father's murder investigation.

"Thank you," he said softly.

Dora waved him off.

Logan studied her for a long moment before speaking. "Good night, Dora."

She met his gaze and gave him a small smile. "Good night, Logan."

DORA WALKED THROUGH the police garage, headed for her newly minted police-issued sedan, when her cell rang. "This is Madison."

"Detective Madison, you have to help me." The breathy words came over the line in a whisper.

"Randi? What's going on? What's wrong?"

"There is someone here. Someone in Violet's house. I think Violet is hurt badly."

Dora ran the rest of the way to the car and jumped in. "Where are you right now?"

"I'm hiding in a closet, but I can hear the guy. He's still here."

Dora tore out of the garage. "Can you get out of the house?"

"I can't." Dora could hear the tears in Randi's voice. "I'm scared."

"Randi, I'm on my way. I'm minutes away. Just be quiet. I'm going to switch over to the other line now and make a call. Don't hang up. I'll be right back, okay?"

"Okay."

Dora put Randi's call on hold and used the police radio to call for backup to Violet's house. Then she punched in Logan's number. Logan's phone rang but rolled over to voicemail.

She made the turn off the main road and into Violet's neighborhood. "Logan, it's Dora. Randi is in trouble. Someone broke into Violet's house. I'm almost there. I've called for backup, but…call me."

She flipped back to Randi's call as she turned onto Violet's street.

"Randi?" Dora said but received no answer. Her heart hammered. She didn't want to yell just in case her voice carried over the phone in case the perpetrator was still there, and the sound clued him into Randi's hiding place.

She tried again. "Randi?"

Still no answer.

Dora threw the car into Park in front of the house next door to Violet's. There was no time to wait for backup.

The street appeared quiet. Violet's house was dark. She peered through the sidelights next to the front door.

The inside of the house was still. The door was locked. She made her way around the back, her gaze catching on the busted lock on the back door. Her pulse raced, adrenaline soaring through her body.

She stepped into the small vestibule between the kitchen and the laundry room and listened. The refrigerator hummed. A pipe clanked somewhere in the walls. She could hear a rhythmic ticking that she recognized as being the pendulum on a grandfather clock coming from the front of the house.

She moved as quickly and quietly as she could along the main floor. The house wasn't large. The kitchen, living room, dining room, and a small den comprised the main floor.

Dora climbed the stairs to the second floor. Randi had said she was hiding in the closet, which could've been any closet, but at this time of night the bedroom closet seemed as likely as any.

The quiet stillness of the house was disconcerting. The first, largest bedroom looked disheveled, as if a struggle had occurred, but there was no one in the room. Dora stepped back into the hallway, her senses picking up the whisper of a sound a split second too late.

She turned, but not fast enough. A burst of pain blinded her.

Then there was darkness.

Logan sat at Landon's kitchen table, nursing a beer. Landon sat across from him, flipping through the Metropolitan Police file on their father's case. His brother had given him a summary of all the research he'd done over the last several days and his visit with Carisse

Lynn's sandwich shop. Logan still wasn't sure whether his brother was on to something or on a wild-goose chase, but he knew that Landon needed to assure himself that everything that could be done to catch their father's killer had been done. But it seemed farfetched to believe that their father's death might have had something to do with Addison Kober's disappearance. It was far more likely, in Logan's opinion, that Landon was grasping at straws.

"You have to thank Dora for me."

"You may want to thank her yourself." Logan took another pull from his beer bottle.

Landon looked up from the file. "Things are going that well?"

Logan sighed. "I'm not sure how things are going."

"It looked like you two were getting along at family dinner the other night at Lisa's."

Logan ran his finger through the condensation on the beer bottle. "I told her how I feel about her."

Landon's left eyebrow arched. "And how do you feel about her?"

"I love her. I've loved her for a long time." It felt good to say that. "I was an idiot to leave her."

"Well, it seems like you're making a good start at fixing things."

"I thought so." Logan frowned.

"Dora wasn't receptive?"

"Well, I invited her to come home with me tonight, and she said she needed time to think."

"Ouch."

"Imagine how I feel."

"Well, she didn't say get lost, so there's still a chance."

"Just what every man wants to hear after he bares his soul to the woman he loves—*there's still a chance*." He finished his beer.

Landon stood. "Let me get you another beer."

Logan's phone vibrated. He took it from his pocket and saw that he had a message from Dora. The phone hadn't rung, but their mother's house had always been iffy when it came to cellular service.

Logan accessed his voicemail and listened to the message. He was out of his chair and headed to the front door before the message was over.

"Logan, where are you going?" Landon said, racing behind him to the door.

"It's Dora," Logan called back over his shoulder without stopping. "She's headed into trouble."

DORA WAS MISSING, likely in the hands of the serial killer, and Logan had no idea where to begin looking for her. A neighbor had given them a description of a vehicle that had been seen speeding away from the house: a white SUV with a black racing stripe. It matched the description of the vehicle registered to Violet Fullerton. They already had an APB out on it. Violet had been in critical condition when Logan arrived. She was barely breathing but hanging on. An ambulance had raced her to the hospital. Now the evidence-collection team was in the house and Logan had been relegated to the front yard to question witnesses and wait.

Keene joined Logan in the driveway.

"I got our tech department looking at traffic cams to see if we can get a sense of which direction the perp is going," Keene continued.

Logan took out his cell phone and texted Kaj's information to Keene. "Tell them to reach out to Kaj Ryland. He's a computer expert at the FBI. If there's something to be found on those traffic cams, he'll find it."

"Will do."

Logan's phone rang. Crenshaw's number scrolled across the screen. He answered with "Tell me you have something."

"Traffic cams caught a white SUV heading across the Washington, DC–Maryland border about forty-five minutes ago. We've got state units on the lookout for it."

Logan brought up a map on his phone, looking for any ideas as to where their perp might be headed. But without knowing who they were looking for it was impossible to say.

"Elkins. Keene." Roberts jogged toward them. "We've got him. We got a face on a neighbor's doorbell camera."

"Crenshaw, I have to call you back," Logan said.

"Keep me posted, and send me that video, Roberts," Crenshaw said before ending the call.

Roberts pressed Play on the video already cued up on his phone. After a few seconds of nothing but the street in front of a nearby house, a man walked into the frame from the left. His head was down so his face couldn't be seen.

"Roberts, this doesn't show us anything we can use."

"Wait for it." Roberts fast-forwarded. "Watch when the car backs out of the driveway and turns. Here." Roberts paused the video and enlarged the screen, turning it to face outward so they could all see it.

Logan's stomach dropped.

"It's a money shot," Keene said.

"I can get it out on the wires right away," Roberts said. "Someone will definitely recognize this guy."

"You don't have to put it out," Logan said. "I know who it is."

Chapter Twenty-Two

Pain thundered through Dora's head, so loud it was all she could hear. It pounded against her brain like a hammer. Her thoughts came slowly, as if she was swimming against a powerful tide of pain and fear. *Where am I?* In a car, she realized as the ground rolled underneath her.

Panic raced through her. She opened her eyes to darkness. A blindfold covered her face. That realization brought another stab of fear.

Don't panic. And don't let on that you are awake.

She wasn't sure why, but she instinctively knew that letting her captor know she was conscious would not be good if she had any chance of getting out of this alive. She didn't want to draw any attention. She didn't have her gun, so surprise was her best asset at the moment. Her hands were tied behind her back, but the car's carpeting against her face was rough enough that it did not take much to shift the blindfold covering her eyes so that she could see. She and Randi lay in the trunk of what appeared to be an SUV. Randi was unconscious, but the slight rise and fall of her chest let Dora know she was still alive. For now. Matted blood covered her left temple, and there was little color in her face. Dora had to get Randi to help soon, or escaping would be the least of their problems.

A cold sweat seeped from her pores as she tried to think of what to do. Where was their captor taking them? The headache pulsing in her head made it hard to think, much less come up with a coherent plan.

The car rolled on for how long, Dora wasn't sure. The drive had gone from smooth to bumpy at some point, telling her that they'd turned off the paved streets and onto what was probably an unpaved road somewhere. Somewhere no one would ever find them, the thought ran through her head.

No. She couldn't think that way. She had to come up with a plan. She glanced at Randi again. She was still out cold; her breathing had become raspy. If Dora didn't come up with a plan, she and Randi would just be two more missing women among thousands, dumped in some remote outpost somewhere where no one would ever find them. She'd never get the chance to tell Logan how she really felt. That she forgave him. That she wanted to have a life with him. That she loved him and had loved him almost since the moment they'd met. She would have that chance. She just had to not panic and think.

She took as deep a breath as she could without making any sound.

Her head bounced against the floor as the car drove over a deep pothole before jerking to a stop.

Her pulse raced. She held her breath as the SUV's front door opened, then slammed shut. She wheeled herself to say still, to keep her breathing even, but nothing could stop the frantic pounding of her heart.

The trunk opened, and she was grabbed by the ankles and dragged out of the car, her body dumped against the gravel strewn ground.

A dark silhouette loomed over her. A low voice sounded near her ear. "I know you're conscious, Detective."

Dora went rigid. She recognized that voice.

She squinted up at her captor and found herself staring at Dr. Najimy.

LOGAN FELT LIKE he was going to jump out of his skin. Najimy had Dora and Randi, and they had no idea where he had taken them. There'd been no sightings of them by any of the cops on the streets or any other traffic cams that they had access to.

"Where could he be going?" Logan mumbled to himself for the thousandth time. He was at Violet Fullerton's house, waiting to see if the evidence unit found anything inside that might lead them in the right direction. With an MPD detective kidnapped, the combined forces of the District, Maryland, and the FBI had been deployed. There was an FBI chopper in the air, but so far, they had found nothing.

"How can three people just disappear?"

He couldn't just stand around any longer. He started toward his car.

"Hey, where are you going?" Keene fell into step beside him. The younger detective had been keeping a sharp eye on Logan ever since they'd learned Dora was missing. No doubt at Crenshaw's direction. The lieutenant was sharp. He'd give her that. She likely hadn't missed the change in his and Dora's relationship. He was sure she didn't want him going off and doing something stupid. Well, he had to do something. The waiting was going to drive him insane.

"I have to get out there and look for her."

"I'll come with you."

Logan stopped short, examining the young man for several seconds.

"Hey, I want to find her too," Keene said.

"Fine. Let's go."

They jumped into the car. Logan peeled away from the curb.

"Where are we headed, Logan?" Keene asked.

"Dr. Najimy's office."

It hadn't taken long for Crenshaw to get a judge to sign warrants for Najimy's office and home once Roberts found the video. There were already evidence-collection units headed to both locations. Najimy was too smart to keep anything incriminating at his house, where his wife might find it and get suspicious. And he certainly wouldn't have taken any of his victims there. But maybe there was something that could help them at his office where he might have felt it was less likely that anyone would notice. Something that would help them locate Dora.

"We will find her," Keene said with enough conviction that Logan was sure he was attempting to convince himself as well as Logan.

The crime scene investigators were already hard at work when Logan and Keene arrived. The building manager who'd been awakened in order to let them in was fretting in Najimy's waiting room.

Logan hadn't felt this much fear…well, ever. Nearly paralyzing fear. The only thing that kept him moving forward was the knowledge that Dora needed him. Needed him to be strong.

He followed Keene back to Najimy's office. The evidence techs were working, but they hadn't been working the case like he had. They didn't have the insight into Najimy's mind that Logan did.

"I'll take the desk," Logan said, already rounding it. "You search the filing cabinets. We need to get into this computer as well." Logan tapped the silver laptop on the desktop.

"On it," Keene said, pulling his phone out. "Maybe your friend Kaj can come down. That would be faster than transporting the unit to the station."

Logan agreed. He shuffled through the papers on top of the desk, finding only bills for the practice and message slips from Najimy's receptionist. The rest of the desk drawers similarly yielded nothing of interest.

Logan bit back a scream of frustration just as Keene called out from the other side of the room.

"Logan, I think I got something."

"What is it?" Logan crossed over to Keene quickly.

Keene held out a manila folder. Inside were dozens of photographs of their first victim, Monica Gonzalez. From the look of it, she hadn't known she was being photographed.

"That is creepy," Keene pronounced.

Logan couldn't argue that point. He reached for another folder in the same file cabinet. This one had photos of another woman, but Logan didn't recognize her. He and Keene flipped through the folders in the drawer quickly. Folder after folder of photos of women who clearly hadn't known they were being photographed.

"He stalked them," Keene said.

That was exactly what Najimy had been doing. The thought was terrifying. But none of this helped them find Dora.

Keene's phone rang. He answered it on speaker so Logan could here. "Keene, Elkins, the uniforms said you'd taken off from Violet Fullerton's place. Where are you?" Crenshaw barked.

"I couldn't just sit a Fullerton's doing nothing anymore, so Keene and I headed for Najimy's offices. I figured it was more likely we'd find something here that would tell us where he's taken Dora and Randi." Logan said.

"You're probably right. I'm at the Najimy house now. Mrs. Najimy isn't being very cooperative."

"Then haul her in, in cuffs, and let her sit in the cell. I'm sure that will change her mind," Logan said.

"Have you ever heard the phrase *you catch more flies with honey*?"

Logan was sure that there was nothing sweet about Crenshaw, which might have been why she was having so much trouble getting Mrs. Najimy to talk. No one ever wanted to believe they'd been living with a killer.

"She did tell us that her husband did volunteer work with several drug-rehabilitation programs in the area. I was thinking that could be how he first encountered his victims, since we know Michelle and Monica had problems with drugs and addiction. We'll have to look into that more, but it could be the connection we are looking for."

"Could be," Logan agreed. "But finding Dora is the priority right now. Ask Mrs. Najimy if there is any reason her husband would be headed into Howard County. Any family or friends live out there?"

"Okay, hold on."

The line went silent while Lieutenant Crenshaw was away from the phone. After what seemed like forever, she came back on the line. "No family, but she said her husband used to go out to a cabin in Poolesville when he was working on writing his book a few years back."

A zing of excitement tore through Logan. "What's the address?" He said, moving toward the door already. Keene was hot on his heels.

His phone dinged in answer. "I just sent it to you and Keene."

Keene pulled the text up on the car's navigation system and engaged the map function. "It's about forty-five minutes away."

Logan shot past the elevator bank and to the stairs, not wanting to waste a moment waiting when Dora was in trouble. "Crenshaw, have the locals get out to that address now. Keene and I are on our way."

DORA'S MOUTH WENT DRY. Najimy was the serial killer.

"Don't move," he said. He reached into the SUV's trunk and lowered Randi onto the ground next to Dora. They were in the gravel driveway of a rundown hunting cabin surrounded by woods.

Randi groaned and opened her eyes. Her gaze was unfocused and glassy.

"Don't move," Najimy repeated before rounding the car back toward the front. Dora hadn't seen a weapon, but that didn't mean Najimy didn't have one, and her gun was missing. With her hand still behind her back, Dora worked at loosening the ropes that bound her enough to slip her hands free.

"Randi," she whispered.

Randi turned to face Dora, tears streaming down her face. Dora spared a glance at Randi's bound hands. The rope looked bound tightly. But Randi could run.

Dora lowered her voice even more. "Randi, when I give you the signal, run." She tipped her head toward the trees. "Don't look back and don't stop running."

Randi whimpered again but gave a slight nod.

"Hey, shut up!" Najimy called from the front of the SUV.

"The FBI and the entire MPD are looking for you," Dora said loud enough for Najimy to hear. "They know where I was headed. They probably have the license plate of this SUV by now, and traffic cameras are marking the route that you took. Your only chance is to let us go."

"Let you go and still go to jail," Najimy called back. "I don't think so."

"If you kill us, you could get the death penalty." Dora could feel the ropes around her wrists loosening now.

"But you will have paid."

"Paid for what? Why are you doing this?"

Just a little more. She just needed Najimy to stay at the front of the SUV. What was he doing up there anyway? She wasn't sure she wanted the answer to that question.

"Because she was innocent, and I couldn't save her." Najimy stepped back around to the back of the SUV.

"Who? Who couldn't you save?"

"My sister. Our father hit her. And me. But she was so

small. He killed her. I should've stopped him. I should have—"

"You were young, a victim too. I'm sure you did what you could," Dora said, trying to empathize with Najimy.

For a moment, she'd thought it had worked. But then the soft expression on Najimy's face hardened.

"Enough talk! On your feet, both of you."

"I think Randi is really hurt," Dora said, trying to buy herself more time.

Najimy pulled Dora's gun from his back waistband. "I said on your feet."

Randi whimpered beside Dora. They both struggled to their feet, Dora grabbing a handful of gravel as she did. She flexed her wrist one more time as hard as she could and felt the ropes give just enough that she could pull one hand and then the other out. She held on to the rope so that it would not fall, and Najimy wouldn't realize she was free.

"Move!" Najimy shoved Dora forward toward the cabin. She kept her back angled toward the SUV. She only had a moment before Najimy would realize she was untied.

She threw the gravel at Najimy's face. He screamed. A gunshot blasted through the air. A stinging pain seared Dora's left arm.

"Run," she yelled, already moving in the direction of the trees.

LOGAN HAD CUT the forty-five-minute drive down to a little more than thirty minutes, but he had to slow down once the paved roads gave way to dirt and gravel.

"Here. Turn here," Keene pointed to a narrow drive no wider than a single car's width.

Logan hung a sharp right.

They drove along the rutted road until they turned a corner, and the white SUV came into view.

"This is it," Logan said, throwing the car into Park. "Call it in."

Keene grabbed the radio and began barking out their location and a request for backup. Where the hell were the local cops anyway? There was no time to wait for them.

Logan and Keene got out of the car and went to the trunk.

"I always carry a spare Kevlar for just such an occasion," he said, handing Keene a vest. Logan pulled a second vest over his own head and then grabbed a shotgun out of the sedan's trunk.

"Do you have a spare one of those?" Keene asked, looking pointedly at the shotgun in Logan's hand.

Logan flashed a small smile. "Sorry. This is my baby. My one and only."

"I guess my Glock will have to do." Keene checked that the safety was off, while Logan closed the trunk.

He surveyed the area. Trees to the west, south, and east, with a ramshackle cabin to their north. It looked vacant, but he wasn't taking any chances with Dora's life.

"I'll go right. You go left," he said to Keene. "Keep your eyes open. Najimy has nothing left to lose."

"Got it. You do the same," Keene answered before heading to the left of the cabin.

Logan rounded the right side of the cabin, listening for sounds inside. There was nothing. The exterior windows were coated with too much grime to see inside. He made his way carefully onto the stoop. The front door was unlocked. He pushed it open slowly and had one foot over the threshold when a gunshot ripped through the adjacent woods.

He took off running. *Hang on, Dora. I'm coming. Just hang on.*

BRANCHES TORE AT her slacks, but she heeded her own words and didn't stop running. She pushed through the overgrown foliage and darkness.

"Detective!" Najimy's scream cut through the dense woods.

She slid behind the tree and tried to quiet her breathing. She had no idea how far she'd run or where Randi was. Najimy must have taken her cell phone—not that she'd have gotten service out here anyway. She knew Najimy was out there. Waiting. She couldn't stay there hiding. He wouldn't hesitate to kill her if he found her.

As she made her way around the tree, she saw nothing but darkness. She moved slowly, hoping the sounds of nature covered whatever noise she might be making.

"Come out, come out, wherever you are."

Najimy's voice echoed off the trees.

She had to move faster. She had to stay alive until Logan came for her. And she knew he would come.

Another gunshot sounded. A hot flash of pain seared through her as she moved, reminding her that she had been shot. How much blood was she losing? Her arm felt as if it was on fire.

"I'm getting tired of this game, Detective. Come out now, and I'll make the end quick."

Dora started moving again, making herself as small as possible.

"There you are." Najimy stepped out in front of Dora, her service weapon in his hand. He had it aimed at her.

Najimy's smile was menacing. "I'm a man of my word." He stretched the gun out farther in front of him. "Goodbye, Detective."

Dora closed her eyes.

A gunshot blasted through the air.

"Dora!"

Dora opened her eyes.

Logan ran toward her just as her legs gave out. He caught her before she hit the ground.

"Randi. She's out there somewhere..."

"We got her. Don't worry—we got her, and she's safe."

"Good. Good. Logan, I love you." His face was the last thing she saw before darkness claimed her.

Chapter Twenty-Three

Was this what death was like? Dora's thoughts raced. After a moment, she realized she was in a soft, comfortable bed. So not dead. That was good. A moment later, she homed in on the sound of snoring. She cracked her eyes open, her gaze landing on a sleepy Logan slumped in a chair next to her bed.

The events from the last several days flooded back into her mind. Chasing the serial killer with Logan. Getting kidnapped with Randi. Getting shot.

The pain of that was still vivid, but whatever the doctors had her on had dulled it enough that she felt a little as if she was floating. It was a strange feeling but better, she supposed, than the alternative. When she opened her eyes again, Logan's were open too and locked on her face.

"Dora!" He leaned forward in the chair and took her hand gently, squeezing it. "Thank God."

He looked awful. His eyes were red rimmed, and his jaw covered in a five o'clock shadow.

She tried to speak but quickly realized her lips were chapped and her throat was raw.

Logan grabbed the empty pitcher from the bedside table and left her long enough to fill it from the attached bathroom. He was back a minute later, filling the glass from the table and lifting it to her lips.

"I should let the doctor know that you are awake," he said.

"Wait." The word cracked out of her. "How long have I been here?"

"A little more than twenty-four hours."

"You look awful."

He laughed and some of the tension eased from his body. "You're one to talk. The bullet went straight through, but you lost a lot of blood." His mouth fell, and he released a ragged sigh. "We thought we'd lost you, Dora. I thought I'd lost you, and it nearly killed me."

"You can't get rid of me that easily," she joked.

But he was not in a joking mood. "I don't want to lose you. Not ever." He cleared his throat, suddenly nervous. "Do you remember what you said to me right before you lost consciousness?"

She remembered, but before she had a chance to answer, the door to the room opened and an older man with olive skin and a white lab coat walked into the room.

"Welcome back to the land of the conscious, Detective Madison. I'm Dr. Hawkins. You gave your friends and coworkers quite a scare there, but it looks like you're going to be just fine."

"Great. When can I get out of here?" she asked.

The doctor chuckled. "Well, not so fast. I want to keep you here for a couple of days, and then we can talk about getting you out of here."

Dora groaned.

Dr. Hawkins simply smiled and went about the business of getting her vitals. He left when he was finished, promising to return later.

Logan came back to her side once the door to the room closed. "I asked you a question before the doctor came in, and you have an answer."

"You did?" she teased. "It must be the drugs. What was the question again?"

Logan smiled and played along. "Do you remember what you said to me before you passed out?"

"After I'd been shot?"

"Yes."

"I'm not sure you can hold a girl to anything she says in the moments after she's taken a bullet."

Logan's face fell. "Does that mean you didn't mean it?"

She could tell he was holding his breath. Dora sobered, gazing at him. "I remember. And I meant it. I still mean it. I love you. I loved you from the moment I met you."

Logan let out a shuddering breath, almost as if he'd been holding it for years. "I was a fool to walk out on you...on us. I didn't know what I wanted or how to want anything, but now I know. I want you. A future with you. A family with you. If that's what you want?"

She looked at him, at the love shining from his eyes and knew. "That's what I want. More than anything, that's what I want."

Logan leaned forward, sealing their declaration with a kiss.

Chapter Twenty-Four

Lisa and Landon stood at the barbecue grill in Dora's backyard arguing over how well to cook the burgers. Layla and Randi lounged on the deck, both with cell phones in hand, debating the next musical selection, having deemed Dora's selections as "too old." Dora didn't mind. In fact, she was happy to see them getting along and hoped that the two girls might even forge a friendship. Noreen had called to say that she'd be late but to save a six pack for her. Dora had it chilling in the refrigerator.

Dora watched from the kitchen, tossing a salad to go along with the food from the grill.

Her family. That was what the people congregating in her yard were. Her family. As much as her mother and Noreen were. And there was nothing she wouldn't do for them. A fierce urge to protect surged in her gut, and she had to tamp it down, reminding herself that there was nothing to protect them from at the moment. At the moment, all was well, and they were safe.

She was still surprised, happily, at how quickly the Elkinses had come to feel like family. She held out her hand, admiring the ring Logan had slipped on it just last week. A square-shaped sapphire rock rimmed by tiny diamonds. There was nothing traditional about it, but that was one of the things she loved most. They'd been through so much, and now this felt like a true new beginning for them. She knew neither of them planned on taking that for granted.

When they'd searched the cabin that Najimy had taken Randi and Dora to, they'd discovered enough evidence to put Najimy away for life. His basement had looked like a house of horrors, and they'd found dozens of desert roses in the greenhouse built into the back of the cabin. The evidence had guaranteed Najimy would face a life sentence, and the prosecutor was confident he'd get a quick guilty verdict when the case went to trial. Najimy's wife had been cleared of any wrongdoing by the justice system, but the court of public approval was a different story. She had to leave DC to get away from the press.

Bruce Najimy had lawyered up and wasn't talking, but a search of his home had answered many of the outstanding questions. He and his sister had suffered abuse at the hands of their father for many years as children. When Bruce had turned eighteen, his father had thrown him out of the house. A month later, seventeen-year-old Sarah's body had been found in a field, badly beaten, a desert rose in her hair. Based on what Najimy had said while he'd held Dora and Randi captive, it seemed as if he had been trying to replace his sister, and when the women he'd kidnapped failed to meet his standards, he had killed them. A sad waste of several young women's lives.

Fortunately for him, John Leonard had recovered

from the injuries he sustained in the car accident. Unfortunately, he had been promptly arrested by the FBI for money laundering, among several other charges. It hadn't taken long before he decided to flip on his co-conspirators.

Senator Quitoni and his wife had publicly thanked the police department and Dora by name. The arrest had earned her a commendation. The Chief Bayne had taken a two-week victory lap after Dora arrested Najimy, and rumors that he was considering a run for Congress had begun making the rounds. Dora was just glad to have them off her back. And she'd be even happier when she could get back to work. Her wound had healed nicely, and her primary doctor had finally given her the okay to return to the job two days earlier as long as she eased back into field work. As much as she wanted to get back to work, she had to admit she was going to miss her time being on her own.

The experience of being kidnapped had brought them together in a way that neither had been able to explain. Randi still didn't want to go home or reach out to her parents, but she'd agreed to continue living with Violet. Randi had really taken to being a caretaker, doting on Violet and making sure she got to her doctor's appointments and her physical therapy sessions. As thrilled as she was that Randi had found some purpose, Dora wanted to make sure that the teenager had time to just be a teen. She'd begun meeting Randi for lunch at least once a week, and they'd explored the city visiting the museums, taking a cruise on the Potomac, and even hopping on one of those city tour buses and taking the dime-store tour of Washington, DC. And a week ago,

Randi had confessed that she was considering signing up for pre-nursing courses at the University of the District of Columbia. Dora couldn't have been prouder and had offered to help her pay for it if she decided to go back to school.

But she'd spent most of her time off with Logan. He'd practically moved into her house. She knew conventional wisdom would have said to take things slowly, but whatever misgivings she'd had about trusting him had faded away over the weeks. Getting shot had put a lot of things in perspective, nothing more so than the fact that time on this earth was precious and shouldn't be wasted. She loved Logan, and she was willing to risk her heart if it meant that she might have a future with him.

Dora smiled as strong arms wrapped around her, pulling her from her thoughts.

"What are you thinking about?" Logan asked.

She didn't want to ruin the day by saying what she'd really been thinking about, so she fibbed. "You."

"Good, because you're always on my mind. And I can't wait to make you, my wife."

They sealed the thought with a kiss.

* * * * *

THE UNKNOWN COLTON

LISA CHILDS

To the amazing and talented authors who I had the pleasure of working with on this Colton continuity: Justine Davis, Tara Taylor Quinn, Karen Whiddon, Beth Cornelison and Jennifer D. Bokal, as well as editor Caroline Timmings!

Prologue

Fifteen years ago…

Once the bell rang for recess, ten-year-old Lakin Colton rushed through the open doors of the school and headed toward the swing set on the playground. Before she made it there, a small group of kids, three boys and two girls, formed a circle around her, trapping her. Then the taunts began.

"Nobody wants you!"

"Your parents dumped you at the grocery store like bad fish they didn't wanna keep."

"Like cans they were dropping off."

"You smell like fish."

"You're ugly."

Lakin closed her eyes, trying to hold back the tears that rushed up. It wasn't just what they were saying that made her want to cry. Raised voices terrified her, making her shake and sob, and sometimes she even threw up. They'd done this to her before. Maybe because they'd seen how she reacted, they were trying it again.

If Parker was here, these kids wouldn't be picking on her.

Parker was her older brother by two years and an adoption, but he'd just moved from elementary school to middle school. They had two older brothers, too, but Eli was in college and Mitchell would graduate from high school this year.

She had Colton cousins, too. Spence was in middle school with Parker, though. Kansas was the only other girl among Lakin's siblings and cousins, but she was tough. Usually she would be at school, but she was home sick today.

So Lakin was alone like the day she'd been left at the grocery store seven years ago. Although she didn't remember much about that time, about her life before, she hated being alone. Since Will and Sasha Colton adopted her, she rarely was.

If Kansas was here, they would meet up at the swings which was where Lakin had been heading. But she couldn't see over the kids skipping in a circle around her like they were playing ring-around-the-rosy.

"Nobody wants you."

"Nobody wants you."

"Shut up!"

She'd opened her mouth to say it, but the words didn't come from her. A boy broke up the circle, separating the kids and shoving them away from her.

"Stop being mean!" he said, his face scrunched up with anger. But he was still the prettiest boy Lakin had ever seen.

Troy Amos. He had dark skin and really light green eyes. And he was bigger than the other kids even though he was just a few months older than she was. Maybe that was why they didn't pick on him even though his skin was darker than theirs, like hers was. He was half Black while she was probably half Inuit. But nobody really knew for sure what or who she was since she'd been so little when she'd been left at the grocery store.

"Stop picking on her," he said.

"What? Is she your girlfriend?" Billy Hoover asked. As usual, Billy's nose was running, and his red hair stood up all over his head.

"You like her!" one of the girls said. She was a pretty girl with blond hair and blue eyes, but that prettiness disappeared when she glared at Lakin.

"Yeah, I like her," Troy said. "She's nice. Everybody likes Lakin." Then he leaned closer to the blond girl, narrowed those pretty green eyes and added, "Nobody likes mean people."

The girl's bottom lip quivered, and tears filled her eyes. "I'm gonna tell on you."

"Go ahead," Troy said. "And I'll tell on you." He fixed his gaze on all the kids. "I'll tell on everybody this time. The next time you mess with Lakin, I'll do more than that. Me and my family and the Colton family will make you regret picking on her. So nobody better mess with Lakin again." There were even more Amoses than Coltons. Troy had four older siblings and two younger ones.

The boys scrambled away in fear while the one girl ran off crying. The other stayed for a second and mumbled, "Sorry, Lakin," before running off, too.

And Lakin was left alone with Troy Amos, her hero with the prettiest eyes. She decided right then, at ten years old, that she was going to marry him someday.

Chapter One

"Are you married yet?" Billy Hoover asked the minute Lakin walked through the door of Roasters, the local café in Shelby, Alaska.

Billy blocked her way to the queue. His red hair wasn't quite as messy, and his nose didn't chronically run anymore, but he was still the bully he'd been in elementary school.

However, Lakin had learned long ago to not let him or anyone else get to her. She'd even learned how to control her reaction to raised voices now. But instead of ignoring him, like she usually did, she pointed out, "I could ask you the same question, Billy."

Rumor had it that his wife had left him. Again.

His face flushed, and he glared at her before stomping out of the café like he'd stomped off the playground all those years ago.

While she moved to the end of the line of customers who also needed their morning fix of coffee, she was conflicted, feeling both a pang of regret for upsetting him and a surge of triumph that she didn't need anyone to rescue her anymore. She'd learned how to defend herself from bullies. Yet Billy's question bothered her—the hollowness she'd had before her adoption was back inside her, making her yearn for more. For marriage.

She loved Troy, and she knew he loved her. Although it had taken him a bit longer to realize it. Once he had, though, they'd become inseparable.

But he hadn't proposed to her yet. She didn't even have a promise ring to assure her that he planned to. They had talked about their future, about buying and running a business together like her father and her uncle.

Dad and Uncle Ryan had started RTA, Rough Terrain Adventures, when they moved from San Diego to Shelby twenty-eight years ago, after the family tragedy. They had retired a few years ago, though they were still a huge part of the business. Parker ran the company now, with Lakin helping out in the office. Their older cousin Spence was one of the most sought-after RTA tour guides.

While Lakin enjoyed working in the family business, she wanted to build something of her own. *No*, she thought to herself, she wanted something with Troy. She wanted to work with him every day and watch their business thrive…and hopefully someday a family of their own, too.

But Troy was insistent that to be successful, they needed to save before they made any large investments. Despite the fact that he made good money working on oil rigs, he didn't think he'd saved up enough yet. He was also helping out his younger siblings with college tuition and helping his widowed mother, too.

Because he was gone so much, sometimes Lakin didn't even feel like she had a boyfriend. She missed him and felt so lonely when he was away for months at a time. But Troy was coming home; she'd just received an email from him that he would be back in a week. That email was the first she had heard from him in much too long. While he spent months out on oil rigs, he usually managed to talk to her at least once a week via the radio on the rig or with a text or email that managed to get through despite poor internet and cellular reception.

Since she'd gone so long without being able to communicate with him, she wasn't sure if he was aware of what his older sister Hetty and Lakin's cousin Spence had recently endured.

Hetty had been shot. The wound hadn't been serious, but she and Spence could have died. The man trying to kill them had been a professional assassin hired to murder the guests that should have been on the tour Hetty and Spence were guiding. While they'd survived the ordeal, they had discovered the body of a woman who hadn't survived hers.

Lakin's heart ached with sympathy for the woman and her family while she also shivered a little with fear that there was still another killer out there. The assassin who'd attacked Hetty and Spence hadn't been responsible for that murder or for the murders of the other two female victims whose bodies had recently been discovered along Muskee Glacier Pass.

So who *was* responsible?

The authorities were working on it, some of them being Lakin's own family members. Her brother Eli and her cousin Kansas were on the case. She knew they would find and stop the killer; she just hoped it was soon. Because ever since those bodies had been found, she had a strange feeling she was being watched. Like a prickling on the skin between her shoulder blades or this chill that kept passing through her, raising goose bumps along her arms. She had the sensation now even though Billy Hoover had left.

Or had he? He could be outside watching her through the big windows that opened onto Main Street.

As the customer in front of her stepped aside to wait for a to-go cup, Lakin passed her bright blue Roaster's travel mug to the barista. She didn't have to tell her what she wanted; Lakin got the same thing every morning before heading into the RTA office: the Roasters house blend with a dollop of cream and a drop of caramel syrup. Hopefully the hot coffee would chase away the chill permeating Lakin.

When Fay, the barista, passed back her travel mug, Lakin smiled and dropped her money on the counter, enough to cover the coffee and a tip. She saw Fay so often that the young woman had become a friend. "Thank you."

"Thank you, Lakin, and hey…" Fay stepped closer to the oak counter and lowered her voice. "All anyone is talking about is those bodies showing up. Be careful out there."

Lakin wasn't the only one spooked about those murders. "You, too," she said. In addition to the three bodies that had been found, another woman was missing now, her picture all over the news. And then there was the Whaler, a local fishing legend who'd died in an accident that hadn't actually been an accident.

Shelby had always felt like such a safe place to live

until recently. But it was still home. And she didn't want to live anywhere else.

What about Troy?

Did he really want the same things she did? She'd once thought he did, that they had a future together. But he was gone so much that she wasn't sure what he wanted anymore. Did he still want her?

That hollow ache of loneliness inside her intensified, and she flinched and closed her eyes. She opened them when she bumped into someone. "I'm sorry—"

"It's my fault," Eric Seller said with a grin.

The man was in his midthirties with a lean, athletic build. He was a frequent customer of RTA and flew up often from wherever he worked in Silicon Valley for day trips and weekend excursions. Clients had to book at least six months ahead to get a tour with RTA. Lakin worked in the office, not as a guide, but she still saw Eric Seller more often than she saw Troy.

"How are you doing, Lakin?"

He was a customer, a good one, so she didn't want to burden him with her fears about Shelby's safety. And, since he was a man, he was probably safe.

So she just smiled and lied, "I'm doing well. And you, Mr. Seller?"

"Eric, call me Eric," he said with a weary sigh. In every interaction they had, he pleaded with her to use his first name.

While she did with other clients, she felt odd doing it with him, like he wanted that familiarity a little too much. Like it meant more to him, like *she* meant more to him, than she should. And she didn't want to give him any encouragement. So instead of complying, she just smiled again.

He chuckled. "I don't know if you're shy or if you just don't like me," he said.

"I assure you it's neither," she said. "And I'm sorry you've felt that way. I guess I have been preoccupied because I've been very busy." Or at least she pretended to be whenever he came into the office. But instead of taking the hint and leaving her alone, he usually waited and messed with the personal items she kept on the reception desk. Like the framed pictures of her and Troy.

He glanced around the café. "Are you here with the boyfriend?"

She shook her head.

"Is he still just a boyfriend?" he asked. "Or has he finally proposed?"

Heat rushed to her face, but she was irritated more than embarrassed. Everyone seemed very interested in her love life today. Or maybe Seller had already been in the café and overheard what Billy said to her. Maybe he was just piling on like the kids used to do on the playground.

The question unsettled her, though. The press had given a name to the person responsible for the gruesome murders of those women: the Fiancée Killer. The bodies had all been staged with a fake engagement ring on a finger.

"Troy and I are both very busy," she said. Then she moved to step around him, but Seller stepped in front of her again. Blocking her from leaving, like Billy Hoover had blocked her from entering the café moments ago.

"Nobody should be too busy for love," Seller said, his head cocked to one side, as if he pitied her.

"And nobody is," Lakin replied with a smile. No matter how busy she and Troy were, she still loved him. She always would. She just wasn't sure how *he* felt now, especially when so much time had passed without hearing from him during his last stint on the oil rig.

Seller arched an eyebrow and smirked as if he didn't believe her. If he wasn't such a regular customer, she would have shut him down like she had Billy Hoover. Instead she just smiled, sidestepped once again and walked away.

Maybe Seller was the one who'd been watching her earlier. Or perhaps he was watching her now as she left. Either way, she had that creepy sensation again, that chill racing down her spine.

Someone was watching her.

With a serial killer running around the Shelby area, murdering young women, the idea of being watched scared the hell out of Lakin. The Fiancée Killer had to be stalking his victims before he chose them, figuring out when they would be the most vulnerable. Once he chose them, he abducted them.

That was probably what happened to poor Dawn Ellis who'd been reported missing just a couple of days ago. Lakin hoped against hope that that wasn't the case this time, that Dawn would be found alive.

But until this murderer was caught, like Fay, the barista, had advised Lakin needed to be extremely vigilant…so that she didn't become the serial killer's next victim.

IN HIS ENTIRE twenty-six years of living, Troy had never been as scared as he was five weeks ago when he fell off the platform on the oil rig and then felt nothing. One moment he'd been in excruciating pain from hitting the water and then nothing. Instant paralysis. He probably would have drowned, too, if not for his coworkers jumping in to save him.

If only he'd lost consciousness, too, but he'd been all too aware of what he might be facing. He'd chosen to face it alone; he hadn't allowed anyone to contact his family or Lakin.

He would deal with whatever he had to deal with on his own. He hadn't wanted anyone to make sacrifices for him like he knew Lakin would, despite all the dreams she'd had since they were kids. So he'd spent weeks in the hospital waiting for news, for feeling, for anything but the panic that pressed down on him.

And then…

Feeling returned. At first it had been just tingling, but then that tingling had turned painful, like all his extremities had been asleep or frozen and were returning to wakefulness with a vengeance.

While Troy had been reluctant to get his hopes up, the doctors had been cautiously optimistic. The swelling that had caused the nerve damage in his spine had gone down, and the paralysis he'd experienced had proven not to be permanent. He still had some tingling in his hands and feet, and he couldn't move as fast or carry what he normally would've on the job. He might never recover enough to work on the oil rigs again. And he had to take it easy while the contusions to his back continued to heal or the swelling could return and cause paralysis again.

And next time, the doctors warned, the nerves might not recover as quickly as they had the first time. Or they might not recover at all. And he would be permanently paralyzed.

He moved slowly and stiffly as he pushed open the driver's door of his truck and stepped into the parking lot of Rough Terrain Adventures, the Colton family business. The main office was actually a large cabin with a metal roof and a big porch. An enormous garage sheltered their vehicles and equipment, and several cabins behind it housed family, like Lakin, or were rented to guests.

This place was usually his first stop when he came home. But this morning, he'd stopped to see a different Colton. Mitch Colton wasn't part of the family business—he owned and operated Shelby's local corporate law practice. Troy had asked for Mitch's advice with the situation with his employer, with the safety issues on his job. He wanted to address that situation as much for his coworkers as for himself. Mitch had promised he would take care of it.

But Mitch wasn't the Colton Troy really *needed* to see.

He missed Lakin so damn bad. He needed to feel the power of the wide smile that lit up her whole face and made her dark eyes glow. He needed to touch her silky dark hair and her soft skin. To kiss her sweet lips.

Every minute he was away from her, he ached for her. It had been even worse when he was lying in that hospital bed waiting for feeling to return, praying that it would. If it hadn't, he would have even less to offer her.

While she'd gone to college after high school and had a bachelor's degree in business and accounting, he'd chosen to go straight to work to help support his younger siblings. Mom had already been working two jobs after Dad passed away. He'd been injured on an oil rig, too—but fatally. Mom hadn't wanted Troy's help, though. She had insisted that she had everything under control.

And she probably had. She'd always been strong and resilient. But Troy hadn't wanted her to keep working so hard. He would have felt guilty if he'd left her to manage on her own. As the fifth of seven kids, he used to feel a bit lost in the shuffle. Helping her and his younger siblings made him feel useful to her and his family in a way that he hadn't before.

Until he'd started helping his mom, the only person he'd really felt useful to was Lakin, as first her friend in elementary and middle school and then…

Then in high school, he'd realized that his sudden attraction to his best friend wasn't just unruly teenage hormones but that he really loved her. That he had probably always loved her.

Just like the Coltons had fallen for her when they first set eyes on the little girl their friends had been fostering. With her thick dark hair and big, deep dark eyes, she was physically beautiful, but there was also a spiritual beauty to Lakin. She had this sweetness and kindness about her that drew people to her. Some bad, like the old playground bullies who'd mistaken her kindness for weakness, but mostly good, like Troy hoped he was. And yet he still worried that he wasn't good enough for her.

Wanting so badly to see her, he hastened his step as he started across the parking lot toward the office. But the faster he moved, the more he limped as those tight muscles in his back and legs cramped.

"Troy!"

He recognized that voice and turned to find his sister Hetty standing behind him. Then she started toward him, limping even worse than he probably was.

"What happened to you?" he asked, his voice gruff with emotion at seeing his tough sister hobbling. Hetty was only two years older than him, but she'd always seemed so much older and wiser and tougher to him than he would ever be.

"I was shot," she said, matter-of-fact.

He gasped like a bullet struck him along with her words. "What?"

"Exactly," she said. "How the hell don't you know? Where have you been?"

"Working."

"Bullshit," she said, her eyes narrowing with suspicion. They were the same green as his and their father's. "I saw you get out of the truck. You look like you've been shot, too."

He shook his head, then winced as a twinge went from the base of his skull down his spine. "I had an accident. That's all."

It was her turn to gasp. "Dammit, Troy. Do you know how Mom would feel if we lost you like we lost Dad?"

He knew. That was another reason he hadn't wanted to contact anyone after the accident. Not until he knew how much—if at all—he was going to recover.

Hetty answered her own question. "It would kill her."

"I'm not the only one with a dangerous job. And

you're the daredevil in the family," he reminded the pilot. "How the hell did you get shot?"

She sighed. "It's...a long story. There's been a lot going on since you've been gone."

"But you're okay now?" he asked, his heart beating fast with concern.

Hetty smiled, and her eyes lit up with a happiness he hadn't seen in her since their dad died. "I've never been better. I'm in love."

"Really?" Troy asked. She'd always been so tough and independent. "Who's the lucky guy?"

"Spence Colton."

Shocked at her declaration, Troy whistled between his teeth. "Did hell freeze over?" For years, she'd fought with and complained about the RTA tour guide, probably mostly because Spence had been so popular, especially with their female guests.

She laughed. "Well, getting seriously hurt puts things in perspective," she said, then narrowed her eyes again. "Doesn't it?"

Troy nodded. He just wasn't sure how to handle that perspective, or how to even move forward with a future that was still so uncertain. Maybe he shouldn't have come to RTA or even home to Shelby. Maybe he should just stay away from Lakin.

She had so many dreams. She wanted a business of her own, one they could build and manage together. When he'd finally emailed her, he realized she messaged him much more frequently than he did her.

But when he was on the rig, he worked such long hours that he fell into bed exhausted at the end of a shift. In her emails she'd told him about the old Shelby Hotel going up for auction. Unfortunately the date of the auction had already passed. Not that they would have had enough money to buy it and invest in the extensive remodeling the two-story building needed to make it operational again. Those extensive renovations would also require a lot of manpower.

And right now, Troy didn't have the money or the physical ability to turn the hotel into the business Lakin wanted it to be. After so many weeks of not talking to her, he wasn't sure that he even had Lakin anymore. After so much time with no contact from him, maybe she'd realized she didn't need him anymore, that she didn't want him anymore. But Lakin, being Lakin, wouldn't break up via email or text. She would wait until he was home to do it in person.

"Let's talk," Troy said to his sister. "I want to hear about everything that happened to you. Everything that happened while I was gone."

She glanced toward the office. "You don't want to talk to Lakin first?"

He wanted to do more than talk to his longtime love. His body ached for hers; he'd been gone too long. But then his body just ached a lot now. And he was scared of what the future might hold. How angry was she with him for being out of touch for so long? She would also be so upset that they'd missed out on the opportunity to buy the old hotel.

Unfortunately, they wouldn't have been able to even if he'd been in communication with her. He was helping his mother with his brother's college tuition; he hadn't managed to save enough yet for the future Lakin envisioned for them. He needed to work a couple more years on the rigs to get enough for them to open and operate something like a hotel, especially one that needed as many renovations as the old Shelby Hotel.

What if he wasn't able to physically work on the rigs anymore? He might never be able to help make Lakin's dreams come true.

And then he wouldn't be the partner she needed and deserved.

"Lakin's working," Troy reminded his sister. "Instead of interrupting something, I should wait until she's done for the day."

Hetty's brow furrowed beneath a lock of her thick black hair. "You know she's going to be thrilled to see you. She always is."

True. Every time he came home after months spent away from her, it felt like they were on a vacation or a honeymoon. Lakin's entire face would light up with a smile and she'd run into his arms, arms that longed to hold her. She would take some personal days off work, and they would spend as much time as they could in bed or on the couch or in a tent in the woods, just being together in every way. Making up for lost time was what they called it.

The weeks Troy had spent in a hospital bed, waiting for his back to heal, had been lost time. While Mitch figured Troy might have a case against the oil company, Troy wasn't as convinced. When his dad died, there had been no payout because that would have been an admission of poor safety protocols in the workplace. And the oil company was not about to admit to violating safety rules. The lawyer his mother had been able to afford hadn't found enough evidence to convince a civil court judge to make the company pay them anything either. Troy wasn't sure he had enough evidence either.

And if he didn't, there was no making up for what he'd lost, money, work and maybe even relationship-wise.

THE PHOTOGRAPH WAS more than twenty years old, so it was frayed on the edges and the colors were so faded that it was nearly black and white. Yet the man holding it knew exactly who the people in that picture were.

One of them was him, but a younger, more muscular version with thick hair and a cockiness in the way he stood that he didn't feel anymore. He knew more now than he had then, so much more. He wouldn't wind up where he had before; he was smarter now.

He drew in a deep breath and focused on the other people in the picture he held in the palm of his hand. He'd been studying it for a while as he sat in the battered pickup truck he'd *borrowed* a few weeks ago. He knew the other people in that old photograph, too, the dark-haired woman and the dark-haired toddler she held in her arms.

That toddler had grown up and looked like the woman now, almost eerily so, like she was her ghost. The first time he saw her in Shelby, he thought he really had seen a ghost.

But she was real, the young woman. He'd finally found her, and he'd spent the past couple of weeks following her around from the coffee shop she stopped at every morning to her job at the adventure tour company. She lived there, too, in one of the small cabins on the property.

He knew everywhere she went and everything she did

now. He'd been watching her to learn her routine and to figure out what he was going to do about her.

Or get out of her.

Because there was a reason that he'd tracked down that young woman. There was some unfinished business between them. And it was well past time that he finished it, and maybe her as well.

Chapter Two

When Troy's truck pulled into the parking lot of RTA, Lakin noticed immediately. Even if she hadn't seen the rusted old pickup through the office's big windows, she would have known. She'd always been able to sense when he was close; it was as if her whole body tingled with awareness of him. Before she could disengage from the client talking her ear off on the telephone, he was gone again.

He'd been heading toward the office when Hetty caught up with him. She knew, of course, that Hetty was still recovering from her gunshot wound. But was Troy limping, too?

Maybe he'd just been stiff from the long trip from the offshore oil rigs. Of course he wouldn't have been shot like Hetty. Nothing bad could have happened to him, or someone would have notified her or at least his family.

Troy and Hetty probably had a lot to catch up on, and that was why he'd left. But without even stopping by the office to give her a quick kiss? If she hadn't been on the phone with a client, she would have run out to greet him like she always did. She'd missed him so much when he was gone that she couldn't wait to see his handsome face again, to kiss him, to hug him.

And he hadn't even stuck his head in the office to smile at her before leaving again?

Maybe he'd found out what she'd done, and he was mad at her.

But only a few people besides her knew. And her dad wouldn't share her secret until she started sharing it herself. He understood her reasons for wanting to keep it quiet until she was ready to announce it to other members of their family. They might be the hardest to tell. And Troy...

Would he be happy about it?

Unfortunately she doubted it. He was so determined to wait, and not just when it came to starting their business together. He seemed determined to wait for them to start their life together as well. Marriage. A family. All the things they'd been talking about since they started dating in high school and he'd finally realized what she'd known all along: they were soulmates. But now, it seemed like he wasn't in any hurry to give her the commitment she wanted.

Maybe she was just letting Billy Hoover and Eric Seller's comments get to her. Instead of understanding Troy's reasons for working on the oil rigs, she was beginning to think they were just excuses to put off their future. Maybe she was just getting sick of waiting for Troy. And sick of missing him.

She was so sick of it that she felt nauseous. Or was that nerves churning her stomach because she was worried that he was going to be angry with her? Not that he really had any reason to be, not after going so long with so little communication. If anyone should be angry, it should be her.

If only she didn't love him so damn much...

He was a good guy. So protective and loyal and caring. All he wanted to do was help the people he loved.

But was she still one of those people?

"You don't look so good," Parker said the minute he stepped out of his private office. The administrative building was a big old cabin and felt more like a home than a workspace. The floor was polished concrete, and there was wood everywhere and big, thickly cushioned leather furniture where guests and family often lounged while waiting for a tour to start.

Parker hadn't even walked up to her desk before he made his pronouncement. He was perceptive as ever. He'd taken RTA to the next level, rebranding the company after their father and uncle retired and making it even more successful than it had been. Lakin loved working with him and had learned so much from him that she had the skills to run her own business now. She just needed help—the partnership she'd dreamed of having, in every aspect of their lives, with Troy.

"Lakin?" Parker asked, his voice deep with concern. "Are you okay?"

She nodded, then grimaced at the tension headache forming behind her eyes. That, coupled with some nausea, made her wonder if she had picked up a virus.

She was pretty sure it was just stress. If she admitted that to her brother, though, he would want to fix it. Her three older brothers had always been super protective of her, just like Troy; that was probably the only reason they'd accepted him as her boyfriend, because he was so much like them.

Maybe she should have been offended that they didn't think she could protect herself, but like Troy, she loved them so damn much that she could never be angry with them. They were the best big brothers she could ever imagine anyone having.

"I'm fine," she tried to assure him. "Just probably not sleeping well right now."

Because of what she'd done…and that feeling she'd been having that someone was watching her. But *who*… and why?

"I don't think anyone is sleeping well right now," Parker said. "Not with some maniac out there abducting and killing women. Are you sure you shouldn't be staying with Dad and Mom instead of in that cabin all by yourself?"

"I'm fine," she repeated. "I lock my doors and windows and keep an eye out." Even though she'd been super careful, she hadn't figured out who was watching her. Maybe nobody was, and she was just being paranoid because of the killer.

"That's good," Parker said. "And I'm sure Eli will find the bastard soon and put him behind bars for the rest of his life."

"I hope he finds Dawn Ellis soon," Lakin said, "and alive and well." She'd never met the missing young woman, but she was worried about her.

Parker nodded. "Yeah, me, too." He stepped closer to the reception desk and narrowed his eyes as he studied her face. He must have noticed the dark circles under her eyes. "Go home and get some rest. I'll handle the office for the rest of the day."

She smiled. "It's almost quitting time."

He chuckled. "Yeah. That's why I can handle it on my own."

He was obviously on his way out, so she shouldn't take him up on his offer. But she was feeling too sick, with nerves and a bad stomach and a headache, to stay. So she grabbed her bag and headed toward the door.

"Hey, you didn't drive here?" Parker asked. He must have looked out at the parking lot and noticed her SUV wasn't there.

"No. I left my vehicle at the cabin."

"Let me lock up and walk you to your place," Parker said.

She laughed and shook her head. "You're not getting off desk duty that easily," she said. "We're getting a delivery with the toner I need for the printer, and someone has to be here for them to leave it."

Parker groaned.

"You just have to—"

"I know how to sign for a package," he told her. "I don't like you walking by yourself."

"I walk by myself all the time," she said. "I'll be fine."

"Lakin—"

"I know," she said before he could bring up the serial killer again. "I'm always aware of my surroundings, and I'm very cautious. I'll be fine."

Parker still looked worried, but he nodded begrudgingly.

She understood his concern. Her own worries didn't end when she stepped outside into the cool afternoon air.

What would Parker do when she wasn't here to help him? She felt a twinge of guilt that she wanted to leave. RTA was family, and she felt like she was betraying them. But if she had help with her new venture, she would be able to train her replacement. If she had Troy...

She needed to talk to him. Really talk. Of course, usually after these long stretches apart, talking was the last thing they did. First she ran to him and leaped into his arms, then wrapped hers around his neck and pulled his head down for her kisses. Just thinking about his mouth against hers, his strong arms holding her, had her flesh tingling and heating up.

Her legs weakened a bit, and she nearly stumbled as she walked toward her cabin. It was farthest from the office and close to the woods. She'd chosen it because she liked the solitude of being farther away from the other cabins, especially when Troy was home from the oil rigs.

But now...

She shivered at the isolation as she passed the last unoccupied cabin. She'd parked her SUV at her cabin when she came back from Roasters that morning, but she wished now that she'd parked at the office.

No. She spent entirely too much time at her desk and liked to walk outside as much as she could, whenever she could. While she liked to be outside for the fresh air, she wasn't into the extreme outdoor adventures her family business offered. She preferred her cabin and her soft bed to a tent and a sleeping bag. And the farthest she liked to hike was to her cabin from the office.

That was a moot point now. After what she'd done, she wasn't going to get much time outside, especially if she couldn't convince Troy to help her with her new venture. Maybe she shouldn't be worried about him helping her; maybe she should be worried that he might break up with her over making such a big decision without discussing it with him.

But she'd tried.

He was the one who was out of touch for weeks, sometimes months, at a time. And that was getting old.

Especially now with a killer on the loose. Being alone so much was unnerving. Maybe Parker was right; maybe she should stay with Mom and Dad until the killer was caught.

Eli would catch him. Her big brother was the best agent with the Alaska Bureau of Investigations. And this case was personal to him. She knew why; it reminded him of how he and Dad had found Aunt Caroline all those years ago. Dressed up with a fake engagement ring on her finger, the young model had only been seventeen. She hadn't been anyone's fiancée, but an obsessed fan had thought she was his. He'd taken her life, her parents' lives and his own. And Dad and Eli, when he was just six or seven years old, had found their bodies.

That was why Dad and Uncle Ryan had moved from San Diego and started over in Shelby, where no one knew what had happened. For nearly thirty years, there had been no reminders of that horrible time.

But now…

It was as if that dead killer was starting over, too.

Lakin wondered if Eli was having nightmares again like he occasionally had as a kid. His nightmares had helped her feel better about the ones she had, like she wasn't so weak and messed up. Because Eli definitely wasn't. She wasn't even sure he remembered having them, but he and their father had been extra comforting when she had hers.

She hadn't had a nightmare in years, though. Probably because her memories of the time before Mom and Dad adopted her had faded. She shivered again, wondering why she'd started thinking about those fleeting flashes of a face or voices...

What could her old memories have to do with the current murders? Nothing.

Maybe she was just looking for something to think about besides her tenuous relationship with Troy. They spent so much time apart, and whenever she tried to talk about the future, he either ignored her like he had the past few weeks or he insisted they needed to wait until he saved more money.

Lakin was getting tired of waiting. While she had no intention of buying herself an engagement ring, especially with the Fiancée Killer on the loose, she had bought herself something else. And she wasn't a damn bit sorry. She wanted Troy to share her dreams, but if he wasn't ready, it didn't matter. She wasn't putting her dreams on hold anymore, not even for him.

The thought made her sick again, and she was glad she was drawing closer to her cabin. She'd had some sleepless nights lately as she lay awake, listening for any suspicious sounds, for someone trying to get into her place.

The killer was making her paranoid, and she hated it. Hated feeling like she did now, chilled all of a sudden. Maybe the cabins she'd passed weren't all empty. Maybe someone had chosen to skip their adventure tour or had returned early.

Or maybe...

Maybe it wasn't a guest. Maybe someone really was following her and scrutinizing her every move. She shivered, trying to shake off the paranoia. But she glanced back over her shoulder nonetheless.

The wind wriggled some tree branches, but nothing else moved behind her.

Definitely paranoid.

Smiling at herself, she let the tension drain away and slowed her approach to her cabin. She wouldn't be living here much longer if she had her way, so she took a moment to study the little wood structure tucked into a stand of pine trees. She and Troy had had so many magical moments in this place that she would miss it.

Like she missed him…

So damn much that she ached for him. Why hadn't he come inside the office earlier today? Why had he just driven off again without even a wave in her direction?

She blinked against the sudden rush of tears, and as she refocused, she noticed that her door wasn't shut tightly. A crack showed between it and the jamb. While she hadn't always locked her door, ever since hearing about the serial killer, she made certain that she closed and locked it.

Unless…

Was it Troy? She didn't see his truck parked anywhere, but maybe he'd hidden it to surprise her. But she didn't feel the way she usually felt when he was near; she didn't feel any tingling awareness of him.

She felt only fear.

Hired assassins. Dead bodies and a serial killer. As Hetty brought Troy up to speed on what had been happening in Shelby, he was horrified and worried.

That morning Mitch had alluded to a lot happening lately in Shelby, but the lawyer hadn't had time to go into detail. He'd left for court right after his meeting with Troy. Troy wished Mitch would have filled him in on all this; he wouldn't have decided to catch up with his sister before seeing the woman he loved. The woman he was so damn worried about now.

Lakin lived alone in her little cabin that was too far from the other ones at RTA, too far away for someone to hear her cry for help, for someone to rescue her if she needed it.

Scared for her safety, he jumped up from his chair at the table he and Hetty were sharing at Roasters. Even this late in the day, the café was pretty busy with people using laptops or reading books while sipping from their bright blue Roasters coffee mugs.

"I need to check on Lakin," he told Hetty. While he'd wanted to give himself some time to figure out how to tell Lakin what happened on the oil rig, he wished now that he'd rushed right in to see her, to hold her, to assure himself that she was all right. That was all he wanted to do now, make sure that she was safe. He started toward the door.

"Hey," Hetty called after him. "You should have been worried about Lakin before this. You should have been worried about losing her."

Losing her?

Because he'd never been good enough for her? He'd known that for years; that was why he hadn't proposed yet. He wanted to be able to buy her a big engagement ring as well as that business she wanted to run with him. He wanted to be able to make all of her dreams come true.

Was that what Hetty was talking about? That Lakin was going to realize he wasn't good enough for her? Or that he might lose her to someone like the serial killer going after women in Shelby?

Right now he just wanted to make sure Lakin was safe, so he didn't bother to ask his sister to clarify. Instead, ignoring the twinge in his back, he hurried out of the café and hopped in his truck. Speeding back to RTA, Troy silently cursed himself for leaving earlier without talking to her.

While he appreciated his sister apprising him of everything that had happened while he was gone, she'd wasted her breath warning him about losing Lakin. He'd been worried about losing her ever since their first date.

But then he'd only been worried about losing her to someone who had more to offer her than he did. Now he was worried about all the other horrific ways that he could lose her.

He hoped Dawn Ellis was found soon. Hopefully she wouldn't be another victim of the serial killer.

A serial killer in their safe community. Hired assassins who'd shot Hetty.

What the hell was happening in the place he'd always considered the safest? While crime and chaos ruled in other areas, Shelby had always been quiet and controlled with nothing more than petty thefts and drunken disorderly conduct around town.

But now…

Now he just wanted to see Lakin, to hold her, to make sure that she was safe. He was so impatient that the truck tires squealed as he turned into the parking lot of RTA. Jumping out of his truck, he limped across the porch of the RTA office, pushed open the door and stepped inside, calling out, "Lakin! Lakin!"

Parker poked his head out of his office and grinned at him. "Hey, Troy, I'm damn glad to see you're home!"

The Coltons had always been so friendly and accepting of Troy even when they had to know that Lakin, with her beauty and intelligence, could do better than him. But that was the kind of people that they were. Lakin had once shared that their family motto was *believe*.

The motto had originated because of some tragedy from their past. But it meant that whenever someone told them something, they would believe them until proven otherwise. So maybe they believed he would make Lakin happy…until he proved them otherwise.

"I'm damn glad to be home," Troy said. And he was happy now that he was back if only just because of everything that had been going on while he was gone. Not to mention that he should just be damn happy that he was alive at all. "Where's Lakin?"

While he usually would have talked with Parker about RTA business and life in general, he'd already spent way too much time away from his love.

"Ouch," Parker said with a hand to his chest. "Thanks for making it clear I'm not the Colton you were hoping to find in the office." Instead of being offended, Parker chuckled. "I totally get it. I'm not the Colton who would like to be in the office."

Neither was Lakin but her brother didn't know that yet. She wasn't ready yet to leave, though. Or maybe she was, but Troy wasn't ready yet to help her leave the family business to start their own. If only he'd been able to save more money, but with helping his younger brother with college and his mother with living expenses, he hadn't been able to save as much as they needed yet. And now…if he wasn't able to work on the rigs anymore…

He couldn't even let himself think about that yet, about how he would make the kind of money he needed if he couldn't go back to work. Hopefully Mitch would come up with a plan for him to at least hold the oil company responsible for disability pay while Troy fully recovered from the fall.

"I don't care where Lakin is," Troy said. "I just want to see her."

Parker chuckled again. "You have been gone a long time."

"And Hetty's brought me up to speed on what's been happening around Shelby while I was gone," Troy said to further explain his urgency to see the woman he loved.

Parker's smile slid away, and his body tensed. "Yeah, it's not been good."

"Or safe. So I really want to check on her, make sure she's okay," Troy explained.

Parker smiled again, but then he shivered as if he was chilled. "She just left a little while ago. She wasn't feeling well. I offered to see her back to her cabin, but she insisted she would be fine."

While her big brother might have believed that, Troy wasn't so sure. Nobody was safe with a killer on the loose in Shelby.

ELI COLTON STARED down at the young woman's body, but instead of seeing her, he saw his sister's face and his aunt's and his cousin's. Then he blinked away the horrors of his imagination and his memory and focused.

Dawn Ellis was someone's sister, someone's cousin, someone's daughter, and now she was dead.

He'd hoped like hell that she would be found alive, but just forty-eight hours after she'd been reported missing, she was found here, on the outskirts of Shelby. The town where Eli's dad and uncle had moved their families because they'd believed it would keep all of them safe from harm.

But here, just off the road, she'd been found—her body staged just like the other victims, with all but her head and left hand buried. She wore a gaudy fake ring, and she had the telltale marks around her neck from the hands of whoever had strangled her. When the rest of her body was uncovered, Eli had no doubt she would be wearing a little black dress. Like she'd just been at her engagement party.

But Dawn Ellis hadn't been engaged.

Three other bodies had been found buried just like this, wearing similar gaudy rings and black dresses. Only one of them had been identified, leaving two other Jane Does whose families were undoubtedly still looking for them.

Hopefully they would find DNA matches soon, so those people would have some peace, some closure, if there was actually such a thing.

Was it only Eli's imagination that had him comparing Dawn to the women he loved? All the victims had long, dark brown hair like his sister Lakin and his cousin Kansas and were roughly the same age. A lot of women had dark hair and were in their age range, though, so it was probably just a coincidence. Maybe it was just his fears making him draw comparisons to the women he cared about.

Thinking of Lakin and Kansas, Eli stepped away from the crime scene that the techs were meticulously processing to make some calls. To make sure that everyone he loved was safe.

Kansas picked up immediately. "You found her?" she asked. She was in law enforcement, too, and clearly knew why he would randomly check up on her.

"Yes."

"Where?"

He gave her the location. "I'll talk to you when you get here," he said. He glanced at his partner Asher, wondering if he should warn him that his nemesis was going to be here soon. Kansas and Asher did not get along, often putting Eli in the middle of their squabbles. He loved them both too much to take sides, but he often tried to point out at they were all actually on the same side.

Enforcing the law. While he and Asher were lieutenants in the major crimes division of the Alaska Bureau of Investigations, Kansas was a state trooper and member of the search and rescue unit.

But he would warn Asher in a minute that Kansas was on her way. Right now he had another call to make.

But his call to Lakin went unanswered.

Lakin always answered her phone. Where was she? And was she okay?

Chapter Three

Her cell ringing startled Lakin, but she wasn't the only one. A clang rang out from behind the partially open door to her cabin. She gasped. Somebody was definitely inside.

"Troy?" she called out tentatively.

It had to be Troy. Right? He'd been at the office earlier. When he drove off without talking to her, he could have been planning to surprise her at home.

And yet she hesitated before walking into her own cabin. It didn't feel like her home right now; it felt unfamiliar, strange…like her relationship with Troy had suddenly become.

He'd never gone so long with so little contact before. Something had to be wrong, and she knew that he wouldn't try to remedy that with a surprise. And if he'd wanted to surprise her, he wouldn't have sent the email last week letting her know that he was finally coming home.

But home probably just meant Shelby. Despite how much he stayed with her when he wasn't working, they didn't live together. Most of his things and his room were at his mother's house. Mrs. Amos undoubtedly missed her son as much as Lakin did. And she probably worried about him even more since she'd lost her husband on the same oil rigs that her son insisted on working on as well.

Lakin wasn't sure if he was just trying to help his family out or if he missed his father so much that he was trying to replace him. Either way, she loved him for loving all of them so much.

But as much as she loved him, she was beginning to lose hope for a future with him.

So she didn't believe he'd made the noise inside the cabin. Something…or someone…else was in there.

Once a raccoon had managed to break in through an open window. But a door? As clever and capable as they were with their little handlike paws, she doubted that was possible.

No, it had to be a human inside her place.

But who? Why would anyone break in? She had nothing worth stealing. The only things of value were her heart, which Troy already had, and her life.

She started backing away from the cabin, scared that whoever was inside was going to come out. She turned to run but instead collided with a long, hard body. She gasped as strong arms wrapped around her.

But these arms were familiar.

"Hey, what's wrong?" Troy asked, his voice a low rumble in his muscular chest.

She tingled with awareness of his closeness and with fear. "Someone's in my cabin," she whispered.

How was Troy here? She'd been so focused on her cabin that she hadn't heard his truck drive up.

"Run back to the office," Troy whispered gruffly.

Maybe he didn't want to alert the intruder to their presence—but her ringing cell had already done that. He turned with her in his arms, positioning himself between her and the cabin, then released her. "Go," he urged her. "Get Parker and call the police."

The police—well, her brother Eli—had already called. But she'd been so stunned to find her door open that she hadn't known how to react.

As if Troy expected her to obey him, he turned back toward her front door.

"Where are you going?" she asked, her voice rising slightly with panic.

"I'm going to try to catch whoever the hell is in there." He started toward the door again.

"No, it's too dangerous. They could have a gun or some kind of weapon," she warned and reached out, trying to stop him.

But then another noise rang out, louder than their argument: the crack of the cabin's back door slamming.

Before Lakin could grasp his arm, Troy was off, running after a figure that was just a blur of dark clothes heading into the woods. But Troy wasn't really running. Not like he usually did. He was moving oddly, stiffly, like he was limping or hurt.

If he caught up with the intruder, he might get hurt even worse.

The shadow was tall and broad and moving faster than Troy. But if the person turned back, they could overpower Troy, especially if they were armed. If they were armed, they might do more than just overpower him.

"Troy!" she yelled, her heart racing with fear. "Troy! Come back!"

But it was too late. He disappeared into the woods. Would it be the last time she saw him?

Troy ignored the twinges of pain in his back as he pushed himself to run faster through the forest. Branches were rustling and snapping back toward him; he was close to whoever had come out of Lakin's cabin. But all he could see was a dark shadow through the trees.

A black coat maybe? Black hat? Hiking boots. He could tell by the deep treads pushing the pine needles into the dirt.

Just about everybody in Shelby wore hiking boots, though, and coats and hats, too, since the evenings were cold in September. It could have been anyone, and too many trees and branches blocked Troy from getting a better look at the person. He had to get closer. But as he ran harder, the uneven ground twisted his back, and he winced.

"Stop!" he yelled at the intruder like Lakin had yelled after him. But he didn't expect this person to listen to him any more than he had listened to her.

Troy had to find out who'd broken into her place and why. Was this the person Hetty had told him about? The serial killer targeting women in Shelby? Even though he and Lakin had been in a relationship for ten years, she was alone so much. Was that why someone had broken into her place?

Was she the serial killer's next target?

Frustration gripped him, making his muscles tense even more, and he had to stop running for a moment. He had to catch his breath. His lungs burning, he leaned forward, hands on his thighs and drew in deep breaths of fresh air.

Fresh air with a hint of stale cigarette smoke. Usually the woods smelled of pine needles and fresh rain. The intruder had to be close.

Troy peered around, wondering where the person was hiding. Maybe they weren't hiding at all. Maybe they were waiting to ambush him once he got close.

He didn't want to get knocked out, or worse, and leave Lakin unprotected. Hopefully she had run back to the office to get Parker and had called the local police. Eli and Kansas could be anywhere in Alaska, but Shelby PD was close. And at the moment Troy was more of a liability than an asset. Instead of saving her from the intruder, he might need saving himself.

THE MAN DUCKED under the pine boughs and hunkered down near the trunk. He shouldn't be discovered in the shadows. And if he was…

Maybe that would be a good thing. Getting rid of whoever was chasing him would be the smart thing to do. He couldn't afford for someone to disrupt the plan he had painstakingly put into place. He had put in too much effort and research for it to be put into jeopardy now.

Who the hell was this guy anyway?

He'd not been around the past few weeks, not like the other men, those *Coltons*. They were always around. The boys and their dad. He would deal with them in time, too.

But right now…

Now he had a more immediate problem. This young stranger had rushed headlong to her rescue, chasing after him through the woods. Except…there was no running now. No snapping of twigs and branches or rustling of leaves. Just what sounded like gasps for breath.

Whoever was trying to be her hero either wasn't in very good condition or wasn't used to the altitude.

It would be easy now to take him out. He would never become a problem.

Chapter Four

Troy was hurt. Lakin knew it even before she found him gasping for breath in the middle of the forest. She'd recognized pain on his face as he took off after the intruder. His entire long body looked as if it had protested every step he took.

"What's wrong?" she asked when she found him. "What's happened?"

She would have thought that the intruder had turned the tables on Troy and attacked him, but there were no visible marks on his smooth chocolate skin, no swelling on his handsome face. He looked as perfect as always but for the pain in his beautiful green eyes. His mouth twisted into a grimace, and finally he released a long breath and straightened up.

"What are you doing here?" he asked. "You were supposed to go to Parker, to the office, to safety…" He glanced at the trees around them, as if expecting the intruder to be hiding nearby.

Maybe they were; Lakin could smell something other than the pines, something like stale cigarette smoke. She felt that strange sensation again, like she was being watched. She shivered and whispered, "We should go back to the cabin."

"You should," Troy said, and he put his hand against the small of her back, turning her away from him. "Go back to the cabin. Now."

"Not without you," she said. "You're hurt. What happened?" Why wouldn't he just admit that he'd been injured and tell her how? Not that they had time to talk here. They needed to get out of here, but Lakin wasn't leaving without Troy.

"I'm fine," he said. But his jaw was so clenched, she was surprised he managed to get out the lie. He clearly wasn't fine.

"Troy!" she exclaimed with exasperation.

Branches rustled around them; something was moving in the trees.

Troy pulled Lakin into his arms and wrapped them around her, as if using his body to shield her from whatever was coming.

But no person appeared.

Maybe when she shouted at him, she'd startled a bird or something. Or maybe it had been just a sudden gust of wind.

She could feel Troy's heart beating fast and hard, could feel the heat of his skin, the hardness of his muscled body. This was where she should have been, in his arms, the minute he got back into town.

But he hadn't come straight to her. And then someone had been inside her damn cabin. Doing what?

"I called Parker and Eli," she assured him and whoever might be out there listening to them. She felt that strange sensation again, that creepy awareness of someone watching her. Who was it?

The intruder in her cabin proved that she wasn't just imagining things. Someone could really be following her around. If not for Troy showing up when he had, they might have gotten her.

She wound her arms around him now and held on. But as she tightened her grasp around his back, he flinched.

"You are hurt," she said. "Troy—"

"Lakin!" Parker's voice echoed around the woods. "Troy! Where are you?"

"Here, we're here!" she called back to her brother.

"The police are on their way," Parker said loudly, as if warning off whoever might be hiding in the woods with them.

Lakin was pretty sure that someone was out there, watching them, waiting… For what? For her to be alone?

Branches rustled again, but it was Parker who pushed them aside. "Thank God you two are all right," he said. "Who was it? Did you see them?"

Troy shook his head.

"I saw the front door of the cabin was open," Lakin explained, "so I didn't go inside. And when the intruder ran out the back, I just saw a shadow heading toward the woods."

"It was a good thing you noticed the door was open," Parker said. He shuddered as if horrified over what could have happened to her.

"I'm sure it wasn't…" *The serial killer*, she thought. But she didn't say the words out loud. She didn't want to think of him or give him any more attention. Wasn't that why serial killers killed? They wanted the notoriety and attention? The press had already given him a name, had already reported too much about him.

But not everything.

They didn't know what had happened years ago within the Colton family. They didn't know how eerily close the crimes felt to one that had almost destroyed her family before she'd even become part of it.

Her family was strong and resilient. They had not allowed that tragedy to define them. But if someone brought that tragedy to the attention of the press, they might make her family relive it all over again.

"Let's head back to the office," Parker said. "Shelby PD's finest, Bobby Reynolds, is on his way, and Eli and Kansas are, too. We'll leave the policing to all of them."

"And leave the chasing after bad guys to them, too," Lakin said pointedly to Troy. "You shouldn't have gone after him. What if he'd had a weapon?"

He shrugged. "I just wanted to see who it was."

"Eli will figure that out," Parker said.

Lakin worried that everybody expected too much of her oldest brother but nobody more so than Eli himself. He had so much responsibility bearing down on him; she didn't want to add to his burden. But she did want to know who the hell had been in her place, just not badly enough to chase after them herself.

With her arm around Troy, she urged him from the woods. Parker fell behind them, as if making sure that nobody could sneak up on them. Proof that Parker wasn't any more willing to leave everything up to his older brother than Lakin was. He was trying to protect her, too, just as all her brothers had always done, Eli, Mitch and Parker.

Troy had always wanted to protect her, too. But she wondered now if the one she really needed the most protection from was him.

Going so long without seeing him or even communicating with him had hurt her. Badly. And it had hurt their relationship to the point where Billy Hoover and Eric Seller weren't the only ones questioning it.

Like those men, she was also wondering if there was a future for the two of them. Did Troy love her as much as he once had? Did he love her enough to start their future now instead of waiting? Because Lakin was tired of waiting.

The deaths of those young women, including the aunt she'd never met, proved to her that life could be cut much too short.

"WHAT THE HELL happened to you?" Parker asked. It was the same question that Lakin had asked Troy in the woods.

The three of them had made it back to the RTA office, even locking themselves inside the building. But despite the sound of sirens growing louder, Troy didn't feel any safer than he had in the woods. Because now both Lakin and her brother were staring at him.

The muscles in his back were cramping up again, making him flinch despite his best effort to ignore the pain. He didn't want Lakin to find out about his fall off the oil rig like this. He wanted the time and the privacy to explain why he hadn't called her or his family.

"Did the guy get the jump on you out there?" Parker asked. "You said you didn't see him but…"

"I didn't see him, and he didn't attack me," Troy said. "I don't even know if it was a man or a woman."

"Troy was already limping before he ran after the intruder," Lakin said. "But he won't tell me what happened to him."

Drawing it out was just making her angrier, he could see that. She would also be angry that he hadn't told her when it happened, just like Hetty. His mom and other siblings would probably also be pissed at him.

"I fell off the oil rig several weeks ago," he said. And he'd missed all those weeks of pay. Hopefully Mitch could help him get reimbursed for those lost wages.

Lakin's dark eyes widened with shock. "You fell into the water? How? What happened?"

He shrugged and flinched again at the twinge of pain in his back. "I don't know. I thought my safety harness was secure, but the cable or something snapped when I was up on one of the towers, and I fell and hit the water." So damn hard.

Parker gasped. "You could have died."

Troy knew that all too well; it was how his father had died. "I didn't. I'm fine," he said, trying to reassure Lakin. Her dark eyes were still so wide, and her face was pale.

"You're not fine," she said, sounding like she was gritting her teeth. "You're limping, and you're obviously in pain right now."

Running on uneven ground hadn't been good for his back. But hopefully the physical therapy he'd signed up for in town would make it easier for him to use his muscles again.

"I'm better," he said. "For a while…" He trailed off and not just because the sirens were even louder now as the police pulled into the parking lot.

He didn't want to say any more about his accident, at least not until he and Lakin were alone. Knowing how protective her family was of her, he wondered if he would get the chance anytime soon. But keeping her safe was more important than anything else, even their relationship.

And let alone keep her safe, right now, he didn't know if he could help her achieve all those dreams she had, not without knowing how well he might heal.

But why was she in danger? Who the hell had broken into her cabin? Was the serial killer targeting Lakin now?

The thought horrified him more than anything else. He couldn't imagine anyone wanting to hurt Lakin. And he didn't want to imagine anyone succeeding.

ELI LOOKED AT his sister and saw Dawn Ellis's lifeless face instead. The color drained from her skin, the blue around her painted red lips and that garish ring on the finger of her exposed hand.

Then he blinked and saw Lakin again. She was moving carefully through the cabin that Eli and his team had already searched with the help of the local police department. Officer Reynolds wasn't really thrilled that they'd taken over, but he hadn't argued. He knew how close the Coltons stuck together; he just didn't know why. He didn't know what they'd already been through and how many loved ones they'd already lost, albeit nearly three decades ago.

"Is anything missing?" Eli asked Lakin.

She stopped in the kitchenette; the doors of the few hickory wood cupboards stood open. The refrigerator door had been open, too, but someone had closed it after processing the handle for prints and DNA. Probably Scott Montgomery. The tech was detail-oriented like that and wouldn't have wanted any of her food to spoil.

"When I saw my front door was open and heard someone inside, I thought of the raccoon who got through the window last year," Lakin said with a small smile.

"It wasn't a raccoon who jimmied open the door," Eli said. Though, since she hadn't dead-bolted it, the lock wouldn't have been hard to open.

"But this seems like someone scavenging, doesn't it?" she said, pointing at the food that had been dropped on the floor as well as on the small table. "Maybe they were looking for something to eat, not for me."

Eli hoped like hell that was the case. After all, none of the other crime scenes had been left a mess like this. Not that the women had been murdered where their bodies were found. He had yet to find the actual crime scenes. He shrugged. "It doesn't make sense."

Kansas nodded in agreement.

Officer Reynolds sighed and pushed a hand through his short brown hair. "There have been a couple other break-ins like this in the area," he said. "People who are out of work and desperate to make ends meet. Like I said, I don't think this is a case for major crimes or search and rescue." His dark eyes narrowed as he shot a glance at both Eli and Kansas.

"There are food banks," Eli said. He didn't believe there was any excuse to commit a crime. And if someone was desperate for food, why break into a small cabin that might have only been used for vacationers? It could have been empty or poorly stocked. Unless they'd been watching it for a while, watching Lakin.

"Well, some people are too proud to admit they need help," Kansas said.

"Some people are too proud for their own damn good," Lakin muttered just loudly enough for Eli to hear and wonder. She was staring through the window to where Troy stood outside next to Parker.

He'd noticed the tension between them from the minute he walked into the office over an hour ago. Usually when Troy was around, the two of them couldn't stop grinning and laughing; it was like love bubbled out of them.

"Are you mad because he tried to chase down the intruder?" he asked.

She hesitated a moment, then nodded.

Was that really the reason for the tension between them? Eli could understand her being upset that Troy had put himself in danger like that. Eli would have been upset, too, but he understood why Troy had gone after the guy. Troy loved Lakin as much as her family did. Maybe more.

Troy really looked sick, his face twisted with a grimace. Probably because he hadn't caught the guy. Eli understood that feeling all too well, too. He had to catch this damn serial killer before he took anyone else's life, anyone else's loved one.

Fortunately, Eli didn't think that was who'd broken

into Lakin's place. "What do you think, Kansas?" he asked his cousin. "Is Officer Reynolds right? This intruder is just somebody down on their luck looking for food or cash?"

His cousin nodded.

But Eli caught a look passing over Lakin's face, like she had something else to say.

"What is it?" he asked her. "Is something else bothering you?"

She shook her head. "No, I think I'm just letting all the press about that killer get to me."

"Sometimes it's good to be scared," Kansas said. "It makes you more aware and cautious. You noticed that door before you got too close to the cabin. That's good."

It was good to be aware and cautious, but that didn't mean it would keep a person safe. Eli had a horrible feeling that this killer might just consider awareness a challenge. But hopefully Officer Reynolds and Kansas were right and that was not who had broken into Lakin's place. Finding another body had probably just put Eli too on edge to accept a simple explanation for the break-in.

Hopefully nobody was after Lakin at all. And the only thing she needed to be concerned about was whatever was going on between her and Troy.

Chapter Five

Lakin knew she should have told Eli about the strange feeling she'd been having that someone was watching her. But after seeing her place and realizing that all the intruder had taken was some food, she'd gone back to feeling paranoid instead of genuinely worried about being stalked. She had no proof that anyone was really watching her, just a sensation she sometimes got. The only proof she had of any crime was of someone being so desperate for food that they'd broken in to steal some.

Eli and Kansas had much more dangerous criminals to find than her hungry intruder. So once the techs finished processing her cabin for prints on the doorknob and the kitchen cabinets, she hugged them both and sent them back to their more important cases. She earned a smile of approval from Officer Reynolds, who seemed so serious that he probably rarely smiled.

"I'll be fine," she assured her brother and her cousin. "And I'll make sure that I use the dead bolt now on all the doors even when I'm not home." Nobody would have gotten inside if she had.

Eli hugged her again and whispered, "Please, be careful, little sis."

She hugged him back and promised, "I will."

She wasn't sure if his concern was only regarding the serial killer or if he'd noticed the tension between her and Troy as well. Eli never missed a thing, though, so he was probably cautioning her about both.

When he and Kansas followed Officer Reynolds out of Lakin's cabin, she began to close the door, but a hand caught the edge of it.

Troy stepped inside with her. Then he closed and dead bolted the door behind himself.

The tension was there, but it wasn't just frustration she felt now. She also felt the usual awareness, the attraction. Despite all the years they'd been together, she'd never gotten used to the rush of desire she felt for him. Maybe if their relationship hadn't been long distance so many of those years, she would have gotten used to it. But he'd never given her the chance.

"Do Eli and Kansas think they'll be able to find the intruder?" Troy asked.

She shrugged. "I think he's the least of their concerns right now."

"But he broke in here—"

"Apparently because he or she was hungry," she said, gesturing toward the kitchenette. She still had to clean up the food on the floor, the table and in the sink, as well as the residue from the fingerprinting.

"They still broke into *your* home," he said, his voice gruff with emotion, "and if you had been home—"

"They probably would have gone on to the next cabin," she interjected.

"Parker checked the other ones," Troy said. "He

couldn't find any sign that anyone had tried getting into them. Just yours."

That knowledge chilled her a bit. Why just hers? Maybe because hers was the farthest away from the others, so the chance of getting caught was slimmer. She hoped that was the only reason, but she wasn't going to obsess over that, not right now. She was obsessing over something else, over some*one* else.

She shrugged off his concerns about the break-in. "I don't want to talk about that right now. I want to know how badly you were hurt when you fell off the oil rig." Several weeks ago. Several weeks ago he'd been hurt, but he hadn't let her know. Why? Because he hadn't been able to? But why didn't someone from the oil company contact his family?

Troy sighed and rubbed his hand over the head of black hair he kept super short. "Lakin…"

"Tell me," she insisted. "How bad did you get hurt when you fell off the rig?"

He touched his back almost unconsciously, like he didn't realize he was doing it. "I… I was paralyzed."

"You were *paralyzed*?" she repeated, her voice cracking. Pain pressed on her chest, making her heart ache for what he must have gone through. "Why didn't you call me, Troy? I would have rushed to the hospital—"

"That's why," he said. "I didn't want to put you or my family through the fear and uncertainty—"

"That you were feeling," she interjected. She couldn't imagine how scared he'd been. That he hadn't reached out to his family didn't make her feel any better. She loved his mother and siblings almost as much as she loved him, almost as much as she loved her own family. "You shouldn't have had to go through that all by yourself."

"I wanted to," he said. "*I* had to know what I was facing before I told anyone what happened."

"Why?" she asked, her heart pounding hard with fear, over what he'd gone through and over what it meant to their relationship that he'd chosen to be alone. "You have to know that it wouldn't have mattered to me or to your family. We would have wanted to be there for you no matter the outcome from your fall."

He groaned and rubbed his hand over his head again. "That was why, Lakin. I didn't want you or my family to make sacrifices for me—"

"Like you make?" she interjected. "You sacrificed your college education to go right to work on the oil rigs so you could help your mom and siblings." She'd understood that then. But what she had assumed would be just a few years had become seven, nearly eight years of long distance. "And you choose to keep working there instead of starting a business with me."

"Because I don't have enough money saved yet for us to give up our day jobs and start up a business," he said. "We have to be sure we have enough reserves to give us time to get the business up and running."

While Troy hadn't physically gone away for college like she had, Lakin knew that he took online courses in business. He probably knew more than she did even though she had the degree. And he wasn't going to agree with what she'd done any more than she agreed with what he'd done.

But right now, even though it made her feel like a hypocrite, she couldn't confess to what she'd done. She was too upset over his injury. That concerned her more than anything else. She hated that he'd been hurt even more than she hated that he'd chosen to go through his medical ordeal alone.

"So what are you facing?" she asked him. "You're obviously still in pain, still limping…"

He nodded. "I'm still healing. The swelling went down, and the paralysis went away, so I can start physical therapy now. But I still have some numbness and tingling, and I have to be careful until I'm completely healed or…"

"It could come back," she said, alarm shooting through her. "The paralysis could return?" She couldn't imagine Troy, who'd always been so strong and fit, feeling that helpless. He must have been terrified; he probably still was. She didn't dare show him how scared she was for him.

He shrugged, then grimaced slightly, as if the movement had tweaked those healing muscles again. "I don't know," he said. "I'm not even sure if the doctors know for sure, but they warned me that I have to be careful."

"Chasing after intruders wasn't being careful," she pointed out. Anger joined her fear. "You shouldn't have done that." And not just because of his back. He could have wound up in the hospital again or worse if the intruder had been dangerous.

She wasn't only angry that he'd put his life in danger again. She was angry that he'd shut her out. "And you shouldn't have kept what happened to you from me and your family," she said.

She was so damn hurt that he had. While she hadn't had the chance to tell him what she'd done, the two things were not the same. He'd been hurt and hadn't reached out to her for comfort or emotional support.

He reached out for her now, but she stepped back and shook her head. If he touched her, the same thing would happen that always happened. She would forget all about how she felt when he was gone and focus only on how wonderful it was that he was home, that he was with her again. While they always made the most of their time together, it was never long enough. He always went back to the oil rigs.

The thought of him going back again to where he'd been hurt…and knowing that he could be hurt again or, worse, wind up dead like his dad, filled her with more terror than finding out someone had broken into her cabin.

"Lakin…" His voice was gruff with emotion, and his beautiful green eyes glistened with it. But was it regret? Did he feel bad for not contacting her?

"Why, Troy?" she asked. "Why did you shut me out?"

"Because I love you," he said.

She shook her head again. "No. You would have wanted me there with you then." He had kept her in the dark and at a distance for far too long. She'd wondered before how long they could continue that way, but now she realized it might already be too late to salvage their relationship.

TROY'S ARMS ACHED to hold Lakin, but she kept stepping back from him, as if he was one of the bullies who used to pick on her on the playground. But he'd been the one who'd protected her from them, just like he'd wanted to protect her from what had happened to him.

He knew that she would have been upset and scared for him; he could see that she was now, just from hearing about his fall. He'd wanted to save her and his family from the uncertainty and fear of his paralysis. But apparently he'd only put it off; he hadn't saved her from it.

And he really hadn't saved her from the intruder he'd chased through the woods. The person probably would have run off anyway if they had just been desperate for food, like Eli and Kansas seemed to think. Although if they had really wanted only food from her, they would have just had to ask. Lakin was so sweet and selfless that she would give someone her last morsel of food even if she was hungry, too.

"I do love you," he said, his heart aching. He reached out again to touch her cheek, to slide his fingertips across her soft skin. "I love you so much."

Tears filled her dark eyes, and she shook her head again. One of the tears slipped down her cheek, and he wiped it away with his fingertips. He hated that she doubted his feelings. He hated even more that he'd hurt her.

"I am so sorry," he said. "I just didn't want to put you and my mom through that uncertainty. I wanted to know what I was facing before I told anyone what happened." It had made sense at the time. But now…

"What are we facing, Troy?" she asked. "What kind of relationship do we have if we're not there for each other in the bad times as well as the good times?"

He sucked in a breath, alarmed at the question. Had she had doubts before about their relationship, or were her doubts new…and because of what he'd done?

"I'm sorry I didn't call you," he said.

"If you had it all to do over again, would you?" she asked. "Would you call me if you get hurt again?"

"Lakin…" He couldn't lie to her.

She stepped back again so that his hand dropped back to his side. "You should leave."

"But…" She had never turned him away before. In fact she was the one who usually pulled him inside this cabin with her, who led him toward the bed. But today she hadn't even kissed him yet.

Of course there'd been the intruder, and now… He wasn't sure what was going on now. His body was aching, but it wasn't just because of the fall. He wanted her, needed her, and she was turning him away for the first time in their lives.

Like he'd turned her away? Was she getting back at him for not calling her?

No. Lakin wasn't petty. She was kind and forgiving and loving.

And maybe he'd taken all of that for granted for much too long.

"You shouldn't be alone tonight," he said. "What if the intruder comes back?"

She shook her head. "They won't. They got food. Lunch meat and chips and cookies. It was probably a teenager. Maybe a runaway." Her brow furrowed, and her dark eyes glittered again with more tears, sympathy for the person who'd robbed her.

That was how sweet Lakin was.

And sometimes naive.

"Teenagers can still be dangerous," he pointed out.

That shadow he'd chased through the woods had been big and broad. Even if the intruder was a teenager, he was bigger and more muscular than Lakin, probably than Troy was right now. Hopefully the physical therapy he was starting in Shelby would get him back in shape soon, as well as get rid of the limp and the pain. It was frustrating enough that he couldn't work right now, but it was even more frustrating that he couldn't really protect the woman he loved.

"I'm going to dead bolt the doors like I promised Eli I would," she said. "I'll be fine."

"I won't," he said. "Not with you mad at me. I won't leave you here alone. I'll be outside in my truck." He turned and started for the door. Standing in one place had stiffened his back even more, making his limp more pronounced. He grimaced at the twinge of pain.

"Don't go," she said.

He released a breath of relief. Another thing he loved about Lakin was that she could never stay angry for long. She was always quick to forgive. Maybe he'd been counting on that when he hadn't called her.

But then she said begrudgingly, "You can sleep on the couch."

Before he could even turn around, he heard the door to the bedroom close and then lock.

He'd shut her out when he hadn't called her after his fall, but he'd done so out of consideration. He hadn't wanted to worry her until he knew what he was facing. But she was shutting him out now, and he wasn't sure why.

Was she just too angry to forgive him yet? Or was she completely over him?

Another body was found.

Will stared down at the text on his phone, but the sudden rush of tears blinded him for a moment as he thought of Caroline. Of how he and Eli had found his beautiful sister sitting with her killer, both deceased, on the couch in the home where Eli had grown up, where he'd once felt so safe. It hadn't been safe for any of his family that day. His parents had been murdered in their bed. And his dear sweet baby sister had been strangled to death at seventeen.

But it wasn't her body that had been found today. It had to be the woman who'd been reported missing: Dawn Ellis.

Poor Dawn and her family. Her poor family.

Will knew all too well the devastating heartbreak they would be suffering. He and his brother had suffered like that. On that one horrific day, they'd lost so much: their parents and their beautiful younger sister. All taken from them much too soon and much too cruelly.

"What is it?" asked Sasha, his beautiful wife.

He jumped a bit, startled by her sudden appearance. She'd been out in her studio, the one he'd built behind their house for her pottery. She was so damn talented. And beautiful. Her once light brown hair was silvery gray now, making her blue eyes even brighter in her delicately featured face.

"Eli sent a text," Will said.

"It upset you," she said.

"I think they found that missing woman," he said.

Eli was pretty careful to not give him too many details, but the ABI lieutenant always gave Will a heads-up so he wouldn't be surprised, like they'd both been surprised on that horrible, tragic day.

Sasha released a shaky sigh. "She's dead."

Will nodded. "I think it's her." Unless there was another victim. Two of the bodies that had already been discovered were yet to be identified. Somewhere, their families were probably hoping they would be found alive. But a killer had made certain that wasn't possible.

"Eli will catch him," Sasha said, and she slipped her arms around Will's waist.

He wound his arms around her, too. He wasn't sure if he was offering her comfort or taking it. Or both. "I hope soon," he whispered. He didn't want anyone else to suffer the way his family had, the way the families of these recent victims had to be suffering.

"I need you to be careful," he said as he pressed a kiss to the top of her head.

She tipped her head up and smiled reassuringly at him. "I do not fit that profile. I'm not a young woman with brown hair." Her smile slipped away, probably with the realization he'd come to a while ago.

Lakin and Kansas were young dark-haired women. While his niece was armed and prepared to defend herself, Lakin was more vulnerable, if just because of her open, trusting heart. And she was alone so much; Troy was gone for work more than he was in Shelby. Will loved Troy like one of his children, but he wished the man would settle down with Lakin, especially given the current circumstances.

"We should have Lakin move back home for a while," he suggested. Then he could keep an eye on both her and his beautiful wife.

Sasha nodded and released a shaky breath that was warm against his throat. "Yes, that would be good."

If Lakin agreed…

But he had a feeling that if Lakin moved, it wasn't going to be back home. It would be into the new enterprise she was starting. He felt a rush of excitement for her over that and was glad she'd reached out to him for help, though it was their little secret for now.

He didn't know if that was because she wasn't ready yet to tell Parker that she was leaving the business or because she wasn't ready yet to tell Troy what she'd done.

But at this moment the most important thing was to keep her safe.

Chapter Six

Guilt gripped Lakin for making Troy sleep on the couch. His back was injured, and he was too long for the sofa. While it was better than if he'd tried to sleep in his truck like he'd threatened, she should have given him her bed. But she would have been tempted to share it with him if she hadn't closed and locked the door between them.

There was nothing between them now as she stood over the couch and stared down at him. His handsome face was relaxed, no grimace on it as he was curled up on his side. He looked fine. Too fine for her to resist, so she hurried past him and out the door, closing it softly behind herself so she wouldn't wake him up.

So she didn't lean down and brush her mouth across his firm lips. She didn't run her hands over his muscular chest. She didn't straddle him on the sofa and make love to him like she wanted. She wanted him so much, but she felt as if the only reason he'd stayed was to protect her.

She didn't need him to take care of her; she needed him to let her take care of him for once. But even when he'd been hurt, he hadn't reached out for her help. And that hurt her so much.

She wanted to be there for him like he tried to be for her. But he hadn't tried that hard lately. He'd been gone so much.

While he was sleeping peacefully, she hadn't been able to rest at all the night before. The break-in had rattled her, and even though she was comforted that she wasn't alone in the cabin, she hadn't been able to sleep. Troy was so close, yet not close enough. She'd wanted him beside her, his arms wrapped around her, her head against his chest.

Maybe she should have unlocked her door and asked him to join her in bed. But they wouldn't have slept then, either. And all that passion would have clouded her judgment even more.

Because she hadn't slept, she headed straight to Roasters, in desperate need of caffeine.

That wasn't likely to assuage her guilt, though. She didn't feel guilty just over making Troy sleep on the couch; she felt guilty over being mad at him for keeping things from her when she was doing the same. She was a hypocrite because she hadn't told him yet what she'd done about the auction of the Shelby Hotel.

She would talk to him. After her coffee…

It was earlier than she usually stopped at the café, so hopefully she wouldn't run into Billy Hoover or Eric Seller. The last thing she needed was either of them asking about her future with Troy again when she was so uncertain of it herself. She would probably burst into tears if they questioned her about her relationship today.

She was tired of waiting for Troy to be present in their relationship. She wanted to start their lives instead of just planning for a future that seemed to never arrive. And she wanted him to want that, too.

The guilt she'd felt earlier dissipated some. She had every right to be angry with him. She was also too hurt and proud to welcome him back with open arms like she did every time he came home after a long time working away.

Although he hadn't been just working this time; he'd been hurt.

She hated thinking of him lying alone in a hospital bed waiting for paralysis to go away, worrying that it wouldn't. He must have been terrified.

But he was the one who'd chosen to go through all that on his own. If he'd let her or his family know, they would have been there to support him. To love him…

Did he no longer want her love or support?

She needed to ask him these questions instead of asking them of herself. But first she needed her coffee.

She easily found a spot to park her SUV. Roasters wasn't that busy yet. There were only a few other patrons sitting at the tables, and one couple was in line in front of her when she walked into the café with two bright blue Roasters mugs. Troy had one that he left at her place.

She almost wished the line was longer. Then she would have more time to think about how to talk to Troy. She needed to get through to him that if he loved her, he should let her be there for him. And then she had to tell him what she'd done when she hadn't been able to reach him.

She released a small sigh that drew Fay, the barista's attention. "Coffee's coming, Lakin. I just brewed a fresh pot when I saw your SUV pull up outside."

She passed both mugs over the counter. "I need two today, please," she said just as a yawn slipped out.

The younger woman nodded. "I understand why. I didn't sleep at all last night, either, not after hearing that terrible news about poor Dawn Ellis. I was really hoping she would be found alive."

Lakin gasped. "They found her?" Why hadn't Eli told her? Probably because they had to verify her identity and notify her family. Her poor family. "Are they sure it's her?"

The woman nodded. "Yeah, late yesterday just on the outskirts of town. They tried to keep the story from coming out, but someone must have leaked it."

Neither Eli nor Kansas had mentioned it yesterday, but then they'd been more concerned about Lakin and her intruder. And maybe they hadn't wanted to scare her any more than she already was. No wonder Kansas had kept advising her to be cautious.

"That's so sad," Lakin murmured, and she felt guilty again. She should have been happy that Troy was alive, that he hadn't been hurt worse. Instead she'd gotten hung up on how he hadn't called her when he'd been hurt. At least she and his family could see him again, could be with him. Unlike Dawn's family.

The barista sighed, and her eyes misted a bit. "We definitely need to be careful out there."

Lakin nodded. "Definitely." She was especially glad that Troy had spent the night. Even though she hadn't slept any better with him there than she probably would have without him, at least she'd been safe. "And please, make that second coffee a regular with a shot of espresso."

"You must be really tired this morning," the barista said with a smile. And then the young woman must have remembered—that was Troy's drink. "Oh..." Fay glanced around the restaurant "...that hot boyfriend of yours is back in town?"

Lakin nodded and tried not to be disappointed that after ten years, he was still only her boyfriend. Not her husband or even her fiancé. Apparently, she didn't need Billy Hoover or Eric Seller to ask about the future of her relationship; she was asking herself.

"I'll hurry it up so you can get right back to him," the barista promised.

A few minutes later, Lakin was trying to juggle both mugs and open the door when someone opened it for her. "Thanks," she said as she stepped out.

But instead of walking into Roasters, the man followed her to her truck parked at the curb just outside the café.

Her skin chilling with uneasiness, she looked up at him. He was tall with a rangy build, iron-gray hair and a lot of lines in his face. One of them was actually a scar, and it ran jagged down the left side of his face. Despite the wrinkles, he was probably just in his sixties, maybe even late fifties. While his hair was gray, his brows were black, like his eyes, and bushy.

Her uneasiness increased. She glanced into the café, hoping that the barista saw what was happening even though Lakin herself wasn't sure what this was.

"I can take it from here," she assured him. She set the coffee mugs on the roof of her SUV so that she could find her key fob in her purse. She wasn't sure if she would need it to unlock her doors or to sound the alarm button on it. There was something menacing about the man. Or maybe that was just her paranoia.

"Lakin," he said. "I've been looking for you for a long time, girl."

She tensed with even more fear. How did he know her name? How did he know her at all? "I… I don't know who you are," she said. And some instinct told her she really didn't want to know him.

He pressed his hand against his heart. "That hurts. But I guess I shouldn't be surprised. It's been a long time since I saw you, girl."

She shook her head. "I don't remember you."

"You were just a little girl," he said. "My little girl. I'm your father."

Instinctively she shook her head. Her father was handsome with kindness and gentleness that radiated from him. She glanced around, wishing he was running around town like usual. But he'd probably already been out for his morning run and was back home again with her beautiful mother.

She shook her head again, denying his claim. "No…"

He narrowed those beady dark eyes of his and leaned closer. "I am your biological father," he said. "You must know that you're adopted. You must remember me and your mother. You weren't a baby when you went missing."

"I didn't go *missing*," she said. "I was *abandoned*." And nobody had come looking for her. That was why the Coltons had been able to adopt her after they'd taken over fostering her. Nobody else had claimed her. "And I was only three years old."

"So you don't remember me at all?" he asked, suspicion in his dark eyes. "But I remember you, my sweet little girl." He smiled at her, but it didn't seem to quite reach his eyes.

Maybe he wasn't happy because she'd made it clear she didn't believe him. Should she? That was what Will and Sasha Colton had taught her; to give everyone the benefit of the doubt. To believe what they said until they were proven wrong. Because nobody had believed young Caroline Colton that she had a stalker…until it was too late.

Was this man a stalker? Was he the one who'd been watching Lakin?

He didn't look like he could be her father any more than the Coltons could be biologically related to her. From her darker complexion and hair and features, she was clearly part Inuit. This man wasn't. The only thing they had in common was the fact they both had dark eyes.

He reached into the pocket of his flannel shirt. "I got this," he said. "I've carried it with me for years, looking for you. And then to find you here…" He pulled out a photograph and held it out to her.

Her fingers shook as she reached for it. The colors had faded with age, leaving the photo in sepia tones, but the woman in it looked like Lakin. Her dark hair was long and straight and parted in the middle, highlighting the same nose and mouth and cheekbones that Lakin had. That woman held a toddler who had dark hair and chubby cheeks, and she wore a little dress. The color was faded, but Lakin knew the dress was pink and came with ruffled underpants. The dress was tucked into a box somewhere in her cabin, the one thing she had left from that time before the Coltons adopted her.

But it wasn't just the woman and the child in the photograph. A man stood next to them, almost towering over them, casting them even more in shadow. He was tall and lean, and even in that photograph, he had a scar on one cheek. In the picture his hair matched the dark color of his bushy black brows. He looked younger but no happier. But then maybe he just didn't smile in photographs. Her brothers had gone through a phase where they had refused to smile, thinking they looked cooler with a scowl.

"That's me, your mama and you," he said, pointing a tobacco-stained fingertip at them. "Don't you remember us, Lakin? Your parents? Your real family?"

She shook her head again, not just because she didn't remember but because he was not her real family. The Coltons were. "No, I don't remember you."

"Well, that's a damn shame," he murmured. "Damn shame…"

She didn't remember him, and she didn't want to believe him although the family motto compelled her to. Her heart was beating fast and hard with fear. She didn't know if she was scared of him or scared of what he might tell her.

She had the urge to escape. To get away from him as fast as she could.

"I… I have to go," she said. "I'm going to be late for work."

"You don't want to talk to your daddy?" he asked with a slight smile as if he was more amused than offended. "You don't want to get to know me better?"

"I don't know you," she said. And despite her family

motto, she was struggling to believe him. But that picture… She couldn't stop staring at it.

"Keep the photograph," he said. "I wrote my cell number on the back. And when you're not so busy, you give me a call, and we can catch up on each other's lives since I lost you, little girl."

He made it sound like he'd just misplaced her somewhere, not like he'd abandoned her.

Unless…

Unless what she'd always believed was true was not what had really happened. What had really happened? Part of her had always wanted to know. So why not ask him? Why not talk to him?

She tore her gaze from the photo to look up, but he was gone. She glanced around, but she didn't see him anywhere. He'd left her again. Was that how he'd done it twenty-two years ago?

And what about her mother? Lakin glanced back at the picture. Where was she?

She flipped the photograph over and saw a phone number scrawled on the back of it along with a name: Jasper Whitlaw. Was that her father's name?

Was that her last name before it became Colton? Her first name had always been Lakin. She'd been talking at three, and she'd been able to tell people that. "Me…" And she would press her thumb in her chest. "…Lakin."

The Coltons often retold that story. But they'd never known her last name. Maybe she'd been too young to remember that.

"Whitlaw," she whispered it aloud, but it didn't sound familiar.

But the woman in the picture, she was definitely

familiar. It was like looking in a mirror. Her mother. Where was she? What was her name?

Lakin could call Jasper Whitlaw and ask him. But she wasn't sure she was ready yet for his answers. Or even to see him again. And at the moment, feeling as raw as she was, she wasn't sure she was ready to see Troy again, either.

TROY JOLTED AWAKE with such a start that a grunt of pain slipped through his lips. He closed his eyes and tensed, waiting to see if he'd awakened Lakin. But there was no other sound in the cabin.

Maybe she was still ignoring him. He opened his eyes and peered around. The bedroom door wasn't locked anymore; it was wide open, so he could see that the bed was made. From the stillness of the cabin, he could tell that it was empty but for him.

She was gone.

He slowly sat upright and blinked to clear the sleep from his vision. The cabin was empty but bathed in sunshine. It wasn't as if she'd sneaked off in the middle of the night. Or worse yet, that someone had sneaked in and taken her.

She'd probably just left for work.

Usually when he came home from a long while away, she would take some personal days to spend time with him. The bed never got made because they rarely left it. Last night she hadn't even wanted him to touch her to comfort her, let alone kiss and make love with her.

He hadn't realized she would be so angry with him for not calling her when he was hurt. But if the situation was reversed…

He grimaced over a twinge of pain, but it was in his heart, not his back. If the situation was reversed, he would have been hurt, too, that she hadn't needed him and turned to him.

"Dammit," he murmured with sudden understanding of how badly he'd screwed up.

She was probably at the office by now, or maybe still at Roasters getting her morning coffee.

He slid his feet into his boots and stood to head to the door, but before he got there, the knob rattled.

The door opened, and Lakin stumbled across the threshold as if someone had pushed her.

"What's wrong?" he asked because she was clearly shaken. He glanced behind her to see if someone had chased her back to the cabin.

She shook her head.

"Where were you?" he asked.

She blinked at him as if she hadn't realized he was there, or maybe she didn't realize where she was. "I… I was at…at Roasters…"

He glanced at her hands. She wasn't holding the bright blue coffee mugs. Instead she clutched what looked like an old photograph in one hand.

"You don't have coffee, Lakin," he pointed out, keeping his voice soft and calm since she seemed so rattled.

Her dark eyes went wide. "I must have left the mugs on the roof of the SUV…"

"Is that why you look so stunned? You haven't had your caffeine fix yet?" he asked, trying to tease her a bit. Maybe she was still just really mad at him—and he understood now why.

She continued to stare at him with that blank expression, like she was in shock. She must have been to drive off with the mugs on the roof of her vehicle.

He was getting scared. "Lakin, what's wrong? What happened that you look so…" *Devastated.* He stepped close and put his hands on her shoulders.

This time she didn't jump back and shake off his touch like she had last night. It was as if she didn't even feel or see him. Her blank stare was unnerving.

"Lakin, I know you're still mad at me, but you have to talk to me," he persisted. "Or I'm going to call your parents or Eli—"

"No! Don't call my parents," she said, her voice cracking. Tears rushed to her eyes.

"Then talk to me," he said, his heart aching over the look on her beautiful face. He hated to see her cry. "Tell me why you're so shaken up right now. What happened? Did somebody bother you? Scare you?"

God, a serial killer was on the loose in Shelby. That scared the hell out of Troy. How had he fallen asleep last night? He hadn't done a very damn good job of protecting her when she'd managed to slip right past him this morning. He hadn't even realized she'd left. What if someone else had slipped past him and hurt her? He would never forgive himself if something happened to her whether he was here or not.

"Did you see the intruder again?" he asked when she still didn't answer. Maybe the person had tried getting into her vehicle and that was why she'd driven off like she had.

Her forehead furrowed as if she was trying to remember. "I… I don't think it was him…" she murmured.

"Him?" So she had seen someone. "Who are you talking about?"

She held out the photograph she'd been clutching. "Him..."

At first glance, Troy thought the woman in the picture was Lakin. They had the same hair, the same facial features that suggested Inuit heritage, but the snapshot was old, the colors faded. He turned it over to see if there was a date on it. Instead he saw a name and what must be a phone number scrawled across the back of it. "Jasper Whitlaw. Who is he?"

"He says he's my father," she whispered, as if she didn't want anyone to overhear what she said.

Troy thought immediately of her father, of Will Colton, with his tall, lean build and dark brown hair and bright blue eyes. He was probably pushing sixty, but he looked like he was in his forties.

Troy flipped the photograph back over and studied the man standing next to the woman who looked like Lakin. That man was lean, too, but in a way that was more hungry than fit. The scar on his cheek and the coldness in his dark eyes were nothing like the warmth in Will Colton's face, especially when Will was with his family. He loved them all so much, but Troy suspected he loved Lakin even a little more, maybe because he knew she needed more love.

Maybe Troy wasn't giving her enough love or time or attention. Hell, there was no maybe about it; he'd been neglecting the woman he loved. But that was because he was trying so hard to save for their future, so that he could buy her the ring she deserved to have, so he could help her finance the business she wanted to start.

After focusing on the woman in the photo and then the man, he turned his attention to the child. With her dark hair and dark eyes and little chubby cheeks, she was adorable. She could have been Lakin twenty some years ago.

"I've pretty much forgotten you were adopted," he admitted. She was so close to her family and so much a part of them that it didn't matter if they shared no DNA; they shared love.

But back in school other kids remembered the story of the little girl in the grocery store, and they hadn't let her forget about it...until Troy and her brothers made certain they stopped taunting her. Billy Hoover had taken a little longer to convince than the others, but eventually Troy had gotten through to him. His knuckles ached a bit with the old memory.

"What does this Jasper Whitlaw want?" Troy asked.

The man had had years to come looking for the child he'd left in a grocery store. Why come back for her now, when she was an adult? When she was a Colton?

She shrugged. "I don't know."

"What did he ask you for?" Troy asked. The guy had to have a reason for showing up now after all these years. He had to want something.

"He said that he just wants me to give him a call when I'm ready to talk to him."

"So he just wants to talk?" Troy asked. He didn't believe that for a minute. *Believe* was the Colton family motto, but it wasn't his, especially not after someone had broken into her cabin the day before.

Lakin nodded. "That's why he wrote his number on the back of the photograph and gave it to me," she said.

Troy wanted to wad up the picture for some reason, and he wasn't sure why. But something didn't feel right about this. Maybe the timing.

"Do you think he's the person who broke in here yesterday?" Troy asked.

She gasped. "Why would he do that? I doubt he needs food that desperately."

The man in the picture looked hungry to Troy. Of course a lot could have changed since then. It occurred to Troy that the stolen food could have been a misdirection, someone wanting the break-in to look more innocent than it was.

"I don't like this," Troy admitted. "I don't think you should call him."

"Why not?" she asked.

"I don't think you should trust him," Troy said. "I think he's after something."

"What?" she asked.

"Colton money."

She stepped back and shook her head. "*You* are the one who is obsessed with money."

"What? I don't want any Colton money," he assured her. He wanted desperately to pay his own way and hers; that was why he wanted to wait to propose and start their business until he had more money saved.

She flinched as if he'd slapped her and said, "But I'm a Colton."

He moved closer to her and gently touched his fingertips to her cheek. "Yes, you are, and I don't want your money."

"If we were really a couple, it would be *our* money,"

she said. She stepped back again so that his hand fell to his side.

"We are really a couple," he said, but he felt the same panic from when he'd finally realized why she was mad at him. And that she had every reason to be.

"No, we're not. You would have called me when you got hurt. You would have wanted me there for you, to support you, to comfort you."

"Lakin…" Troy didn't know what to say or how to make it up to her. He had wanted her there, but he'd been so afraid that the paralysis wouldn't go away. He hadn't wanted to stick her with someone as helpless and hopeless as he'd felt those weeks in the hospital bed.

Clearly she wasn't interested in hearing his excuses. She took the photo back from him. "But this isn't about money to me. It's about information."

"What kind of information?" he asked.

"I should know about my heritage, my genetics, what medical conditions I might pass onto kids someday." She looked up at him, her dark eyes intent on his face. "The kids *we* talked about having someday."

"We were kids ourselves when we talked about having kids," he murmured, thinking of all their teenage dreams. But then his dad had died, and Troy had been consumed with grim reality rather than dreams.

"Did you outgrow me, Troy? Our relationship? Do you want different things now?" she asked, her voice cracking slightly with emotion.

He wanted the same things he always had. A life with *her*. But if his back got screwed up again… He didn't want her to wind up like his mother, raising kids alone, struggling to make ends meet, crying from the stress after she thought they were all asleep.

"I can't think about the future right now," he said. "Not until I know how completely I'm going to heal." He was starting physical therapy soon. How his body reacted to that would determine if he would be able to go back to work on the oil rigs. Or anywhere…

"It doesn't matter to me how badly you're hurt," she said. "If you'd stayed paralyzed, it would have changed nothing for me. I love you."

"You're being naive, Lakin," he said. "It would have changed everything."

"Not my love," she said. "But apparently it changed yours." She stepped back again, drew in a shaky breath and pointed toward the door she'd left open when she stumbled in moments ago. "Just leave. I need some time alone."

"Lakin, I do love you," he insisted.

But she just shook her head, refusing to believe him.

He was tempted to remind her of her family motto: *believe*. She'd told him that once, but clearly she wasn't thinking like a Colton right now. Was she a Whitlaw? Or was this Jasper person running some scam on her?

"Please, let me be here for you," he said. He had a horrible feeling she was in danger.

"Why?" she asked. "You didn't let me be there for you. Go." She didn't wait for him to leave before she went into her bedroom like she had the night before. And like the night before, she closed and locked that door, shutting him out like she must feel he'd shut her out.

Their future was in danger, but not for the reason he'd believed—not because of his injury but because of him.

Why couldn't she see that he'd been thinking about her, that he hadn't wanted her to make any sacrifices for him? He loved her so much that he wanted all her dreams to come true.

Even if those dreams no longer included him.

THE HOOK WAS BAITED. Now the fisherman just had to wait for the right moment to reel her in.

Then, finally, after all these years of planning, he could be certain this part of his life was over.

And so was hers…

Chapter Seven

Once the door to the cabin closed behind Troy, Lakin left her bedroom and went into the RTA office. She spent the day there, doing what she always did: taking calls, talking to clients and vendors, putting out little fires. And yet she felt like it wasn't real, like she was in a *Groundhog Day*-like dream. She was doing the same thing over and over, but she wasn't really present.

She wasn't sure where she was, but she knew where she wanted to be. And once she left the office, she hopped in her SUV and headed there. Home.

Not to her empty cabin but to the house where she'd grown up with her brothers and her mom and dad.

Because it was home and would always be, she didn't knock. She just pushed open the kitchen door and walked in, surprising her parents at the counter. Her dad had his arms around her mom as she was chopping up something on the cutting board, and he was nuzzling her neck as she squirmed and giggled.

Lakin's heart warmed with love for them and for the love that they had for each other all these years later. They'd been high school sweethearts like her and Troy, but unlike her and Troy, they'd shared their vision for family and their future.

And their love thrived even or maybe especially during the tragedies they'd suffered.

"Oh, there's our baby girl!" Mom exclaimed as she dropped the knife and rushed over to hug Lakin.

Lakin smiled over being called baby. She was taller and bigger boned than her mother. Sasha Colton had a delicate build and facial features, but she was strong and fiercely loving and fun. She had so many friends because everyone who met her became her friend.

What about…? The woman in the photograph suddenly popped into Lakin's head, the woman who'd looked so much like her. She felt a twinge of guilt.

Sasha Colton was the woman who'd raised her, who'd read to her at night and helped her with homework and talked to her about friends and boys and life.

Lakin tightened her arms around her mother, holding tight to her for a moment and to those memories. She breathed in the scents in the kitchen. The roasting chicken. The cinnamon and nutmeg spices from the Dutch apple pie cooling on the counter. And her mother's hair brushed across her cheek, soft and smelling like a combination of the cooking aromas, spring and clay.

She smiled again. "I love you so much, Mom," she said.

Sasha clasped her tightly. She was as famous for her hugs as for her pottery and her cooking. "I love you, too, baby."

"What about me?" her dad asked.

Lakin and her mother laughed. "Of course we love you, too," they said together.

When they stepped back from each other, her dad hugged Lakin. Almost too tightly, like he was trying too hard to hang onto her.

Did he know about Jasper Whitlaw's visit? Had Troy told him? He might have out of concern, but then he should have been concerned that he would make her even more mad at him. She doubted he would risk that.

Maybe Eli or Kansas had told Dad about the break-in at the cabin last night. But she didn't think either of them would want to worry him when they'd really seemed to believe it was just a hungry vagrant.

But was that really the case? While she hadn't felt that strange sensation of being watched since this morning, she felt it now. Was it because of how intently her parents were staring at her or…

Was there someone outside watching?

She glanced through the front windows of the house and noted a few trucks and other vehicles parked on the street. With the sun shining on the windows, she couldn't see inside them. Maybe they weren't all empty. Maybe someone was out there peering back at her. Whitlaw? Or someone else?

Once her dad released her, she walked over to the window and closed the blinds.

"Too bright?" Sasha asked.

Lakin nodded. The truth was she wanted to shield her parents from that watchful gaze. She wanted to protect them. So she couldn't tell them about Jasper Whitlaw and that photograph. She knew they would seek him out and try to get answers for her like they'd tried all those years ago. For some reason, she didn't want them anywhere near Whitlaw or her long-ago past.

After they adopted her, the Coltons had given her such a wonderful, perfect childhood. Even though she was an adult now, they were still here for her, helping her make her dreams come true. If she hadn't reached out to her father during that auction for the Shelby hotel, she would have lost her opportunity for the business she always wanted. But, despite what Troy believed, the money wasn't as important as the fact that her dad believed in her.

He and her mother always had.

"I don't know if I tell you enough how much I love you two," Lakin said.

Her mom smiled. "You definitely tell us enough, but I love hearing it." She hugged Lakin again. "And I hope you know how much we love you."

"I have never doubted your love," she assured them.

"Uh-oh," her dad murmured.

"What?" her mom asked with a glance at him.

"I feel like there is a story behind that statement," he said. "Trouble with Troy? I know he's been gone a long time…"

"He's back," Lakin said.

Her dad arched an eyebrow. "And you're here without him?"

She nodded. "I need some space," she admitted.

"Uh-oh," her father said again.

Tears rushed to her eyes, but she blinked them away. She didn't want to start crying because she was afraid she might not stop. "Can we talk about that later?" she asked.

She had to figure out first if she could just be happy that Troy was okay and not worry about how he hadn't called anyone when he got hurt or how uncertain he was about the future. She wanted to be understanding, but she'd been patient so long with him. She wasn't sure she had any patience left.

"Of course," her mom said. Then she turned toward her husband and gave him a pointed look. "We're not going to pry, are we, Will?"

He sighed. "No, we're not."

Lakin smiled in appreciation; she knew how hard it was for him to not step in and help her. Ever since they brought her home, her father and brothers had been the white knights trying to slay her dragons. Mom had always been the one encouraging her to slay her own dragons and having the faith in her that she had the strength to do that.

But now her mom's face flushed a bit and she murmured, "We were actually going to call you about moving back home for a while."

Lakin groaned. "Eli told you?"

"About that girl's body being found," her dad said with a nod. "Yes. And I know you probably think we're being overly cautious, but you shouldn't be alone in your cabin. It's too far from the other guest cottages."

It didn't sound to Lakin like they knew about the break-in the day before. That was good. It was also the least of the things she was keeping from them right now. But she didn't want to worry them any more than they already were.

"And you said you want some space from Troy, so you really will be alone out there," her dad added.

"Troy spent last night on the couch," she admitted,

Her mom smiled. "Of course he would be worried, too, and want to protect you. He loves you so much."

Lakin sighed. "I'm not so sure about that anymore." Did he really love her, or was he just used to protecting her and everyone else in his family? He probably believed that he'd been protecting them when he didn't call after his fall.

"What happened?" her dad asked, his long body stiffening with outrage. Like he intended to go defend her honor.

Tears sprang to her eyes again, blurring her vision for a moment. He was her father no matter what Jasper Whitlaw claimed he was; he hadn't been there for her like Will Colton had always been.

"I don't want to pry, honey," her mom said as she slid her arm around her shoulders. "But you seem really upset, and you might feel better if you talk about it."

"Troy got hurt…" her voice cracked "…badly on the oil rig."

Her mother gasped. "Is he all right?"

Lakin nodded. "Now. And I am relieved and grateful that he is." If he hadn't recovered… She couldn't even consider the horror of that without more tears rushing to her eyes.

"But?" her mother prodded.

"But he was in the hospital for weeks, and he didn't call me," she said. "He didn't let me know."

"He probably didn't want to worry you," her dad said.

"He still should have called," her mom said. "Men and their foolish pride, trying so hard to be strong for us." The look she gave her husband was telling.

Lakin understood. These killings had to have brought back all the pain of his family tragedy, the loss of his parents and sister. She hugged him.

Her father patted her back, comforting her instead of accepting her comfort. "You and Troy will work this out," he said. "I don't remember a time that you weren't in love with him and he with you."

Neither did Lakin. She'd loved him for so long. But she sighed again. "I don't know if we want the same things anymore," she explained. She wanted it all, the business, kids, a family...

"Oh," Mom said, her brow furrowing beneath a lock of silvery gray hair. "That's hard."

It was. But so was this, being here with her parents and keeping so much from them. Lakin wanted to tell them both everything like she always had. But she didn't want to worry them. Like Troy hadn't wanted to worry her...

Maybe she was a hypocrite to be mad at him for doing what she was doing. While she could forgive him for not telling her about his accident right away, she wasn't sure if she could continue on the way that they'd been for so long, this long-distance limbo waiting for their future together to start.

Life was too short for that, as his accident should have made him realize. As the horrible deaths of those women had made her realize.

"Well, dinner is almost ready," her mom said. "I hope you're hungry."

Despite the delicious smells, Lakin's stomach churned at the thought of food. She shook her head. "I had a late lunch. I didn't stop in for dinner, just to check on you two."

"We're fine," her dad said. "But we would be better if you'd stay with us."

She smiled at his not-so-subtle manipulation. "I will be fine in my cabin. Like I told Troy, I need some time alone."

"Right now isn't the safest time to be alone," her father persisted.

She sighed. "I promise I'll be fine." She hugged them both again. "Love you, and I will see you later."

As she left, she couldn't help but feel like she shouldn't have come at all. That she'd brought whoever was watching her to the loving home that Will and Sasha Colton had made for Lakin and her brothers.

She wanted that person, that stalker, to leave with her; she didn't want whatever was going on with her to touch her family or hurt them in any way.

Troy felt like a stalker. He'd been following Lakin around all day, sitting in his truck, keeping an eye on her, making sure that nothing and nobody threatened her. So it was kind of ironic when he received a threat.

It was a call from his supervisor. Troy answered it, thinking the man was just calling to check up on him, not so much because he cared about his health but because he wanted him back on the job.

"What the hell are you thinking, Amos?"

"What do you mean?" Troy asked. "You know I'm not cleared yet to return to work."

"So you're suing the company? You're not going to win. In fact you're going to lose big and probably more than just your job."

"What do you mean?" Troy repeated. More than just his job? What else could his employer take from him?

But Harrison didn't answer him, just disconnected the call.

"What the hell was that about?"

Troy texted Mitch: I take it you contacted the oil company. I just got an interesting call.

Mitch texted back: Don't talk to them again. Let me handle everything.

Gladly.

The last thing Troy wanted to deal with was work when he was home. He didn't even want to think about it. He wanted to focus only on Lakin, especially now with that weird man accosting her and claiming to be her father.

And the break-in...

They had to be related, more so than she probably was to the man. But the woman in the picture was clearly her biological mother, so he understood why she'd been so shaken. And why she would want to learn more.

He just didn't want anyone hurting her. Not Jasper Whitlaw, not her biological mother, the intruder, that serial killer or even himself.

But it was too late for him. He'd already hurt her. Now he had to do everything he could to make it up to her. Like keeping her safe.

However, after an uneventful day sitting outside the RTA office, he'd begun to think he was just paranoid.

But when she drove from the office to her parents' house, he wasn't the only one following her. Another truck was between his SUV and hers. It followed every turn she made. When she parked in her parents' driveway, the truck pulled up to the curb across the street from her childhood home.

Somebody was following her. Someone besides him.

Troy wanted that person to know he'd seen them. He edged away from the curb and started down the street to where they'd parked. He wanted to see who this person was. He wanted to know who was following Lakin.

But when he got close to the truck, the old vehicle pulled away from the curb and sped off down the street. Undeterred, Troy followed.

Despite its rusty condition and worn-looking tires, the truck was fast. Puffs of black smoke from the exhaust clouded Troy's vision, so he couldn't see the license plate nor could he tell what make or model it was. He pressed harder on the accelerator and held tight to the steering wheel as they rounded the road's sharp curves out of town, toward the mountains.

The driver had to know the area or was just a damn good driver. They barely kicked up any gravel on the side of the road whereas Troy's tires dropped off the asphalt a few times and spewed gravel up behind him. He eased up on the accelerator, slowing down for the next sharp curve. But when he rounded it, he didn't see any sign of the truck he'd been following.

Had it gotten that far ahead of him?

He continued on, driving more slowly, checking the side of the road. But as the road wound higher into the mountains, there was less room on either side. On the right was the side of mountain; on the left, a steep drop.

"Where did you go?" Troy muttered. He came around another curve, and there it was, in the center of the road, blocking his way.

He tapped his brakes and tightened his grasp on the steering wheel, swerving so he wouldn't hit the rusted-out truck. His tires dropped off the asphalt, sending gravel and rocks tumbling down the side of the mountain. He jerked the wheel the other way, trying to correct, trying to stop himself from driving right off the mountain.

But it was too late.

AFTER LEARNING THAT the serial killer had claimed another victim, Will had been anxious to see Lakin and make sure that she was all right. But her visit hadn't reassured him at all.

"She'll be okay," Sasha assured him. "Our little girl is tough."

Abandoned at three, she'd had to be tough, but she'd never gotten bitter or resentful. She was such a loving, forgiving person. So beautiful outside and in, like Caroline.

His niece, Kansas, looked more like his late little sister, but something about Lakin reminded him more of the girl who'd never aged beyond seventeen because of an obsessed stalker. Caroline had drawn people to her with her beauty and her spirit, and Lakin had that same spirit. Her smile lit up a room. He remembered the first time they'd seen her, and his boys, older than her and rough-and-tumble, had been immediately drawn to her. They'd fallen for her as hard as he and Sasha had.

As hard as Troy Amos had.

He sighed. "I would feel better if Troy was staying with her."

"He did last night, and even though Lakin wants some space, he won't be far away from her," Sasha said. "Troy Amos is proud, but the man is no fool. He knows Lakin is the love of his life."

"As he is hers," Will said. "It's so hard to see any of our kids hurting."

"She's tough," Sasha repeated. "She'll survive some heartache."

"Do you think that's all that was bothering her?" Will asked.

"You don't?"

He shook his head. He knew their little girl well. "She got out of here fast, and closing the blinds…"

"You think she's worried someone was watching her?" Sasha asked, her blue eyes widening with alarm.

His blood chilled at the thought that someone could be watching Lakin like someone had been watching Caroline all those years ago. Back then the authorities, and even their parents, hadn't believed that Caroline's *fan* was actually dangerous.

Jason Stevens had proved how dangerous he was.

If someone was watching Lakin, hopefully they weren't a killer.

Chapter Eight

The minute Lakin stepped out of her parents' house, she'd noticed the trucks speeding off down the road. They were both old, one more rusted than the other. The less rusted one showed traces of teal blue paint, and there was a shiny chrome toolbox in the bed of the truck.

"Troy…"

Was he the one who'd been watching her? But his gaze had never creeped her out; it had always warmed her with love and desire, somehow both reassuring and exciting. And he'd just returned to Shelby, so there was no way he was the one who'd been watching her over the past couple of weeks.

Had that been Jasper Whitlaw? Was that who Troy had sped after? Or was it someone else in the other vehicle?

Anxious to find out what was going on, she hopped into her SUV and headed after the two trucks.

She wasn't brave enough to drive as fast as they were around those sharp curves. The road was too narrow the higher it wound up the mountain, leaving rock on one side and nothingness on the other. She didn't bother trying to call or text Troy. She didn't want to be distracted and she didn't want to distract him from whatever he was doing.

A high-speed chase up a mountain? Who was he so intent on catching that he was risking his life? And this after he'd had such a close call falling off the oil rig. She shuddered as fear gripped her.

"Stop!" she called out, wishing he could hear her. They were going so fast, though, that she quickly lost sight of them. She slowed down, peering off the side and around the curves ahead.

A truck nearly sideswiped her as it raced past. It was so fast that she couldn't see the driver nor the vehicle itself clearly. She jerked her wheel toward the right and nearly struck rock. When she pulled back to the left, she glanced in her rearview mirror. The truck gave a quick flash of brake lights as it slowed. But it didn't stop and soon disappeared from view.

Where was Troy? Why was the one vehicle heading back down, but he wasn't following it?

"Troy?" she called out as if he could hear her. But then she heard the sound of another motor. Smoke was billowing from an exhaust pipe sticking up from the side of the road. That and a rear bumper were all she could see. Troy's truck.

She braked, engaged the hazard lights and jumped out and raced across the road. Her heart pounded with fear that she was too late.

And she'd been such a bitch to him.

Sure, he hadn't called when he got hurt, but he'd been hurt. And scared. And sure, he hadn't reached out to her, but it hadn't been about her. Since he'd come home, she'd made it all about her. No wonder he hadn't reached out when he was hurt; he hadn't wanted to comfort her or focus on her. He'd wanted to focus on healing.

If he was hurt again, he might have undone all that healing. How hard it must be for him to have to live with the fear that paralysis could return if he wasn't careful.

"Troy!" she yelled.

The rear tires of the truck spun, gravel flying as he tried to back up, but the truck didn't move backward. Instead it slipped a few more inches forward, over the steep incline of rock and gravel that made up the side of the mountain.

"Troy! Get out!" she yelled over the roar of the engine he was gunning. The truck was going to go over the steep side with him in it. This would not be a fall that either his truck or he would survive. "Troy!"

He must have heard her or seen her in the side mirror because he rolled down his window. "Get out of here, Lakin! You're going to get hurt."

"No. You get out of there!" she shouted back. "Jump out before it goes over!"

But he kept spinning his back wheels, spewing more gravel. Yet again, instead of going backward, the truck slipped forward a bit more.

"Get out!" she yelled again.

"If I take my foot off the gas, it's going over," he told her as he kept gunning the engine.

Her heart pounded hard. "What can I do?" She'd left her phone in her purse. But if she ran to get it and the truck went over... Tears burned her eyes. "I love you," she said.

"What the hell are you two doing?" a voice asked, the words slightly slurred.

Lakin glanced behind her to see Billy Hoover hanging out the side window of his truck, staring down at them. "Billy!" Was his the truck that had nearly run her off the road and probably Troy as well?

"Do you have a tow strap?" Troy yelled out his window.

Billy nodded, then pushed his greasy red hair out of his face.

"Hurry!" Lakin said. At the moment she was less concerned that Billy might have caused the crash than she was about making him help rescue the man she loved.

She was the one who wrapped the tow strap around Troy's hitch and then Billy's, making sure both ends were secure. Billy didn't even get out of his truck, but that was fine.

"Gun it!" she yelled at them both.

Gravel flew and metal crunched as Troy's truck came up the side of the mountain and bounced back onto the road, colliding with the back bumper of Billy's truck as the redhaired man abruptly stopped.

Troy hopped out of his truck. Lakin would have rushed to hug him, but her legs were shaking too badly. She couldn't get over how close she'd come to losing him forever. If that truck had gone over... She glimpsed over the steep drop. There was no way he would have survived that fall.

"You're going to have to pay for that, Amos," Billy shouted over his loud motor.

"Like you can tell what damage my truck did to yours," Troy remarked as he unwound the strap from his hitch.

Before he could take it off Billy's, the other man sped

away, the strap trailing behind him. The dents and dings on Billy's rusted truck were undoubtedly caused by how the man drove. Despite his help, Lakin was tempted to call the police. Billy had obviously been drinking. And if he'd caused the crash, she would.

"What happened?" Lakin asked Troy, her heart still pounding frantically even though he was back on solid ground. She wanted to run and hug him even now, but she wasn't sure her legs would hold her up.

He leaned against the side of his truck still idling in the road near hers. Maybe he was as shaken as she was. "Someone ran me off the road."

"Was it Billy?" she asked.

He glanced in the direction their old school nemesis had gone. "I don't know for sure. It was a rusted truck, too, but I didn't get a good look at it or the driver."

Could it be Billy who was watching her? She hadn't considered it, but he'd been a bully as a child. What could he be now? A stalker? A serial killer?

She shivered as she had that sensation again that someone was watching her. Watching both of them now, and maybe getting ready to try something…while she and Troy were just standing in the road, both easy targets.

"Let's get out of here," Troy said, and he levered himself away from the side of his pickup. "It's not safe standing in the road or even parked alongside it. Get in your vehicle, too, and let's head back to your cabin."

Lakin didn't argue with him. He could have died if Billy hadn't come along when he had. Even though Troy hadn't been able to see who'd forced him off the road, they needed to call the police. She would insist that they did.

Later. When they were safe…

INSTEAD OF LOCKING him out, Lakin held open the door for him when Troy walked up to her cabin. Or limped, actually. He tried not to grimace as he climbed the couple of steps and crossed the porch to her.

Going off the road had jarred his back again. Maybe it had already been hurting from taking the turns as fast as he had. And then Billy Hoover jerking the truck up the embankment with the tow strap hadn't helped, either, but it had kept the truck and Troy from sliding down the mountain.

Was Billy the one who'd driven him off in the first place though? If so, from how he'd slurred his words, it might not have been intentional. Either way Troy should have called the police, but he'd wanted to make sure that Lakin was somewhere safe first.

Once he hobbled inside her cabin, he closed and dead-bolted her door. He wasn't sure even that would be enough to keep them safe if someone was really determined to hurt them, though.

Her?

Or him? His supervisor's words echoed inside his head. He might lose more than his job? His life? Or the woman who was the most important part of his life?

Lakin threw her arms around his neck and pressed her body against his. She was trembling. "I was so scared," she said. "I thought I was going to lose you."

He closed his arms around her and held her tightly against him. God, he'd missed her so damn much. Not just the weeks he'd been gone, but since he'd been back there'd been such a distance between them. He tipped her face up to his and lowered his mouth, brushing it across her lips.

Her breath whispered out, heating his skin, making him tingle. He wanted to deepen the kiss, but she stepped back and dropped her arms from around him.

"Why are you following me?" Lakin asked.

"I wanted to make sure you got safely home," he explained. Her safety was what mattered most to him.

"I mean earlier," she said. "I know you were parked outside my parents' house. I saw your truck pull away when I walked outside. Why were you there?"

He sighed and pushed his hand through his hair. "I don't like that after all these years some guy shows up claiming to be your father and that he approached you right after someone broke in here."

"For food."

"You don't know that's really why they broke in," he pointed out. "Because of the break-in and how shaken you were after Whitlaw came up to you, I wanted to keep an eye on you." He wanted more than his eye on her, but she'd put distance between them again. "And I don't think I was the only one following you."

She shivered but didn't argue with him. And she didn't seem at all surprised, either.

"You know someone's been following you," he surmised.

She shrugged. "I don't know for sure. I've never seen anyone. Did you get a look at this person?"

He shook his head. "When I tried, they drove off."

"And you sped off after them," she said, her breath

catching. "You could have been hurt or worse, Troy. That was so dangerous."

"Yes, it was," he agreed. "This person following you is dangerous."

She closed her eyes and sighed. "I just can't be certain someone really is and that it's not just paranoia about the serial killer and the other things that have happened in Shelby lately."

Maybe because he finally knew about all those dangerous occurrences, he'd assumed his supervisor's call was a threat. But it could have been empty. What had happened on the mountain could have been an accident. But he didn't really believe he was overreacting to any of it.

"I think it's better to be safe than sorry," he said. And he would be more than sorry if something happened to Lakin; he would be devastated. "We should call the police."

Though he wasn't sure what they could do about him being run off the road. There were no cameras up in the mountains, and he wouldn't be able to give them a license plate number or even a good description.

"Bobby Reynolds was here the other night with Eli and Kansas," she reminded him. Bobby was the officer who'd been with Shelby PD the longest. "He wasn't concerned about the break-in here at the cabin."

"I'm concerned," Troy said. "About the break-in. About this man claiming to be your father. And whoever's following you…" He wasn't just concerned; he was scared to death that something was going to happen to her. "Is there anything else you haven't told me?"

Her dark eyes widened for a moment, and her mouth opened. Finally she said, "Yes."

He gasped. "What?" Had something else horrible happened?

"When you didn't reply to my emails and texts about the Shelby Hotel, I went to the auction anyway," she said. Then she paused, drew in a deep breath and said, "And I bought it."

"What?" That was not what he'd expected her to say. It had nothing to do with the break-in and Whitlaw. "I don't understand."

"I bought the Shelby Hotel," she said. "I actually got a great deal on it."

"But the auction meant you had to pay cash. No matter how great a deal, how would you have enough cash to purchase it?" he asked.

Her face flushed slightly, and she glanced down. "My dad helped me."

Her dad had helped her because Troy wouldn't. He hadn't seen her texts or emails until after he'd recovered in the hospital. But even if he had seen them before the auction, he wasn't sure he would have been able to help her no matter how cheap the hotel had sold.

"I'm going to pay him back," Lakin said. "I'm working on getting a business loan now for that and for renovations and carrying costs. I have a plan."

"I…" It used to be *we. We had a plan.*

"I got sick of waiting for our future to start, Troy," she said. "I love the idea of turning the old hotel into an experience with gorgeous suites for guests to celebrate their special occasions, like honeymoons and anniversaries."

"The renovations are going to take a lot of money," he said.

He'd driven past it earlier when he'd followed her to her parents' house. Because she'd slowed down as she'd passed it, he had, too. And he'd really studied the place. The wood siding was weathered, and while he hadn't been able to see the roof of the two-story building, he was worried that it probably needed to be replaced, too. If the roof had been leaking, there would be a lot of renovations required inside, too.

"And it's going to take a lot of hard work, too, to get it up and running," he said. He wasn't really capable of the hard work, not yet. And the money. He'd already lost too many weeks' wages, and if he lost his job, too, now, there was no way he could help her with anything.

She nodded. "Yes, I know all that, and I'm willing to do the hard work."

"You have a job." One that he thought she'd enjoyed since she was working with her family.

"I'm going to give Parker my notice soon, once the business loan is approved," she said.

"You've made a lot of decisions while I was gone," he said. He felt left behind and left out, like he was still stuck in that hospital bed, paralyzed while she was running circles around him.

"I tried to get in contact with you—"

"I was in the hospital!" he said, his voice a bit sharp. He would have answered his emails or texts. But his phone had gone in the water with him, and he hadn't been able to replace it until he'd gotten better.

"I didn't know that," she said, "because you didn't

let me know that." The hurt was in her voice and in the depths of her dark eyes.

He released a ragged sigh. "I'm sorry," he said, and he stepped closer to her. "I never meant to hurt you. I was trying to spare you…"

"What? All the fear you must have been feeling?" she asked. "You should not have had to go through that alone, but you chose to. And I don't understand why."

"You don't?" he asked. "You're clearly not eager to call the police about someone following you, about Whitlaw…"

"I don't know that there is anything to tell," she said. "You have more to report with someone running you off the road."

"I'll go by the police department tomorrow," he said. "And you should go with me."

"I'll talk to Eli," she said. "I don't want it getting around town about Whitlaw."

"So you didn't tell your parents about him and the photograph he gave you," he surmised.

She sighed. "No. I didn't want to worry them."

He touched her chin, tipping it up to him. "Why not? Because you love them? I love you, Lakin. That's why I didn't want to worry you."

"It's not just your accident, though," she said. "You're gone so much, and I hear so little from you when you're on the rig."

They were drifting apart. He hadn't realized how much until now.

"Lakin, what's going on with us?" Their relationship had always been so loving and easy. Until now. And he didn't know how to fix it.

She shrugged. "I don't know. We just don't feel like us anymore. Maybe our lives aren't going in the same direction anymore."

"I love you," he repeated, trying to get through to her that he hadn't changed and that his feelings hadn't changed. When she'd been angry with him earlier about not calling her after his accident, she'd doubted his love.

"And I love you," she said, but she sounded more resigned than happy about it.

Until now, he'd never realized that their love might not be enough.

THE TRUCK WITH the rust eating away at the bright blue paint was parked outside her cabin next to her SUV. It should have gone over the side of the mountain with the man inside it. He should have died.

While he'd survived this time, the boyfriend had to go. He was a pain in the ass, and he was going to get in the way and mess up the plan.

He had to die.

Chapter Nine

Lakin saw the hurt and the fear on Troy's face after her declaration of love. She knew he was thinking the same thing she was, that it wasn't enough. They were slipping away from each other.

Earlier tonight, he'd nearly slipped over the side of a mountain. He could have been lost to her forever. She wanted to hang onto him like she had when he walked into the cabin earlier. Like she had every other time he'd come home after a long time away from her. She wasn't thinking about the space that she'd told her parents she wanted from Troy. She was thinking of having no space between them at all.

"I was so afraid when I saw your truck over the side like that…" she murmured, her voice hoarse from yelling at him and at Billy, trying to be heard over their engines.

"I'm fine," Troy said. "I'll go into the police station tomorrow and report it."

"Just that," she said. "I don't want to talk to the local police about Jasper Whitlaw." She refused to call the man her father.

"You need to talk to someone about him. Have someone check him out," Troy persisted.

"I don't want to talk at all," she said. Talking with Troy just led to frustration and disillusionment over their future. She didn't want to talk or think or worry right now. She just wanted to feel.

Him.

She stepped closer to him now and pressed her palms against the sculpted muscles of his chest. Through his T-shirt she could feel the heat of his skin and the hard beat of his heart. Then she moved her hands up over his shoulders and pulled his head down toward hers.

His beautiful green eyes darkened with the desire already burning in her. "Lakin…" he whispered, his voice sounding even more hoarse than hers.

"I need you," she said. "I need to feel that you're alive and well…that you survived…" Not just tonight but that fall as well. Every time she closed her eyes, she imagined him dropping down from the rig into the dark cold depths of the ocean. Disappearing under the water and out of her life.

"I'm alive and well," he said with a smile. "I'm also aching for you…"

He'd limped when he walked up to her cabin earlier. "I don't think you're aching for me," she said.

He took one of her hands and pulled it between their bodies. She could feel the hard ridge of his erection pressing against the fly of his jeans. "I've missed you… so damn much…"

She'd missed him as well, too much to continue to deny herself. Especially after tonight, after he could have died once again. This time, not on a rig but because he'd been trying to catch her stalker. If that was even who it was…

She closed her eyes, trying to shut out those thoughts, those fears.

And he kissed her.

His mouth moved hungrily over hers. She parted her lips, deepening the kiss. As they kissed, they moved together toward the open door to her bedroom. But it was like a slow dance, not the usual frenzy when they first saw each other after a long separation.

Troy didn't pick her up and carry her to the bed. Instead he moved stiffly, walking with her through her bedroom door toward her bed. When they got near it, they fell down onto the comforter. She felt Troy grimace and heard his sharp intake of breath.

She pulled back, panting for air herself, and asked, "Are you okay?"

He nodded, but his jaw was clenched like he was gritting his teeth. Was he in pain?

"Can you do this?" she asked. "Or will this hurt you more?"

"It'll hurt me more to not be with you," he said. "I have been aching for you, Lakin. To kiss you, to touch you…" And he kissed her again.

Then he began to undress her. Every inch of skin he uncovered, he caressed and kissed. He glided his mouth over her shoulder and then along the ridge of her collarbone and down to her breasts. As he drew one nipple into his mouth, he stroked the other with his thumb.

She was the one hurting now, her body tense and needy for his. She tried to touch him, too, but gently, so she wouldn't hurt him.

But he was so focused on her. He moved his head from her breasts over her stomach to her core. And he made love to her with his mouth. As he did, she came, crying out softly with the pleasure and the release flowing through her.

But it wasn't enough. He wasn't close enough.

"Please," she murmured. "I need you."

"*I* need *you*."

But he hadn't. When it counted most, he'd shut her out. She tried to shut that thought off, push it out of her mind. She focused only on him, gliding her hands and mouth over his muscled chest and arms.

It was as if their clothes had dissolved. She'd barely noticed him undressing himself. But now she took advantage of his nakedness and wrapped her hand around his pulsating erection.

He sucked in a breath, then he moved between her legs. She guided him inside her, arching to take him deeper. He moved slowly; she wasn't sure if it was because of the injury to his back or because he wanted to drive her out of her mind. The slow strokes built the tension inside her again, and she arched and writhed, moving faster.

Then he reached between their bodies and stroked the most sensitive part of her. She came, yelling his name. Then he tensed again, and at first she thought he was hurt because of the grimace on his face. Then his body shuddered, and he filled her with his release.

While they'd made love with all their normal passion, she didn't feel as close to him as she usually felt. The distance remained between them.

If love couldn't bridge it, she wasn't sure what could.

EVEN THOUGH THEY'D made love the night before, Troy knew he was losing Lakin. And not just because she was gone when he woke up. He wasn't even sure if she slept beside him last night.

After he dressed, he went out into the living room and saw her pillow on the couch with a throw blanket. Sometime during the night, she'd left her bed. She'd wanted physical distance between them again.

But she shouldn't have gone off alone, not with a serial killer on the loose. And whatever Whitlaw really was to her… Father? Intruder? Stalker? Troy had no idea, but he needed to find out.

Yet, when he went to the police department to report the incident on the road last night, he didn't mention Whitlaw at all. Last night Lakin had told him not to, and when he'd stopped at the RTA office to make sure she wasn't alone, she'd reminded him in a whisper to not mention it, that she was going to talk to Eli.

That was good. But she needed to do it soon. At least she was safe at the office with Parker and Spence both there. So Troy would go to his first physical therapy session once Officer Reynolds finished taking his report.

"Billy Hoover filed one earlier this morning," Reynolds remarked.

"He admitted to running me off the road?" Troy asked with surprise.

Reynolds shook his head. "He said you were already off the road when he rescued you, and that for his trouble, you damaged his truck and ruined his tow strap. He figures you must have been drunk."

Troy gasped at the outrageous claim.

Reynolds chuckled. "Yeah, I pointed out that it was

too late for me to tell now and that you both should have called me to the scene. I know why he didn't." Obviously the officer knew who'd really been drunk. "But why didn't you?"

"Lakin was with me, and it was getting late. After getting run off the road once, I didn't want to risk it happening again." Troy didn't want her to be in any danger. Although until that serial killer was caught, everybody was.

Reynolds nodded. "Yeah, everybody needs to be extra vigilant right now. Keep an eye out for anything strange."

"I wish I'd gotten a better look at the truck and the driver that did cause me to go off the road."

"Me, too. That road is too dangerous for anyone to be driving that recklessly."

Troy's face heated a bit. He'd been driving recklessly himself to try to catch the guy. "I thought he might have been following Lakin, that he might be who broke into her cabin the night before that."

Reynolds sighed. "That was probably just a vagrant or a teenager looking for alcohol and made off with some food instead."

"I hope you're right." But Troy didn't really believe that he was. Or that he would find the intruder at all. Hopefully Lakin would talk to Eli soon.

The officer passed a card across the desk to him. "Here's your report number if you need it for insurance."

"Thanks." Troy didn't have full coverage, so he wouldn't be filing a claim. But it made him think of the workers compensation and disability suit Mitch was filing for him to get back some of his lost wages and to make sure his medical bills were covered.

But it wasn't just the money he was concerned about replacing now. He didn't want to lose his job or whatever else his supervisor had so very vaguely threatened. When Troy was done with his physical therapy session, he would drop by Mitch's law office.

As he left the police station, Troy had that strange sensation that Lakin had mentioned the night before, as if someone was watching him.

Who?

And why?

MITCH'S LIPS STILL tingled from Dove's kiss even though she'd left his office a while ago. He'd never felt like this before and wouldn't have believed he ever would, especially with someone as totally different from him as Dove St. James. But maybe that was what made her so damn exciting.

"You look happy," a deep voice remarked.

"I am," Mitch said, and he looked up from his desk to see Troy Amos walking into his office. Limping actually. The man was obviously in pain. Mitch jumped up. "You okay? Need anything?"

Troy shook his head and grimaced. "First physical therapy session."

"Hope you didn't overdo it," Mitch said.

"I've got to get back to work," Troy said. "But it sounds like I may not have a job to go back to."

"That's illegal for them to threaten your employment over a work comp claim," Mitch said. "It's only going to make our case stronger."

"I'm not sure my job is all he threatened," Troy said.

Mitch tensed. "I have been hearing some things," he admitted.

"Like what?"

"Like this oil company doesn't like to pay out for anything."

"I figured that out already," Troy said with a slight grin.

But it had to be frustrating for Troy with all the years he and his father had worked for this company. "I'm going to make sure that they do this time, no matter what," Mitch said. "But be careful."

In a lot of lawsuits against this company, the plaintiffs had withdrawn their claims. Mitch wondered now if they'd been threatened into doing that.

Troy nodded. "I will. But I'm not as worried about me as I am Lakin."

"You think they'll go after her?" Mitch asked with alarm.

"I really don't think they'll go after either of us," Troy said. "Now that I've had some time to think about it, I think Harrison was probably as drunk as Billy Hoover was last night. He's probably the one who's going to end up fired."

Mitch nodded. "Supervisor on the job site. He probably will be sacrificed as the scapegoat."

"He should have made sure the equipment was in better condition," Troy said. "But I didn't intend for him to lose his job."

"We'll see what happens," Mitch said. But he was definitely going to add some things to the lawsuit to put the pressure on the defendants to settle quickly.

"Thanks for taking this on for me," Troy said.

"Of course."

Troy started turning toward the door, but Mitch stopped him. "If you're not worried about the oil company coming after Lakin, why are you worried about her?" He loved his little sister so much, but he'd been so busy that he hadn't seen much of her lately.

Troy lifted his shoulders in a slight shrug. "I guess I'm just worried because of everything that's been happening in Shelby."

"The serial killer," Mitch said, and his stomach tightened into knots of tension and dread. "We're all worried about that." The murderer needed to be caught before he hurt anyone else. He had faith that his older brother would catch the killer.

Troy nodded. "Yeah…"

"Yeah?" Was that really the reason?

But Troy slipped out of the office before Mitch could question him further.

And the lawyer wondered. Was there another reason that Troy was worried about Lakin? Another reason that meant Mitch should be worried about her, too?

Chapter Ten

A few days had passed since Jasper Whitlaw had given Lakin the photograph that she stared at while sitting at her desk in the RTA office. She hadn't told anyone but Troy about it yet. He'd wanted to bring Jasper Whitlaw up to Bobby Reynolds, but she'd made Troy promise to keep all of that quiet until she found a way to tell her parents.

Lakin didn't want to upset them more than they already were about the recent murders. They were already worried enough about her. They kept calling to try to get her to stay with them. But after knowing that someone had probably followed her to their house the other night, she was determined to stay away. She didn't want to put either of them in danger if she was.

But why would she be? It didn't make any sense that someone would want to hurt her. Or want anything from her.

What did Jasper Whitlaw want?

Troy was convinced that the man had an agenda for seeking her out. He was even more worried about her than her parents were. He'd insisted on staying with her, but he'd moved back to the couch, telling her that he didn't want to chase her from her own bed like he had the other night. After they'd made love…

That had been a mistake. Making love with him again hadn't brought her closer to him but had somehow highlighted the distance between them.

Usually after they made love, they would cuddle and discuss the future, making plans. But Troy clearly didn't want to talk about the future at all.

Maybe that was just because of the uncertainty over his injury. But he was going to physical therapy; he seemed to be getting better. Still, he didn't talk to her about the hotel or ask if she'd gotten the business loan yet. He didn't seem any more interested in their future than in getting back into her bed.

Maybe he'd thought it was a mistake, too. And maybe not just making love but their whole relationship.

She wasn't sure now if they had a future together. The doubts churned in her stomach, making her queasy despite the fact she hadn't even had any coffee lately. After losing her mugs off the roof of the SUV, she hadn't gone back to Roasters. She hadn't wanted to risk running into Jasper Whitlaw there again.

But when she looked up from her desk, she found him standing over her. His sudden appearance startled her for a number of reasons, not least of which was that she'd thought she was alone in the office. Spence and Parker had left some time ago to lead hiking and fishing tours respectively. She must have been so lost in her thoughts that she hadn't noticed him open the door and walk into the building.

"So you haven't lost my number," Whitlaw remarked, his dark eyes cold as he stared down at her.

She suddenly felt too choked to speak, like something was clogging her throat. She hadn't even considered calling him over the past few days, not with what had happened to Troy and his suspicions about Jasper Whitlaw barging into her life. She wanted him to be wrong about the man, but…

She couldn't bring herself to trust him, either, let alone believe anything he told her. While she wanted to know more about her past and the woman in that photograph with her, she had a feeling Whitlaw might not tell her the truth. Besides, learning more about her genetics didn't seem to matter much right now when she wasn't sure she and Troy had a future together, much less a future family.

"Why haven't you called me, little girl?" he asked. "Don't you care where you came from? Or do you think you're too good for me because you're a Colton now?"

She cleared her throat of the fear and dread that had caused it to clog. That fear wasn't for herself now. "What do you know about the Coltons?" she asked.

Whitlaw smirked. "More than you probably think I know. Probably more than a lot of people in this town know about them."

About the tragedy that had brought them here to start a new life in Shelby? Was that what he was alluding to? And how would he know about that?

She jumped up from her desk, sending her chair rolling across the polished concrete floor. "Stay away from them," she said.

The older man snorted. "Why? Don't you want them to know that your daddy's come back for you?"

"I'm not a little girl anymore," she said.

His beady gaze flicked over her in a way that a father should never look at his daughter. "You look so damn much like her…"

"Where is she?" she asked, wondering about her biological mother.

"If you'd called me, I might have told you," he said. "But I've been sitting around this crappy town waiting for my phone to ring, and I'm not feeling quite so talkative anymore."

"What do you want?" she asked. She was pretty sure that Troy was right now. Her father, or whoever this man was, hadn't reached out to her because he cared about her. He didn't even know her.

"Well…" He smirked again. "I could use some money. I've been sleeping in my truck because I can't afford a place around here."

"You were the one who broke into my cabin," she said. "And stole that food."

He snorted. "I shouldn't have to *break* into anything. You should be begging me to stay with you. I'm the only real family you have left, little girl."

She gasped with shock, even though she had always suspected that her biological mother wasn't alive. Surely she would have sought Lakin out sooner if she had been.

She leaned closer to him and lowered her voice even though no one else was around to overhear them. "The Coltons are my real family," she said. They had been there for her after her biological family abandoned her.

But what if her mother hadn't abandoned her?

"Well, if you don't want me bothering your *real family* for money, you better help me out." Whitlaw held his tobacco-stained hand across her desk, palm up.

Her face flushed with embarrassment and anger. Embarrassment that Troy was right and that she could potentially be related to this mercenary man. And anger that he was threatening the Coltons, the people who'd loved and raised her like their own.

"You don't want to help out your own father?" Whitlaw asked.

She nearly shuddered at the thought of this man being related to her. But she didn't want him bothering her mom and dad, so she opened the bottom drawer of the big desk and reached inside her purse for her wallet. She didn't carry much cash, so she only had a couple of twenties to hand over to him.

He stared down at the two bills lying in his palm as if waiting for her to produce more. "That's all you got?"

"Yes, it is," she said.

"This isn't nearly enough."

"For what?" she asked.

"For a room. Hell, even for much of a meal," he said. "And I'm really hungry right now."

"It's all I have," she said. And unfortunately, until her business loan was approved, she didn't have much money in the bank, either.

He snorted again. "Like you keep telling me, you're a Colton now, little girl. I don't believe you can't get your hands on more than this." He wadded up the bills in his fist.

She found herself instinctively stepping back from

the desk. Maybe he wouldn't have hit her, but she had the uneasy feeling again that he knew more about the Coltons than maybe even some of the Shelby townspeople knew. Like he knew how much money they'd had before Will and Ryan had moved here and started their adventure business. Like he knew about the real estate business in California…

But how? Who the hell was he really?

Before she could ask, the office's front door opened. Whoever had taken the fishing tour, Spence or Parker, had probably returned, maybe with some clients.

But she couldn't see around Whitlaw. He leaned closer and whispered, "You better get more because I'll be back for it." Then he turned and walked away from her, right past Troy and Spence who'd just stepped inside the office.

Lakin held her breath until the door closed behind him, then released it in a ragged sigh of relief that he was gone.

For now.

She believed him, though. He would be back because he definitely wanted more than forty dollars from her. But she wasn't sure that money was really all he wanted.

TROY GLANCED AT the door as it closed behind the older man, then he turned back toward Lakin. She looked as shaken as she'd been the day she came home from Roasters after meeting a man claiming he was her father.

"Is that him?" Troy asked, his heart thumping with anger that the man had upset her again.

"Who?" Spence asked curiously. "Who was that? A client?"

Lakin shook her head. "Nobody. That was nobody." She stared hard at Troy as if silently willing him to shut up. Then she turned toward her cousin. "Spence, I left some messages on your desk."

Spence glanced between her and Troy. "Trying to get rid of me? Okay." He headed toward his office, leaving them alone.

The old man must have been watching her and waiting for another chance to catch her alone. Troy cursed himself that Lakin had been alone. But he'd had another physical therapy session. And he'd thought her brother and cousin would be here with her.

Troy turned around and headed toward the door, but before he reached it, Lakin caught up with him.

She stepped in front of him. "Let him go."

He shook his head. "We need to find out who the hell he really is and what he wants." And if he was the one who'd been following her and who ran Troy off the road.

But Lakin remained planted in front of the door. "I don't want you going after him," she said.

Troy wondered if she was trying to protect that man or him. "What happened, Lakin? Why was he here?"

Her face flushed.

"Money," he surmised.

She closed her eyes.

Troy touched her face, running his fingertips along her jaw. "I'm sorry."

She opened her eyes, and tears glistened in them. "You were right."

"I wish I was wrong." About that, and about not committing to her. But he'd spent the past few days in physical therapy and was no closer to getting back to work on the oil rigs. If he even had a job to go back to…

And Jasper Whitlaw, or whoever he really was, wasn't the only one who needed money. Lakin needed it, too; her business loan hadn't come through yet. The last thing she needed was someone else wanting something from her instead of giving it. While Troy couldn't help her financially, he could keep her safe.

"We need to call the police," he said.

"Over a relative asking me for money?"

"You don't even know if he's a relative," he reminded her. "Someone needs to check him out." Troy would do that, or at least talk to the man, if she'd get out of his way. But Whitlaw was probably long gone by now. He would be back, though; Troy had no doubt about that.

"I'll call Eli," she said.

"You were supposed to call him days ago," he reminded her.

"I…" Clearly, she dreaded making the call. Maybe she'd hoped that Whitlaw would go away, that he'd abandon her again like when she was three.

But the man wasn't going anywhere until he got what he wanted. Money… Or more?

"Call Eli now," Troy told her. Even though he wished he could help her with Whitlaw, he didn't have the resources that Eli had. All that really mattered was that someone investigated the guy. "Call him now." He stepped back and gestured for her to return to her desk.

But when she did, she didn't reach for her phone. She glanced instead toward the back office where Spence had gone. "I will call him. I promise I will," she said, "but after I leave work." Evidently, she didn't want

Parker and Spence to overhear her conversation with the ABI lieutenant.

But Troy believed the more people who knew about Whitlaw, the more they could keep an eye out for the opportunist or whatever else he might be. "Lakin, the man could be dangerous," he warned, especially if he was the person who ran Troy off the road.

"He's not going to get any more money out of me if he hurts me," she pointed out. "He's not going to hurt me."

That was really Troy's biggest concern: her safety. But he also hated seeing her as upset as this man made her.

"Just promise me you'll call Eli as soon as possible," Troy urged.

"I will, once I'm done working…" She peered around him as the outside door opened again.

Troy tensed. Had the man returned already?

But the guy who walked into the office was younger than Whitlaw. He wore the name brand adventure gear of someone with a lot of disposable income. The watch on his wrist advertised his wealth as well.

"Mr. Seller," Lakin greeted the man.

"Eric, please, Lakin, do I have to beg you to use my name?" he asked and chuckled. Then he looked at Troy standing over her desk and grinned. "So the boyfriend is home from the oil rigs." He thrust out his hand toward Troy. "Good to finally meet you."

Troy shook the man's hand but just nodded.

"You should be down on your knees," Seller said, "begging this woman to become your wife."

Troy sucked in a breath at the unsolicited advice.

"If you don't, I'm afraid you're going to lose her to someone else," Seller warned him.

"I trust Lakin," Troy said. And he did. He'd never had any reason to doubt her love or her loyalty to him.

Unfortunately she no longer believed the same of him. He hadn't called her when he was hurt, and now she didn't think he loved and needed her as much as he did. The problem was that he didn't want to need her too much. He didn't want to be like Jasper Whitlaw, a drain on her emotionally and physically.

Seller chuckled. "Even trustworthy people get sick of waiting around."

"I don't think this is really any of your business," Troy said, bristling with anger.

Lakin stood up. "Please, Troy, just leave. I need to help Mr. Seller."

Seller gave him that infuriating, condescending grin again. Troy's hand tightened into a fist that he was tempted to swing at the smug, rich guy.

"Hey, Troy," Spence said, stepping out of his office. "Let's go for that beer you promised me."

"I didn't—"

Spence wound his arm around his shoulders and started pushing him toward the outside door. "Right now."

"But—" He didn't want to leave Lakin alone with this man any more than he wanted her left alone with Jasper Whitlaw.

"Lakin's going to be a while yet, and you and I have some catching up to do," Spence said.

Troy hadn't had a chance to talk to his sister's fiancé much yet, but he'd rather put it off for another time. Spence wasn't giving him a choice, though, as he guided him toward the door and out into the parking lot.

"Come on," Spence said. "Hop in my truck. You know you're only going to piss off Lakin more if you stick around and get into it with a client."

Troy sighed, knowing her cousin was right. He had already pissed off Lakin when he hadn't called her after his accident. If he didn't want her to break up with him completely, he had to make sure that he didn't upset her any more than he already had.

And Parker was walking up to the office now with what looked like a couple of fishermen, so she wouldn't be alone with Seller. And once the office closed for the day, she would call Eli. Lakin kept her promises.

When Troy moved around to the passenger's side of Spence's vehicle, he noted the collection of cigarette butts on the ground in the empty spot next to it. Somebody had either cleaned out their ashtray in the parking lot, or they'd been standing there for a while.

Watching Lakin?

SINCE HETTY'S BROTHER had been back in town, Spence had noticed the tension between Troy and Lakin. Hetty had even mentioned it to Spence along with her concern that her brother was going to blow it with Lakin. Spence had managed to stop him this time from swinging his clenched fist at a client, but he didn't know what else he could do to help ease the tension between them.

"What's going on with you and my cousin?" Spence asked once they settled onto stools at the bar.

Troy groaned, but Spence wasn't sure if it was because of Lakin or because of his back. Hetty had also filled him in on the nearly fatal accident her brother had had while working on the oil rigs.

"She's mad at me for not reaching out when I was in the hospital," Troy said.

"Hetty and your mother aren't exactly thrilled with you over that, either," Spence warned him.

Troy smiled. "I can deal with them being upset with me."

"Really?" Spence asked. "Because Hetty's got quite the temper." He'd set it off a lot before they finally realized how they really felt about each other.

"Does she get mad because you try to protect her?" Troy asked.

"Yeah," Spence said. But he wondered if they were still talking about Hetty now. He studied the younger man's face. The poor guy looked miserable and a little scared. "Is everything okay with Lakin?"

"I told you she's mad at me," Troy said.

"Yeah, I can see that, but…" Spence sensed now that something else was going on.

"We were talking about my sister," Troy said. "And of course she's going to get pissed off if you try to protect her. Hetty prides herself on being able to take care of herself."

"She does, and she can," Spence heartily agreed. "She's tough and independent and so damn beautiful…" God, he loved that woman.

Troy groaned again. "Maybe let's not talk about my sister," he said. "Not if you're going to get all mushy about her."

Spence grinned. "I'm definitely all mushy about her," he agreed. "But you and Lakin…"

Troy's shoulders slumped as if he was carrying a heavy burden. "What about me and Lakin?"

"You two have been together for so long." Spence couldn't imagine them not being together. They'd always reminded him of his aunt and uncle; Lakin's parents had met and fallen in love in high school. Like they were going to last...

But a lot of people had lost their lives lately, proving that anything could be cut short. Lives and love.

Chapter Eleven

Once Lakin got rid of Eric Seller, she did as she'd promised Troy and called Eli. Worried that Parker might overhear their conversation, she had asked the ABI lieutenant to come talk in person.

That had to be his knock at her cabin door. Unless Troy was back.

Or Jasper Whitlaw…

She shivered and called out, "Who's there?"

"It's me, sis," Eli called back.

She released the breath she hadn't realized she'd been holding, turned the dead bolt and let him in. "Thanks for coming out."

"I would have come earlier," he said. "But I wasn't in Shelby."

"You didn't have to drop everything," she assured him. "I could have waited."

He studied her face. "No. I don't think it could. And I wanted to see you anyway."

"Check up on me, you mean," she said with a smile.

"I've been worried about you," he said.

She released a shaky breath. "You're not the only one. Troy has been bugging me to call you."

He glanced around as if looking for her boyfriend. "He's not here? I was counting on him sticking close to you after the break-in."

"He has been," she said. But was it out of concern or obligation? She wasn't as confident of his love as she'd always been. Or maybe it wasn't his love she questioned but his commitment to a future with her. "He's with Spence now." Or at least she hoped he still was and not out trying to find Jasper Whitlaw or Eric Seller.

Eli glanced around the cabin. "You shouldn't be alone at all right now," he said.

"You sound like Troy. And like Mom and Dad who've been trying to get me to stay with them," she said. She was so glad she'd resisted the temptation of going home, though, or Whitlaw might have shown up there.

"I sound like someone who loves you then," Eli said with a slight grin.

She sighed even as a smile curved her lips. "People who love me should know that I can take care of myself," she pointed out.

"You're tough, Lakin," Eli said. "But a lot of victims were."

She sucked in a breath. *Victim.* "I'm not in danger of anyone killing me," she assured him. "I'm just…"

"What?" he asked. "What's going on?"

"I don't know," she admitted. Then she pulled the photograph out of her purse and handed it to him.

Before he even looked at it, he asked, "What's this?" Then he studied the snapshot, and his jaw clenched. "This is you…in the picture…"

"The little girl," she clarified, just in case he thought she was the woman who had to be her biological mother.

"Where did you get this?" he asked. "Did Mom and Dad have it?" Then he flipped it over, probably looking for a date like Troy had. "Jasper Whitlaw. Who is this?"

"The man in the picture," she said. "He claims he's my father."

"He can claim whatever the hell he wants," Eli said. "But he needs to prove he actually has a biological relationship to you. And even if he does, he's not your *dad*."

"No, he's not," she agreed. "That's why I haven't said anything to Mom and Dad about this, so please don't…"

"Lakin." Eli's blue eyes studied her face with the intensity he'd given the photograph moments ago. "When did this guy give you the picture? Before the break-in?"

"The morning after it," she admitted.

"I don't like this," he said. "Has he bothered you again?"

She didn't deny that he had. There was no point; she was still trembling a bit from the interaction earlier. "Today," she said. "He showed up at the office."

"What does he want from you?" he asked.

"Money," she admitted with a pang of regret that Troy had been right about him.

Eli cursed. "We really should tell everyone else about this, warn them to be on the lookout."

She shook her head. "Mom and Dad are already on edge because of this serial killer. I don't want to needlessly put them through anything else. I gave Whitlaw forty bucks, so he knows I don't have much money. Maybe he'll just leave town now."

"He wants more than forty bucks, Lakin," Eli said. "He's going to be back. And I want you to keep your distance. Make sure you're never alone with him."

She nodded. "I'll be careful."

"You said Troy bugged you to call me," Eli said. "So he knows about this guy?"

She nodded again. "Yes."

"And clearly he doesn't trust him anymore than I do," Eli surmised.

She smiled. "You're both cynical and overly suspicious."

"That doesn't mean we're wrong."

She sighed. "No, it doesn't." She didn't trust Whitlaw, either. She hadn't when she first met him and she definitely didn't now after how he acted in the office. He'd barely disguised his threats to go to her family for money. "I… I'm worried," she admitted. "I don't want him bothering Mom and Dad."

"Or you," Eli said. "I'll check him out. And then I'll track him down and have a little talk with him."

She smiled. "You mean you'll run him out of town like it's the Wild West?"

"Something like that," he said with a grin.

"Before you run him out of town, can you do me a favor?" she asked.

Eli's grin slipped away. "What?"

"Can you find out what happened back then? Why I was left at the grocery store and what happened to her…" She pointed toward the photograph he held. "To my biological mother."

"He didn't tell you anything?"

She shook her head. "But he said he's the only family I have left."

"That's bullshit. You have us."

She hugged him and held on for a long moment. "I know. That's what I told him."

"And you have Troy and all of the Amos family, too," Eli reminded her.

That was what Troy had told those playground bullies all those years ago. She smiled. "But I don't want Troy fighting my battles anymore." She didn't want Eli fighting them, either, but at least he was armed. She wasn't, and neither was Troy. And she had a feeling that Troy was right about Jasper Whitlaw being dangerous. At least to her and her family.

What about Troy? Was Whitlaw the one who'd run him off the road?

Was Troy in danger, too?

"So the honeymoon is over," Hetty remarked as she joined Troy and Spence at the bar.

"Honeymoon?" Troy asked. Hetty had admitted she'd fallen for her former nemesis, but he hadn't thought they were doing more than dating right now.

She chuckled. "Metaphorically. Instead of rushing home to me, my man is out drinking in the bars."

Spence chuckled, too, and looped his arms around her waist, pulling her in for a kiss.

Troy shook his head. "I can't believe you two are together. Not after all the trash you talked about him, Hetty."

Instead of being embarrassed or remorseful, his sister laughed.

"She stills talks trash about me," Spence said.

"No, I tell you to take out the trash," she corrected

him, but from the twinkle in both their eyes, it was clear they were teasing each other.

Maybe that was all they'd ever been doing even back when they fought with each other.

"She's as bossy as ever," Spence said.

Troy groaned. "Don't I know it."

"I wouldn't have to be so bossy if you two would just do what I told you to," she said.

Spence laughed, then saluted her. "Yes, ma'am, from now on."

"Don't encourage her," Troy warned him. "She'll just get worse."

Hetty slapped his shoulder, and he flinched as his back muscles tightened. "Oh, God, I'm sorry, Troy!"

"I'm fine," he said. "I just did a lot of physical therapy today." He had been daily; he needed to get stronger.

"Is it going well?" she asked, her green eyes bright with concern.

"It's getting better," he said. He probably wouldn't hurt like he did now if he wasn't so tense from finding Lakin alone in the office with Whitlaw. And then the other guy, Seller, warning him about losing her…

"And your relationship with Lakin?" Troy probably flinched again because Hetty added, "That's too bad."

He sighed.

"She still hasn't forgiven you for not calling her when you fell?" Hetty asked. "That doesn't sound like Lakin. She loves you so much, and she's so forgiving. Unlike me and Mom. We're still pissed as hell at you." She reached out as if to smack his shoulder again but pulled her hand back before making contact.

"I understand why you're all mad about that," Troy admitted. "I would be, too."

"But you would do the same thing all over again, wouldn't you?" Hetty asked. "You wouldn't call any of us until you knew if and how you were going to recover."

His sister knew him well. He nodded. "I didn't want to upset anyone until I knew what I was dealing with. And I sure as hell don't want to be a burden to anyone."

Hetty snorted. "No, you want to be the hero, Troy. And you don't have to be. You just have to be you. That's who we all love."

"I like him a lot, but love..." Spence shrugged. "I don't know."

Hetty laughed and lightly swatted her boyfriend's shoulder. "I know you love him, too. All of you Coltons love my brother Troy."

The Coltons had always been so warm and friendly to him. While they were that way with everyone, they'd made him feel special in that they'd taken the time to get to know him. Sometimes, growing up in a big family like his, Troy had felt lost in the shuffle. Unimportant. But the Coltons had always made him feel special; no one more so than Lakin. She'd always looked at him like he was her hero.

And he didn't want her to stop looking at him that way, or worse yet, to look at him with pity instead. "I just want to make sure that I'll be able to work again," he said. "I want to take care of Lakin, not have her take care of me."

Hetty shook her head. "Your damn pride, Troy. It's going to be your downfall. Lakin doesn't care about money or anything else but *you*."

Hetty didn't know Lakin like he did; she didn't know about Lakin's dreams, about the hotel she'd already purchased and the family she wanted to have.

Troy didn't want to hold back the woman he loved from achieving everything she wanted. He didn't want to tie her to his uncertain future. That was why he hadn't begged her to marry him like Seller had told him he should. If Troy knew he had a job and a way to help her out with the business and with the children she wanted to have, he would hit his knees and propose right now.

But he had a feeling that even if he did, Lakin might not accept. He might have already done too much damage to their relationship. He might have hurt her too much for her to trust him completely with her heart.

ONCE ELI RELUCTANTLY left his sister's cabin, he wasted no time running a background check on Jasper Whitlaw. To verify the man's real name, Eli had even taken fingerprints from the photograph he'd borrowed from Lakin.

She wanted it back. Hell, she hadn't wanted to part with it at all.

He could understand why. That photograph was the one link to her past and the people who might be able to answer questions about it. Like why she'd been left in that grocery store all those years ago.

Jasper Whitlaw might have those answers, but he would obviously only give them to her if she paid for them. And then it wasn't a guarantee that he would actually tell her the truth about anything.

A quick background search was enough for Eli to conclude that this man was probably not her father. So what was he? Besides a convicted criminal? The man had been in prison until recently, so maybe that was why he hadn't sought out Lakin sooner.

But why now? What did he want from her?

Money or silence?

Did Lakin know more about her past than she was willing to remember?

Chapter Twelve

Lakin drove her SUV into the empty parking lot of the former Shelby Hotel, then looked around before getting out and heading toward the door to the lounge area. She was pretty sure she was still being followed. She just wasn't sure who it was now. A random stalker? Jasper Whitlaw? Troy or one of her brothers?

They were all worried about her. She was worried, too, but not so much about being watched as about her future plans. She and Troy were stuck in this kind of limbo where he wanted to protect her but not be her partner. So he slept on the couch, and she wasn't sure that she slept at all.

She lay in bed with her body aching for his. Usually when he returned from being away, they rarely left her bed. This time they had only made love once. She was going slowly out of her mind with frustration and desire for him. She wanted him so damn badly.

She wasn't at all sure that he felt the same. Maybe it was easier for him to ignore the attraction because he wasn't fully recovered from his fall.

While he went to physical therapy nearly every day,

he seemed to be in more pain, not less, after his sessions. Maybe he was pushing himself too hard to heal. He probably wanted to get right back to work on the oil rigs that had killed his father and had almost killed him as well.

She wasn't sure she could keep sending him off with a smile and the hope that he would come home to her. Because he might not…

She pressed a hand over her heart at the horrific thought and the physical pain it brought her. She didn't want to lose Troy, but she felt in some ways she already had. She'd lost the Troy that for the past ten years she'd planned a future with; she'd lost the man she'd envisioned as her partner in business and life.

Tears blurred her vision, and she had to blink them away to unlock the door. Her hand trembled, and she still struggled to get the door opened. Then she realized she'd locked it.

It must have already been unlocked.

But how? She was the only one with a key, or so she'd been told. But from the condition of them, it didn't look as if the locks had been changed recently. Maybe whoever had keys from when it was still the Shelby Hotel had used them to stop in and look at the place.

She hoped that was all they'd done. She wanted to get the place up and running as quickly as possible. She had to if she was going to pay her dad back as fast as she'd promised.

He'd told her to take her time; he'd even offered her more money. But she wanted to do this on her own.

No. She wanted to do this with Troy.

But if he was here, he was probably out in his old truck watching her. Hopefully he was the only one.

A thump and then a tinkle of breaking glass startled her. It came from somewhere inside the hotel.

And she realized she was not alone. Nobody would have broken into a long abandoned hotel to find food.

So why were they here?

What did they want?

THE PHYSICAL THERAPIST had turned him away today. "You're exhausted. You need to rest."

But Troy wasn't tired because of therapy; he was tired because he couldn't sleep with Lakin so close and yet so far from his reach. She hadn't just shut him out of her bedroom; it was as if she was shutting him out of her life, too.

Or maybe he'd shut himself out, just like Hetty had warned him. Being too stubborn and too proud.

He really didn't want to be Lakin's hero, like Hetty had accused him of wanting; he just didn't want to be a burden to her. He wanted her to be happy and, more important, safe.

To ensure her safety, he'd followed her from the RTA office over to the old Shelby Hotel. He waited until she'd parked and gone inside before he pulled into the parking lot. Weeds were growing through the asphalt because nobody had been using it. The building looked as abandoned as the parking lot; its windows were all boarded up. The wood siding was weathered and, in some places, rotted. The place needed a lot of work.

But of course, Lakin would see the potential in it. Just as she must have seen the potential in him all those years ago. She was always so positive and hopeful until recently. Until he'd hurt her.

His heart hurt more than his back that he'd done that. He'd let her down in more ways than one. First, he hadn't told her when he was in the hospital, and second, he didn't reply to her texts and emails about the hotel.

But Troy loved her too much to saddle her with a cripple, which he might wind up being if he got hurt again. He wanted to be an asset to her, not a liability. He just wasn't sure how he could help her except to keep her safe right now.

While she'd talked to Eli like she'd promised, Troy wasn't sure what else her oldest brother was doing to protect her. Ideally the ABI lieutenant would have run Jasper Whitlaw out of town, but Troy was pretty sure he'd seen the man skulking around town still.

Whitlaw drove an old pickup truck like Troy's, like Billy Hoover's. And Whitlaw was always somewhere in the vicinity of Lakin, like Troy was. Strangely enough, sometimes Billy Hoover was, too.

Troy didn't trust their old school bully any more than he trusted the stranger claiming to be Lakin's father. With those two never far away from her, not to mention that bored rich RTA client Eric Seller, Troy needed to stick even closer to her.

He pushed open the door to his truck and stepped out onto the cracked asphalt of the old parking lot. He waited for his back muscles to tighten from twisting himself out from under the steering wheel. But he didn't feel even a twinge of discomfort. Maybe the physical therapy was helping. Maybe he would recover enough to be the partner Lakin deserved to have.

Feeling a little lighter and more hopeful, he studied the hotel for a moment. Instead of seeing the boarded-up windows and weathered wood, he saw the potential that Lakin must have seen. The location was great, and the structure itself looked solid. The roof wasn't sagging, and the walls were straight. It might not take as much time and money and manpower as he thought to renovate it into something special.

Lakin wasn't just optimistic; she was smart. And she was gutsy as hell to have gone ahead and bought this property at an auction with no chance for inspections or way to back out of it. But because she was so smart and determined, he knew that she would work hard and make it a success.

He felt a yearning to be part of it, part of her dream, of her future with this business and with a family. With a little girl who looked like that little girl in the photograph Whitlaw had given Lakin. He headed toward the front door, eager to see inside the building.

When he put his hand on the knob, he heard Lakin's scream.

Chilled, he tried the knob. It didn't move.

She'd locked herself inside with whatever danger she faced.

"I JUST WANT to shake him," Hetty said, frustration overwhelming her.

Her mother chuckled. "You used to say that all the time about Spence Colton."

Now Hetty wanted to do more than shake Spence Colton. She smiled but then remembered why she was frustrated and frowned. "I'm talking about my idiot brother."

Her mother sighed. "He's more stubborn than your father."

"He's trying to be Dad," Hetty said. "Sacrificing everything to take care of everyone else. He's going to lose Lakin if he doesn't realize he doesn't have to be her hero. He just has to be her partner." Like she and Spence were partners. Equals. Both independent and strong separately but even stronger together. They'd had to be, or they wouldn't have survived when a professional assassin had tried to kill them.

"Why would he feel like he has to be her hero?" Mom asked. "Is something going on with Lakin?"

Hetty tensed. Was there something going on with Lakin? Was there a reason her brother felt as if he had to protect the woman he loved? From what? How could Lakin, who didn't have an enemy in the world, be in danger?

Then Hetty remembered how she and Spence had just been in the wrong place at the wrong time and nearly lost their lives because of it. And those women…

The poor women who'd become victims of a serial killer. Had they even realized they were in danger before it was too late? Was that who Troy thought he needed to protect Lakin from? A serial killer?

Or was there another threat against her?

If there was, Hetty had no doubt that Troy would do whatever he could to protect her from it, like putting himself in danger to save her.

Chapter Thirteen

Lakin's throat burned from the scream. She'd uttered it as much to scare off whoever was in the hotel with her as to call for help. She just wasn't sure if anyone was close enough to hear her.

The front door behind her burst open with such force it slammed against the wall. Troy ran inside and put his hands on her shoulders.

"What is it?" he asked. "What's wrong?"

"Someone's in here," she whispered.

He let go of her and rushed off, intent on rescuing her as usual. Just like he'd chased the intruder from her cabin into the woods that first day back in Shelby.

But he wasn't limping today.

Lakin struggled to keep up with him as he ran through the lounge and down a wide hall. He opened each door off the hallway. Finally he stopped outside one, and Lakin caught up with him, peering over his shoulder into the room, she saw shattered glass sparkle in the sunlight pouring through an open window.

"Someone took the boards off from the outside," she said, keeping her voice low.

"They didn't get inside," he said, pointing to a small hole in the glass. Someone had hit it with some kind of tool, probably whatever they'd used to pry off the boards. But they hadn't gotten through the window.

Maybe her scream had scared them off. She released a shaky breath of relief.

Troy spun away from the window as if to head outside.

She grasped his arm. "Stop." She didn't want him getting hurt because of whatever was going on with her. "I'll call the police."

"Whoever it is will be gone by the time Officer Reynolds gets here."

"Whoever it was is probably already gone," she pointed out.

Troy tugged his arm from her grasp and hurried from the room, as if trying to prove her wrong. Or catch the would-be intruder.

She hoped she was right and that the person was long gone. Or Troy could be running into danger.

TROY WAS TOO late to catch this intruder, just as he'd been too damn late at her cabin. The only thing left behind, besides the splintered boards pried from the window, was a cigarette butt.

He stared down at it and at the boot prints left next to it. The prints were similar to the ones he'd found in the woods when her cabin had been broken into. "It has to be Whitlaw," he said.

"Why?" Lakin asked. "What does he have to gain by breaking into places I own?" She gestured at the back of the building where the window had been broken. The wood was even more weathered than on the front. "There's nothing to steal in there. Or in my cabin."

"Maybe he's just trying to scare you," Troy said. "So that you'll give him what he wants."

"Money." She snorted. "Joke's on him. I'm broke after buying this place."

Troy flinched, not with pain but with regret. He had some money saved up that he could give her, but he wasn't sure how long he would be without work. He'd already lost weeks of wages. In trying to get some compensation for that, he was probably going to lose his job, too. While he didn't have many expenses of his own, he also didn't want to have to borrow money from anyone.

"I know that was my choice," she said. "But I didn't want to lose this place. I can see it so clearly, how amazing it can be." She smiled as she stared at the building. "I think I'll call it Suite Home."

"Sweet?"

"S-u-i-t-e," she spelled out. "Each room will be a suite with a little kitchenette and a spa-like bathroom. There will also be space for a work area and of course a very nice bed."

He could see it, too. "It's going to take money to make all those changes."

Her smile slipped away.

And he could have cursed himself for dimming her excitement.

"It's all about money with you, Troy." She glanced down at the cigarette butt.

"It's all about money for a lot of people," he said.

"Well, Whitlaw isn't going to get any more out of me," she said.

"You paid him?" he asked with alarm. "When? Have you seen him again?" He should have stuck closer to her.

"I haven't seen him since that day you found him in the office with me. That was when I gave him forty bucks," she said. "That was all I had in my wallet at the time."

"It's not all the money that the Coltons have," he pointed out.

Her father had helped her buy the hotel at auction; he would help her pay off that creep, too. But giving Whitlaw any money probably wouldn't get rid of him. It would just make him greedy for more.

"I'm not asking my dad for any more money," she said. "The bank is waiting on the professional appraisal of the hotel, and then I should be approved for my business loan." But she looked more nervous than confident. "I'm going to make this place a success."

He nodded. "I know you will, Lakin."

"Do it with me," she implored him. "Be my partner."

His chest ached with the urge to say yes. "I just need another year on the oil rigs, and then I'll have enough money—"

"No!" she exclaimed, her voice sharp. "You can't be serious about going back to work on them. Putting your life in danger again?"

He might not be able to go back to work there if he was fired. "I have Mitch helping me with something that could make the workplace safer from now on. All the safety harnesses will be regularly inspected and any ones with the frayed ropes like mine would be thrown out."

"How is Mitch helping you with that?" she asked.

"He filed a lawsuit against them in civil court," he admitted. But after his mother's civil suit had failed years ago, he knew not to get his hopes up again. "All I really want is the wages I lost when I was in the hospital and then a safer workplace going forward for my coworkers and for me." It was too late to help his dad, but Troy wanted to make sure nobody else lost their life like he did. Or got hurt like Troy had.

"It's not safe for you to go back there," she said. "Especially because you've sued them."

He snorted. "I may not be able to go back," he said. "My supervisor already made that clear to me."

"He threatened you?"

He shrugged. "I don't know. I think Harrison was just drunk when he called me and was acting like Billy Hoover. Mitch says they can't fire me over this."

"I hope they do," she said.

He gasped.

"You want to protect me," she said. "That's why you keep following me around, but you won't protect yourself." She shook her head. "You won't even listen to me. And I'm sure your mom and Hetty are begging you not to go back, too."

His face flushed a bit. "Well…"

"They don't want to lose you," she said.

"What about you, Lakin?" he asked. Had he already lost her.

"I don't want anything to happen to you, Troy. I don't want you to get hurt on the oil rigs or here in Shelby while you keep trying to protect me."

"Lakin, you must realize that you're in danger," he said, pointing toward the splintered boards. "Someone tried to get into the hotel just like they got into your cabin. You know that someone's following you."

"Yeah, you are," she said, her lips curving into a slight smile.

"I'm not the only one."

She shivered. "Have you gotten a good look at who it is?"

"Just that old truck that drove me off the road that day," he said. "But there are a lot of old trucks in Shelby."

"You could have died that day, Troy," she said. "You have to stop putting yourself in danger. Eli knows what's going on. He'll take care of it."

"Eli has a lot on his plate right now," Troy pointed out. "And he's not even around Shelby very often. He can't protect you."

Troy wasn't sure how well he could, either. He was never quite fast enough to catch whoever was after her. And that was the only way to make sure that she was safe—to catch and stop whoever was after her.

THE BOYFRIEND WAS a pain in the ass. He was always around, always in the way.

Maybe it was time to get a gun.

That might be the most effective way to get rid of Troy Amos.

Chapter Fourteen

Bobby Reynolds came by the hotel to check out the attempted break-in, but he wasn't too concerned. "Teenagers break into this place a lot," he said. "Looking for a place to hang out."

Lakin wished she could believe that, but it all felt too coincidental that it happened so recently after her cabin had been broken into. And why would teenagers be breaking into abandoned buildings during the daytime when they should be in school? Of course she'd been a good student who didn't skip classes, so maybe she was being naive about teenagers. Or paranoid about the break-ins. But she didn't argue with the officer.

Troy, on the other hand, wanted Bobby to track down Jasper Whitlaw and check his alibi.

Bobby warned him against making accusations with no proof. He also refused to have the cigarette butt tested for DNA since a broken window wasn't a high priority case. "Leave the policing to the police," he cautioned.

Lakin definitely didn't argue with that. Neither did Troy, though she didn't expect him to stop trying to protect her. Fortunately he also helped her secure the hotel again so no damage should come to the place.

Despite Bobby claiming teenagers had broken into the building before, she and Troy didn't find much damage inside. The roof, while old, hadn't even leaked. It really wouldn't take much for her to fix it up and get it going. She could renovate a couple of rooms and the lounge and start on a small scale, if she couldn't secure that loan.

She was going to make it a success. Even Troy believed that. If only he would help her...

But she didn't want to beg him to build a future with her. If after ten years he couldn't commit, then, she told herself, she didn't want him.

Only she did.

Once they were back in her cabin, she found herself lingering in the living room with him instead of going into her bedroom and locking the door. As frustrated as she was with his stubborn determination to return to work on the oil rigs, she was also frustrated from denying herself the passion that always burned between them.

If he left again, she didn't want to regret not being with him. Even if it might be their last time.

"Thank you for helping me board up that window again," she said.

He nodded. "I'm sorry that's all I can do to help you at the hotel."

"That's not all you can do," she said. "It's all you're willing to do."

"Lakin, it's not that I'm not willing," he said. "I just don't know what the future holds for me, not after the accident."

"Nobody knows what the future holds, Troy," she pointed out. "We just have to have faith that everything will work out for the best."

"But it doesn't all work out for the best," he said. "My dad died. Your aunt and grandparents were murdered. Bad things happen all the time, and we don't know when or where or how they're going to happen."

She shivered at the reminder. "You're right." And because of that, she was even more determined to take what was right in front of her, while *he* was still here. She'd already nearly lost him when he fell off that rig and then the side of the mountain. She didn't want to lose him because of an accident. Or something that maybe wasn't an accident.

"I'm sorry," he said again.

"Me, too," she said. She reached out then, sliding her arms around his broad shoulders. "I'm sorry I've been locking you out."

"I understand why you're mad at me," he said.

"I don't even think I'm mad anymore…" She wasn't sure what she was now. Maybe resigned. The next time he left, he wouldn't be coming back to her even if he returned to Shelby in one piece. She wasn't going to wait around for him any longer.

"You've forgiven me?" he asked, his green eyes brightening.

She didn't want to dash his hopes like he'd dashed hers. Instead of replying, she kissed him, sliding her lips seductively back and forth across his mouth.

He clasped a hand in her hair, holding her head to his, and kissed her back. Deeply. Passionately.

Her pulse raced as heat flushed her entire body. She wanted him so damn badly. Despite all the years they'd been together the passion between them had never cooled. It burned as hot as ever, maybe even hotter now than before. Because of the danger, because of knowing how close she'd come to losing him, Lakin wanted him more than she ever had.

As she pressed her mouth hungrily to his, she tugged him back toward her bedroom. This time she wasn't locking him out; she might just lock him inside with her, to keep the rest of the world out.

He lifted his mouth from hers, panting for breath, and asked, "Are you sure, Lakin?"

She nodded. She was sure that she wanted to make love with him, but that was all she was sure of at the moment. She wasn't sure that they had a future. But she didn't want him going back to the oil rigs without being with him again, even if it was the last time.

Once in the bedroom, he kicked the door shut. And then he dragged off his clothes. He was so muscular. His biceps bulged, his ab muscles rippled, and his chest thumped, his heart beating as fast as hers.

Needing to press her skin against his, she undressed quickly, too, until she was as naked as he was. His erection pulsated, as if begging for her attention.

But before she could reach for him, he was swinging her up in his arms.

"Troy!" she exclaimed, worried that he was going to hurt himself.

He grimaced as he carried her the short couple of steps to the bed. When he laid her on it, he followed her down. She wasn't sure if it was because he wanted to be close to her or if it was because he was hurt.

"You shouldn't be overdoing it," she said. "Are you all right?"

"Frustrated," he said. "It's been killing me to lie out there on the couch, aching for you."

She didn't want him aching *because* of her, though. She wasn't petite. She was five nine with an athletic build. But Troy had always picked her up like she was light. Until today.

"Are you really all right?" she persisted.

"I will be," he said. "Once I'm inside you, once we're as close as we used to be."

Physically they could be that close again, but she wasn't sure about emotionally. But then he was touching her, sliding his hands and mouth all over her, and she couldn't think at all. She could only feel the passion burning inside her, making her tremble.

She touched him, too, running her hands and mouth over him. But before she could slide her lips around his erection, he pulled back.

"I'll go too fast," he said. "I want to take my time."

Maybe he knew, too, that this might be their last time. Their last chance to be this close. Maybe that was why he gave her so much pleasure, moving between her legs to make love to her with his mouth and his wicked tongue.

She squirmed against the blankets as he drove her wild with desire. The tension was so tight inside her, and then he moved his hands to her breasts, stroking them. She cried out as she came.

Then he was inside her, thrusting slowly, building the tension inside her again. But he knew how and where to touch her to release that tension. And she came again, screaming his name.

Then his body tensed and shuddered and he cried out her name.

And, "I love you."

She loved him, too, but she couldn't say those words right now, not when their future was so uncertain. And it wasn't just Troy going back to the oil rigs that could end their relationship but whoever was following her around and breaking into her cabin and the hotel. That person could end their relationship and maybe their lives.

SHE DIDN'T SAY it back.

For the first time since they had exchanged *I love yous* as teenagers, Lakin didn't say it back to him. Even though they'd made love and both stayed in her bed afterward, Troy felt like he was still shut out. Not out of her bedroom but maybe out of her life and her heart.

Long after Lakin had fallen asleep, he lay awake, worrying that his sister was probably right. He was going to lose Lakin if he didn't make a commitment to her and their future.

Maybe losing her would be the best thing for her. She could have a better life with someone like that rich customer who'd also warned him about losing Lakin. Was that because he wanted her for himself?

And what about Whitlaw? What did he want from her? Just money or something more?

Eventually Troy must have fallen asleep because he awoke to sunlight slanting through the blinds to shine in his eyes. He blinked and squinted, trying to focus. But he didn't need to see anything to know that Lakin was gone. The bed was cold beside him.

Maybe she'd already left for work, or maybe she'd gone to Roasters. He didn't want her going there alone. That was where Jasper Whitlaw had first accosted her.

She'd given the photograph to Eli. But what had her big brother found out about Whitlaw? Was the older man even in town still?

Troy needed to make sure Lakin was safe. He dressed in a hurry and headed off to the coffee shop. But when he pulled into the lot, her SUV wasn't there.

Maybe he'd just missed her. But what about Jasper Whitlaw? Had he been hanging around?

Troy was sick of waiting for this guy to show up and harass her again. He wanted to find the man and make him leave town. So he parked his truck and rushed into the café.

"Hey, are you here to pick up Lakin's order?" the barista asked him.

"Did she place an order?" he asked. Maybe she was on her way.

"No, but she usually comes in every morning, and I haven't seen her for a few days."

Because Lakin didn't want to run into the man who claimed he was her father.

"There was an older guy here the last day she was in," Troy said. "He gave her a photograph. Did you see him that day? Have you seen him around town?"

The barista's eyes widened and then narrowed. "Older guy, looks kind of homeless? I have seen him hanging around here, but that was more before he talked to Lakin. I haven't seen him often after that day he gave her something. Then she drove off with her coffee mugs on the roof of her vehicle. I picked them up and washed them for her."

"That was very sweet of you," he said.

"Lakin is sweet," the young woman said. "One of my favorite customers."

People were naturally drawn to Lakin's kindness and her beauty. He was lucky that he hadn't already lost her to someone who could give her more time and attention. Fortunately for him Lakin was as loyal and loving as she was beautiful.

Troy leaned closer to the counter. "Will you let me know if you see that guy around here again? Or anywhere?" he asked. "I really want to talk to him."

"No." The deep voice that answered wasn't the barista's.

Troy turned around to find Lakin's oldest brother, Eli, standing behind him. His arms were crossed over his chest, and he didn't look happy.

But Troy wasn't particularly happy with him, either. Lakin had reached out to him for help, but things were still happening, like that broken window at the hotel.

Officer Reynolds might believe it was teenagers, but Troy didn't. Lakin was in danger, and Troy felt like he was the only one doing anything to protect her. He was afraid it still wasn't enough…

ELI WAS APPARENTLY at Roasters for the same reason that his sister's boyfriend was, and it wasn't for the coffee although it did smell damn good in the café.

"No," he repeated. "If she sees Jasper Whitlaw around again, she's going to call me." He passed the barista a card as she handed a coffee over the counter for him. He laid down some bills and turned toward Troy again. "Do you want anything?"

Troy stepped away from the counter. "Not coffee. I want answers."

Eli sighed. "Don't we all?" He had so many questions and not just about Whitlaw.

"So you haven't found out anything more about that man who accosted Lakin?" Troy asked.

Eli had, but he intended to tell Lakin first and definitely not in a public place. "I know he's dangerous," he said. "And that you shouldn't be looking to confront him."

Troy sucked in a breath, looking like Eli had punched him. "So Lakin really is in danger."

"I don't know that he would hurt her," Eli said. "He won't be able to get money out of her if he does." Though he wasn't certain that was all Whitlaw wanted from her or why he'd turned up in Shelby when he had. "But I don't think he would hesitate to hurt you if you get in his way," Eli warned the younger man. He'd always liked Troy Amos; the guy was a hard worker who clearly worshipped Lakin. If something happened to him, Lakin probably wouldn't get over it.

"I don't care what he does to me," Troy said. "I just want to make sure he doesn't hurt Lakin."

Eli figured it was already too late for that. Whitlaw's sudden appearance with the photograph had stirred up a lot of emotions for Lakin and a lot of questions about her past. Eli understood that only too well; the Fiancée Killer was stirring up a lot of memories and nightmares for him and undoubtedly for the rest of his family, too.

The last thing any of them needed was someone trying to hurt another one of their family.

"I'm on it," Eli promised him. "I'm looking for the guy, and when I find him, I'll make sure that he knows he's not getting anything out of Lakin."

"You might want to check out a couple of other guys that seem to keep turning up around her," Troy remarked.

Eli felt a smile twitch his lips. "Lakin is beautiful. I'm sure there are a lot of guys who keep turning up."

Troy looked again as if Eli had struck him.

"Didn't it occur to you that other men might find her attractive?"

"Of course," Troy said. "I'm not talking about that kind of attention. I'm talking about her old school bully, Billy Hoover, showing up here and other places unexpectedly. And then there's some RTA client, Something Seller, that seems a little too interested in her."

Eli tensed. The thought that the serial killer could be targeting someone in his family was keeping him awake nights. Why else were the murders so similar to his aunt's death? But who in Shelby really knew about his aunt Caroline and his family's reasons for moving here from California all those years ago?

"I'll check into them, too," Eli assured him. "But you need to stay out of this."

Troy shook his head. "Not until I know she's safe."

Troy Amos obviously loved Lakin a lot, so much so that he was more concerned about her life than his. But if he really knew Lakin well, he would know that she wouldn't want him getting hurt because of her.

And Eli had a feeling that, as determined as Troy was to protect her, he probably was going to wind up getting hurt or worse.

Chapter Fifteen

Leaving Troy lying alone in her bed had been hard. After last night, after being that close to him again, Lakin wanted to stay curled up in his arms with her head on his chest. But she knew that eventually they would have to talk, and every time they spoke lately, she was disappointed that Troy was so uncertain about their future.

He should know that it didn't matter to her if he wasn't able to work again; she loved him for who he was, not for the money he might make someday. Maybe he knew how she felt, but he was just too proud to accept her unconditional love if he couldn't give her what he wanted to in return.

She blinked hard to focus on her computer screen, and a sigh slipped out along with all her frustration. She was too much in limbo right now, waiting to find out if Troy would recover fully, waiting for her business loan, waiting to find out if Jasper Whitlaw was really her biological father so she could get some answers about her past.

She cared the least about Whitlaw. He'd waited more than twenty years before finding her, so he didn't care about her. She couldn't trust whatever he told her. And the past didn't matter as much as her present and her future.

If she and Troy even had one…

"You look very stressed for someone so young," a voice remarked.

Startled that she wasn't alone, Lakin jumped, making her chair creak. A hand touched her shoulder, maybe just to steady her, but she jumped up from her chair at the unwelcome contact and so that Eric Seller wasn't standing over her anymore like he had been. "Are you okay?" he asked.

She shook her head. "I didn't hear you come into the office."

"You need one of those bells that ding when the door opens," he suggested.

Usually people didn't slip in so silently, so it had never been an issue before. Although Jasper Whitlaw had the other day.

"Do you need something?" she asked. She hadn't even realized that he'd signed up for another tour. But then she'd been distracted lately and not really doing her job as well as she should. She needed to talk to Parker and give her notice.

"I was just thinking about you, Lakin, and wanted to make sure that you're okay," he said.

Instead of reassuring her, his words made her more uneasy than she usually was around him. "I'm fine," she said. "No need to worry about me." And definitely no reason to make a special trip to Shelby.

"I've seen all the news about some serial killer targeting single women in this area," he said. "So naturally I thought of you."

"I'm not single," she said.

"You're not married," he said. "Or even engaged. You could be a potential target."

She shivered. "With some of the victims not even identified yet, nobody knows if they were single or not. So are you just trying to scare me?" she asked. And it was working since she wondered how he knew something that hadn't been disclosed in the press.

His eyes widened as if in surprise. "Oh, I guess I just assumed that they were all single. And I think, that with you looking similar to previous victims and being alone so often, you need to be extra careful."

"I am," she assured him or maybe she was warning him.

He glanced around the office. "Really? You're all alone here. Even that boyfriend of yours isn't hanging around..." He took a step closer, as if he'd been waiting for the opportunity to get her alone.

She opened her mouth and considered releasing a scream but instead she shouted, "I'm not alone!" And hoped like hell she was telling the truth because she wasn't sure what Seller was trying to do.

"Lakin!" Parker exclaimed, appearing suddenly in the doorway of his office. "What's going on?" He looked from her to Seller. "Is there a problem?"

Seller shook his head and stepped back from her desk. "No problem at all. I'm just very concerned about your sister."

"Why?" Parker asked with his usual bluntness.

"Just seems like Shelby is a dangerous place for a single woman," Seller said.

Parker snorted. "Lakin isn't single. She's been with

Troy Amos for most of their lives, and he will make damn certain nothing happens to her."

"Really?" Seller asked. "I understand that he isn't usually around that much."

Lakin nearly screamed now—with irritation, not fear. "I can take care of myself," she assured them both.

"But there's a serial killer on the loose," Seller said. "His other victims probably thought the same thing you do, that they could take care of themselves."

Other victims. Was he saying that she was going to be next?

"Are you trying to scare her?" Parker asked. "And what are you doing here? You don't have a reservation, and we're completely booked."

Which was a lie. There had been a few cancellations, probably because of the serial killer scaring away some of their clients.

Seller held up his hands. "I'm sorry. I should have called ahead to make sure there was availability. I just had some downtime and came up for a quick fishing trip."

"You must have a lot of downtime," Parker remarked. "You're here a lot."

Had any of Seller's visits coincided with when those women disappeared? Lakin wanted to ask, but she didn't want to accuse one of their most frequent guests of being a serial killer. Although she suspected that her brother shared her suspicions. Parker moved even closer to them.

"I really enjoy my time in Shelby," Seller said. "I like to visit as often as I can. Let me know if you have a cancellation today. I'll take myself to that coffee shop in town for now. I can see that I've made you both uneasy. That was never my intention."

Lakin wasn't so sure about that.

Apparently neither was Parker. He didn't say anything else to Seller, just watched him until he left the building. Then he turned toward her. "Are you okay? I can refuse his business from now on and keep him away from you."

"I love you for offering to do that," she said. "But he's a great client."

"Not if he's creeping on you," Parker said. "I don't like how he was talking to you."

"Neither do I," she admitted. "But I'm just going to ignore him from now on."

"I don't think that's a good idea, either," Parker said. "We should talk to Eli about him. The comments he made about those victims…" He shuddered.

She nodded. "I agree that Eli should check him out." She didn't want anyone getting hurt because she had been too naive to believe someone she knew could be dangerous. She had a feeling that Seller wasn't the only person she knew who could be, though.

Parker nodded. "I'll give our big brother a call—"

"Wait," she said.

"You changed your mind? You think Seller is okay?"

"No. I just want to talk to you for a minute," she said. "I've been meaning to do it…" since she'd bought the hotel.

"What's going on, Lakin?" Parker asked with concern.

"I've been wanting to start my own business for a while now," she said.

"This is your business, too," Parker said, gesturing with open arms. "This is our family business."

"This is your business now," she said. "Since Dad and Uncle Ryan retired, you've taken over. You're the one who's made it more successful than it's ever been."

He shook his head. "No. That's been all of us working hard together."

She smiled. "I love working here, but I want to do what you've done. I want to take something and put all my energy into rebuilding it into what I want."

"Like what?" he asked.

"Like the Shelby Hotel."

"I thought that recently sold at auction," he replied.

"It did," she said, "to me."

"That's great, Lakin!" Parker hugged her, then pulled back. "But damn, that place needs a lot of work."

She nodded. "I know. That's why I'm going to need to devote all my time and energy to it."

"You're leaving?"

Tears stung her eyes at the thought of no longer working with her brother in the family business, but she nodded. "Yes, but I'll keep working here until you find my replacement."

"Nobody will ever be able to replace you," Parker said and hugged her again. "What about Troy? Will he be helping you?"

More tears rushed to her eyes, but she blinked them away, too. "I don't know."

"He was hurt on that damn oil rig," Parker said. "He's not going to go back, is he?"

"I hope not," she said. "But I think he will if he can."

"And leave you again? Leave you to do all the work at the hotel alone?"

"You know I won't be alone," she said.

Parker chuckled. "No, Dad is always looking for a new hobby."

"He helped me buy it," she admitted. "I'm going to pay him back, though, as soon as my business loan gets approved."

"I'm glad he has something else to think about," Parker said.

"Other than RTA?"

"Other than the Fiancée Killer."

She shuddered at the mention of the serial killer.

"You really need to be careful," Parker said. "The way Seller was talking…"

"I know," she agreed. "And I will be." But like Seller had pointed out, the serial killer's victims probably all thought they were being careful, too.

Troy was beyond pissed that Eli wouldn't tell him why he knew Jasper Whitlaw was dangerous. After his frustrating conversation with the ABI lieutenant, he left Roasters and headed straight to the RTA office…and walked into another tense conversation between Lakin and Parker.

They both assured him that everything was fine, but he had his suspicions, especially when they confirmed he had seen that Seller guy leaving. Troy was glad he'd given the man's name to Eli.

The office got busy after that, and neither Lakin nor Parker had time to talk. Neither did Hetty when she rushed in for a minute before leaving for a flight. All she said was, "Mom and I have been talking about you."

"That's nothing new," he replied with a chuckle.

"Do us all a favor," she said with a glance at Lakin who was on a call and hopefully not listening. "Stay here in Shelby. No more oil rigs. No more danger."

Even if he promised no more oil rigs, he couldn't promise no more danger. Nobody could. But Hetty rushed off again before he could point that out to her. Hell, not too long ago she'd been shot. She knew as did everyone who watched the news that Shelby wasn't safe at all anymore.

Once Lakin had a free moment, Troy told her about his conversation with Eli.

She nodded, unsurprised. "He texted me earlier. He's going to come by later this afternoon and fill me in," she said.

"Good."

"That means that you don't have to babysit me," she said. "You must be bored sitting around all day watching me."

"Never," he said. And it was true. He missed her so much when he was gone that he could never see enough of her to make up for it. Maybe Hetty was right; maybe it was time that he gave up working on the oil rigs. But what could he do in Shelby that would make enough money to help his family and Lakin with her business?

"Seriously, Troy, you don't need to be here," Lakin said. "There are a lot of people coming and going, and Eli will be here soon."

"Sounds like she's trying to get rid of you," Parker remarked when he stepped out of his office.

"That goes for you, too," she said. "You've been hovering."

"After that conversation this morning, I don't think you should be alone."

"Conversation?" Troy repeated. "What conversation? With Seller? What happened?"

Lakin sighed. "I don't want to rehash all this. And Eli is on his way. You can both take off. Go get a beer. Something."

It was obvious she didn't want him or Parker around when she talked to the ABI lieutenant. Or maybe she didn't want Troy around at all anymore. Maybe last night had been a goodbye. A last time…

The thought jabbed his heart with a sudden pain.

"You look like you could use a beer," Parker said. "And I know I could, too. Let's go."

Troy hesitated. "You won't leave on your own again?" he asked Lakin. "You'll have Eli see you safely back to the cabin?"

She sighed but nodded.

"She said she would be careful," Parker said, as if vouching for her. Or maybe he was trying to convince himself.

He repeated the same words just a short while later when they settled on stools at the bar.

"What did Seller say that rattled you so much?" Troy asked. It was clear that Parker and Lakin had both been rattled.

"He just kept talking about her being single and the damn serial killer." Parker shuddered.

Troy grimaced. "I'm glad I mentioned him to Eli."

"I texted Eli, too, to check out the guy," Parker admitted.

"I thought he was a great customer for RTA," Troy said.

"You know I love my sister more than I care about business," Parker said.

Troy clasped the man's shoulder. "I know."

"What about you?"

"What do you mean?"

"She told me about the hotel, but it doesn't sound like you're doing it with her," Parker said.

"I…"

"I know you got hurt on the oil rig the last time you were gone," Parker said. "But that's just another reason you shouldn't go back."

"Wow, everyone's piling on today about that," Troy said. "My sister, apparently my mother and now you."

"You can understand why we all want you to stay in Shelby," Parker said. "Especially now."

Troy sighed. "With that serial killer and Jasper Whitlaw running around…"

"Jasper Whitlaw?" Parker asked. "Who's that?"

Troy grimaced again. "I thought Lakin or Eli might have told you."

"About this Whitlaw person?"

Troy nodded. "I guess I should have known Lakin wouldn't tell you."

"So Eli knows about him," Parker said. "But why wouldn't Lakin tell me?"

"Because she doesn't want your mom and dad to know," Troy said. "And I shouldn't have said anything."

"But now that you have, you're going to have to spill," Parker said.

"Eli knows more than I do," Troy said.

"That's why he's coming by the office to talk to Lakin," Parker said. "It's about Whitlaw."

Troy nodded. "Yeah…" And it was killing him to not be part of that conversation. He had to know exactly how dangerous Jasper Whitlaw was. "Maybe we should go back and make Eli tell us, too."

"You heard Lakin," Parker said. "She didn't want us there." He looked over at Troy, his brow wrinkled with suspicion. "What's going on with you two? She doesn't seem really happy with you."

"She's not," Troy admitted.

"And here I thought you would do anything to make her happy."

Anything but burden her with a cripple or with debt that he couldn't help her pay off. He remembered all too well how his mother had struggled after his dad died. He didn't want to put Lakin through that; he loved her too much.

Maybe he had to accept that he wasn't what would make her happy.

THE BOYFRIEND WASN'T playing watchdog at the moment. Which was too bad because the gun lay on the seat next to him, and he couldn't wait to use it.

The boyfriend hadn't been around as much today as he usually was. When he was, he'd been with too many other people.

Unlike Lakin, who was alone right now. There wasn't another Colton anywhere around her as she sat alone in that office, watching the door, as if expecting someone to show up.

But he'd seen the others leave not long ago. The boyfriend and her brother were gone.

The others were as well.

She was all alone.

It was finally time to show little Miss Lakin just how much danger she was in…

Chapter Sixteen

Lakin waited and waited for Eli until she finally got a text from him.

Something came up. Will have to talk to you tomorrow.

What was the something that had come up? Had another body been found? Or maybe the serial killer?

She really hoped that was the case, so that nobody else would get hurt. Nobody else should lose their life or a loved one like her dad had lost so many people he cared about. She would have asked Eli why he couldn't make it, but too often he ignored questions like that. He had to keep the details of an investigation close to his chest so that things didn't get leaked to the press.

Despite his efforts, things did seem to be getting leaked.

Lakin understood why he had to be so secretive, but she would feel so much better if she knew what had come up. She would also feel so much better if she wasn't completely alone. But she was the one who'd shooed out Parker and Troy, so that she could talk to Eli without them present.

Now…

She could call either one of them, and they would rush back to her side. Still, she appreciated having a little distance from Troy, especially after last night.

She wanted to be with him again, wanted to sleep in his arms like she had the night before. She loved him so much, but she was pretty sure she was going to have to let him go when he went back to the oil rigs. After he'd been hurt, she would be terrified the entire time he was gone that he would be hurt again. She didn't want to live in fear of losing him. Or of losing herself.

That was how she felt right now, like she was losing part of herself. For so many years, it had been the two of them, loving and laughing and making plans for the future. But apparently she was the only one who really intended to follow through on those plans.

No. She wasn't going to live in fear for Troy or for anyone else. Seller had made her uneasy with his comments this morning, but she was not going to let him make her feel like a victim before anyone even tried to hurt her.

She'd already proven when she'd been abandoned at three years old that she was a survivor. She was strong.

She drew in a deep breath, stepped outside and locked the office door behind her. It was just a short distance from the office's porch to where her SUV was parked, but night had fallen like a black blanket. The porch light bore only a small hole in it. She pulled out her key fob and flashed her lights on, and that was when she saw *him*.

Not his face. But his height, his broadness. A man stood out in the darkness. Waiting for her…

With where he was standing between her and her SUV, she wouldn't be able to get into her vehicle. And if she turned around to unlock the office door, he might have time to run up and force his way inside with her before she could lock the door behind herself again.

She clicked her key fob again, turning on the vehicle alarm. Hopefully the blare of the horn and the blinking lights would draw a guest from their cabin or catch the attention of someone driving by.

She didn't wait around to find out. She ran.

The man ran after her; she could hear his feet pounding the ground behind her. She might have screamed, but she wasn't about to waste her breath. She needed all of it as she ran for her life.

ELI GLANCED AT his phone to confirm that Lakin had read his text. She'd given it a thumbs-up because, of course, she would. She wouldn't argue with him and insist that he tell her what he'd found out about the man claiming to be her father, not like Troy would.

Or Kansas.

His cousin stood next to him in the lab, intently watching the tech, Scott Montgomery, process the photograph. Since Eli had shared the situation with Kansas, she was as worried about Lakin as he was. She'd suggested they run more tests on the old snapshot.

"I'm sorry," Montgomery said. "I can't get enough DNA off the photograph to process, let alone compare it to anything left at the other crime scenes."

Kansas cursed.

Eli swallowed his. "Thanks for trying."

Scott nodded. "No problem. I really wish I was able to do more."

"We know," Kansas assured the man who smiled shyly back at her.

Eli figured the tech had a crush on her. But he suspected he wasn't the only man Eli worked with who had one on the beautiful state trooper.

"You really think this guy could be the serial killer?" Montgomery asked.

Eli shrugged. "I don't know. But I hope not." It would make sense, though, since the killings hadn't started until after Whitlaw's release from prison. That was why Eli had agreed with Kansas that the trip to the lab to try to pull DNA off the photograph was more important than meeting with Lakin. Eli could help her more by putting Whitlaw back in prison than by filling her in on what little he'd learned about the man.

But this trip to the lab hadn't given them any new information and definitely no connection between Whitlaw and the Fiancée Killer.

As much as Eli wanted to find and stop the serial killer, he wasn't sure that he wanted it to be Whitlaw. The man was focused on Lakin right now. And not for the reason he claimed. What was his real connection to her?

More important, what did he really want from her?

TROY KNEW HE shouldn't have left Lakin alone at the RTA office. When Parker got the text from Eli that he'd canceled on her, Troy rushed out of the bar and back to RTA. He didn't wait for Parker. He was too worried.

And for good reason. When he drove into the lot, he saw the lights flashing and heard the horn blaring on her SUV. Either someone had tried to break into it, or she had deliberately set off the alarm. Either way she was in trouble.

The second he threw open the door to his truck, he heard her scream. It chilled his blood. And then he started running.

She must be trying to get back to her cabin. He headed that way, yelling her name. He wasn't just calling out to let her know he was coming, but also to whoever might be chasing her.

Unless they'd already caught her...

He heard other running footsteps, but he couldn't see anything. Not even a star or a sliver of moon lit the way. What had happened to the lights in the other cabins? Were they all vacant?

"Lakin!" he called out again, trying to figure out where she was.

But she didn't call back to him. Was someone holding a hand over her mouth? Or was it worse than that?

"Lakin! The police are coming!" he yelled again. But he hadn't called them yet. Hopefully someone had who'd seen her lights flashing and heard her horn honking.

But if not...

There was no help coming but him. He had to find her.

It was too dark for him to track footprints unless he pulled out his phone. He heard no sirens in the distance. He needed to call the police himself.

He flashed his cell light on and immediately heard a gun cock. Then, seconds later, the blast of it being fired.

His first fear was for her, that Lakin had been shot.

But before he could call out to her, she screamed his name. Leaves rustled, and branches snapped near his head as bullets fired at him.

He ducked down, trying to take cover. It was clear whoever had been after her was willing or maybe even determined to kill him so that he didn't get in their way.

But he wasn't as worried about his life as he was hers. He had to figure out a way to stay alive and make sure that she did, too.

Chapter Seventeen

The person pursuing her had been so close that for a second Lakin had felt his breath on the back of her neck, his hand reaching for her hair. She'd screamed and ran harder, faster, more desperately because she hadn't thought anyone would hear her scream any more than they'd heard the blare of her vehicle alarm.

But then Troy had called out to her. She should have been relieved, but now she was afraid for both of them.

Instead of calling back with the man so close to her, she'd ducked under some low-hanging pine boughs. She held her breath, terrified.

Until she heard the gunshots.

She screamed Troy's name. But the shots weren't as close as she expected. Had the man turned around and gone back toward the office? Or had he gone after Troy instead?

Like the white knight he'd always been for her, Troy had rushed to her rescue, putting his own life in danger.

She didn't know what to do. If she ran from her hiding place, she could get shot, too. And then she wouldn't be able to help Troy. If she turned on her phone, the light or the sound of it could give away her location. But she had to get help.

Pulling her RTA shirt out of her waistband, she concealed her phone inside it, then texted an SOS to her sibling/cousin group chat. Her fingers were trembling so badly that all she managed was in fact SOS. She couldn't text that she was afraid Troy was hurt.

That he might have been shot…

She didn't even want to think it, as if putting her fear into words would somehow make it come true.

Tears burned her eyes, and so many regrets rushed through her. She'd been so frustrated with him since he'd come back, so disappointed with his stubbornness. She'd wasted so much time being angry when she could have been with him like she'd been last night. Like she wanted to be now, wrapped up in his strong arms, feeling his heart beating against hers.

Was his heart still beating? Was Troy alive?

Or had one of those gunshots stopped his heart? If it had, Lakin suspected hers would stop, too.

THE SOS SCARED the crap out of Kansas. It wasn't like Lakin to ask for help ever. Not even back when she was being bullied in school. She'd just ignored the bullies until one of her brothers or Kansas or the Amoses had put a stop to it. Of all of them, Troy had been the most effective at ending the bullying.

Where was he that Lakin had sent out an SOS? He was back from the oil rigs, so he should have been where he usually was when he was in Shelby, at Lakin's side.

"Can't you drive any faster?" she asked Eli, even

though he probably already had the accelerator pressed to the floorboards of his ABI SUV.

He didn't even spare her a glance. Was he mad at her? If she hadn't talked him into the trip to the lab, he would have been here with Lakin, protecting her from whatever compelled her to send that SOS text.

"Scott really thought he might be able to get something off the photograph," she said. "And if this Whitlaw guy is the Fiancée Killer…" He was even more dangerous than they'd thought.

And he was out there, somewhere in Shelby, stalking Lakin.

Kansas swore, then added, "I'm really sorry."

Eli still didn't say anything, but a muscle twitched in his cheek from how tightly he'd clenched his jaw. And Kansas knew if something happened to Lakin, Eli wasn't going to forgive her any more than she was going to forgive herself.

As they neared RTA, other sirens blared and lights flashed. Kansas had called the local police, knowing that they would reach the location given for Lakin's cell sooner than she and Eli would. But it wasn't just the local police already on the scene, an ambulance was as well. Had someone been hurt? Kansas prayed that it wasn't Lakin. But if not her, who? So much of their family worked at RTA. Even her dad and her uncle stopped by frequently despite having "retired" from the adventure business they'd started when they first moved to Shelby. When they'd fled from family tragedy to start over.

But had family tragedy found them again?

TROY FLINCHED AS the EMT pressed something against the stinging skin on his cheek. He wasn't sure if a bullet had grazed his face or one of the tree branches he'd jumped into for cover. But he didn't care about himself.

"Are you really all right?" he asked Lakin again. He tried to see her around the paramedic treating Troy in the back of the ambulance.

Once the emergency vehicles had pulled into the parking lot of RTA, the shooting had stopped, and Troy wasn't the only one who'd rushed out of a hiding place. Fortunately Lakin had been hiding, too.

"Like I already told you, I'm fine," she said. "He never took any shots at *me*. I didn't even know he had a gun until I heard the shooting start."

"Who was it?" Kansas asked just as Bobby Reynolds opened his mouth. Probably to ask the same thing. Clearly Lakin's cousin and brother weren't willing to leave this investigation in the officer's hands.

Lakin shook her head. "I never saw more than a shadow. He was standing by my SUV when I clicked my key fob to unlock it. Then I set off the alarm."

"That was smart," Kansas said.

"But then I couldn't see anything with the lights flashing," Lakin said.

"You couldn't tell if it was Jasper Whitlaw?" Eli asked, appearing beside Kansas.

"Where were you?" Troy asked the ABI lieutenant. "I wouldn't have left her if you hadn't said you were meeting her at the office."

"That was my fault," Kansas said. "I thought one of our techs could get DNA off that photograph, but he wasn't able to after all."

"So he couldn't get any DNA to see if it matches..." Lakin said, her voice soft with obvious disappointment.

"He's not your father," Eli said.

She nodded. "I know that Dad is—"

"That's not what I meant," Eli interrupted her. "He can't be your biological father because he was in prison for assault. He was serving a two-year sentence during the time you would have been conceived and born."

"He's been in prison," Troy said, his gut churning with fear for Lakin. Just as he'd suspected, the man was dangerous as well as a liar.

Eli nodded. "More than once. He's been in and out a lot for assault. And he just got out recently."

"And came looking for me," Lakin remarked. "Why? Since I'm not his daughter, what does he want?"

"I don't know," Eli said.

Troy had an idea. Money. But when he'd mentioned that before, Lakin had gotten upset with him. And he didn't want her to be upset with him again, especially not when they'd come so close to losing their lives.

"What are you going to do to keep her safe is the real question," Troy said.

"We don't know that the person who shot at you is Jasper Whitlaw," Eli pointed out.

Troy had given the lieutenant some other potential suspects. But he couldn't see Billy Hoover waiting all these years before trying to take him out. Unless he was so damn drunk he wasn't thinking straight. And Seller...

Did a guy as rich as that do his own dirty work? And why would he go after Troy anyway? Why would anyone? Unless it was just because he was in their way, standing between them and Lakin.

Harrison's threat rang in his ears again, about losing more than his job if he went through with the lawsuit. Had he been talking about Troy's life?

But the shooter had been waiting in the parking lot for Lakin, trying to get her alone. Well, if anyone knew Troy at all, they would know that it would hurt him more if Lakin was hurt. Hell, it would destroy him.

"We have to make sure Lakin is safe," Troy said.

"You're the one who nearly got shot," Lakin pointed out. "You need protection, too."

He needed her. He needed to close his arms around her and never let her go. But he wasn't sure that would keep either of them safe.

"We'll keep an officer in the area," Reynolds said.

"We'll be close, too," Eli said, gesturing toward him and Kansas.

Reynolds nodded. He probably knew better than to argue with a Colton. When one of them was in danger, they were going to rally around their loved one.

Troy was counting on that. He wasn't doing a very damn good job on his own keeping Lakin safe. But he definitely wasn't going to leave her side from now on, either.

He told her as much when they were finally escorted safely inside her cabin.

Instead of the pushback he expected, she linked her arms around his neck and hugged him. Then she pulled back and touched his face below the bandage on his cheek.

"Never leaving my side isn't safe or practical," she said. "You could have been killed tonight."

"And here everybody has been worrying about me

working on the oil rigs," he said. "I've been in more danger since coming back to Shelby."

"But all you have so far is a scratch," she said. "You were hospitalized from working on the oil rig."

Hospitalized and paralyzed. The fear of feeling that helpless ever again never left him. Though he'd nearly felt that helpless tonight when he hadn't known where she was or if she was safe.

"I was so worried about you," he admitted. "When I saw the alarm going off on your vehicle and then I heard you scream…" He shuddered as he relived those moments.

She hugged him again. "I'm safe, Troy."

For now. "I'm going to do everything I can to make sure you stay that way," he assured her.

"So now you're my bodyguard?"

He nodded. "Until you're no longer in danger."

"We're safe here," she said. "You know there are officers and troopers outside watching the cabin."

Troy stepped back. "So you don't want me close?"

"I want you even closer," she said with a smile. She entwined her fingers with his and tugged him through the open bedroom door.

His pulse quickened almost to the speed it had been when he'd heard her scream. He'd been so afraid that he'd lost her. But she was here, with him. Safe.

But he was still so afraid he was going to lose her. Maybe not to a killer, but to his own stubbornness. "I love you, Lakin," he said.

And he waited for her to say it again. But she kissed him instead, her mouth moving over his. As she kissed him, she undressed him.

Once he was naked, she dropped to her knees and closed her lips around his shaft. He groaned, and she lifted her head. "Are you all right?"

"No," he said.

"Where are you hurt?"

"I ache," he said.

She jumped up from the floor. "Do I need to call the paramedics back?"

He shook his head. "You're the only one who can relieve this pain," he said.

"Oh…" She smiled as she realized what he was saying.

"I need you so badly." His entire body was filled with a tension only she could relieve. But he didn't want her to do it with her mouth. He wanted to be inside her, part of her.

He undressed her, baring every silky inch of her skin for his touch and his taste. He ran his lips and his tongue over her breasts and then lower.

Her knees buckled, and she dropped back onto the bed, pulling him down with her. He rolled over so that he wouldn't crush her, but Lakin wasn't small or delicate. She was strong, and she pushed him onto his back and straddled him. Then she guided his cock inside her, and it was like coming home.

She moaned and bit her lip. Then she began to move with frantic urgency, as if she was as desperate for release as he was. He reached up and cupped her breasts in his hands.

She leaned down, her dark hair falling like a curtain around them as she kissed him. Their mouths mated like their bodies.

He stroked his thumbs over her nipples. She moaned again and moved faster, rocking back and forth, sliding up and down, driving him out of his mind. Then she came, her inner muscles convulsing around him, squeezing his cock.

She screamed his name. His body tensed, and finally his release came. He thrust his hips up, filling her as she filled his heart with the love he felt for her.

He didn't dare express it again, afraid that she wouldn't say it back. That she couldn't. Maybe she didn't love him anymore, or at least not like she once had when she could see a future for them. Their business, a family… All the dreams she'd had for their life together… He'd taken them away from her with his unwillingness to commit.

And tonight someone else had nearly taken his life. Had the shooter been after him or her?

He must have tensed up again because she wrapped her arms around him and murmured, "Go to sleep. We're safe here."

He was worried they wouldn't be safe anywhere from whoever was after them. Was it Jasper Whitlaw? Someone else? Someone who might be even more dangerous, like the Fiancée Killer?

Chapter Eighteen

Lakin should have been exhausted, but maybe there was just too much adrenaline coursing through her body. From the close call she and Troy had had and from how they'd made love again. While he'd fallen asleep afterward, she lay awake next to him, listening to his even breathing and the beat of his heart beneath her cheek.

She loved him so much even when he frustrated her with his stubbornness. But was he the only one being stubborn?

She'd thought she didn't want him leaving again because she didn't want him getting hurt on the oil rigs, but as he pointed out, he'd been hurt here, too. Was his safety just an excuse she was using because she wanted him with her?

She did want him with her. Always. But she also didn't want him getting hurt, and in trying to protect her like he had tonight, he had been. The bandage on his chiseled cheekbone made her feel queasy with regret and fear.

Her cell vibrated against the bedside table with an incoming call. Not wanting to wake up Troy, she grabbed it from the nightstand and slipped out of bed. Maybe it was one of her siblings calling. Or one of the officers watching the cabin.

But when she stepped out of the bedroom and looked down at the number, she recognized the one Jasper Whitlaw had scrawled on the back of the photograph.

He wasn't her father, but why had he been in that picture with her and her biological mother?

Wanting answers, she slid her finger across the screen to accept the call, but she couldn't bring herself to say anything. She had no idea what to say. Even if she asked the questions she had for him, she doubted he would tell her the truth.

"Hey, little girl," he greeted her. He sounded amused. Was this all some sick joke to him?

"I know you're not my father," she told him.

He snorted. "What? You trying to pretend you're really a Colton now?"

"I am," she said. "But I know you were in prison around the time I would have been conceived and born. You're nothing to me."

"I'm a link to your mother," he said. "If you want to know the truth about her…"

Her heart yearned for the truth, to know more about the woman she looked so much like. The woman who had left her in that grocery store all those years ago.

"I'll find her on my own," she said. That way she would trust what she found out. She wouldn't be hearing it from a man who'd already lied to her.

"You won't find her," he said.

A heaviness settled on Lakin's heart. She was dead. That had to be what he meant. But again she didn't trust him for the truth. "I'm not going to pay you for information on her," she warned him. "So if you're after money, you're not going to get any out of me."

"Then maybe I will go to your Colton daddy," Jasper threatened. "Or maybe I'll go straight to the press. They buy stories. They might be interested in one about a serial killer stalking Shelby, Alaska, the way Caroline Colton was stalked and murdered years ago along with her parents. I'm sure the press would love to dig up that family tragedy, probably set up their vans and stuff right outside Will and Sasha Colton's house. It's a nice one. I can make sure they find it like I did."

So he had been outside their house that day. Had he also driven Troy off the road?

"Stay away from my parents," she said. "And don't go to the press."

"Why?" he asked, as if he was only idly curious. "Are you going to make it worth my while?"

"I… I…" Lakin had no money of her own anymore. She'd put it all into the hotel. She couldn't go to her dad for more, not for this. Not for blackmail.

"I'll get some money," she said. But what she really intended was to get Eli and Kansas to track down and arrest the blackmailer. They would probably have to have a recording of him actually blackmailing her, though, so it was more than her word against his.

"It better be more than I can get from the press for selling this story," he threatened.

"It will be." She wished she'd been recording this call. If only that had occurred to her sooner… "Where do I find you when I get the money together?" she asked.

"Since all you've given me was forty bucks, I've been

camping outside, not far from your place," he said. "I couldn't afford a hotel."

From the way he said *hotel*, she wondered if he knew about the Shelby Hotel. Had he been there that day the window was broken? He had to be the one who'd been stalking her. He knew too much, like where her parents lived. It made her sick that she might have been the one who led him to them.

"Were you here tonight?" she asked. "Did you shoot at Troy?"

He snorted. "Why would I shoot at anyone, girl? That's not going to get me what I want, which is money enough to start over somewhere. And since I'm still on probation, I can't have a firearm. It wasn't me."

What he said made sense but also made her more uneasy. If not him, who had taken those shots at Troy and why?

"Where can I find you?" she asked.

He named a road that had a riverbank on one side where people often camped. He probably wasn't alone out there. She would make certain that *she* wasn't alone when she met him.

But she was also going to make sure Troy wasn't with her or anywhere near her. She didn't want him putting his life in danger trying to keep her safe.

TROY JERKED AWAKE, imagining he felt that sting against his cheek all over again. But it was just a dull throb, unlike his pulse that was suddenly racing when he realized he was alone in bed.

"Lakin!" he called out.

Maybe she was just in the bathroom. But he jumped

out of bed to find it and the rest of the cabin empty. She was gone.

He didn't think she would have headed to the office this early. Dawn had only lightened the sky a bit; the sun had yet to rise. So where was she?

He grabbed his cell and called her, but her voicemail immediately picked up. She either wasn't taking his call or she couldn't.

He called Eli next. "You're supposed to have someone watching Lakin. Do you know where she is?" He braced himself for Eli to point out that Troy had said he was watching her. He already felt so damn guilty for falling asleep. More than once she'd slipped out of the cabin without him noticing. Good thing he wasn't a real bodyguard.

"She called me," Eli said. "And told me where she's headed."

"Where?" Troy asked. But part of him already knew and dreaded what her brother was about to tell him.

"To meet Jasper Whitlaw," Eli confirmed his worst fear.

"Why the hell would she do that?" They'd told her the man was dangerous. He'd been in and out of prison for assault for years.

"He threatened our family," Eli said.

Troy knew Lakin would do anything to protect the family she loved so much. He cursed.

"I'm on my way to catch up with her," Eli said. "She can't have much of a head start. She called me just a few minutes ago."

Hopefully she didn't have much of a head start on

Troy either then. "Where?" he asked. "Where is she meeting him?"

"She didn't wake you up because she doesn't want you getting shot again," Eli said. "So I'm not going to be the one who puts you in danger."

"No, you're not," Troy agreed. "I am."

But he realized he didn't need Eli's help to find her. He disconnected the call.

Years ago, he and Lakin had shared their phone locations with each other. Because he was out of cellular range so much when he was working on the oil rigs, he had nearly forgotten. He checked it now.

A little dot blinked within a circle close to a riverbank just a short distance from RTA.

He would be able to find her. Hopefully he wouldn't be too late to help her. Because he didn't think Jasper Whitlaw was just a threat to her family.

He was a threat to her, too.

HE'D PUT FEAR in her; he knew and relished that fear. Now all he had to do was wait. When people were afraid, they didn't think rationally. They were too emotional, too panicked, to think clearly. To make a plan.

Like the plan he'd made.

The plan he was going to carry out so that he would finally get what was owed to him.

And so would the Coltons.

Chapter Nineteen

Lakin knew she was taking a risk sneaking out on her own, but she didn't want Troy to get hurt again. She didn't want her family hurt, either, but she had called Eli for help. She glanced at her phone, checking the time. He should have been here already.

He'd told her to wait for him before she got out of her vehicle, but she was impatient. She needed to record Jasper Whitlaw's threats and extortion attempt. Then she could use that to make him leave Shelby and her family in peace. She couldn't wait any longer for her brother. Maybe he was already here. He'd told her that he would stay out of sight so Whitlaw wouldn't know he was there.

But where was Whitlaw?

Lakin walked around the area where he claimed to be camping, but she didn't see even a place where a sleeping bag might have lain let alone remains of a fire. It got cold at night in September. Maybe he was sleeping in his truck and just parking it here.

But she didn't even see any tire tracks.

Had he lied to her?

But why? She couldn't give him the money she'd promised him if she couldn't find him.

Had he realized she was lying and trying to set him up? That would explain why he'd given her a phony location.

She might have been relieved that he wasn't here if she wasn't more worried about where he might be. Had he accosted her dad like he had her? Was he trying to get money directly from the Coltons? Why did he seem to resent them for adopting her anyway? She'd been abandoned. It wasn't like Whitlaw or anyone else had wanted her but the Coltons.

And eventually Troy had wanted her, too. Or so she'd thought. Of course, now she wasn't as confident of having a future with him as she had been. Actually, after the shooting last night, she wasn't as confident of having a future at all.

But nobody had been shooting at her. They'd been shooting at Troy. Was he the real target in all of this?

She'd left him back at the cabin, alone and asleep and completely vulnerable.

What the hell had she been thinking? Could she get back to him in time to make sure that he was safe? Or was she already too late?

Troy jumped in his truck and headed right where he thought Lakin was. But once he was away from the Wi-Fi of the cabin, her location disappeared, and he wasn't able to pull up cellular data either. He had no bars out here; the tower was too far away. So he had no idea where she was, just where she'd been.

Wandering around the riverbank where he'd pinpointed her location earlier, he wasn't even sure where he was.

Why would Lakin have met Whitlaw here? Or Eli? Wasn't Eli supposed to be coming as her backup, to make sure she stayed safe? Had the ABI lieutenant let her down again?

A branch snapped behind Troy, and he whirled around with his fists up to defend himself. They were his only weapon.

But the gun that faced him wasn't the one that fired at him the night before. Eli immediately holstered his weapon when he saw Troy.

"Of course you wouldn't stay away like I told you to," Eli remarked.

"Of course I wouldn't," Troy agreed. "Not that there is anything or anyone to stay away from. Have you seen Lakin or Whitlaw?"

Eli shook his head. "I saw some tire tracks, but they appear to be from only one vehicle. Probably Lakin's SUV."

"Not Whitlaw's truck," Troy said. "Why would he tell her to meet him here?"

"Maybe he knew what she was up to," Eli remarked. "And wasn't going to fall for it."

"What was she up to?" Troy asked. "Why would she agree to meet him? She has no money to give him." She'd invested it all in the hotel. Troy would have given her money if she'd asked, though...and if he'd thought that was really all that Whitlaw wanted. But now, knowing Whitlaw wasn't her father, he had a feeling the man had a whole other agenda where Lakin was concerned.

"She was going to record him demanding money in exchange for keeping his mouth shut to the press about my family. If she could get him to admit to that, I could arrest him for extortion," Eli explained.

Troy chuckled for a moment at her brilliance. She was going to turn the tables on an ex-con. But then his amusement dried up. "So where is she?"

"I don't know," Eli said. "I had to take a detour around a logging truck that lost some of its load in the road. So I was late getting here."

"But like you pointed out, there is only one set of tire tracks here," Troy said. "Whitlaw drives an old truck. His tread marks would have been bigger and deeper than Lakin's."

Eli nodded. "He was never here."

"I don't get why he would have told her to meet him here even if he knew what she was up to," Troy said. "Why this place?" He glanced around at the river and the trees surrounding them.

"I don't know," Eli murmured. "Maybe he wanted her away from the cabin. Or away from someone else."

Troy's stomach muscles clenched with dread. "I don't like this."

"Me, neither," Eli agreed. "He was threatening to go public with my family tragedy."

Troy sucked in a breath. "When you said family, I didn't think about your aunt and grandparents' murders. How did he find out about that? And no wonder Lakin agreed to meet him and pay him off." With money she didn't have. But maybe she would have gone to the same person she'd gone to for the hotel. "Call your dad," he suggested. "See if he's heard from her."

"I don't think she wants him to know what's going on," Eli said.

Troy suspected she wasn't the only one who didn't want to worry their father. But he knew how much Will and Sasha Colton loved their daughter. "He's going to want to know," he pointed out. He'd realized too late how many people he'd hurt because he hadn't reached out when he was injured. "The people who love you want to show up for you."

Eli groaned. "You're right."

Troy took no comfort from that. He wasn't going to feel better until he knew where Lakin was and that she was safe. "While you call him, I'm going to head back to the cabin. She probably would have gone back there or the office."

Eli reached out and squeezed his shoulder. "Be careful."

Troy nodded. He wasn't worried about himself; he was worried about her. She'd agreed to meet with a dangerous ex-con in order to protect her family. She didn't care about her own safety at all.

And finally he could relate to how she felt when he went off to work the oil rigs, doing the same job that had killed his father, knowingly putting himself in danger just as she had done in agreeing to meet Whitlaw.

Troy had to find her before something happened to her. She was the most amazing person, so kind and loving and supportive to everyone. Troy had failed her in so many ways; he just wanted to have the chance to make it up to her.

WILL HATED GETTING calls this early in the morning because they were rarely good news. At least it hadn't woken him up; he'd already been out for his run and was just opening the back door when his cell vibrated.

Sasha was awake, too, in the kitchen. He could hear the pots and pans and smell the coffee brewing. But he stepped back outside to answer the call.

"Good morning, Eli. Or at least I hope it is."

The hesitation was all the confirmation Will needed that there was nothing good about this morning.

Then Eli asked, "Have you seen Lakin today?"

Will's stomach pitched a bit, and he was glad it was still empty. "No. Is there any reason she would have been by so early? Why are you looking for her?"

"Uh, it's just…"

Eli's breath of relief rattled his phone. "Never mind. Troy texted that her phone location shows she's back at her cabin."

"What's going on, son?" Will demanded.

"We'll bring you up to speed soon," Eli promised, and he ended the call before Will could argue.

What the hell was going on? When Lakin stopped by a few days ago, she'd seemed tense and distracted. She'd kept looking out the window, almost as if she thought she was being followed.

His skin chilled at the thought of his daughter having a stalker like Caroline had. Nobody had believed that man was dangerous until it was too late.

Until too many lives had been lost…

That couldn't be the case with Lakin. Will could not let that be the case because he couldn't lose any more of his family than he already had.

Lakin had to be safe.

Chapter Twenty

When Lakin pulled up to the cabin, Troy's truck was gone. That meant he'd driven off somewhere, and she could imagine where: to find her.

Sneaking off without him wasn't going to keep him safe, especially if he'd been the target all along. She knew he'd talked to her brother Mitch about what happened on the oil rig. Maybe the lawyer had talked to the company and they'd sent someone to shut Troy up. After all, a dead man couldn't sue them. Not that she was sure he was having Mitch sue for him or just to make the workplace safer.

Troy *should* sue them for his pain and suffering. But when Troy's mother had sued the company, the case had been dismissed. Now it had cost her a husband and very nearly a son as well. Lakin wanted to make sure that Mrs. Amos didn't lose that son here in Shelby, either.

Even though it didn't look like he was in the cabin, Lakin headed inside to see if he'd left a note. Although he probably would have texted instead. She reached for her cell as she approached the door, but finding it partially open distracted her. Since his truck wasn't here, she assumed that Troy had left in such a hurry that he hadn't closed it tightly.

She needed to find out where he was. She unlocked her phone as she pushed open the door to the empty cabin.

But it wasn't empty. There was the acrid smell of cigarette smoke, so thick that someone had to still be inside. She backed toward the front door, but it banged into her.

Before she could whirl around to see who had been hiding behind the door, a hand covered her nose and mouth with a cloth and blocked her vision. Another smell, cloying and syrupy, filled her nose, smothering in its sweetness.

She tried to wrest herself away, but a strong arm encircled her, keeping her arms locked to her sides. As the smell overwhelmed her, consciousness began to fade. Her phone slipped through her fingers and dropped to the floor.

Then her legs buckled, and she dropped to the floor as well. She blinked, trying to clear her vision, but before she could focus on the face of the intruder, the last of her consciousness slipped away.

ONCE TROY HAD driven a short distance away from the riverbank, he'd been able to pull up Lakin's location again. She'd gone back to the cabin, so he texted Eli to let him know. Unfortunately when he pulled off the road to send that text, a tractor had managed to get ahead of him. A very slow-moving tractor.

When he was finally able to pass it, he worried that Lakin might leave the cabin again before he got back to her. Instead of checking his cell again, he pressed harder on the accelerator until he was speeding down the lane to her cabin.

He breathed a sigh of relief when he saw her SUV parked near the porch. She was still home.

And that was what she was to him: home. His heart, where he always wanted to be, was here in her cabin on RTA property or in the old Shelby Hotel. Suite Home would be a sweet home for them.

Eager to tell her that and confirm that she was really all right, Troy pushed open his driver's door and nearly sprinted up to the porch.

But when he neared the door and found it partially open, his heart started beating even faster. He drew in a breath, inhaling something unusual, cloying and chemical at the same time. He coughed, cleared his throat, then yelled, "Lakin!"

His shout echoed off the wood walls and floor. There was no response. Outside not even a bird chirped or a leaf rustled. She was gone.

He wanted to believe that she'd walked to the office, but she wouldn't have left without closing and locking the cabin door. And then there was that smell…

That chemical smell and a lingering odor of cigarette smoke.

When he stepped through the open door, he saw a big handkerchief lying on the floor. Was that where the smell was coming from?

He didn't touch it. He didn't dare because he had a feeling Lakin's home had just become a crime scene. But what was the crime? Abduction? Or worse?

He couldn't let himself think that. He couldn't let himself believe that he wouldn't see Lakin again, or he would become as paralyzed as when he fell from the oil rig. He wouldn't be able to breathe, let alone move.

He had to find her.

THE SEARCH AND rescue team had just gotten a call. Another woman was missing. The last woman who'd gone missing from the Shelby area had turned up just a few days ago. Dead. Dawn Ellis.

This woman could not turn up the same way. This woman was family. Kansas drew in a deep breath, trying to pull herself together, for her family's sake and mostly for Lakin's. She had to find her cousin.

So she rallied the search and rescue team. This had to be a rescue, not a recovery. They had to find Lakin.

Alive.

Chapter Twenty-One

Lakin was stuck in an old nightmare. The one where she could hear voices shouting at each other. She'd had such a hard time for so long with raised voices. School had been so tough in the beginning until she'd learned to ignore her reaction and suppress the old memories.

But they were back now, pulling her into the nightmare. The shouts. The sharp slap of skin against skin. Someone was fighting.

And the crying…

Someone was hurt.

Tears burned the back of her throat, like they were running down behind her closed eyes. Behind her closed eyes, images wavered, faded and yellowed like that old photograph Jasper Whitlaw had given her.

He wasn't her father.

But she heard her father's voice now: Will's deep rumble. He used to wake her up from the nightmares and hold her until she stopped crying and trembling.

She needed him now.

She needed Troy to rush to her rescue like he always did. She imagined she felt like he had after falling off the oil rig—she couldn't move. She couldn't even open her eyes. She couldn't pull herself out of the nightmare.

She had to…

She couldn't keep counting on other people to rescue her. Especially not Troy. He wasn't sticking around. He would go back to those damn oil rigs, back to putting his life in danger. Maybe it was better being in danger doing a job than defending her. She didn't want him getting shot at again. She didn't want him or anyone else to risk their life for hers because she wouldn't be able to live with the guilt of causing someone else harm.

She had to rally her strength. And she also had to clear her head enough that she would be able to figure out who the hell had grabbed her and what they wanted with her. Then she had to get the hell away from them.

She drew in a little shaky breath and managed to lift her heavy lids. Not much… Just enough to see that she was in some kind of cave. Walls of rock surrounded her. The dirt was cold and hard beneath her body. The ground wasn't smooth, either; rocks and twigs poked into her back.

She tried to move her hands, but they were numb, the circulation cut off from duct tape binding her wrists tightly together.

There was duct tape around her ankles, too.

And over her mouth…

She couldn't move. She couldn't speak, and in the dimness of that cave, she really couldn't see, either. But she knew, from the rumble of voices, that she wasn't alone. Had more than one person abducted her? Was more than one holding her here? Or was it just one person on the phone?

A sudden flash of light illuminated a corner of the cave. The light was from a phone. She could see its screen but not the face of the person holding it. Once again, he was only a shadow looming in the darkness, like the monster she used to imagine lurked in her closet or under her bed.

Now she knew that the monster was real.

TROY KEPT HIS phone app open, looking for an update on Lakin's location. But her last location still showed the cabin from nearly an hour ago.

"Why do we have to wait for search and rescue?" Troy asked. Eli had shown up soon after Troy at the cabin. But it hadn't mattered; they'd both been too late to save Lakin from being abducted. "You and I should be able to follow the tracks."

"Do you want to waste your time?" Eli asked. "We don't know if she was dragged off to a vehicle or…" He choked as if he couldn't even say the words.

Was he going to say what Troy was afraid to even consider? That she'd been partially buried like those other women?

"She could have been put in a vehicle," Eli said. "And if they're not on foot, they could be anywhere. We have to wait for the dogs to see if they can follow a scent."

Troy understood that, but waiting was killing him. It was like those weeks he'd lain in the hospital bed unable to move, to feel anything but fear and panic. He'd hated that helplessness.

He hated even more that someone had taken Lakin.

"Where are they?" he asked, his voice gruff with the fear choking him. He felt as if he couldn't breathe, like he'd hit the water again after a long fall.

Eli shrugged. "I don't know where the team is, but they should be here soon."

Troy realized Lakin's brother was as frustrated and frightened as he was. Maybe more so because he'd seen what had happened to the other women who'd disappeared.

"This isn't the serial killer, is it?" Troy asked, although he'd been reluctant to even consider that horrific possibility. "This has to be Whitlaw. Or maybe that rich RTA client. Or Billy Hoover." But any of them might also be the serial killer. His stomach pitched, bile rising with the terrifying thought.

"It's not doing either of us any good with you speculating about what's happened," Eli said, his voice gruff with emotion. "We just need to stay calm."

When the person who mattered most to him was in danger? Possible grave danger? Troy was hanging on to his sanity the best he could at the moment. Calmness was out of the question.

"If the SAR team doesn't get here soon, I'm going to start looking myself," he warned Eli.

"And potentially contaminate the scene and the dogs' ability to track?" Eli shook his head. "You don't think I want to be out there myself, looking for my sister? I know I have to follow protocol."

Troy didn't have to; he wasn't in law enforcement. But he also didn't want to do anything that might lower their chances of finding Lakin alive.

ELI TOTALLY UNDERSTOOD and shared Troy's frustration. Where the hell was search and rescue? They had to get the damn dogs here before the scent went cold. Before they lost their chance to find his sister.

Troy was right; maybe they needed to just start looking for her themselves.

Eli's cell vibrated in his pocket. Maybe it was Kansas, calling with an updated ETA. But when he glanced at his screen it was lit up with: Dad.

Eli was tempted to swipe Ignore. But he couldn't help but wonder about the timing of his dad's call. Had someone notified their parents that Lakin was missing? If so, Dad had to be as out of his mind with fear as Eli and Troy.

He clicked to accept. "Dad—"

"Eli, I just got a ransom call for Lakin."

"What?"

"You told me she was home," Will reminded him. "So I wanted to check with you—"

"She's not here," Eli interjected. "Troy got back to the cabin and found the door open. Her SUV is here, but she isn't."

"And?" Will asked because he had to know there was more.

"Troy found a rag with chloroform on it," Eli admitted. It was the only way someone could have taken Lakin without her managing to get away like she had the other night when someone accosted her outside the office. She hadn't had to fight hard that night, though; she'd just had to run until Troy showed up.

But Troy hadn't been fast enough to save her this time, and Eli could tell it was killing him. Troy paced, his limp all but forgotten, as he waited for the SAR team.

"Did you get to talk to her, Dad?" Eli asked.

"No."

"Any proof that this person who called actually has her?"

"No," his father admitted. "But I don't care. I'm going to get the money together that they want, so I will be ready when they call back to tell me where to leave that money."

"Dad…" Eli wanted to warn him that it wouldn't guarantee her safe return. Nothing would. But his dad knew that as well as he did. "You have to make sure that you get to talk to her when the person calls back. What did the caller sound like?"

"A man. I couldn't tell his age or anything by his voice, though, and the phone number was blocked," his dad said.

"I'll have your records checked," Eli said. "We might be able to get it unblocked." Montgomery might know a way. The crime-scene tech was very savvy.

"You do what you have to do to get our girl back," Will said. "And so will I."

Eli's blood chilled. He'd never heard his dad sound so determined. But he knew why; he didn't want to lose Lakin like he'd lost his younger sister. Aunt Caroline.

Before he could say anything else, Dad disconnected the call.

"What is it?" Troy asked.

"My dad just got a ransom call."

Troy cursed.

"No, this could be good news," Eli said. "There were no ransom calls when those other women were abducted."

"So you don't think it's the Fiancée Killer who has

her?" Troy asked. He sounded a little more hopeful now as he stopped pacing and studied Eli's face.

Eli nodded. But just because it wasn't the serial killer who had her didn't mean she wasn't still in danger. He knew that; he just wanted to assuage some of Troy's fear and his own. But he wouldn't be sure of anything until they found Lakin. They had to find her.

Eli had been in law enforcement long enough to know how few kidnapping victims were ever recovered alive.

Lakin had to be the exception to that grim statistic, though. They had to be able to get her back safely. And soon.

Chapter Twenty-Two

Lakin closed her eyes, pretending to be asleep when the shadow moved from the corner of the cave over to where she lay. She knew it was best to not see the face of her abductor. He was more likely to let her go if she couldn't identify him.

That was her father's voice she'd heard in her dream. It had been coming from this man's cell phone. There was only one probable reason for that: a ransom call.

Dad had already loaned her so much money. She didn't want him paying out more for her. She definitely didn't want him to pay it only for her not to be released.

She intended to release herself, though. She'd managed to roll to her side and get one of those twigs near her wrists. She would be able to use the sharp end that had been jabbing into her back to fray the duct tape. If the man left her alone…

He stood for a long moment over her. Then he murmured, "Like looking at a damn ghost…"

Her skin chilled, goose bumps rising as she recognized the voice and simultaneously what he meant. Her birth mother was definitely dead. He wouldn't have called Lakin a ghost if she wasn't.

She schooled her features to remain relaxed, her breathing deep and easy. Finally he stepped over her. She lifted one lid just a fraction of an inch and watched as he exited the cave, which suddenly seemed brighter without Jasper Whitlaw inside it.

He was the dark shadow. The person who'd been stalking her. Just for money? Or was that nightmare about shouting and slapping and crying more than a dream? Could it be a memory? One Whitlaw might not want her to remember again.

Had she been there when her mother died?

In that case, even if her father paid him the ransom he demanded, Whitlaw might not have any intention of releasing her. She had to act fast.

She grabbed the stick and contorted her body so she could tear through the tape around her ankles. Then she wedged the sharp tip back between her wrists and managed to tear through the tape binding them as well. Once her hands were free, she reached up and eased the tape from her mouth, swallowing the cry of pain that wanted to slip out as the tape pulled at her skin and her lips.

She didn't want to alert Whitlaw that she was free. But she wasn't actually free yet. She pushed herself up from the ground, but her legs were shaky, and dizziness had black spots dancing before her eyes. She blinked and steadied herself, then moved to the mouth of the cave.

He was standing out there, near a battered old truck parked in a stand of pines. She hadn't seen that truck at the cabin when she came home earlier. Had it already been parked here? How had he managed to get it through the thick forest of trees that covered this side of the mountain? Was this the mountain behind RTA? Was she close to home?

She tried to consider which direction to go, but again dizziness threatened to overwhelm her. She really didn't have time to think. The man was just standing there smoking. If he turned and saw her...

She slipped out of the cave and started moving as quietly as she could away from him and that truck. Holding even her breath so that she wouldn't alert him, she placed each foot softly against the ground. But a twig snapped beneath the sole of her hiking boot.

He whirled toward her. "Damn it, girl. Stop! Stop right now, or I'll shoot you!"

She did the opposite. She ran like she had that night he'd been waiting for her outside the office.

She knew now that it had to have been him that night. He'd lied when he told her on the phone that he didn't have a gun. But of course she shouldn't have expected him to tell her the truth about anything. The man was a liar and probably a killer as well.

"You are just like your worthless mama, girl," he shouted as he ran after her. "No matter how many times Stella ran from me, I always caught that faithless wife of mine." He coughed, probably from all his smoking and the exertion of running. "I'm going to catch you, too, and then I'm going to kill you like I did her, like I would have killed you all those years ago if she hadn't dumped you in that grocery store."

Tears stung her eyes. Her mother hadn't abandoned her; she'd saved her. She must have already been wounded when she'd left her at the grocery store.

"Before I could find you, social services got involved, and then those damn Coltons adopted you," he said, his breathing getting more labored as he chased after her.

Her lungs burned with the need for more air as she wound higher up the mountain. Her feet slipped on rocks and sand, and she clutched at tree branches to pull herself up.

But he was so close that she could still hear everything he said. "Rich people like the Coltons think their money can buy them everything they want. But after that mess they went through back in California, they should know the one thing it can't buy 'em is life. It can't buy your life, little girl. Nothing can."

So even if her dad paid him the ransom, Whitlaw had no intention of letting her live any more than he'd let her biological mother live.

Lakin tried to run faster. She knew she was literally running for her life.

TROY HAD BEEN pushed back to the perimeter of the crime scene around the cabin now that the SAR team had finally arrived.

Kansas, her face pinched with the same fear Troy and Eli were feeling, led one of the dogs to the door of Lakin's cabin. It sniffed at the boards on the porch and then the door. As it sniffed the floor, it whined and backed off.

"The scent of chloroform might be lingering yet," a man with dark blond hair called out to Kansas. "I'm sure that's what was on the handkerchief."

So was Troy, and he had never smelled chloroform before. He just knew it was something used to make people lose consciousness. That was probably the only way the kidnapper would have gotten Lakin out of the cabin without a fight.

Troy didn't really believe people had stopped bullying her just because of her family and his. It was because Lakin had gotten stronger; she'd learned to fight back. She would have done that today if she'd been able.

But the chloroform would have made her as helpless as he'd been after falling off the oil rig. At least he'd had his coworkers around to jump in and save him. Lakin had no one.

They'd waited so damn long for search and rescue to show up, or so it had seemed, that the scent of the trail to her might have gone cold. She could be many miles away by now. And waiting around had only increased those miles.

But then the dog started barking and pulling Kansas across the front porch toward the woods. "He's got a scent!" Kansas yelled, and her face didn't look quite as pinched. She was hopeful.

Eli had been on the phone coordinating with the surveillance team setting up at his parents' for the kidnapper's follow-up call, but he hung up and started after Kansas.

Troy had overheard the ABI lieutenant earlier telling Kansas about the ransom request.

"Every kidnapper has to know that the person will want proof of life before turning over any money," Kansas had said. "That's good. That means she's alive."

Troy wanted to believe that, too, so badly. But he was too damn scared to think rationally at all. He waited just until Eli rushed into the woods after the SAR team before he ducked under the crime-scene tape and started after them.

The crime tech who'd identified the chloroform saw him but looked away, letting him go. He must have noticed how upset Troy was, how determined he was to find the woman he loved. And the guy hadn't just looked away from Troy—he'd looked off in the direction Kansas had gone. Maybe he understood what Troy was feeling because he cared about someone like that, too.

Troy stayed back a bit from the team, so that the officers and the dogs didn't notice him like the tech had. He didn't want to get in the way or cause a distraction. He didn't want to detract in any way from the search for Lakin. He just wanted to help.

And he wanted to be there when she was found.

She had to be found. Alive.

Will held onto his wife's trembling body, trying to comfort her while seeking comfort himself. He was so damn scared. They'd gotten together a lot of money. Sasha's pottery business was doing well, and Will still had a lot of investments from selling the real estate business in California that he and his brother had inherited after losing the rest of their family. His brother, Ryan, who loved Lakin like she was his own daughter, had chipped in some of his inheritance investments, too.

Everybody wanted to get their girl safely back where she belonged: with them.

"Why hasn't he called yet?" Sasha asked, her voice muffled as her face was buried in his throat. Her tears wet his skin.

"He'll call back," Will said. "He has to call back…" If he wanted the money.

But was this really about money? Or was there another reason Lakin had been abducted?

Did her kidnapper really have any intention of letting her go?

Chapter Twenty-Three

Whatever Whitlaw had drugged her with back at the cabin was still affecting Lakin, slowing her down so that she felt as if she was running in quicksand. The slope was getting more treacherous with rocks and loose leaves making her slip and fall. Her hands were scraped.

But she didn't notice the pain or the blood seeping from her scratches. She clawed at branches, using them to pull herself up. She couldn't go back…

He was right behind her. Branches rustled, twigs snapped, and every now and then he coughed or cursed.

She waited for gunfire, like how he'd shot at Troy the other night. But none came. Maybe Whitlaw didn't want anyone to hear and figure out where they were.

How close to RTA were they?

Why hadn't she gone on some of the damn adventures herself? She hadn't wanted to run all over the mountain like she was now. If only she knew the area more, like her siblings and cousins. Hell, even Mitch the lawyer had gone on more adventures than she had.

"You can run, girlie, but you can't hide," Whitlaw called out to her. He chuckled, but he sounded out of breath.

She was, too, her lungs burning from the altitude. She was going so slow, struggling so hard to fight the dizziness that kept threatening to overwhelm her.

As out of breath as he sounded, he also sounded close. Much too close.

She pushed her way through branches as the ground leveled out for a moment. And then…nothing was ahead of her or underneath her.

She dropped through the air, falling, falling…

Branches scratched at her hair and her clothes until finally she struck the ground.

Hard.

Pain radiated throughout her body and her head. And like at the cabin, blackness suddenly claimed her, pulling her deep into oblivion.

TROY CONTINUED TO follow the sounds of dogs barking and the SAR team members talking back and forth. He recognized Kansas and Eli's voices and knew he had to hang back. If they saw him, they might have someone escort him back to the cabin. But he wanted to get close enough to clearly hear what they were saying. The dogs had to be following the scent still, but where?

"Tire tracks…"

"There's a truck…"

A vehicle was involved then. If a truck was still here, hopefully Lakin was, too. But where?

"And a cave…"

The dogs started barking louder, drowning out the voices. While Troy couldn't hear everything, he suspected he would have heard something over the barking if they'd found Lakin and her kidnapper. Gunfire or screaming maybe…

But there was just barking. So the cave was empty. Since the truck was still here, they couldn't have gotten anywhere fast. They had to be running around the woods. Maybe the kidnapper was trying to find a new place to hide Lakin and himself.

Or maybe Lakin, strong and resourceful, had managed to escape. Maybe the kidnapper was trying to find her.

Either Troy or the SAR team would have stumbled across them if they'd been going down the mountain, so they must've headed up. So he did, too.

Using the branches for balance, he pushed up the steep rocky incline. In one tree, he noticed a strand of long dark hair caught on a twig. Lakin had gone this way.

He wanted to call out to her, but if the kidnapper was looking for her, Troy didn't want to alert him to her whereabouts or to his. The last time Troy had tried to rescue her, he'd gotten shot at. He needed to be careful. He couldn't help Lakin if something happened to him. He was damn lucky that last time he'd only gotten a scratch on his face instead of a bullet in his brain. So he kept his head down and moved as quietly as he could through the trees, climbing up the rocks.

The dogs were not moving quietly. They barked loudly as they crashed through trees. He heard shouting again, in another direction.

He'd gone the wrong way, apparently.

But then he found another strand of hair on a branch. As he reached for it, his foot slipped. He dropped down hard on his butt, jarring his back as he hit the ground. His foot dangled over a steep drop.

Ignoring the twinge of pain in his back, he scooted closer to the edge and peered down into a deep ravine filled with trees and boulders. He looked at the branch above him, with that long strand of silky dark hair dangling from it.

The pain in his back moved to his heart. Had she fallen in the ravine?

"Lakin!" he yelled. He didn't care now who else heard him as long as she did. As long as she answered him. "Lakin!"

As long as she *could* answer him.

He could see where something, or *someone*, had broken branches in the ravine below. She had to be down there. Unable to answer him.

So he had to figure out how to reach her without falling himself.

Troy ducked under the branches of the trees that grew on the edge of the ravine, obscuring it so much that it was easy for someone to fall into it. With the edge of the bank eroding under those trees, one had fallen, giving him a gangplank to the bottom. But with branches sticking up from it, he couldn't walk down it. So he climbed down its branches, scratching his hands and his face. He didn't care. He didn't care about anything but finding Lakin.

The tree branches thinned toward the bottom of the ravine, snapping beneath his weight, and he dropped down into weeds and rocks beneath it.

Pain shot up his spine as his knee jammed into a rock. He flinched but willed the pain away. He had to find the woman he loved. He'd wasted so much time that they could have been together. He should have been living with her in the present instead of planning and saving for a future that might never come. If he couldn't find her...

He had to find her.

His throat raw from yelling, he shouted again, "Lakin!"

Pushing his way through the weeds at the bottom of the ravine, he found her lying in crushed ferns.

Blood dampened her hair from a wound on her head, and her eyes were closed. Was she just unconscious or...?

"Lakin!" he yelled.

But she didn't move at all. He couldn't even tell if she was breathing.

"Help!" he shouted, hurling the word toward the mouth of the ravine. "Help me!"

He could hear the dogs and the voices of the SAR team, but they sounded as if they were moving away from him, not toward him.

He stood up and shouted again. "Help! Come help! I found her!"

But had he found her too late?

ELI HEARD TROY shouting. But he was staring into the barrel of a gun that the man from Lakin's photograph pointed at him.

Whitlaw was older now, with several lines in his face. The same jagged scar trailed down one side of it. And his mouth was twisted into the same cruel sneer.

"It's too late," Whitlaw said.

"It is too late," Eli agreed. He held a gun, too, pointed directly at Whitlaw who stood a few yards up the mountain from him. Behind Eli were a couple of the SAR team members, holding back the dogs that Whitlaw had already threatened to shoot. Eli heard another gun cocking. Probably Kansas. His cousin would not let this man take him out. "Throw down your weapon. There's no way out of this, Whitlaw."

"It's too late for her," the older man said.

Eli heard the panic and desperation in Troy's hoarse voice as he continued shouting. The man was too proud to ask for help for himself. He needed help for Lakin.

"What did you do to her?" Kansas asked, moving closer to Eli.

Whitlaw chuckled. "Not a damn thing. She's the one who hurt herself. She ran right off the mountain."

Kansas gasped.

Fear gripped Eli, but he didn't lower his weapon. He didn't trust this man for a moment. If they got distracted, Whitlaw was going to shoot one of them. And with his obvious resentment of the Coltons, it was going to be either Eli or Kansas.

He had to take this guy out. Now. Without anyone else getting hurt.

But Eli couldn't stop thinking about Lakin hurt and needing his help.

Chapter Twenty-Four

Shouting pulled at Lakin in the darkness. Was Whitlaw yelling at her mother in her nightmare? Her mother was crying. Lakin was crying.

Or were the shouts from the man she loved? Troy?

"Help! I found her!"

It was him. She hoped.

Whitlaw couldn't find her, or he would kill her for certain, just like he'd killed her mother. That thought was so unbearable, like the pain, that she slipped back into oblivion. But not into the nightmare.

Instead she dreamed of Troy, of their first dance, of their first kiss. Of all of their kisses.

She'd loved him for so long.

"Come back to me," his deep voice, gruff with emotion, pleaded. "Come back to me…"

Where was she? She couldn't tell. Couldn't see beyond the darkness.

"I love you…"

The words pulled at her more than the shouting.

"I love you," he repeated, his voice cracking. "Please come back to me…"

Where was she? Was she dead? But she could feel. Her love for him and the pain. It pounded so hard inside her head, reverberating off her skull. She flinched from the intensity of it. But she didn't want to leave him.

Not Troy.

She fought her way from the blackness, opening her eyes. She squinted against the light and the pain. Why so much pain?

"What happened?" she asked in a whisper. Her throat was raw, and her voice muffled by the mask over her mouth. It wasn't the tape or the handkerchief. It was plastic and full of oxygen.

The grasp on her hand tightened, and she peered up to find Troy leaning over one side of her while a stranger sat on the other. Wherever they were, they were moving, bouncing along a road. Sirens blared, making her flinch again. The pain intensified so much that she couldn't hang on.

She had to let go of Troy.

Had to let go of the pain.

Of consciousness.

IGNORING THE PAIN in his back and his knee, Troy paced the waiting room. "How long does it take to do a CT?" he asked Eli.

Leaning against a wall, Eli shook his head. "I don't know. They need to make sure there's no bleeding or swelling on her brain."

Troy flinched at the thought. "She regained consciousness in the ambulance," he reminded her brother. "She asked what happened."

Was that a good thing or a bad thing, though? Didn't

she remember what had happened, that Whitlaw had abducted her? Or was it the fall she'd forgotten?

She'd gotten hurt because of that horrible man. He was in custody now; he couldn't hurt her.

But a brain injury could. Even though she'd regained consciousness, the bleeding or swelling could still take her life. Troy knew that many people, even movie stars and celebrities, had lost their lives because of traumatic brain injuries like that.

His breath caught in his lungs with the panic pressing on his chest. For a second, he couldn't move.

Eli reached out and grasped his shoulder. "She'll be all right. She regained consciousness. My little sister is tough. She'll be fine."

Troy wasn't sure if her older brother was trying to convince him or himself. "Lakin is tough," he agreed.

She'd gotten away from that creep. And she'd put up with Troy for years, with the long-distance relationship so many other people, besides Billy Hoover and Eric Seller, must have pointed out to her was going nowhere. Troy had been such an idiot.

"You're an idiot!" Kansas exclaimed.

Troy jerked his head toward the door to the waiting room, expecting to see Kansas pointing at him. But she was talking to another man. Troy had seen him around enough to know that he was Eli's partner with ABI. Asher or something like that.

Eli groaned and levered himself away from the wall as if he needed to break up the fight. But then the tech with the dark blond hair stepped between the two of them.

"Ah, Scott Montgomery to the rescue," Eli remarked.

Unlike Asher who'd obviously upset her, Scott spoke

softly to Kansas. She offered him a faint smile before glowering at Asher again.

Troy focused on them for a moment, mostly so he would stop worrying about Lakin and how badly she might be injured. "What's the deal with all that?" he asked Eli.

"I think both my partner and the brilliant tech have crushes on my beautiful cousin," Eli said with a chuckle that sounded almost pitying. "But Kansas is too focused on finding the serial killer to give either of them the time of day."

It was true; Kansas walked away from both men and headed toward Troy and Eli. "What have you heard? How is she?" she demanded.

"Nothing new yet," Troy said.

"Uncle Will and Aunt Sasha were pulling into the lot as I was walking into the lobby," Kansas warned Eli. "They're going to want news."

"We all want news," Troy said. The longer it took for this damn CT scan, the more worried he got. What was taking so long? Had they found the very things they were worried about? Bleeding, swelling... Was she going to be okay?

If only he'd found her sooner...

Once he had, it hadn't taken the SAR team long to get them up from the ravine and down the mountain to the ambulance. Hopefully they'd gotten her medical attention fast enough. He couldn't consider the alternative.

He couldn't consider losing her.

But even if she recovered, he might still lose her. He'd been the idiot that Kansas had called Eli's partner. Troy had been waiting for his future to start instead of living it. Instead of just focusing on his love for Lakin and not worrying about anything else.

Now, he was worried only about her.

EVER SINCE HE got the ransom call, Will had been scared to death that they might lose their daughter. He'd held onto the hope that if he paid the ransom, they would get her back. Or that Eli and Kansas would find her.

But Troy Amos had.

Eli had told them when he'd called them. Troy had found Lakin, and they were in an ambulance on their way to the hospital.

"Why?" Will had managed to choke out.

Eli knew better than to sugarcoat things with him. He'd replied honestly, "She was running to escape her kidnapper and fell."

Will hadn't asked any more questions. Maybe because he hadn't wanted to know how badly she was hurt. He just wanted to see his daughter.

So did Sasha. Together, they rushed into the hospital waiting room, holding onto each other.

"How is she?" Will asked his son who stood next to Troy and Kansas.

"We're waiting for them to come back from CT and let us know," Eli replied.

"CT?" Sasha whispered. "She hit her head?"

His face grim, Eli nodded.

"She regained consciousness in the ambulance," Troy said, his voice gruff.

"She'll be fine, Uncle Will. Aunt Sasha, she'll be fine," Kansas said, but she sounded as desperate to believe that as they were.

"Lakin's strong," Eli said.

Will knew that, but he still remembered the sweet little toddler who'd woken up with nightmares so often after she came to live with them. She wasn't the only one who had nightmares back then. He and Eli had had some, too, after finding the bodies of his parents and Caroline and her killer.

But Lakin was alive. And she would stay that way. She had to…

Will couldn't lose anyone else he loved.

"Sir," Troy said. Tears shimmered in his green eyes. "May I speak to you and Mrs. Colton for a moment… alone…?"

Troy had found her; he'd ridden with her in the ambulance. Maybe he knew more than the others. Will was almost afraid to talk to him.

But Sasha, probably knowing that Troy needed comfort as much as they did, released Will to hug their daughter's longtime boyfriend. "Thank you for finding her, Troy," she said, tears streaming down her face.

Troy deserved their gratitude, let alone some of their time. So Will walked with the young man and Sasha toward a quiet corner of the waiting room that was beginning to fill up with Coltons and Amoses.

So many people loved Lakin, but no one more than Troy. She had to be okay for his sake as much as for hers and theirs. She had to be okay.

Chapter Twenty-Five

Lakin heard voices, but these were soft whispers, not the shouts from her nightmares or even from earlier... Was it today that she'd heard Troy yelling for help? How much time had passed since she'd slipped and fallen trying to escape from Whitlaw? From her biological mother's murderer?

She gasped at the sharp jab of pain over the loss. The woman had given Lakin life and had done her best to protect that life.

"She's awake," a soft voice said with awe. "Sweetheart, are you all right?"

And she opened her eyes to the mother she knew, the one who'd been there for her as long as she could remember. Who'd loved and supported her unconditionally. "Mom..." Lakin whispered, her throat raspy.

Then she saw her dad leaning over her mother and her brothers and even Hetty and Mrs. Amos and a couple of the other Amos siblings.

Where was Troy?

She didn't see him even though she looked around for him. He was tall; she should have been able to see him over the others. But instead of asking for him, she forced a smile for all the worried faces staring back at her. "I thought there's a limit on the number of visitors a person can have."

She knew she was in the hospital. An IV line was taped into a vein in her arm, and she lay partially inclined in a bed with railings.

"There are too many of us Coltons and Amoses for them to hold us to that limit," her father said with a grin, but his eyes were damp like her mom's.

"I think we can break this one law," Eli said, his voice gruff.

Lakin shook her head and flinched at a jolt of pain near the base of her skull. "No more law breaking," she murmured. "I'm okay…"

Or she would be when she saw Troy. Where was he? Why wasn't he with her?

"That's all we wanted to know," Mrs. Amos said, "that you would be all right, sweet girl."

Lakin smiled at the beautiful woman she'd hoped would one day be her mother-in-law. But Troy wasn't ready to make a commitment obviously. He wasn't even here for her.

Although he'd been in the ambulance. Had something happened to him? She wanted to ask about him, but first she had to know…

"Did you catch Whitlaw?" she asked her brother.

Eli nodded.

"He killed my birth mother," she said. "He told me so when he was chasing me. He would have killed me, too, back then if she hadn't left me in that grocery store."

"We knew you were loved before we loved you," her adoptive mother said, tears shimmering in her blue eyes. "And now we know how much."

Her birth mother had loved her.

"Eli and I need to talk to Whitlaw," Kansas said and jerked her head toward the door. "We can go now that we know you're all right."

Lakin hugged them both goodbye. She was all right physically. Emotionally she was still a mess, especially because Troy wasn't here.

But when Eli and Kansas opened the door, he was standing there out in the hall.

Had he just gotten here? Or had he been out there the whole time? Afraid to see her? Afraid that she might not want him here like he hadn't wanted her at his bedside all those weeks ago?

Everybody else followed Eli and Kansas's lead, hugging and kissing her before walking out into the hall.

While everyone else was walking out, Troy stepped inside the room. He was limping again, and a grimace crossed his face as he moved around the room until he was beside her bed. Finally the door shut behind her last visitor, leaving them alone together.

Lakin stared at Troy for a long while. She felt caught in his green-eyed gaze, her image reflecting back at her. She was bruised and scraped up with a bandage on the back of her head.

He was bruised and scraped up, too, his clothes torn.

"What happened to you?" she asked.

His breath caught for a second, then released in a ragged sigh. "I went into that ravine to find you."

She wasn't sure it was a ravine she'd fallen into or if she'd just gone off the side of the mountain. She'd accidentally gone over; he'd purposely risked his life for hers.

"You hurt your back again," she said, tears rushing to her eyes for the pain he had to be feeling.

He shook his head. "Whacked my knee on a rock," he said. "It's bruised but not broken. They think my back will be fine."

"Good," she said. And then she had to ask, "Does that mean you're going to go back to the oil rigs?"

Was he going to leave her again?

"I'm sorry," he said, his voice heavy with emotion.

As her heart broke, she closed her eyes. "Then…just go…" she choked out. She couldn't keep doing this; she couldn't keep saying goodbye to the man she loved and not know if he was going to be able to make it back to her.

TROY'S HEART BROKE from the tears sliding down her face. "I'm so sorry," he said, and he pushed down one railing so he could sit on the bed and pull her into his arms.

But her body was stiff with rejection. "If you're going to leave again, just go," she said. "I can't keep saying goodbye to you."

"I'm not leaving," he said.

Finally she opened her eyes, wet with tears. "What?"

"I'm never leaving you again," he said. "I'm sorry I was so stubborn and stupid to think that money mattered when the only thing that matters is love. No, the only thing that matters is you. I love you so much, Lakin, and I'm so sorry. Can you ever forgive me for putting off our future, for worrying about things that don't really matter?"

"I thought they mattered, too," she said. "I thought we needed more money saved before we bought our business."

"But you did it anyway," he said with a smile of pride at her bravery. "When the opportunity came up, you took it. Just like you must have to get away from Whitlaw."

She shuddered and clutched him closer. "I was so scared."

"Me, too," he admitted. "I've never been so scared. Not even when I fell off that oil rig. And I realized when you were missing that nothing else matters but us being together. I was just so scared of being a burden to you."

She pressed her fingers over his lips. "I love you. No matter what. Sickness and health."

"Will you say those words to me?"

"I just did," she said, her forehead furrowing a bit.

"I would drop down to one knee, but it would be a little hard right now," he said. "What I'm asking, Lakin Colton, is for you to be my wife, my partner in business and life. I love you so much, and I will do my best to spend the rest of our lives making up for the time we've been apart while I've been stupid."

She chuckled and pressed her fingers to his lips again. "You've been stubborn," she agreed. "But you're not stupid. I know your family struggled after your dad died, and you worry about security."

"You're my security," he said. "You're my home.

You're my everything. I asked your dad and mom for their permission to marry you. They said it's up to you. Maybe they think I've already blown my chance. Have I, Lakin? Have I waited too long to start our future?"

She shook her head. "No, our future starts now. Yes, I will marry you. I will be your partner in all things. I love you so very much, Troy Amos."

Finally she'd said the words back to him again. He had her love back. He had Lakin back.

"And I love you." He lowered his head and kissed her lips. All the pain he'd ever felt disappeared; he felt only love and gratitude that she was safe and she was his as much as he was hers.

KANSAS WAS IRRITATED with Asher. He'd wanted to start the interrogation of Jasper Whitlaw without her and Eli. Sure, he figured they wanted to be there for Lakin, and he wasn't wrong about that. Even Scott had pointed that out. But he could have just waited; it was as if he hadn't believed that Lakin was going to be okay.

Kansas hadn't wanted to consider the possibility. Anyway, Lakin was fine. And from what Mom and Dad had insinuated when they all left her and Troy alone together, she was probably engaged by now.

Which for some reason made Kansas even more determined to find the Fiancée Killer. There was no proof yet that any of his victims had actually been engaged, though. The ones they'd identified had been single.

Except for Mrs. Whitlaw; Stella, who was undoubtedly Lakin's biological mom, had been a married woman. But she was dead, and her husband had confessed to killing her.

Facing Jasper Whitlaw, Kansas began, "We have you on your wife's murder as well as the abduction of Lakin Colton, kidnapping, extortion and the attempted murder of Troy Amos. You have a long list of charges being brought against you. So tell us about the other women."

"Other women?" Whitlaw asked. "Stella was the tramp. Cheated on me when I was prison and gave birth to that little whiny brat."

"Lakin was never whiny," Eli defended his sister. "She was always as sweet and kind as she is now."

Whitlaw snorted. "People thought the same about her mother, wondered why Stella was with me. She probably thought she could save me or reform me, but in the end nobody was able to save her."

"Why'd you come after Lakin?" Eli asked.

Whitlaw shrugged. "Figured she might remember what happened, and I didn't want to go to back to prison."

"She was there when you killed her mother?"

He sighed. "Stella didn't die right away. She managed to get the kid to the grocery store. But she died shortly after that."

"From the beating you gave her," Eli said. "Lakin used to wake up with nightmares."

"And she didn't like shouting," Kansas remembered. "But what about the other women?"

"What other women?" Whitlaw sounded annoyed now. "I only grabbed Lakin because I figured it wasn't fair. She got the cushy life as a Colton. I was owed some of that money, too."

"You were owed nothing," Eli said. "But you owe plenty to other people. Closure. The truth."

"I don't know if Stella's body was ever found," he said. "That's up to you to figure out."

"What about the other women?" Kansas persisted.

"I haven't killed any other women," Whitlaw said. He leaned back and shook his head. "I'm no freaky serial killer if that's what you're trying to pin on me. Hell, give me the dates, and I'm sure I've got alibis."

Kansas figured he probably did. He wasn't the killer they were looking for.

She and Eli left him alone in the interrogation room and stepped into the hall.

"It's not him," Asher said as he walked up to join them.

Of course he would have already figured that out.

"I checked the dates of the other abductions, and he was on his parole officer's radar then. He was regularly checking in with him and wasn't anywhere near this vicinity until a few weeks ago," Asher continued.

Eli sighed. "Did you check out Billy Hoover and Eric Seller too?"

"Billy Hoover and Eric Seller?" Kansas repeated. "Why would you check out Billy? And isn't Seller a RTA client?"

"Troy came up with some other possible suspects when someone was stalking Lakin," Eli said.

"Maybe we should give him a job," Asher said.

But Kansas suspected Troy would have one with Lakin soon. She'd heard about the old Shelby Hotel.

"I already checked out Billy and Eric," Eli said. "Both have alibis for the dates the other women were killed. Bobby Reynolds actually was the alibi for Billy. He locked him up for drunk driving."

Kansas nearly growled with frustration. "We have to find this killer…"

Before he killed again. She had no doubt that he would keep killing until he was caught.

Chapter Twenty-Six

Lakin stepped back and stared at the two-story building. Pride and gratitude overwhelmed her. Gone was the weathered wood siding that had been rotted in places. In just the few weeks since she'd been kidnapped, she and Troy had replaced it with warm, cream-colored siding and rich burgundy trim. Troy had even handcrafted a new sign for out front: Suite Home. He'd made another for the two suites inside that they would eventually combine into their private residence: Sweet Home.

He wrapped his arm around her shoulders and hugged her to his side. "Do you like it?" he asked.

She shook her head. "No. I love it." Then she slid her arm around his waist and stretched up on tiptoe to kiss his jaw. "I love you."

He'd worked so hard on the renovations that she'd been worried he was going to reinjure his back, but while he limped from time to time, he was doing well. Even though his health wasn't as big a concern as it had been, she knew he was still worried about money. Her business loan had been approved, and she'd paid her father back. But until the hotel was completely up and running again, they would struggle to make ends meet.

But just like the bank that granted them the loan, she had faith in their business plan and in their future. There was nothing the two of them couldn't do together, especially after they'd individually survived what could have been fatal falls.

Troy turned his head and lowered his mouth to hers, kissing her deeply, passionately. He pulled back a bit, panting for breath, and whispered, "I love you, too, partner." He lowered his head and kissed her again.

"Get a room!" a deep voice scoffed.

Laughing, Lakin stepped back from Troy and turned to find her brother Mitch standing behind them. "We already have a few ready for guests," she said. They were counting on the money from those for the loan payments and the renovations necessary to get more rooms ready. "We'll have twenty-four in total."

"It looks great, guys," Mitch praised them.

Pride suffused Lakin again. Her brothers were all so successful that praise from one of them meant a lot to her. "Thanks." She pulled away from Troy to hug him.

"You have more to thank me for than a compliment," Mitch said. He turned to Troy. "Your former employer settled the suit."

Troy released a shaky breath. "Really?"

Mitch nodded. "For even more than we were asking."

Troy's green eyes widened with surprise. "Really?" he repeated.

"And they didn't just give you a settlement," Mitch said. "Your mom will get one, too."

Troy's long body shook slightly, and tears glistened in his green eyes. "Oh my God, that's great. Thank you." He hugged her brother.

Mitch patted his back. "More important, they're going to up their safety protocols. The suggestions you made are already being put into practice."

Troy trembled again. "That's good."

But Lakin saw the sadness cross his handsome face, and she knew what he was thinking. It was too late for his dad, even for himself, to not suffer an injury. "That will help others," Lakin said. "That's so good, Troy."

He smiled at her and nodded. "Yeah, it is. Hopefully nobody else will lose someone they love."

Not on the oil rigs. But Lakin was still worried that with a serial killer on the loose, more lives would be lost. Eli and Kansas were working hard to find that person, though. And she had faith in her family, just as she had faith in her and Troy's future. Even more so now.

"Come on, take a look at the place," Lakin urged Mitch.

As they were showing him around inside, someone knocked on the front door and opened it.

"Hello there? Are you open for business yet?" Eric Seller called out.

Troy tensed.

"Remember that Eli and Kansas ruled him out," Lakin whispered to her fiancé. She turned to greet the man. "We have a few suites ready."

The man glanced at her hand and pointed at the ring. Then he clasped Troy's shoulder. "Good job," he said. "Congratulations on the hotel and the engagement."

Troy must have heard the sincerity that Lakin heard because he relaxed and grinned at Eric. "Thank you."

"You two inspired me to look up my old high school sweetheart," he said. "I spent all the years since graduation kicking myself for not trying long distance when we went away for college. I reached out to her and found out that she's never married, either. We've been talking online and on the phone and have been looking for a place to meet in person. I'd like to book a couple of your suites for that meeting."

"Congratulations to you," Lakin said. "I'm so happy that you reached out to her."

He nodded. "Like I said, you two inspired me. I think that's why I was so invested in you getting engaged."

"We'll be getting married soon, too," Troy said. "Just want to get our hotel ready so guests will have a place to stay."

"Brilliant," Eric said. "I think you'll do well here. If you need any investors, let me know."

Troy and Mitch exchanged a grin, and Troy replied, "No, we're going to be just fine."

Lakin grinned, too. "We're going to be better than fine." They were going to be happy because all their dreams were going to come true.

TROY COULD HAVE kicked himself for all the years he'd worried about money, about making it, about not having enough of it. Finally, when he'd stopped worrying about it, he had it. The irony was not lost on him. After Mitch and Seller left the hotel, he laughed and shook his head.

"What's funny?" Lakin asked.

"Not funny really," Troy admitted. "Just sad that I've been such an idiot, worrying about all the wrong things."

She smiled. "Money?"

He nodded. "I'm very sorry for what I've put you through. And my mother…"

"She got a settlement, too," Lakin said. "You won't have to worry about her, either."

"According to her, I didn't ever have to worry about her," Troy admitted. "She's already tried to give me back the money I've given her. I have a feeling we're going to get a pretty big wedding gift from her."

"Wedding," Lakin said, and her face lit up with a beautiful smile. "I can't wait."

"Me, neither," Troy said. "I can't wait to be your husband. To start our family." Emotion overwhelmed him just thinking about their future and how wonderful it was going to be.

Lakin grabbed his hand and tugged him toward the hall with the finished suites. "Maybe we can put in some practice for starting that family," she said, turning back to wink at him.

His pulse quickened with desire. He loved her so much, and yet he would never be able to make love with her enough, to express all his love for her. But he intended to try.

He swung her up in his arms and carried her over the threshold into the suite they'd had so much fun renovating together. Then he laid her on the bed and followed her down.

They both wriggled out of their clothes until skin slid over skin. He made love to her slowly, with his hands and with his mouth, caressing and kissing every inch of her. Finally he slid inside her, joining their bodies like their souls were already joined. And he thrust in and out, in and out, until she clutched him with her arms and legs and her inner muscles. Then her body shuddered, and she screamed his name as she found her release.

And he found his, the pleasure so intense it was almost painful.

Panting for breath, he levered himself up so he wouldn't crush her and leaned his forehead against hers. "You know what they say, practice makes perfect."

"You're already perfect," she told him.

"You are."

"We're perfect for each other."

And they were; they had always been and always would be.

PARKER HAD TEXTED Lakin a while ago about something he needed to find in the RTA office, but she must have been busy at the hotel. It took a while before she texted him back.

When she did text him again, she added, Call Genna McDougal and offer her my old job.

Her old job. Parker felt a pang of loss. He missed Lakin, and not just because she knew where everything was and how to do everything. He missed seeing his sister every day.

And then he felt another pang at her proposed replacement, aka the bane of his existence. But he couldn't tell Lakin that or he would have to tell her what had happened between them...

* * * * *

COMING SOON!

We really hope you enjoyed reading this book.
If you're looking for more romance
be sure to head to the shops when
new books are available on

Thursday 23rd October

To see which titles are coming soon, please visit
millsandboon.co.uk/nextmonth

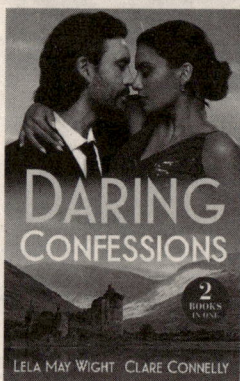

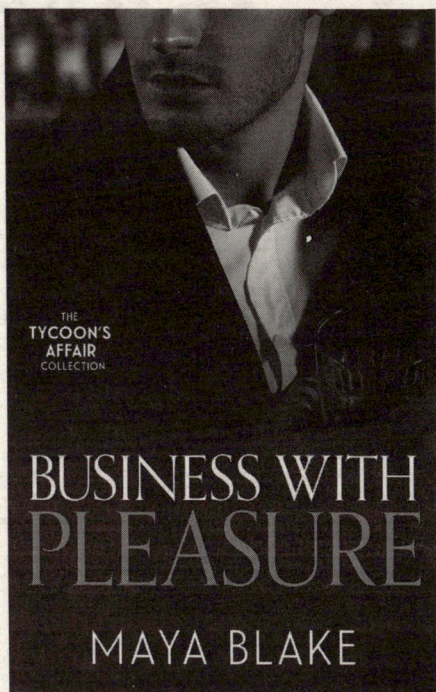

LET'S TALK
Romance

For exclusive extracts, competitions and special offers, find us online:

- **f** MillsandBoon
- **X** @MillsandBoon
- **⊙** @MillsandBoonUK
- **♪** @MillsandBoonUK

Get in touch on 01413 063 232